SE

Rachel drew a dee‌‍   ‍   or to Guy's bedchamber. F‌   ‍nd then her passion swept uncertai‌   , she said, "I want to sleep in your bed tonig‌

She looked at him, need and longing erasing any last vestiges of pride. Without hesitation, Guy gathered her to him, his hands firm and sure, and then his mouth sought her own.

At the touch of his lips, relief swept through Rachel, but the pressure of his mouth and the feel of his body against her own soon stirred something stronger. She clung to him feverishly, returning his kisses with a hungry desperation she had never known and would not have thought herself capable of.

He wanted her. It was heady knowledge, every bit as potent as his touch. But just beyond the intoxication and delight lay the bitter ache of sorrow. There was no doubt that Guy wanted her, but he was not taking her out of love or even desire, but out of kindness and generosity.

It doesn't matter, she told herself as he deftly undid the ribbon which held her dressing gown closed at the neck. It was a lie and she knew it, but just for tonight it was so seductively easy to pretend otherwise . . .

An Improper Proposal

Anthea Malcolm

ZEBRA BOOKS
KENSINGTON PUBLISHING CORP.

For Madeleine Mills and Kate Moore

ZEBRA BOOKS

are published by

Kensington Publishing Corp.
475 Park Avenue South
New York, NY 10016

First printing: August, 1992

Printed in the United States of America

. . . truth is truth
to the end of reckoning.

Shakespeare
Measure for Measure

Prologue

May, 1812

The taste of panic bitter in her mouth, Rachel looked across her cramped sitting room at the man who was her best friend in all the world. "If you stay here, they'll hang you. Dear God, Guy, for once in your life admit that you can't take on the world single-handed."

There were new lines in Guy's face, marks of exhaustion or of grief, but his jaw, which bore a day's growth of beard, golden in the lamplight, was set more stubbornly than ever. "Surely it's premature to talk of hanging," he said in his customary mild voice. "I have yet to be charged with a crime."

Rachel felt an impulse to shake him, to scream at the top of her lungs, to pick up her prized Staffordshire vase from the side table and hurl it into the fireplace. Anything to break through the shell of detachment with which her cousin surrounded himself in times of crisis. Instead she drew a breath and folded her arms in front of her to still their trembling. Her body ached with fatigue and her legs felt weak, but she was determined to remain standing as long as Guy did. "They have a witness," she reminded him in succinct tones. "The runner told me as much. A witness who says he saw you going into the theater last Monday, not an hour before the explosion went off."

" 'Done to death by slanderous tongues.' " Only someone who knew Guy as well as Rachel did could tell how much effort that air of studied disinterest cost him. "I'd rather like to know who paid the man to tell that bold-faced lie."

"*It doesn't matter.*" The words came out more loudly than Rachel intended, echoing off the rose-and-white-papered walls of the small room. "It doesn't matter who the man is or why he accused you. Bow Street don't care. They want to make an arrest. Four men are dead and one is maimed for life. The Home Office are screaming for action, the newspapers are saying it isn't only the Northern counties that are hotbeds of sedition, and the dead men's families—"

Rachel broke off, for one of the four men who had died as a result of the explosion had been her husband. Her husband and Guy's closest friend.

"Rachel—" For a moment the detachment was gone, and raw grief shone from Guy's eyes. He took a step toward her, then checked himself and dragged his hands over his face. "What can I say? There's no way to bring Cadogan back. I would to God I'd been with him at the Angel that night."

He spoke softly but his voice was heavy with self-reproach. Rachel fixed him with a firm gaze. "And lost your own life?" she demanded.

There was a pause of several seconds and then Guy gave a twisted half smile, and a ghost of the familiar mockery lit his eyes. "I'm arrogant enough to think I might have helped rather than added to the carnage."

Rachel turned away, her throat constricting with sorrow and rage. She didn't want to think about Cadogan. Neither about her genuine grief at his death nor about the anger and bitterness which had haunted the last years of their marriage. Not now, when it would be all too easy to say more than she intended. Her relationship with Cadogan was one of the few things about which she had never been able to talk to Guy. She sank down on the sofa, leaning back gratefully into the familiar comfort of the worn velvet. "*I* would to God I'd never agreed to let the wretched play be performed," she said.

"The play wasn't your idea," Guy said in a bracing tone. "Don't turn self-pitying on me, Rachel."

Rachel looked up at him. How typical of Guy to force her out of her depression. "No, but I didn't try to stop it." And

8

she could have stopped the performance of *The Taking of Badajoz* if she had tried. After the death of Cadogan's father, Cadogan and his Uncle Samuel, who owned the Tavistock Theater between them, had been quite willing to relinquish its management into Rachel's hands. It was Samuel Ford, however, who had suggested that the Tavistock, known for producing plays which outraged the censor, the Government, and a good portion of the public, stage a patriotic play glorifying the Battle of Badajoz. Rachel had had mixed feelings about the idea, but she had recognized its benefit to the health of the company and had raised no objections.

"I didn't realize what a storm it would stir up," Rachel said, replaying the events of the past weeks, searching for what she might have done differently.

"Nor did I." Guy ran his fingers through his hair and Rachel had a sudden image of the boy he had been, clever, stubborn, inextricably bound up in the fabric of her life. "I'd hardly call *The Taking of Badajoz* great literature, but I wouldn't have dreamed of denying a fellow playwright his say."

Rachel rested her head against the sofa back and breathed in the faint lingering scent of the wilted flowers on the table behind her. Losing Guy, now of all times, would be an unspeakable wrench, but that was nothing beside the danger he faced. He had to leave England. "Of course you'd never have tried to stop the performance," she said. "But Bow Street need a scapegoat. And you fit the requirements precisely."

"Do I?" Guy was on his guard again, an actor giving a fine-tuned performance, not a cousin offering sympathy. "Do you seriously think they'll put a Melchett behind bars?"

"A Melchett from the black sheep branch of the family," Rachel retorted. "A Melchett who makes his living writing plays and scribbling radical pamphlets on the side, a Melchett who is the leader of a treasonous band of—"

"Treasonous?" Guy said in mock astonishment. "My dear girl, the *Levellers?*"

"Don't be difficult, Guy, you know that's how Bow Street will put it." Rachel studied her cousin. His face was very pale and the strain was beginning to show about his mouth. No matter how lightly he spoke, she knew how much the Levellers meant to him. From the first the authorities had seemed convinced that one of the Levellers—that loosely organized troup of pamphleteers and would-be poets, of dedicated radicals and well-born young men taking a stand against their fathers, a group of which Guy and Cadogan had been the unofficial leaders—had contrived the explosion at the Tavistock to make a statement against the following night's performance of *The Taking of Badajoz,* which was to have been attended by the Prince Regent.

Rachel, knowing the Levellers had never engaged in anything more violent than a coffeehouse brawl, dismissed such an idea. Besides, the most hotheaded members of the group had been inside the theater at the time the explosives went off, holding a secret meeting to vent their anger at the next night's performance. The theater should have been empty, but Cadogan had been in the nearby Angel Tavern. When he learned there were people trapped in the burning building, he had rushed inside and lost his own life. Rachel rubbed her arms. Cadogan had died a hero's death, but there were some wounds which would never be healed and some stings she would never be able to forgive.

"Rachel," Guy said quietly, and Rachel, who had looked away, dwelling in her memories, met his gaze. He was still standing on the opposite side of the room, strained, disheveled, yet somehow composed. "I think it will be best if I don't visit you for a few weeks," he told her. "Or come to the Tavistock. You're going to have enough on your hands as it is."

Rachel stared at him, taking in the implications of the words. "God in heaven," she said, "do you imagine for one minute I've been thinking of myself?"

"I suspect you haven't given a thought to yourself for the past four days. Someone has to do it for you." He regarded her steadily. "I fight my own battles, Rachel, I don't run from them. Nor do I involve innocent bystanders."

Rachel lifted her chin. "Then you admit there's danger?"

Guy smiled, at once acknowledging her argument and rendering it futile. "I never said there wasn't."

Rachel gripped her hands together and said the only words

she could think of which would shake her cousin to the core. "It's because of Christine, isn't it?"

At the mention of her sister's name, Guy tensed. A muscle twitched beside his mouth, but his gaze remained level. "I don't want Christine involved in this either." His voice was still detatched, but it seemed to be worn thin, as if he had no reserves left to call on. "You've both suffered enough as it is."

There was no way Rachel could argue with that. The explosion which had made her a widow had also taken the life of Christine's fiancé, Edmund Hever. A double tragedy, leaving the two sisters bereft. But the reality was more complex. For Edmund's death meant that Christine was now free. Free, perhaps, to turn to the man she had once loved, the man who still loved her. Rachel felt a sick feeling in the pit of her stomach. The thought of Christine turning to Guy upset her as much as it always had. They were hopelessly unsuited.

"You think Edmund's death will change things?" she demanded.

"It already has. Bow Street would be determined to find a suspect in any event, but the fact that Edmund's cousin is the Duke of Arundel is certainly an added incentive."

He had avoided the issue but Rachel knew better than to press him. "All the more reason for you to leave the country."

Guy's face hardened. In the shadows cast by the room's two lamps, the angles of his face were sharpened and his eyes turned a cold, implacable green, like the sea on a stormy night. "Damn it, Rachel, no. It was my friends who died. It was my friends who were maimed in body and spirit. And it's my friends who have to live with the consequences of the explosion. I can't turn my back on them."

"You owe it to them to get yourself hanged?"

"I have no intention of getting myself hanged."

They were back where they had started. Aware of the futility of any argument she might make, Rachel got to her feet and walked to the white-painted fireplace. The plaster shepherd and shepherdess her daughter so liked to play with stood forlornly on either side of the mantel clock, neglected this past week. Rachel had an image of her two children tucked into bed upstairs. They had been asleep when she looked in on them an hour ago, though even in sleep Alec had been frowning and Jessica had covered her face with her arm.

Rachel picked up the shepherdess and wiped the dust from a fold of her pink-painted skirt. "Magnus won't help you, you know," she said, her back to Guy.

"I wouldn't expect him to," Guy said quietly.

Rachel returned the shepherdess to the mantel, wondering, despite her words, how her brother might be persuaded to come to Guy's assistance. Though the Melchetts considered Magnus as much a black sheep as Guy, Magnus had spent the last ten years making a fortune. As the founder of Melchett's Bank, he was not without influence. But Magnus and Guy had been antagonists from childhood and the antagonism had only worsened as they grew older. And if there was little chance of help from Magnus, there was even less from the Parminters, their powerful cousins. Though he shared the name of Melchett with Guy, the current Marquis of Parminter, a spoiled young man of twenty-six known for his extravagant tastes, was unlikely to be moved by cousinly feeling. Nor was his grandmother, the marchioness. Rachel had been taken to Parminter House once as a child, and she retained a vivid memory of Lady Parminter, whose cold blue eyes had said clearly that their branch of the family had long since forfeited any right to the name of Melchett.

Suddenly it all seemed too much. The prospect of losing Guy to exile or prison or worse. Her children's grief and fears, and the knowledge that she could not possibly tell them everything would be all right. Her conflicting feelings about Cadogan, and Christine's hysteria over Edmund's death. The damage to the theater and the need, in the face of all this, to somehow hold the company together. Rachel turned away, arms wrapped tightly around her. Her throat ached with exhaustion and grief and an unbearable sense of loss, and she felt the pressure of tears behind her eyes. The framed theatrical prints on the wall before her blurred as the tears began to spill down her face in silent testimony to all that had been shattered, all that she feared could never be rebuilt.

And then suddenly Guy's hands were on her shoulders and Guy's warm breath brushed her cheek and Guy's arms enfolded her in comfort. Her own breathing was harsh, but his coat was soft beneath her face and his fingers were gentle as they smoothed her hair. Rachel felt the tension drain from her and with it some of her despair. She was safe here, in this moment, secure from the terrors of the world. It had always been so. In a childhood full of chaos and uncertainty, Guy had been an anchor of stability. Rachel snuggled closer to him and closed her eyes, aware of the soft rise and fall of his chest and the steady beat of his pulse. Guy smoothed the hair back from her face and pressed a light kiss against her forehead.

It was meant to soothe, but its effect was quite the opposite. As his lips brushed her temples, Rachel felt the breath catch in her throat. Her heart thudded violently against her ribs and her skin burned with awareness, there, where he had touched her. Guy had hugged her, kissed her, put a brotherly arm around her hundreds of times before and she had never felt like this. No, Rachel acknowledged, trying to moderate her breathing, that was not quite true. There had been moments of awareness, twinges of feeling she had tried to deny or ignore or explain away. Guy was a man, she was a woman. Such things happened. Didn't they? But it was nothing like this, nothing like this terrifying, exhilarating sense that in another moment she would be beyond all control. If she ached now, it was not with exhaustion but with longing. What was happening to her? Her husband had been dead less than a week. But it was far longer since she and Cadagon had slept in the same bed. Was that it? Were the urges of her body finally overwhelming her? Or was she reaching out in her grief, seeking for some way to blot out tragedy?

Guy was still holding her, his unshaven cheek resting against her hair, his arms, once a haven of safety, now a treacherous ground full of dangers and delights. She should pull away from him, retreat to the sofa, force herself back into sanity before she embarrassed them both, but she didn't want to, dear God, she didn't want to.

The creak of the door hinges settled the question for her. Rachel felt Guy stiffen as she raised her head and looked round at her sister. Christine's blue eyes were shadowed and her face looked pale and drawn, but her golden hair shone against the black of her velvet hair ribbon and twilled sarcenet dress. Even in mourning, even in grief, Christine's beauty remained undimmed.

Christine's eyes, wide and dark and intense, were focused on Guy. She made a small exclamation of surprise. She had been near hysterical the day of the explosion, and she had been asleep whenever Guy called at the house in the following days. Save for a brief meeting in a crowd at Cadogan's funeral, this was the first time she had faced Guy since Edmund's death.

Rachel could not have said whether she pulled away or Guy released her, but she knew that Christine became the focus of Guy's attention the moment she entered the room.

"Chrissie." Guy stepped forward, both hands extended. "I'm so very sorry—"

Christine sprang back, as if afraid of his touch. "Sorry?" she said, her voice laced with contempt. "You? You hated Edmund."

Her words surprised Rachel as much as Guy. Rachel knew her sister was distraught over Edmund's death, but she hadn't expected her to turn on their cousin. Guy stood very still. The loosened collar of his shirt revealed the pulse beating at his throat, but he spoke in his customary mild tone. "We had our disagreements. But I never wished him dead."

"Someone did," Christine said. "Someone did far more than wish it."

Rachel drew in her breath. Christine could not possibly mean what her words implied. No one had ever suggested that the explosion was designed to kill Edmund. Christine was grief-stricken and overwrought. Rachel moved forward to stop her sister from saying something which none of them would ever be able to forget, but before she could speak Christine's voice broke. "How could you, Guy? How could you have done it? Couldn't you bear to see me happy?"

Rachel thought the look on Guy's face would be branded in her memory forever. She had never seen him look so very young or so very vulnerable or so very hurt. She wanted to put her arms around him, as she would one of her children,

14

but she knew that she could not. Nothing and no one could make this any less than the hell it was.

Guy stared at Christine for a long burning moment, then without another word turned and left the room. As the door slammed shut behind him, Rachel felt something snap within her. She turned on Christine and spoke the first words that came into her head. "God in heaven, what have you done?"

Chapter One

May, 1814

It was like the first night of a new play, Rachel thought, save that even were the Tavistock given the fresh coat of paint it so badly needed, it couldn't approach the grandeur of Parminter House. And at the theater one was at least able to sit down. There was an ache in the small of her back, her temples were beginning to throb beneath the unaccustomed weight of her jeweled combs, and she could not move her head a fraction of an inch without wondering whether her hair, artfully disposed in ringlets and a Grecian knot, would survive unscathed. Her dress, a satin slip and gauze tunic in a dark red which managed to set off her pale skin without clashing with her auburn hair, felt cool and insubstantial, and its low back left her vulnerable to the draft from the drawing-room doors.

Still, a good costume was an invaluable asset to a successful performance. As the footman pronounced yet another name in a sonorous voice that could quite adequately fill a small theater, Rachel smiled and extended her hand to the next in the seemingly endless line of guests trooping up the gleaming cedar staircase.

Nearly everyone they had invited had come: politicians of both parties; influential hostesses who could make or break reputations; diplomats, both foreign and domestic; wits and dandies; beauties, most of them with a husband in tow. They had come out of curiosity, and Rachel was under no illusion that they had come expecting or even wishing to approve of what they saw. Their smiles and murmured greetings could not have been more polite but said clearly that their presence under the Parminter roof was not to be taken as a sign that they had accepted the new Marquis of Parminter and his sisters as part of their select circle.

Rachel exchanged greetings with the Earl and Countess of Berresford, then took advantage of the momentary lull to glance at her brother. Despite his well-cut coat of dark blue superfine and his carefully tied cravat, there was something about Magnus which set him apart from Berresford and the other gentlemen present. Perhaps it was the trace of ironic amusement on his face or the sharpness of his gray-green eyes, the one feature he and Rachel had in common. Or perhaps it was merely the force of his personality. Six weeks since, he had been Magnus Melchett, feared and admired in the City, not quite accepted anywhere else. Six weeks since, the House of Lords had affirmed that Magnus was rightfully the Eighth Marquis of Parminter. The sordid circumstances that had brought about this change in his fortunes had done nothing to diminish his enjoyment of his new role. He was going to play it with the zest and energy which had already made him, at the age of four-and-thirty, an indecently wealthy man. Berresford, with whom Magnus was presently shaking hands, had had business dealings with him in the past and seemed disconcerted by the banker's elevation to the peerage, a fact which appeared to afford Magnus no small measure of amusement.

But if there was a touch of disdain in Magnus's smile, there was none in Christine's. Of the three Melchetts, she was the only one to look upon their change in status with unalloyed delight. It suited Christine very well to be a marquis's sister. Her eyes were bright and her color high, and she cast the pretty Lady Berresford quite into the shade. But then, one would expect Christine to be in her best looks tonight. It was her betrothal ball. And if her glowing face was not owed to love, Rachel reminded herself that neither she nor Christine had found love a very comforting emotion.

Thinking about her brother and sister, Rachel had not attended to the name the footman had just announced, but as she extended her hand she realized she need not have worried. "Hullo, Philip," she said warmly. "It's a relief to see a familiar face."

Philip Weston gave a twisted smile very different from the boyish grin of the open-faced young man Rachel had first met four years before. "You look smashing, m'dear, never would have guessed you weren't born to it." He leaned toward her as he spoke, and Rachel was surprised to catch a whiff of brandy. Philip had never been one to get cup-shot. "Pity old Guy isn't here," he added with an unexpected touch of venom. "I'd like to see his face when he learns he's the Marquis of Parminter's heir."

Rachel stiffened. She had steeled herself to expect talk about Guy tonight, but not like this, from a man she had thought a friend. Magnus and Christine were still speaking to the Berresfords, but she felt Magnus tense and heard a slight tremor in Christine's voice. "I haven't the least idea where Guy is," Rachel said pleasantly, "but we don't expect him here this evening. And if my brother has anything to say about it, I don't imagine Guy will remain the Marquis of Parminter's heir for much above a year."

Her words seemed to have a sobering effect. "Forgive me, Rachel," Philip muttered, eyes downcast, "forgot myself."

The Berresfords had started for the drawing room. Philip moved on to greet Magnus and Christine, leaning heavily on the stick he'd used since the Tavistock explosion left him a cripple. He seemed to have himself well in hand as he spoke to Magnus, but his careful formality when he addressed Christine told Rachel that Philip was still infatuated with her sister.

A new name was announced, a new hand extended, and there was no time to think about Guy. But half an hour later, when the staircase was at last free of guests and a glance over the gallery railing showed only footmen in the marble-tiled hall below, Rachel turned to her brother and sister and knew that all three of them were thinking the same thing.

Magnus made a minute adjustment to the sleeve of his coat. "It was bound to happen," he remarked. "I daresay this won't be the last we'll hear of it tonight. Every family has its black sheep. We can count ourselves fortunate that ours is out of England."

Christine tossed her head, the light from the candle sconces glowing off the pearls threaded through the bright gold of her hair. "There's no need to look at me, Magnus. I haven't thought of Guy in months, and if anyone is tiresome enough to mention him to me, I shall say so."

It was two years since Christine's careless, hysterical accusation had done what all Rachel's pleading could not — persuaded Guy to leave England. In all that time, the two sisters had not mentioned Guy's name more than a half-dozen times. But one look at Christine's flushed cheeks and bright eyes told Rachel that neither that final quarrel nor the passage of time nor Christine's recent betrothal had served to dim Christine's feelings for their absent cousin. Before either Magnus or Rachel could respond to Christine's words, Justin Hever, Earl of Deaconfield, eldest surviving son of the Duke of Arundel, and Christine's fiancé, strolled from the drawing room. "No offense, Parminter, but I think it's time I stole my betrothed away from such tedious duty." He looked from Christine to her brother and sister. "Difficulties?"

"Philip Weston's here," Christine said in a voice which sounded a touch too brittle to Rachel's ears. "He was foxed and he mentioned Guy."

Justin's face rarely betrayed any emotion stronger than amusement, but at the mention of Guy his eyes hardened for a moment. "How very tiresome of Philip," he murmured. "It's the leg. He drinks to dull the pain and drink always loosens his tongue. Shall I persuade him to leave?"

"I hardly think that's necessary." Magnus liked to fight his own battles.

"You must give us your advice, Justin," Rachel said with a smile intended to divert his attention. "Do you think it's safe to abandon our post? We haven't yet acquired a grasp of such niceties."

"It is certainly safe for Christine to leave," Justin assured her with an assumption of raillery, laying a proprietary hand

20

on Christine's arm. "You and Parminter must decide for yourselves."

"But we can't open the ball until they come," Christine protested. "Let the latecomers fend for themselves, Rachel. It's bad manners to keep your guests waiting."

Relieved to seek refuge in her hostess role, Rachel nodded to the footman and led the way through the open double doors to the second drawing room which had been given over to dancing. It was a long apartment with an ornate plaster ceiling and a narrow band of white-and-gold paneling setting off a series of tapestries commissioned by the fourth marquis to depict his family's glories. A handsome conceit, but tonight it served as a reminder that Magnus and his sisters were not descended from the fourth marquis, who had made the family's fortune, but from his wastrel younger brother.

Otherwise, Rachel could not have been more pleased with the room's appearance. Knowing Magnus's wealth and the family's newness to the world of the ton, the guests would expect extravagance. Rachel, in consultation with Tom Prentice, who painted scenery for the Tavistock, had striven for the exact opposite. Nothing could be simpler than the fragrant branches of hawthorn and apple blossom which overflowed a profusion of fine porcelain vases. Yet, bathed in the light from myriad colored glass lanterns, the room acquired a warm, magical glow. When Rachel had last seen it, it had been empty, a stage before the play began. Now she saw it as she had meant it to look, the light glinting off jewels and washing pale gowns and snowy cravats with brilliant color.

As they moved into the room, eddies of silence rippled through the crowd. Rachel felt the eyes fixed upon them, some curious, more than a few censorious, as if judgment had already been passed. For the first time she truly understood the fears her actor friends claimed to feel as they stepped onto the stage.

The Persian carpets had been removed, and an expanse of freshly polished oak floor was cleared for dancing. The musicians had been providing a quiet accompaniment of Haydn, but they stopped playing when the host and hostess reached the edge of the dance floor. There were upwards of four hundred people in the room, and Rachel could not put a name to half of them. She caught sight of the Fords, her late husband's family, and felt a wave of reassurance. At least she was not entirely cut off from her old life. She looked from the Fords, grouped together about a sofa as if seeking solidarity in these unfamiliar surroundings, to an elderly lady in lavender crêpe and diamonds who was regarding the Melchetts with appraising eyes. Hermione Melchett, widow of the Sixth Marquis of Parminter, gave the faintest of smiles and inclined her head. She had forgot — or at least masked — her earlier distaste for this distant branch of the Melchett family, and for the moment she could be counted an ally.

The musicians regarded Rachel expectantly. She gave a slight nod and they took up their instruments once again. Christine smiled brilliantly, her agitation about Guy forgot in this moment of triumph, and she and Justin moved to the top of the room. They were a handsome couple: Christine graceful and delicate in shimmering gossamer net over white satin, looking far younger than her twenty-five years; Justin tall and elegant in cream-colored knee breeches and a coat as dark as his carefully arranged hair; both utterly self-assured, the offspring of two of England's noblest families, about to join those families through marriage. If only it were that simple, Rachel thought, glancing toward Justin's mother, the Duchess of Arundel, whose careful smile could not hide her disapproval.

Once Christine and Justin had taken their places, sets began to form for the first quadrille. Rachel felt a light touch on her arm, signaling the arrival of her own partner, Gideon Carne.

"Smile," he told her as they moved onto the dance floor, "and nod your head, and think about something interesting. Evenings like this are the very devil, but it's the only way to get through them. I'd say it's going remarkably well."

Rachel laughed. "Flattery, Lord Carne. But I thank you for it."

"No, strict observation. Lady Parminter is smiling."

"That *is* a relief," Rachel conceded. "But the evening isn't over yet."

Gideon's dark eyes grew serious. "There's bound to be talk, Rachel," he said, his hand tightening on her arm for a moment. "Hold your head high and ignore it. They won't be able to touch you."

Rachel smiled in gratitude, but the other couples in their set were moving into place and claimed her attention. Beside her, Gideon was exerting himself to be charming, far more energetically, Rachel suspected, than he ordinarily would at such an entertainment. Every so often Rachel saw his gaze stray to the set where his wife Fiona was partnered by Magnus. The events which had made Magnus the Marquis of Parminter had had an equally drastic effect on Fiona's life, and she, too, was subject to the crowd's scrutiny.

As the first strains of music sounded and the couples began to move through the figures of the dance, Rachel discovered that it was possible to smile and nod and give free rein to her thoughts. It was inevitable that she think of Guy. She found herself wishing he was here tonight. Pure madness, of course. Even were it possible for Guy to show his face in England, this was just the sort of entertainment he would detest. Gideon was right. Evenings like this were the very devil. He and Guy had more than a little in common. But Gideon was at least willing to play the game for his wife's sake. Rachel was not at all sure Guy would do so. Even for Christine.

Rachel inclined her head toward a fair-haired young man as the movement of the dance brought them together. The last time Guy and Christine met she had accused him of causing Edmund's death. And just before Christine had walked into the room, Rachel's own senses had run riot and her feelings had been thrown into tumult by a simple embrace meant only to offer comfort. For the past two years, Rachel had refused to think about that moment in the light of day, but she had dwelled on it more times than she cared to count in the darkness of her bedchamber.

No, for more reasons than one it was a very good thing Guy wasn't present tonight. But her longing for him remained, deep, instinctive, and wholly irrational. Perhaps she wanted him precisely because he would tell her—she could almost hear his voice and see the laughter in his eyes—that the opinions of four hundred starchy people were hardly worth a candle.

Sooner than she expected, the dance came to an end. As she and Gideon left the floor, Rachel was besieged by requests for the écossaise which was to follow. She fended them off with smiles and excuses, under no illusion that her sudden popularity had anything to do with her person. It was gradually being borne in on her that the Marquis of Parminter's sister—no matter that she was widowed, a month past her thirtieth birthday, and of dubious descent—was going to be in for a great many such attentions.

With unerring instinct, Gideon steered his way through the throng and located his wife and Magnus. Magnus, who was engaged for the next dance, excused himself after a few words and moved off to find his partner. "He's enjoying this," Fiona Carne observed, linking her arm through her husband's.

"He enjoys watching everyone adapt to the change in his circumstances," Rachel said. "I don't think he's realized that he may find himself changing as well."

Fiona smiled. Slender and elegant, with pale blond hair and cool gray eyes, she had the classic features of the Melchett family. Looking at her now, fashionably gowned in spangled azure crêpe, it was difficult to believe she had grown up thinking herself the bastard daughter of a country gentleman. It was only within the last year that Fiona had learned her parents had been legally if secretly married and that her mother had been the only child of the Sixth Marquis of Parminter. These revelations had made her mother's second marriage bigamous and bastardized the then eighth marquis. Most of the Parminter fortune had gone to Fiona, but the title had gone to Magnus, the nearest male heir.

Rachel and Fiona were much of an age. Their family connection and their recent change in fortune had quickly cemented their friendship. It was a friendship Rachel valued all the more because of its rarity. Since her marriage, her life had revolved around her family and the theater, and though there were many people she could call friend, none was really a confidante. "I wish I could stay and talk," Rachel told the

Carnes, "but a hostess can't afford to relax at her own entertainment. It's time I circulated about the room."

"I'll come with you if I may," Fiona said. "These occasions call for family solidarity. It's all right, love," she added, twisting her head round to look up at Gideon with a mischievous smile, "you've done your duty. Go find a Tory to convert. Or a Whig to commiserate with. There seem to be plenty of both present tonight."

Rachel and Fiona began to move about the room, stopping to exchange pleasantries with guests who were not dancing, glancing into the third drawing room, which had been given over to cards, complimenting the first footman on the excellent work of the staff. "You do this splendidly," Fiona said. "I could never manage half so well. I own the house still terrifies me."

Rachel smiled. Parminter House had come to Fiona in the settlement of the Parminter estates, but she had let it to Magnus for the Season. "It terrified me, too," Rachel told her friend, "until I realized it's nothing but an enormous stage. If tonight's audience is a bit hostile, they're far more restrained than most."

"What a useful analogy," Fiona said with the generous smile which transformed her reserved face. "I must remember it."

Rachel paused to nod to the Countess Buckleigh. Lady Buckleigh returned the nod with cool precision. She was connected to the Melchett family, but clearly that was not enough to win her approbation. "The analogy came from my children," Rachel confessed as she and Fiona moved on. "When I had to tell them they weren't allowed downstairs this evening, Jessica asked if they could at least go backstage."

"Very sensible," Fiona said. "Parminter House has a backstage, of course, but I'm afraid the footmen and the kitchen staff wouldn't relish having a pair of children underfoot."

"That's what I tried to explain." Rachel frowned, recalling the scene in the nursery. The two years since their father's death had not been easy for Alec and Jessica and the removal to Parminter House had only made matters worse.

Telling herself it would do little good to think about that

now, Rachel turned her attention to her present surroundings. Outwardly all seemed to be going well. Footmen garbed in the red-and-black Parminter livery moved among the crowd bearing silver trays filled with plentiful glasses of a very fine champagne; there were enough chairs and sofas to accommodate all those who wished to sit down; and the sweet, fresh scent of the flowers was strong enough to overwhelm the more unpleasant odors caused by so many people engaged in an activity as strenuous as dancing.

Yet behind the nods and smiles and polite commonplaces, Rachel felt a palpable undercurrent of censure and suspicion. She caught fragments of conversation, too insubstantial to amount to anything more than a vague sense of disquiet. Once she heard the words "Tavistock Theater" and knew that her own role in the management of the Tavistock was under discussion. But it was no worse than she had expected and nothing she wasn't prepared to handle. When she and Fiona had nearly completed their circuit of the room, they extricated themselves from a corpulent baronet who had been eyeing them with frank appreciation and sought refuge behind a gilded pedestal from which a marble bust had been removed to make room for a vase of flowers. As they smiled at each other in relief, a disembodied voice from the other side of the pedestal murmured, "Their mother was an actress, you know. A *French* actress."

Despite the warmth of the room, Rachel felt a chill run through her. For a moment she was aware of nothing but the burning pain which those few careless words had fanned to life. Then Fiona took her by the arm and steered her to a brocade settee which stood in a shallow painted alcove. "As a former governess," Fiona said, her light tone belied by the concern in her eyes, "I find the lack of tact in some of our best families deplorable. No one should leave the schoolroom without learning that one always refrains from gossip until one is safely in one's carriage."

Rachel managed to smile. "Thank you. I didn't mean to make a complete fool of myself."

"You didn't," Fiona assured her. "I doubt a stranger would have known anything was amiss." She regarded Rachel for a

26

moment, as if debating whether or not to say more. "I haven't known you long, Rachel, but I count you one of my closest friends. And I've noticed that you never speak of your mother."

Rachel was vaguely aware of the lilting strains of a waltz rising over the stir of movement and the buzz of conversation. She smoothed her skirt with uncharacteristic nervousness, then clasped her hands and forced herself to meet Fiona's questioning gaze. "It may have been gossip, but it's no more than the truth. My mother is French and she is an actress. Shortly after Christine was born, she left us and returned to her homeland." Rachel drew a breath. Strange that so devastating an abandonment could be described so simply. "We know she is now with the Comédie Française, though she's never written to us."

Fiona's eyes were filled with sympathy but she seemed to sense that any expression of it would undo Rachel entirely. "You must have been—five years old?" she asked softly.

"Five and a half." Now that the words were out, Rachel found it was a relief to speak of it. "She'd never been a very attentive mother, but we noticed her absence more than you'd think. Fortunately, my Aunt Julia and her son Guy came to live with us not long after. Guy was my salvation." She hesitated a moment, then added, "I miss him quite dreadfully."

Fiona made a show of smoothing a flawlessly fitting glove. "You don't think Guy might consider returning to England, now Magnus has become Lord Parminter?"

Rachel shook her head. "Magnus and Guy never got on well. Besides, Guy couldn't show his face in England without facing arrest."

It was all Rachel dared say in such a crowded setting, and Fiona did not press her. They were soon joined by Fiona's friend, Nicola Windham, a lively young woman quite free of pretension who expressed her admiration of the ball with an unfettered warmth which did much to restore Rachel's equanimity. Rachel was leaning back and letting the two friends carry the burden of the conversation, when she saw a slender dark-haired girl in pink slip from the crowd and hurry through the doors to the gallery, a look of confusion on her face.

It was Margaret Hever, Justin's youngest sister, and something had clearly distressed her. Rachel excused herself and moved toward the double doors. The gallery was crowded with guests seeking to escape the press in the reception rooms, and there were several latecomers climbing the stairs. It was a moment before Rachel caught sight of Margaret, who had taken refuge on a blue damask settee some distance down the corridor which opened off the gallery. Her head was turned away, her face in shadow, but the light from the candle sconce above picked out the pale pink muslin of her frock. She seemed unaware of Rachel's approach until Rachel reached her side and said softly, "Hullo, Meg."

Margaret gave a nervous start, then looked round and sighed with relief. "Oh, it's you, Rachel. I was just . . ." Her voice trailed off, and she twisted her hands together in her lap, creasing her long white gloves.

Rachel smiled. "You needn't have an excuse for wanting to get away from the crowd. I feel quite the same myself."

"I'm not very good at large parties," Margaret confessed. "I know I'm a disappointment to Mama, for she was a great success in her youth and Fanny took after her. It wasn't so bad in my first season, for no one seemed to notice me, but since Papa's become the duke—you know how that changes things."

"With a vengeance." Rachel dropped down onto the settee. It had never occurred to her to equate her own case with Margaret's, for though the present Duke of Arundel had only attained the title on his nephew's death the previous year, there had never been any question as to his children's place in society. But being accepted was not the same as feeling all eyes upon one. As a duke's daughter, Margaret was now subject to the same attentions Rachel found so tiresome. "I don't want to pry," she said gently, "but as a hostess I have my duties. Was one of my gentleman guests less than gentlemanly?"

"Oh, no. Nothing like that. It's just—I do hate people who won't leave well enough alone." Margaret's eyes darkened with sudden anger. "Lady Swinnerton kept going on about

28

Edmund's death and how tragic it was—as if I don't know that, he was *my* brother—and how nice it is that Justin and Christine can comfort each other for his loss, and how of course it's only natural that after her betrothed's death Christine turned to his brother, all the time implying that it wasn't natural in the least—" Margaret's hand flew to her mouth. "Oh, dear, Rachel, I'm dreadfully sorry. I wasn't thinking of your husband."

"That's understandable." Rachel regarded Margaret with concern. "People are bound to be saying that sort of thing tonight. I'm sorry you had to hear it."

"It wasn't so very bad until she started asking how my mother felt about Justin's betrothal. I could tell she was positively hoping I'd say something indecorous so she could repeat it to everyone she knew. I told her Christine is my friend—which is true—and that Mama is delighted she and Justin are to make a match of it. Which is true, too, of course," Margaret added, a fraction of a second too late.

Rachel made no comment. The Hevers had never become reconciled to Edmund's betrothal to Christine Melchett, daughter of an improvident country gentleman and a French actress. They could not have been pleased when their second son—now, thanks to his cousin's death, the heir to a dukedom—turned his attention to his late brother's fiancée. But Christine had also undergone a change in status. Justin's parents could not object to their son becoming betrothed to the Marquis of Parminter's sister, but Rachel suspected that they had not forgot her sister's origins. More importantly, she suspected they had not forgiven Christine for, in their eyes, entangling Edmund with the Levellers and thus bringing about his death.

"I should go," Margaret murmured in a subdued voice. "I'm supposed to dance the cotillion with Lord Parminter."

Rachel looked quickly at the younger girl. Lady Parminter had fixed upon Margaret as Magnus's future wife. Magnus was not to be pushed, but there was no denying he had begun to pay Margaret more attention than he would ordinarily lavish on a girl of twenty with no particular beauty to recommend her. But while the duke and duchess's disapproval of

Christine had so far remained decently veiled, that did not mean they would approve if Magnus began courting their only unmarried daughter. The Hevers were an old but impoverished family, and Rachel was not sure which would weigh stronger in the balance, Magnus's fortune or the manner in which he had obtained it.

How Margaret felt about the prospect of becoming Magnus's wife seemed the least of anyone's concerns. "Magnus isn't exactly the stuff romantic heroes are made of, is he?" Rachel asked, studying her friend.

"It's not that I don't like him, Rachel," Margaret said quickly. "He's always very kind to me. But he is a bit — forbidding."

"Not to mention arrogant and high-handed," Rachel said cheerfully. "But he does have his good points. He won't pay you fulsome compliments or offer up inane commonplaces. Besides," she added, rising and shaking out the folds of her dress, "at least no one will dare gossip about the past while you're in his presence."

Margaret gave a determined smile, as if steeling herself for the ordeal ahead. It was some time before they made their way through the crowd on the gallery and finally reached the second drawing room, which seemed to have grown more crowded in their absence, the voices louder, the atmosphere more hectic. They paused for a moment, adjusting to the tumult of sound and the dimmer light of the lanterns.

"Lady Rachel. I'm sorry we're so wretchedly late."

Rachel turned and found herself staring into a long, high-bred face with penetrating dark eyes and a thin-lipped mouth, a face she had seen before in a vastly different setting and under circumstances which even now she could not recall with anything other than anger and alarm.

"Mr. Mountjoy," Rachel said, extending her hand. Beside Mountjoy stood a thin, dark-haired woman with plain but aristocratic features. His wife presumably. Rachel had never met her. Her one previous meeting with William Mountjoy had not been social.

Mountjoy's handshake was firm, as it had been on that other occasion, his manner courteous, his eyes far too shrewd. Rachel introduced Lady Margaret, and Mountjoy introduced his wife, Lady Eveline—Rachel vaguely recalled hearing that she was the daughter of an earl—and the four of them exchanged commonplaces until Lady Eveline was claimed for the cotillion. Magnus joined them soon after. As Rachel had expected, her brother was pleased by Mountjoy's presence. It was Magnus who had insisted the Mountjoys be invited, over all Rachel's protests. With their cousin suspected by the Home Office, Magnus had said, they could not afford to make an enemy of one of its two undersecretaries.

Mountjoy greeted Magnus as courteously as he had Rachel and looked after him as he and Margaret vanished into the crowd. "Edmund Hever's sister?" he said, turning back to Rachel.

Rachel nodded. "The youngest of the children."

Mountjoy shook his head, genuine regret in his eyes. "She must have barely been out of the schoolroom at the time of his death. A sad business." Mountjoy cast a brief glance to either side, then lowered his voice. "I've no wish to cast a cloud over a pleasant evening, Lady Rachel, but I'm afraid it must be said. With the change in your family's circumstances, it's not unlikely that your cousin will send word to one of you. If that happens, we would greatly appreciate it if you would tell us. We are still anxious to talk to him."

For all the polite phrases, there was no doubt that it was a command. Rachel gave a cordial smile and found she was glad to speak of Guy directly. "If you think being the Marquis of Parminter's heir would be of the slightest interest to our cousin, you don't know him," she said pleasantly. "It's likely to make him disown the lot of us."

Mountjoy smiled as if she had made a clever joke and did not press the matter further. When he had excused himself, Rachel took another turn about the room, answered a question from the kitchens via one of the footmen, danced with her husband's cousin, Brandon Ford, and then with two eligible gentlemen whom Lady Parminter had introduced to her. She had just disengaged herself from the second of these, a widower with two young children and an ancient title but little money to support either, when she saw Philip Weston weaving an unsteady path through the crowd toward her.

"Rachel." His voice rose above the discreet murmur around them, and Rachel had no choice but to wait for him to reach her side. To her surprise, he took her by the arm and steered her into a nearby window recess. Now his voice was low, as if he were confiding a secret, and at first Rachel was sure she could not have heard him correctly. Seeing her confusion, Philip spoke again, a trifle more loudly. "Guy's here."

For a brief, incredulous moment, Rachel wondered if it could be true. No, it was impossible. Even Guy would not run such a risk. "Don't be ridiculous," she said sharply. Her feet ached in her thin-soled sandals, her mouth was dry, and her throat hoarse from hours of constant talk, and the last thing she needed was for that sort of nonsensical rumor to be bandied about.

"I saw him, I tell you," Philip insisted. His face was serious though his words were slurred, and Rachel suspected he had drunk a good deal more since his arrival. "In the cardroom. He's playing whist. Go see for yourself."

Rachel had seen her husband in his cups often enough to know it would be little use to argue. "All right," she said in a soothing voice, "I'll have a look."

It was only as she neared the door of the cardroom that Rachel experienced another moment of doubt. Her mind told her there wasn't the remotest possibility that she would find her cousin at the tables, but her body tensed and her pulse quickened. Excusing herself to Lord Buckleigh, who had stopped her just outside the cardroom, Rachel moved through the open doorway and paused to glance about. The atmosphere was more boisterous than on her previous visit, but otherwise the scene appeared little changed. No one remotely resembling Guy was visible, though her view was partially obscured by a lady and gentleman engaged in flirtatious banter. Rachel stepped around them and felt her heart thud to a stop and her blood chill. That light, disordered hair was unmistakably familiar, though the man's face was shadowed as he leaned back to study his cards. Perhaps the faint similarity had deceived Philip, Rachel thought, willing her heart to begin beating again.

The man leaned forward and set his cards on the table, then looked up and met Rachel's eyes. He smiled pleasantly at her and turned his attention back to the game. There was no question now. He was unmistakably Guy Melchett.

Chapter Two

The infectious smile was the same, and the glint in his eyes and the maddening air of self-possession. He was here, scarcely ten feet away. As Rachel looked at Guy's face for the first time in two years, shock and alarm gave way to pure delight. Delight changed to indignation when she realized her cousin had no intention of abandoning his card game. How very like Guy. Rachel let her gaze linger over the other tables, so that her lengthy persual of the whist game would not seem out of place, then took a turn about the cardroom, stopping to speak with others who were observing the play or had just completed a hand.

Because she avoided paying much attention to Guy's table, she did not realize the game had come to an end until a familiar voice just behind her shoulder said, "Hullo, Rachel, sorry to have kept you waiting, but I was winning rather a lot and trying to fit myself out in a style suitable for your drawing room has been rather a drain on my pocket."

Torn between a desire to throw her arms around her cousin and an impulse to box his ears for putting himself in danger, Rachel turned round, grateful that those in the immediate vicinity were engrossed in their cards. Guy's hair, straw-colored in his youth, now streaked with brown, fell over his forehead in its customary state of disarray, but he was very properly attired in sage breeches and a dark green coat. The latter did not fit as if it had been made for him, and its color would only serve to make him stand out amidst the black and dark blue which predominated in her reception rooms.

As she met Guy's gaze, Rachel felt a shock of recognition, followed by an awkwardness she could not have explained. She had forgot how very alive his eyes were or how her heart could lighten when she looked at him. "I'm glad you were able to come," she said, quite as if he were simply another late-arriving guest. "I hope you can spare me a moment of your time."

Mercifully, a door from the cardroom led to an adjoining antechamber. Rachel opened it and saw with relief that the room beyond was empty, though a brace of candles stood burning on the mantel. The room was small, the ceiling lower than in the vast drawing rooms, the plaster walls pleasantly light, but it still seemed a ridiculously formal setting in which to confront the cousin who had seen her with scraped knees. Rachel drew a breath and turned to face Guy, but he forestalled her.

"I know," he said in a contrite voice, "you want an explanation. I'm sure your footmen—are they all yours or did you have to hire extras?—I'm sure your footmen had the strictest orders not to let in anyone who hadn't been properly invited, and naturally you want to know how I managed. The truth is, it was the easiest thing in the world. I simply attached myself to a rather large party of latecomers and no one bothered to count heads. I hope you won't blame your staff."

He was smiling, the rueful, winning, slightly crooked smile which transformed his blunt-featured face and which he used to such effect when he wanted to create a distraction. Rachel, knowing it was useless to ask him what the devil he was doing in England, voiced her most immediate concern. "William Mountjoy is here. I suppose it's occurred to you that he'll have you arrested?"

"He may want to," Guy returned, "but I doubt he'll be able to do anything about it until morning."

"And then?" Rachel tried to match his light tone, but she could hear the tension in her voice as she spoke. Feeling in need of support, she sat down abruptly on a small settee.

Guy settled himself in a nearby chair, upholstered like the

settee in pale green satin with stripes of a paler green. He had a knack of adapting himself to his setting and looked fully as much at home as he would in a coffeehouse or the wings of a theater. "I was never officially charged with anything."

"You would have been if you'd stayed in England. The only reason the Home Office and Bow Street didn't make their suspicions public was that they didn't want to look like fools for losing their chief suspect." Rachel slumped back against the stiff settee, realizing the senselessness of her argument. "You *know* all that," she said reproachfully. Knowing it, he should never have come back. She had stressed the danger often enough in her letters, letters which Guy's friend Gordon Murray had somehow managed to smuggle to him, though for her own sake he refused to tell her where Guy had gone.

Her letters. Rachel recalled the last one and all at once understood why Guy had decided it was worth the risk to return to England. She straightened up, a wave of anger sweeping through her. "Christine," she said, staring into the gray-green eyes which were the twin of Magnus's and her own. "You came back because I wrote to you about Justin and Christine."

Guy was sitting in front of the candles, so it was difficult to read his expression. There was a pause of several seconds and then he said in a level and perfectly pleasant voice, "Yes, as a matter of fact, I did."

Rachel had not expected him to admit it, and the fact that he had increased her anger. "You fool," she said, getting abruptly to her feet. "Don't you realize she doesn't love you? Not as much as she loves herself. She never has, and she never will. She wants to marry Justin, Guy; she wants the life he can give her. You won't be able to change that, but you'll destroy her happiness and wind up in prison yourself, and if I have to watch—"

"Rachel. My dear girl."

Caught up in her tirade, Rachel was scarcely aware that Guy had moved until he took her by the shoulders, his hands warm and soothing. Surprised at having displayed such emotion, she drew a steadying breath.

"That's better," Guy said with approval. He studied her face for a moment, as if learning it anew. "It's good to be home," he said softly, and then he pulled her to him in a crushing, brotherly hug.

It was the first time he had touched her since that night in her sitting room two years ago. His arms were familiar and comforting, but as she hugged him back, Rachel felt a tremor run through her which was anything but sisterly. Would it always be like this? Would her senses overwhelm her reason and jeopardize the most important friendship in her life?

To hide her confusion, Rachel drew back, laughing. "You call this home?"

Guy grinned. "Home is where you are," he said, taking her face between his hands. "It has been since I was six years old." He smoothed some loosened strands of hair off her face with gentle fingers, then, to her disappointment and relief, settled his hands on her shoulders once again. "Now do you think we might discuss this rationally?"

Rachel nodded and permitted him to steer her to the settee. "I came back because of Christine and Justin's betrothal," Guy told her when they were seated. "I did not come back to win Christine for myself. I doubt that I could. Not after what she said to me the last time we met."

"She was angry," Rachel said, hearing the undercurrent of bitterness in Guy's voice, "angry and distraught. She didn't mean it."

"Perhaps. It scarcely matters now. It's been two years, Rachel, and I haven't gone unconsoled. Whatever I once felt for Christine, it's over. Believe me."

No one could be more persuasive than Guy, but Rachel was not willing to let herself be persuaded. "Can you honestly tell me you wouldn't marry Christine tonight if she were willing?" she demanded.

"Marry her?" Guy gave a shout of laughter. "Rachel, my sweet, some things haven't changed. I can still barely afford to keep myself, let alone a wife. I doubt I will ever marry anyone and certainly not Christine. We aren't suited. You've said so often enough."

"You never believed me."

"I was a starry-eyed young devil then. Now I'm sober and practically middle-aged."

"You're five months older than I am." Rachel pushed one of her combs into place. "If you didn't come back to win Christine from Justin, why did you come back?"

Guy settled into his corner of the settee and was silent for a long moment. "Because, whatever else she may have once been to me, Christine is my cousin and I don't care to see her marry a man who may be responsible for the deaths of four people."

He must be joking. Rachel stared at his face in the flickering candlelight, but he looked in deadly earnest. "You're serious," she said at last.

"I'm afraid I am." Guy's voice was quiet and curiously gentle, at odds with his words. "Someone was responsible for what happened at the Tavistock, and I know it wasn't me."

So that was it. Guy was still so besotted with Christine that he had convinced himself her fiancé was behind the explosion. Rachel subdued her anger and forced herself to hear Guy out. "What in God's name makes you think it was Justin?"

"I'm quite certain it was one of the Levellers."

Rachel studied Guy closely. She was sure he did not think any of the Levellers would have planted the explosives to protest the play. Which meant— "You think there was a spy among you," she said.

"I'd suspected it before. God knows the Home Office have planted agent provocateurs in any number of groups, though I'm flattered they considered us dangerous enough to warrant the attention. It wasn't what we did, I suspect, as much as who we were. Most of us had been to university and several of us had relatives in Parliament. They were afraid people might listen to us and to a certain extent that was beginning to be true. The Government were more than usually nervous that spring, worried the Luddites might cause the whole country to go up in flames. So an enterprising soul decided to scare our members back into respectability by proving that radicalism breeds violence."

"And murder?"

Guy shook his head. "The theater should have been empty. Whoever planned the explosion didn't know Edmund and the others were meeting in one of the storage rooms. The deaths made the explosion even more of an incident than the Home Office had intended. Edmund's family were screaming for blood. They had to find a scapegoat or some uncomfortable questions would be asked. It wouldn't look good if it got about that the Home Office had ordered an act which took the life of a young man from one of England's oldest families."

"If one of the Levellers was an agent provocateur, he was probably working for Mountjoy," Rachel said. "It was Mountjoy who steered Bow Street in your direction after the explosion." She was silent for a moment, trying to work it out. "It's possible that the whole thing was arranged with the idea of blaming you. Your plays were winning you a reputation, and they reached a wider audience than any pamphlets."

"Perhaps." Guy's face was impassive. "Whatever the motive, it means one of us was in Mountjoy's employ. And it could very well have been Justin."

"Don't be ridiculous. There must have been twenty committed Levellers and a dozen others who drifted in and out of the group. It could be any one of them."

"I'm afraid not." Guy leaned back and regarded her for a moment. "I said I'd suspected there was an agent among us even before the explosion. Actually, I'd been quite certain of it for a good month."

Rachel's anger gave way to surprise. This was the first she had heard of Guy's suspicions. But then, thanks to Christine, she and Guy had not been on the best of terms during those last days before the explosion. "What happened?" she asked.

Guy spoke quickly, with little pause for reflection. "You remember the article I wrote against making frame-breaking a capital offense? The one that got Gordon's paper shut down? Bow Street got to Gordon before he finished printing it. I'm certain someone tipped them off. I knew the article might get us into trouble, so I'd made it a point to keep quiet about it. But then, after one of our meetings, Cadogan brought a group of us back to Great Ormond Street—you were out at the theater, I think. I'd drunk more than I should, and it was just the inner circle, as it were, so there didn't seem any harm in talking. Not one of my more astute moments. Cadogan and I later agreed one of the men present must have informed. He never mentioned it to you?"

"No. We were both very busy that last month." Rachel smoothed her skirt. "Who was at the house that night?"

"Brandon. Charles Pursglove. Gerald Sneath. And Harry Jessop." Guy recited the list as if he had gone over it many times in his head. "And Philip Weston, who never lost a chance to tag along to Ormond Street to see Christine. And Edmund, who brought Justin and Billingham with him."

All familiar names, all people they had once known well. "Did you confront them with it?" Rachel asked.

Guy grinned. "At the next meeting of the Levellers, I said I knew there was an agent among us and I hoped he'd report our proceedings carefully as we'd been trying to get the Government's attention for years." Guy leaned toward her, suddenly intent. "There were eight at the house that night, not counting Cadogan and me. But Brandon and Jessop and Philip and Edmund were all in the theater the night of the explosion, which more or less rules them out. That leaves four: Charles, Sneath, Billingham—and Justin."

Rachel rubbed her arms. Gerald Sneath was an actor in the Tavistock company. Alfred Billingham, who had married Edmund and Justin's sister Frances, and Charles Pursglove, who had married Cadogan's cousin Dorinda, were both presently among the guests in her drawing rooms. But if she found it difficult to suspect them, she found it equally difficult to suspect the man Christine was to marry. "It needn't have been Justin," she said after a long silence.

"No," Guy agreed, "but Justin seems as good a candidate as any. Did you seriously believe he was committed to the rights of the common man?"

"I'm not a fool, Guy. Justin joined the Levellers because of his brother. Edmund was an impulsive young hothead, and Justin felt it was his duty to keep an eye on him. He as good as told me so."

"I don't doubt it. But if someone like Mountjoy suggested that he could do His Majesty's Government a service by keeping an eye on Edmund's companions as well, I suspect Justin would have accepted."

"You're saying Justin killed his brother."

"He wouldn't have known there was anyone in the building."

It was all so neat, so well worked out, so detached and objective. Unable to argue with him, Rachel changed her tactics. "You must have realized two years ago that it had to be one of them. Why wait until now?"

"Because two years ago you and Gordon convinced me that if I remained in England I'd find myself on the inside of Newgate."

"You still could," Rachel reminded him, returning to her first fear. "The witness—"

"Ah." Guy gave a satisfied smile. "I don't think there's any immediate danger of the witness being called against me. When he convinced me to leave, Gordon promised to investigate the matter. A few months ago he wrote that he'd finally managed to track the witness down."

"And persuaded him to recant?" Rachel asked with disbelief.

"Oh, no. We simply beat the Government's price. The man is currently on a ship bound for the East Indies. I'm going to have the devil of a time paying Gordon back for his passage."

Rachel was conscious of a great relief and of an irrational anger because Guy was able to deflect all her arguments. "The witness may be gone, but they must still have his statement," she pointed out. "And if they bribed one witness, they can easily bribe another."

"They could," Guy acknowledged, "but it will take them a while to realize the first one is missing. And I imagine Magnus's new position will make them more hesitant to arrest me. I've been thinking about coming home for some time. Your last letter decided me. I don't know that Justin is guilty, but I mean to learn whether or not he is before he marries Christine."

"And if he is, you'll stop the marriage."

"Wouldn't you?"

She would, of course, but that was beside the point. "This isn't about Justin," Rachel said, surprised at the scathing note in her voice. "If Christine was betrothed to any of the others, you'd have convinced yourself he was the most likely suspect."

"Good God, Rachel." Guy sprang to his feet, his normally mild voice rising to a sudden roar. "Don't you think I haven't considered that? Can't you credit me with some sense? I may have behaved like an idiot over Christine, but I was never a complete fool."

Silence stretched between them, echoing with the hurt of previous quarrels, bitter with the sense that they had both gone farther than they intended and did not know how to turn back. The door opened onto that silence, bringing bright light and the buzz of conversation and a rustle of satin. "Rachel," Christine said, closing the door on the noise and lights from the cardroom, "Philip told me the most preposterous story—"

Rachel turned her head in time to see her sister standing transfixed not three feet from the door, her normally animated face drained of color and expression, her vivid blue eyes dark and glassy.

"Hullo, Chrissie," Guy said, all traces of passion gone from his voice. "I'm sorry if I've caused a stir."

Christine stared at him, her lips trembling from anger or some other emotion. Then with great deliberation she turned and moved to the nearest chair, arranging her skirts with care as she sank into it. "I couldn't believe even you would have the audacity to show your face. Did you seriously expect you would be welcome?"

"I thought Rachel would be glad to see me," Guy said, dropping down onto the settee. "I know I'm glad to see her."

Christine's gaze flickered in her sister's direction. "Why didn't you have him thrown out?"

"In the middle of the ball?" Rachel demanded. "That *would* have created a stir."

A spasm of annoyance crossing her face, Christine turned back to Guy. "Why did you come?"

"To see Rachel. And to offer you my congratulations, of course. I hope you and Justin will be very happy."

Christine was taken aback. "Justin knows," she blurted out, "that Bow Street suspect you."

"Ah," said Guy, stretching his legs out in front of him, "I wondered about that. Does he suspect me, too?"

Christine looked away, her eyes fixed on the brilliant sapphires in her betrothal ring, glowing against the white of her glove. "No," she admitted at last.

Guy glanced at Rachel. Rachel made no response.

"But Justin's parents know nothing about it," Christine continued, looking up with alarm, "and if they learn you are suspected of causing Edmund's death—Oh, it is insufferable." She rose abruptly. "You had no right to come back."

"That's nonsense, Christine." Rachel was on her feet as well. "Guy is his own master, and he has every right to behave in as foolhardy a manner as he wishes."

"Thank you, Rachel, I was wondering when you'd admit that," Guy murmured.

"I might have known you'd take his side," Christine said bitterly, "you always do." She lifted the brace of candles and stared critically into the chimney glass. "Oh, why can't you leave me alone?" she said with sudden passion.

"It seems to me," said Guy, "that you were the one who burst in on a private conversation."

His tone was dry, but Rachel, looking into the mirror, saw that Christine's mouth was trembling again, this time not from anger. Her maternal instincts roused, Rachel shot Guy a warning glance. "Guy didn't come back to make trouble between you and the Arundels," she said, moving toward her sister. Strictly speaking this was true. Guy was concerned with Justin, not his parents, and Rachel had no intention of allowing him to disrupt her sister's betrothal without solid evidence of Justin's guilt. "Don't distress yourself. Even if they learn Guy is suspected, their quarrel will be with him, not with you."

"Oh, I'm all right," Christine said, shaking off the arm Rachel had put around her. She set down the candles and pinched her pale cheeks, managing at the same time to dash a few tears from her eyes. "Just don't expect me to take your side, Guy."

"I don't," said Guy evenly. "Two years ago you made it clear that that was the last thing you would do."

Christine stiffened. "I scarcely remember what I said two years ago, and I'm sure I didn't mean half of it. You know how it is when I'm overset." She glanced at Guy, a look in her eyes which was close to pleading. Guy made no response. Christine drew in her breath sharply, then turned her attention to a ringlet which had fallen loose and threatened to destroy the symmetry of her coiffure. Rachel moved away from the fireplace just as the door opened again and her brother strode into the room.

Magnus took in the scene before him and expelled his breath on a harsh note. "Good God. I should have known it had to be true. Even Weston wouldn't make up something like this."

Guy stepped forward, his hand extended. "It's good to see you again, Magnus. My congratulations on your good fortune."

Magnus ignored Guy's hand and grasped him by the lapels of his coat. "Out," he barked. "Now. By the backstairs. And if you dare show your face here again—"

"Magnus!" Rachel moved to intercede, as she had so often in the past when her brother and cousin had come to blows.

"It's all right, Rachel," Guy said, disengaging himself without difficulty. Magnus was an inch or so taller, but Guy had always proved more than a match for him in their youthful brawls. "I hadn't intended to stay long in any case. Though I must say I regret missing Mountjoy."

"So help me—" Magnus began.

"Another time perhaps. I take it this door leads to the hall?"

"You'll leave by the front stairs," Rachel said, pressing his hand. "There's no need to disturb the servants."

Guy grinned. "Absolutely not." He kissed her cheek, a light, affectionate salute which affected her far more than it should. "Your servant, Magnus. Christine. Tell Justin I appreciate his faith in me."

Christine stood very still, her face once more devoid of expression. Magnus waited until Guy had reached the door before he spoke. "Whether or not you see Rachel is her affair. But if you dare cross my doorstep again, I'll personally throw you in the gutter. Do I make myself clear?"

"Abundantly. I appreciate the warning. But then," said Guy, smiling his farewell at all three of them, "it will hardly be the first time I've been in the gutter, will it?"

Chapter Three

Guy ran down the stairs of Gordon Murray's lodgings in Portpool Lane and made his way through the printshop that occupied the ground floor. Murray was an old friend of Guy's, nearly twenty years his senior. A publisher of pamphlets and a small newspaper that changed its name every time it was shut down, he was acquainted with every protest group in London as well as a fair number of its magistrates. It was Murray who had finally persuaded Guy to leave the country two years before. "When the Home Office are involved," he had told a stubborn Guy, "one doesn't play the hero. Run to earth, you idiot. Stay there a year. Stay two. I'll keep you informed." And Guy, with Christine's accusation ringing in his ears, had acquiesced.

It was Guy's second day in London. Yesterday he had sought out his cousins. Today he had to give thought to the law. It was a long walk to Bow Street, but it was early, the morning was fine, and Guy wanted time to reacquaint himself with the city before confronting the magistrates who might or might not be inclined to take him into custody. Cousin of the Marquis of Parminter or not, he could still find himself behind bars this afternoon. He had known that was a possibility when he decided to return to England. Now he considered his approach. Burley, the runner who had investigated the case two years ago, had seemed a reasonable man. Burley would know how matters stood.

Guy turned down Grays Inn Lane to High Holborn and from there to Drury Lane, watching and listening as he went. He had been back in England less than forty-eight hours and the sound of English was still harsh to his ears. The rhythm of the London streets also seemed subtly wrong. It was not that people moved more slowly here — their pace in fact was hurried — but they seemed grave with purpose and they lacked grace.

Grinning at this fancy, Guy made his way to Covent Garden and paused in front of the church of St. Paul where hustings were commonly erected for the Westminster elections. What better place to feel himself back into London ways? The street in front of the church was crowded and the purse-catchers were already out in force. Guy was obliged to remove one boy's hand from his pocket. The boy, a thin lad of not more than seven, gave him an impudent grin and ran into the market where he was quickly lost to sight.

The market had long since come to life. Guy left the church and moved into the maze of stalls, his ears assailed by shouts and arguments and snatches of song. He smiled at an old woman sitting on a barrel surrounded by masses of gilly-flowers. "I know you," she said, picking out a blood red blossom and pressing it into his hand.

Guy smiled. "No, you don't, granny." He put the flower in his buttonhole and found a penny to give her in exchange.

"Ah, well then, I don't." She grinned, showing a toothless mouth, and put the coin in the recesses of her skirt. "But I never forget a face."

No, she clearly did not, and there would be others who would remember him as well. He had best reach Bow Street before someone reported his presence in London. Guy pushed through the market, an amiable expression on his face but his eyes observant enough to ward off further attempts on his purse. Leaving the great square by Russell Street, he made his way to the house that held the Bow Street Public Office.

The court that opened off the entrance hall was much as Guy remembered it, small, crowded, and close, with dirty walls and a smoke-blackened ceiling. At the far end was a platform, set off by a metal railing, where the business of justice took place. On one side a few stairs led up to a smaller railed enclosure where three men, meanly dressed and confined by leg irons, waited without hope for their case to be heard. Guy had stood there once on a charge of inciting to riot, but the charge had been dropped and the officer who had brought it had suffered a reprimand. He had been luckier then than on an earlier occasion when his roistering behavior had forced him to empty his pockets in compensation for some smashed bottles, two broken benches, and a blackened eye — not his own.

A clock, its face partially obscured by dirt, was still fastened to the wall behind the prisoners' dock, telling all who cared that the time was now nearing half past ten. On the other side of the platform the three magistrates sat behind a desk, conferring about some aspect of the day's business. A decorative arrangement of scrolled metal partially screened them from the view of the people milling about in the room beyond. In the space between desk and dock, the witnesses — a heavily caped coachman still bearing his whip, a man who might have been a shopkeeper, and another who was clearly a watchman — were talking in angry voices while two young bucks, carelessly but expensively dressed, lounged on the bench that ran across the front edge of the platform, sneers and defiance on their faces.

Guy paid no more attention to the drama unfolding before the magistrates and turned instead to the crowd that filled the body of the room, men and women both, the smell of unwashed bodies and gin-soaked breath vying with the scent worn by the better-dressed among them and the milky smell of infants at the breast. There was no sign of Burley, so he addressed a short, squat man in frock coat and knee breeches who was leaning heavily on a cane and scowling at nothing in particular. "You know this place, sir?"

"Aye," the man answered, with neither rancor nor any lightening of his expression.

"James Burley. Is he still attached to this office?"

The man made a grudging assent.

"And where might he be found?" Guy persisted.

The man looked at him sharply, then shrugged his heavy shoulders. "Try the Bear."

Guy tipped his hat, but the man had turned away and was making his way through the crowd toward the platform where the young bucks, their casual pose gone, were on their feet, shouting at the coachman.

Guy quickly left the building and went outside to the welcome smell of fresher air. The Brown Bear was directly across the street, a narrow brick building of four stories, boasting lodgings as well as refreshment. It was a flash-house, a resort of thieves, but was used by the officers of the Bow Street Patrol for the accommodation of prisoners who must be kept overnight. The Bear was patronized, too, by the handful of thief-takers, known commonly as runners, who were attached to the Public Office. The runners claimed they found it useful to sit down among thieves, for then they knew where their prey might be taken.

Guy pushed into a low-ceilinged room, sparsely filled at this hour, and glanced about. No one looked at him directly, though everyone seemed aware of his presence. "Burley," he said to the room at large. There was an uncomfortable silence, and then a man sitting alone at a wooden table set down his tankard and gestured to the room beyond.

The object of Guy's search was seated at a large round table with a half-dozen men, some red-eyed from lack of sleep. The table was littered with glasses and a near-empty bottle of gin, and the smell of tobacco was heavy in the air. Burley had neither pipe nor glass and at Guy's entrance he looked up with wary curiosity. He was a tall man, scantly fleshed, his shoulders slightly hunched as though he wished to hide his height, his arms long, ending in well-shaped hands with narrow tapering fingers which moved in a silent tattoo on the table, a mannerism of which he seemed unaware. His head was narrow, too, covered sparsely by hair of a nondescript brown, his nose long, his mouth thin-lipped. His eyes were of a curious light blue, almost drained of color, as though they absorbed everything they saw and gave nothing back.

"Mr. Burley," Guy said, remembering their single encounter two years before.

The other man's eyes flickered and he inclined his

head a fraction of an inch. "Mr. Melchett."

"I understand Bow Street may be looking for me."

Burley regarded him for a long moment. The trace of what might be a smile appeared at the corners of his mouth. He had been given a challenge, and the challenge, Guy saw, was accepted. The runner unfolded his long length, clapped a high-crowned black hat on his head, nodded at his companions, and led Guy out of the Bear. On the street he turned and looked at his companion. "So, Mr. Melchett. You've come to answer questions."

"And to ask them."

Burley grunted, then nodded in approval and turned down the street, his long legs quickly covering the distance to Charles Street. It was, Guy thought, matching the other man's stride, no accident that he had taken this direction. The theater stood at the intersection of Charles and Tavistock Streets, from the latter of which it took its name.

But the theater was not Burley's destination, nor did he as much as glance in its direction. He continued on to The Strand and into the precincts of Somerset Place, and from there to the terrace overlooking the river. "I come here often," he said, as though that were explanation enough.

Guy looked down into the greasy green water and his eyes turned east toward the Channel. Burley looked at him sharply. "You were on the Continent." Guy made no response and he went on. "You were wanted for further questioning."

"I didn't know," Guy said, meeting the other man's eyes. It wasn't true and Burley, he could see, did not believe him. "Or was it for something more than questioning?"

"You would have hanged had we found you." Burley grinned, an unexpected act that lightened his gloomy face. "At the time we had to hang somebody."

"But in the end you hanged nobody at all."

They were strolling now along the terrace, their eyes on the water. "It became unimportant, you see," Burley said. "After the Prime Minister was assassinated, no one worried much about what had happened at the Tavistock. There was no real evidence against anyone," he went on. "Save against you. We had a witness who swore you went into the theater that night, an hour before everything blew up. The Home Office were inclined to treat the matter seriously, but I laid it before the Chief Magistrate. 'Mr. Read,' I said, 'John Holby would swear to his sister's chastity while he was spending the money he'd already had for her, John Holby would swear to his own guilt if it brought him a penn'worth of gin, John Holby is not a witness you can trust.'"

"You're an uncommon man, Mr. Burley."

"A cautious one. Not, mind, that I'm uninclined to believe in your guilt."

Guy grinned. "And an honest one. Tell me, Mr. Burley, am I wanted?"

"To answer questions in regard to the explosion and fire at the Tavistock Theater on the evening of the fourth of May in the year of our Lord 1812," Burley said rapidly, as though reading from a document. "I have no further instructions," he added in his normal voice, "though I am obliged of course to notify the Chief Magistrate of your return to England, and he will no doubt see fit to speak to the Home Office."

"And the matter of my absence these past two years—"

"Is not a point in your favor."

"I evaded no summons," Guy pointed out.

"As you say." They had been strolling along the terrace, and Burley stopped now to stare down into the water below.

Guy paused beside him. "What do you want to know?"

"Your whereabouts on the evening in question."

"I told you before. I was in my rooms."

"Alone?"

"Alone. I was working."

Burley said nothing for a moment. "Alone. Inconvenient."

"But hardly damning, wouldn't you agree?"

"Oh, I'm not in the business of damnation, Mr. Melchett. Opportunity, that's the question I ask myself. Opportunity, and motive."

"And what motive am I alleged to have that would lead me to destroy the theater that gave me my livelihood and was owned by my closest friend?"

Burley was silent for so long that Guy thought he had no more to say, but then he spoke abruptly as though he had come to a decision. "Shall we review what we know of the event, Mr. Melchett." It was not a question. "On the evening of May fourth, the Tavistock was closed and all the company and stagehands sent home."

"It was customary when there was no performance. There'd been a rehearsal that morning which lasted far into the afternoon."

Burley nodded. "In the later afternoon, or perhaps the early evening—sometime after four or five, when the company was sent home—someone laid a charge of explosives in the theater."

"Could it have been so early? The explosion was much later."

Burley smiled. "Easily done, Mr. Melchett. Surround a candle with wood shavings or some such material, lay a trail of saltpeter, or perhaps a bit of gunpowder, to your powder keg, and set the candle alight. Easy enough to judge how long it would take to burn down and set the whole thing off. There were two explosions actually, one in the second-tier stage box. That, I take it, is the box that would have been occupied by His Highness on the following evening."

Guy nodded his assent.

"And the other backstage amidst the machinery that was there."

"Some devices for raising and lowering the performers and parts of the scenery," Guy explained.

"Both of which went off at near eight o'clock. Nicely calculated, Mr. Melchett, for someone who did not want that particular performance to take place. There was no place for His Highness to sit, and I understand it would have been difficult to perform the play without the machines, as you say, to raise and lower the performers."

"Heaven and Hell," Guy murmured. "Or their equivalent."

"Just so. But the explosion did more, of course. As it happened, there were buckets of paint about and paint-spattered cloths, and the scenery itself was flammable. The fire near gutted the stage and all the area behind it."

Guy was aware of a familiar surge of anger, but he said nothing.

"Someone would have to have gained access to the theater."

"That wouldn't have been difficult," Guy admitted. "The stage door wasn't locked during rehearsals, and anyone — anyone — could have slipped in and waited till the theater was empty."

"The watchman saw nothing."

"He didn't come on duty till eight and only made his rounds once in an hour."

"So anyone could have done it." Burley paused. "You could have done it yourself."

"I told you, I was at home."

"So you did. Tell me about the Levellers."

Guy had been prepared for this abrupt change of subject, but he did not know how to respond. How explain the web of ideas and feelings that bound a score of men? How explain what they had hoped to do? "It was a kind of debating society," he said at last. "We met Tuesday nights at the Angel in Exeter Street. Other nights, too, some of us. The acting company drank there."

"And the purpose of this society?"

"Why, to bring down the government of England," Guy said lightly, and then, noting the astonishment on the other man's face, he laughed aloud. "Come, Mr. Burley. We talked, we read papers, some of us wrote."

"It is not a matter for levity, sir."

"No," Guy agreed. "I am no advocate of armed revolt," he went on, his voice now serious. "A new set of masters may be as bad as the old. And yet . . . I would not have us be ignorant. I would not have us be satisfied. I have devoted my life to opening people's eyes with my voice and with my pen."

"I've been told you're a dangerous man."

"Deprive me of liberty and I will be more dangerous still."

Burley smiled again, a quick widening of his mouth as quickly gone. "The Levellers, Mr. Melchett. You took your name from the group in Cromwell's time?"

Guy looked sharply at the other man. "You're a student of history."

"A student of dissent, you might say."

"Both past and present. Useful in your work. We were a

small little group, Mr. Burley. There was a touch of humor in our choice of the name, but like the original Levellers, we did not support the use of violence to achieve our ends."

"Yet there were some among you who objected to Mr. Ford's decision to perform *The Taking of Badajoz* at the Tavistock."

"There were," Guy admitted.

"Concerned enough to take the occasion of making a statement. Not, perhaps, like yourself, being handy with a pen. Or thinking that the pen was too uncertain an instrument."

It was the common explanation. There were foolish men among them, men furious with Cadogan for agreeing to what they considered a betrayal of all he and his theater had stood for. The Tavistock operated under a patent granted by the Crown, but it repeatedly stretched the limits of that patent and skirted the edges of slander. "There were disagreements," Guy said cautiously.

"Cadogan Ford was the founder of the Levellers and, save perhaps for yourself, its chief spokesman. And yet he was willing to produce a play that was little more than an appeal to the unthinking patriotism of the mob. I have no objection to such spectacles, Mr. Melchett, even when they have little in common with the events they describe, but it was as unlike the plays he was accustomed to put on the Tavistock stage as cheese is from water." Burley looked at Guy, a question in his eyes.

"He had a family," Guy said, holding his temper in check, "and a company of players dependent on his success. The theater was important to him. It was founded by his grandfather, who left it to his sons, Benjamin and Samuel. Samuel had a profession, so Benjamin inherited the greater share. On his death it went to his son, Cadogan."

"Who had the major voice in decisions concerning the theater."

Guy hesitated. "The voice was likely to be his wife's. Cadogan was impatient of details. But in the matter of the play," he went on, afraid that Burley might misunderstand, "he had given his assent. He was loyal to his players, you understand, and his beliefs did not interfere with that loyalty. He disliked

54

the play, but he knew it would be good for the company, and he did not object when his uncle proposed it for the Tavistock."

"An interesting man," Burley said.

"Irreplaceable." Guy still felt the anguish of his friend's loss.

There was a moment of silence. Then Burley gave a great sigh. "Someone did it, Mr. Melchett. Someone destroyed Mr. Ford's theater and near ruined his company. Why? Were there men that wished him harm?" Burley studied the other man's face. "No, we found no evidence of that. Then it was because they objected to the direction the company was taking. And if it wasn't yourself, Mr. Melchett, then who?"

For answer Guy turned and strolled farther down the terrace. Burley kept pace at his side. "I believe there was a spy set among us," Guy said. "You have no cause to be surprised," he went on, noting the look of disbelief on Burley's face. "It's not uncommon, you must know that yourself."

Burley made an inarticulate sound that might have signified agreement. "You have evidence of this?"

"What do you call evidence, Mr. Burley? A hunch? A feeling of unease? A sense that something is not quite right?" It was more than that, but it was not safe to tell Burley, a servant of the Government, why he was so sure it was an agent of that Government who had betrayed them. "I have no evidence," Guy went on. "I would not wish to overestimate our influence, but we managed to annoy a good many people. We were even—did you know?—we were even denounced in a debate in the Upper Chamber. It would have been only prudent to keep watch on us. It would have been only prudent to draw our claws."

"You're saying that this person set among you intended to destroy the Levellers?"

"It would have been an effective way to do so."

"Mr. Melchett, it may not have been intended, but four men died in the explosion and the fire that followed. You're saying that an agent of our Government set this in motion merely to silence you and your friends?"

"I am."

"It's a monstrous accusation."

"It was a monstrous act."

They had stopped once more and stood face-to-face, each man's eyes measuring the other's conviction. Burley was the first to break the silence. "There is someone you suspect."

"There is. That's why I returned to England."

"His name?" Burley's voice was sharp.

"No, I think not," Guy said after a moment. "I may be wrong. Tell me, Mr. Burley, what happens now."

"I bring you before the magistrates to give evidence."

"And then?"

Burley shrugged. "It's not up to me. We have John Holby's deposition. I dare say he could be found if we tried."

Guy looked fixedly into the light blue eyes that betrayed nothing of the man within. "Give me a month. I have nothing to say beyond what I've told you this morning, and if you've waited two years to hear it, surely you can wait a few weeks longer to put it in record. I need those weeks to see what I can learn, and what I learn I will pass on to you."

Burley regarded him for a long moment. "It's not up to me, you know."

"I understand. Mr. Read, perhaps?"

"Sir Nathaniel Conant. He's the Chief Magistrate now."

"Then you might remind Sir Nathaniel that I have acquired influential relatives. My cousin, God help him, has become the Marquis of Parminter, and though he would cheerfully see me in hell if that would take me from his sight, I do not think he will deny the connection." Guy studied the other man, then added, "My word, you know, can be trusted. I'm staying with Gordon Murray in Portpool Lane. I'll be there when you want me."

This time Burley's smile lingered. "Oh, I will find you, Mr. Melchett. I will find you wherever you go to earth." He studied the other man through narrowed eyes. "Very well. I'll speak to Sir Nathaniel. I see no need to bring you in today."

Having received word that her brother had returned home, Rachel left her sitting room and ran quickly down the stairs. Magnus had been avoiding her. He had refused to discuss Guy's return last night and had left the house early this morning, frustrating her determination to force some kind of accommodation between the two men.

Magnus had never liked Guy, blaming him quite unfairly for their mother's flight. Nine years old and desolated by his mother's final defection from husband and children, Magnus was not prepared to accept the widowed aunt who arrived on their doorstep a few weeks later, a small boy in tow. Aunt Julia's husband had died in Paris where they had lived since their marriage. He had been improvident, like so many of the Melchetts, and had left her nearly destitute. She had no one but his brother to turn to for assistance.

Rachel's father had greeted Julia Melchett's arrival with a desperation born of his grief at his wife's departure and his inability to deal with his children's needs. Rachel had welcomed the exuberant cousin, a few months older than herself, who spoke French better than English, but Magnus refused to have anything to do with either the aunt who now managed their small household or her son Guy who cheerfully refused to acknowledge that his cousin did not like him. Even then, Magnus and Guy might have learned to get along had their father not decided to take his sister-in-law to his bed. Magnus had never forgiven his father and, illogically, he had never forgiven Guy, as though the child had been responsible for the mother's offense. But Rachel had determined to make a friend of Guy, and they were soon inseparable.

Rachel stopped and drew a breath. She would not allow childhood hurts to override present needs. She and Magnus had been close as well, particularly in the last few years, and in the end he would be forced to listen to her and acknowledge that she was right.

At the foot of the stairs, Rachel turned toward the small parlor off the library that Magnus had made his own. It seemed a vast distance away. Parminter House was too large and too ornate for comfort. For her own at least. Christine still delighted in walking from room to room, fingering the fabrics and inspecting the pictures and vases and busts that filled the house with profusion, and Magnus had settled into the enormous house with evident satisfaction. If he did not stay here, he was sure to build something equally grand. I miss Great Ormond Street, Rachel thought as she pushed open the door of the parlor.

It was a comfortable room, though rather dark for Rachel's taste. The walls were paneled with mahogany and covered by pictures in heavy gold frames. The furniture was dark, too, but the drapes, patterned in gold and white, had been drawn back, and a welcome shaft of sunlight brightened the faded colors of the Turkey carpet that covered the floor. Magnus had brought home a box of papers which were now strewn across the table at which he was seated. He looked up at his sister's entrance, his smile genuine, as though their quarrel over Guy had never been. "I haven't thanked you for what you did last night," he said, coming round the table to meet her. "It went off rather well."

"It went off splendidly," Rachel said, taking the leather-covered chair he offered. "Subdued lights to make everyone look much more handsome than they are, and all the torn costumes and missed cues decently camouflaged. The audience came to scoff and stayed to admire and went away applauding politely, quite pleased with their own discrimination."

"You don't like it, do you?"

Rachel shrugged. "It's a challenge to be met. Liking doesn't enter into it. You shall be accepted, Magnus. You are accepted: they can't help themselves. The title is old and good, and you came by it honestly. Your claim to it cannot be impugned by acknowledging your relationship to Guy."

Magnus frowned, a quick contraction of his brows that barely concealed his sudden anger. "I want nothing to do with Guy. I told you so last night. I should not need to tell you again. Guy is a danger—"

"The danger is to him."

"No, to us. To Christine, to her marriage. Did you see his face when he looked at her? Did you see hers when she looked at him?"

"She was furious to find him here."

"Her eyes, Rachel, not her words. She can't be trusted when he's around. When she's married, she's Deaconfield's problem. Till then she's mine."

Rachel rose quickly to face her brother, wanting to deny what she feared was true. "Whatever Christine feels for Guy, she will never jeopardize her chance of becoming the Duchess of Arundel. Magnus, listen to me. Guy is in danger. He left England—"

"To escape being hanged." Magnus's voice was bitter. "A fate I don't doubt he deserved."

"He was innocent. If I believe anything in this world, I believe that."

"Then you are as much a fool as he. You have an accommodating heart, Rachel, too accomodating for your clever head. If Guy is in danger still for a crime you swear he did not commit, then let him go back to whatever haven he found these past two years. If he stays here, if the case is reopened, Christine's marriage is doomed. Do you think the Arundels will consent to the match when they learn Christine's cousin was responsible for the death of their eldest son?"

"They have already given their consent."

"It can be withdrawn."

"No, Magnus. You underestimate yourself, and it's not like you. Christine has your name and your wealth behind her. The Arundels cannot afford to object to the match, no matter what her cousin is reputed to have done. And Justin will never give her up. Come, you can't care what people think. You can't care what they say."

She might have saved her breath. Magnus stood looking down at her, his heavy brows contracted, his face closed. "No. Guy may rot in his own particular hell, but I don't want to know anything about it. If he hasn't the sense to leave England, then at least keep him out of my sight."

Rachel would have said more, but a footman arrived to announce that Sir Nathaniel Conant had called and desired a few minutes of Lord Parminter's time. "Show him in," Magnus said, without a trace of the surprise he must have felt, and then, when the footman had withdrawn, "If you will excuse me, Rachel."

Rachel was back in her chair. "No, Magnus," she said pleasantly. "It will be about Guy, and I am going to stay."

They waited in strained silence for Sir Nathaniel to appear. He proved to be an elderly man, respectably dressed and of a compliant mien. No great force to fear, Rachel concluded. Not a man of great imagination, not a man to challenge the powerful or the great. But a man to do others' bidding. Magnus, she prayed, watch your tongue.

Sir Nathaniel had come, she expected, because he had heard rumors of Guy's return, but the Chief Magistrate of Bow Street surprised her. "I have been with the Home Secretary," he began, "on a matter in which I believe you to be concerned." He looked with inquiry at Rachel.

Magnus frowned, but his face gave nothing away. He indicated that Sir Nathaniel should be seated and asked him to continue. His sister, Lady Rachel, was in his confidence.

Sir Nathaniel settled back in the heavy chair, rather too large for his frame, and cleared his throat. "A man calling himself Guy Melchett—I understand he is your cousin, Lord Parminter?"

"I have a cousin of the name of Guy." Magnus moved to a small settee just far enough away to make it necessary for Sir Nathaniel to raise his voice.

"Yes. As I say, Guy Melchett—I have no reason to doubt he is who he claimed to be—called at Bow Street this morning."

Rachel felt a moment of dismay mingled with pride. How like Guy to walk straight into the lion's den.

"He spoke, I regret to say, not to the magistrates—though they were occupied at the time—but to an officer attached to the Court. Burley, one of our finest thief-takers. He was concerned in the events at the Tavistock Theater two years ago, and it was perhaps for this reason that Mr. Melchett sought him out. He said that he had recently learned he was wanted for questioning."

"I told him so last night," Rachel said, her voice calm. The sun, she noted, had passed the window and the room was perceptibly darker. "Our cousin has been abroad and has only just returned to England."

"Quite so." Sir Nathaniel stirred restlessly in his chair. "I do not know many of the details of the case myself, it having occurred in Mr. Read's time, but Burley told me that he talked at some length with your cousin and told him that he should be speaking to the magistrates. The Home Office as well. They are still much exercised about the matter as I am sure you understand. Dreadful, quite dreadful."

"I am not sure how we can help you." Magnus was growing impatient with the recital and Rachel feared he would not long hold his temper. "Surely this is a matter for your own good offices."

"Yes, yes, of course. But the fact of the matter is that your cousin has made a most curious proposal. He accounted for his own movements on the night in question — or rather he failed to account for them, but sadly that is often the case — and he professed to have some ideas about who might be responsible. He said he wished to be free to pursue them. A period of time was mentioned, a month, after which he would surrender himself for questioning and — ah — whatever might follow."

Whatever might follow, Rachel knew, was Guy's confinement pending a trial, a trial in which Guy, having no way of demonstrating his innocence, would be hard put to refute accusations of his guilt.

Magnus leaned forward, showing his first sign of interest in Sir Nathaniel's recital. "And these ideas?"

Sir Nathaniel hesitated. "I do not feel I am in a position to divulge them, Lord Parminter. You will understand that these allegations are in no way proved."

Magnus threw himself back on the settee and regarded his visitor with no particular favor. Rachel could not blame Sir Nathaniel for his reticence. If she read his discomfort aright, Guy had communicated to Burley his suspicions of a spy among the Levellers, and Burley had told the Chief Magistrate. It was not something Sir Nathaniel would have cared to share with Lord Sidmouth, the Home Secretary, nor with Mr. Mountjoy — if he had, Guy would be in custody by now — but the need for secrecy must weigh hard upon him.

"It is a most unusual request," Sir Nathaniel continued, returning to his narrative, "and not one I am inclined to listen to, save that Mr. Melchett is, ah, connected to one of the first families in England and is a man whose word can obviously be trusted. I thought it worthwhile to lay the matter before Lord Sidmouth," he went on, ignoring Magnus's snort of disbelief, "and we are agreed that Mr. Melchett's request may reasonably be granted."

Rachel drew a breath of relief. Guy had gambled, and he had won. For a few short weeks he would be safe, and if at the end of that time he was no nearer answering the questions about the explosion, he could once again leave England.

"Under some safeguards, of course," Sir Nathaniel added, subsiding in his chair as though he had come to the end of his mission.

Magnus frowned. "Conditions?"

"Yes," the other man said, as though these were trifles of no account. "Provided that you, Lord Parminter, stand surety for his good behavior and make him available to us at the end of a month's time. There is no need for any formal statement on your part. It will be sufficient for us to know that Mr. Melchett is residing under your roof."

Magnus was half out of his seat, ready to speak his outrage and denial, but Rachel forestalled him. "Of course my brother will lend his support to Mr. Melchett, Sir Nathaniel." She heard Magnus draw in his breath to contradict her and spoke the only words she could think of to hold him in check. "Our cousin will soon stand in a closer relationship to us both," she continued, smiling with all the assurance she could muster. "Mr. Melchett and I are to be married. That is why he returned to England."

Rachel's announcement was greeted by a dead silence. Magnus looked at her in disbelief which changed quickly to anger as she continued to hold her ground. Sir Nathaniel rose from his chair and approached her, apologized for anything he had said about Mr. Melchett that might have caused her offense, offered his congratulations, and then took his leave. When Magnus returned after seeing him out, Rachel was standing, prepared to meet the fury in her brother's eyes. "Is this true?" he said. "Because if it is not, I am going straight to Lord Sidmouth."

Rachel had been ready to deny her words, to say that she had only bargained for time, but looking into Magnus's eyes, knowing full well that he meant what he said, she realized she could not do so. "Of course, it is true," she said, holding her chin high. "I hope you will at least wish us well." And with that she swept out of the parlor and up the two flights of stairs to her bedchamber, wondering what in the name of heaven she was going to say to Guy.

Chapter Four

"Purely as a matter of curiosity," said Guy, when the footman who had shown him into Rachel's sitting room had withdrawn, "what would you say are the odds of my being thrown in the gutter?"

He was standing just beyond the door, regarding Rachel with inquiry and amusement and no trace of alarm. For once in his life, Guy Melchett had grossly underestimated the situation. Rachel unclasped her hands, which had grown alarmingly clammy, and gestured to a pair of upholstered beechwood chairs by the windows. "I would say the odds are almost nonexistent," she told him, "but perhaps we'd best sit down before I explain why."

It was more than an hour since her extraordinary declaration to Sir Nathaniel, more than an hour since she had dispatched a note to Guy at Gordon Murray's lodgings. She had had plenty of time to prepare herself for this interview. Her nervousness was due not to uncertainty but to the audacity of what she was about to propose. Rachel sank into a chair, grateful for the warmth of the sun at her back. The late afternoon light was spilling through the windows, dappling the subdued cream and gold of the carpet and the brighter yellow of the wall hangings.

Rachel found herself wishing that the chairs were set farther apart. She was entirely too conscious of Guy, of his faint, rueful smile and the teasing, affectionate glint in his eyes. This sort of declaration required distance, so that one had some hope of keeping one's feelings decently hidden. Resting her hands on the chair arms, Rachel forced herself to look levelly at her cousin. "I told Magnus you'd come back to marry me."

"I see," Guy said, settling into his chair. "That certainly changes things. I assume you had your reasons."

"Sheer desperation. Sir Nathaniel Conant called on Magnus this afternoon and told us he and Lord Sidmouth were willing to give you the month's grace you asked for—provided Magnus stood surety for your good behavior. Magnus was about to say he wouldn't do anything of the sort, and it was the only way I could think of to stop him."

"Did it?" Guy inquired with interest.

"Oh, yes. But the minute Sir Nathaniel left, Magnus told me he was going straight to Sidmouth if it weren't true. So I assured him that it was and asked for his blessing."

Guy threw back his head and laughed. "You're a wonder, Rachel." He sobered and leaned toward her with a smile that was the more disarming because it was unforced. "Thank you. I wouldn't have asked it of you, but I can't deny I'm glad you did it. I don't know if Bow Street could convict me, but if Magnus hadn't agreed, I'm quite sure they'd have taken me into custody, which would've hampered my investigation. That month means a great deal to me."

"I know." Rachel's voice held a touch of tartness. It was no accident that the deadline Guy had set for himself coincided so closely with the date of Christine and Justin's wedding.

"So the only question," Guy continued, "is how long we have to continue with this charade before you can safely jilt me."

Rachel drew a breath. Her mouth felt dry and she was sure that if she moved her hands they would not be steady. She had to speak now or not at all, but she could still not believe she meant to carry it through. Guy's hands, clasped loosely before him, almost brushed her knees, and she could feel the warmth of his breath. "As to that," Rachel said, "I thought perhaps it would be convenient for both of us if I didn't jilt you at all."

Guy heard the words, but it was a moment before their import hit him. He sat absolutely still, his eyes trained on Rachel's face. Her own eyes were honest and direct and utterly serious. "You're an extraordinary woman, Rachel," Guy said at last. "But you must know I would never let you make such a sacrifice of yourself. Even were my circumstances far more desperate than they are."

"And you must know that I'm not the sort of woman to let herself be sacrificed," Rachel retorted. "When I blurted the story out to Magnus, I had no intention of going through with it. But the more I thought about it, the more I realized I would quite like to marry you. The truth is, I'm asking you to do me a tremendous favor, Guy."

For a brief, crazy moment, Guy found himself imagining what it would be like to take her at her word. Since his break with Christine, he had been convinced that he would never marry. But there was something extraordinarily right in the image of sharing his life with Rachel, something very different from his romantic fantasies about Christine, fantasies which had always been rather vague as to the future. Guy leaned back in his chair and folded his arms in front of him. It was madness, of course. Rachel was only trying to keep him out of danger. "Very well done, Rachel. I'd give a great deal to have such a convincing actress speaking my dialogue. I don't believe a word of it."

"That," said Rachel, adjusting the long full sleeves of her gown with care, "is because you have no notion how many men would like to marry the Marquis of Parminter's sister. It's becoming a distinct bore."

"Bravo," Guy said, clapping politely. "You write your lines quite as well as you speak them. I'm beginning to be jealous."

"And as if that weren't bad enough," Rachel continued, "Lady Parminter is determined to see me respectably married. I think she hopes it will persuade me to give up the theater. Once Magnus is betrothed, she'll turn all her attention to me. She's a formidable woman."

Guy, who had met the marchioness when he was a child, could not argue with this description, but he was not taken in by Rachel's argument. "Doing it much too brown, my girl. You're more than a match for Lady Parminter and you know it."

"Of course I am, but it would be much simpler if I didn't have to do battle with her. Not to mention fending off the fortune hunters and the men who see any widow as fair game. You may not credit it, but I am still good-looking enough to attract that sort of attention."

Rachel regretted these words as soon as they were out. From the moment it first occurred to her that, for her own sake as well as Guy's, it might make sense if her impulsive story of a betrothal became reality, she had been thinking how to persuade him. But now that the scene had begun, her determination went beyond practical considerations about her own future, beyond even the need to protect Guy from the consequences of Magnus's fury. If Guy refused, the pragmatic nature of her proposal would not make the sting of rejection any less bitter.

Rachel forced herself to meet Guy's eyes and saw that the mockery had fled from them. "I don't doubt it," he said. "Rachel—" He broke off and ran his fingers through his hair. "Cadogan was a remarkable man. There won't be another like him. But there will—you will fall in love again, Rachel, believe me. And we'd both find it damnably awkward if you were married to me at the time."

Rachel rose abruptly and walked to the window. Cadogan was the last person she wanted to talk about. "Love," she said, her voice more bitter than she intended. "Love is a thing for youth, and I left my youth behind long ago." Startled by the wellspring of emotion Guy had inadvertently tapped, Rachel stared down at the flagged walks and clipped hedges and marble statues of the Parminter House gardens. "The past two years haven't been easy for the children," she went on, forcing herself to turn back to her cousin, "especially for Alec. I'd like them to have a father again. Fond as I am of Magnus, he's not the man I'd choose as a model for my son."

Guy smiled faintly. "I agree with you there. But if you want help with Alec and Jessica, you have only to ask. It isn't necessary to marry me."

"It's not the same thing. They need to feel they're part of a family. They need to know that you won't disappear tomorrow. Losing one father was difficult enough for them, though

God knows Cadogan wasn't—" Rachel broke off, for it seemed pointless and vindictive to burden Guy with her disillusionment.

Guy regarded her in surprise. "Cadogan was always busy," he said after a moment.

"Yes." Rachel did not pursue the matter, but it hung between them with the weight of unfinished business. "We think alike, Guy," she continued. "I don't have to worry that you'll ask me to give up the theater or that you'll try to take it away from me. I want a father for my children. And while it may sound silly to you, because these things are easier for men, I would find it very useful to have a husband."

Rachel paused. If Guy agreed, it would be because he believed the marriage would benefit her, not himself. But for her own peace of mind, it had to be clear that the arrangement was advantageous to both of them. "Were it simply a question of preventing Magnus from throwing you to the wolves, we could let the betrothal drag on until the month is up," she told him, determined to make that point clear. "But I thought you might find marriage useful as well. I have a comfortable income—don't look at me like that, Guy, you can't deny there are times when money has its uses. I also have a house which is far too large for me and the children. And I won't mind in the least if you talk about the theater from dawn till dusk."

"Now that," said Guy, "is a tempting offer. But have you considered that at the end of the month you might find yourself with a husband in Newgate?"

Rachel raised her brows. "You admit you might fail?"

"My dear girl, have you ever known me to claim anything was impossible?" In truth, Guy had known from the moment he decided to return to England that there was a risk he would be taken into custody. He had decided it was worth the chance, but he had no intention of involving Rachel in the risks he ran.

"If it comes to Newgate," Rachel told him, "you'll be far better off as the Marquis of Parminter's brother-in-law than as his disreputable cousin. Magnus thinks I'm bluffing, Guy. He's going to call the bluff and suggest we marry at once. We can put him off, of course. I don't think he'll turn you over to Conant, but he'll never really believe we're in earnest."

"Whereas if we marry, I gain the protection of the Parminter name and fortune." Guy grimaced. "You, on the other hand —"

"I," said Rachel, "am going to defend you whether we're married or not. And it will be a lot easier for me if I have Magnus's help. If there's any sacrifice involved in this marriage it will be on your side, not mine." She hesitated, avoiding his gaze. "Last night you said you didn't think you would ever marry. If that's not true, if there's someone wherever you've been these past two years —" Rachel broke off and realized she was holding her breath.

"No," Guy said quietly, "there's no one. At least," he amended with a faint smile, "no one I plan to marry. Rachel —" Guy stood, stretched out a hand to her, then let it fall and shook his head, hoping to clear it. Rachel had almost managed to convince him that he would be doing her a favor by marrying her to save his own skin. "This is madness."

"No more so than most marriages," Rachel retorted. There was a long pause while they regarded each other in silence. Rachel knew they were thinking the same thing. It would have to be faced before they came to an agreement, and she would have to be the one to raise the subject. "For the children's sake, I'd like us to live under the same roof," she said, forcing herself not to look away from him, "even after I return to Great Ormond Street. Otherwise there's no reason why this marriage should change either of our lives. That is — Oh, the devil. You know what I'm talking about."

"A marriage in name only. I assumed as much."

"Yes," said Rachel, irrationally irritated by his calm acceptance of the fact. "Unless — I don't want you to lose by this marriage, Guy. If you want children —"

She broke off, conscious of the shortness of her breath, the color suffusing her face, the unexpected feelings coursing through her. She looked at Guy and saw not her cousin or her husband's friend or her sister's lover. All the defenses she had used to cloak the attraction were stripped away. Unbidden images sprang into her mind, images of feeling Guy's kisses, lying in his arms, sharing his bed. She felt at once horribly embarrassed and gloriously alive.

Guy stood perfectly still and willed his thoughts to order. Rachel, practical, sensible Rachel, had just offered herself to him. For the most pragmatic of reasons, of course. Being a woman of honor, she was bound to have said something of the sort. She was the one who had suggested this mad marriage. It was up to him to set the terms. If he wanted children, she would give them to him. He had only to assure her that he would make no such demands on her and the matter could be forgot. Why then was he behaving like some callow Romeo, transfixed by his first sight of Juliet?

There was no woman in the world he knew as well as Rachel, and yet he felt as if he were seeing her for the first time. Her face was the same, long and oval and finely boned, with high cheekbones and a slightly pointed chin, but it held a mystery and allure he had never imagined. The familiar, almond-shaped eyes were suddenly luminous. Slanting rays of sunlight streamed through the window behind her, streaking her hair with fire and revealing the supple curves beneath the thin fabric of her gown. She had still been a girl when Guy left for the University of Edinburgh. When he returned to England, she was married to Cadogan. Now, for the first time, he saw her for what she was, a woman, and an infinitely desirable one.

Rachel was silent, her cheeks tinged with color, her breathing rapid and shallow, her eyes lowered to the floor. She was plainly embarrassed. What else she felt Guy could not determine, but he knew it was up to him to put an end to the silence. Even as he felt an impulse to stride across the room and take her in his arms, he knew what his answer had to be. If Rachel ever came to his bed—his pulse quickened at the thought—it must be because she wanted him, not because she felt obliged to give him children. "I rather think," he said, "that I'll have my work cut out for me being a father to the children you already have."

It was the answer Rachel had expected, but she felt a wave of disappointment. Rubbish, of course. Guy had never given the least hint that he desired her. If she had expected something more, she had been a fool. Rachel looked at Guy and only then realized that with his last words he had tacitly accepted her proposal.

"Yes," Guy admitted with a smile of acknowledgement, "you've caught me. It's too good an offer to refuse."

Rachel laughed, hoping the sound would wash away the awkwardness between them. She and Guy had just agreed to spend the rest of their lives more or less together, and she had never felt less comfortable in his presence. Some sort of gesture was required to acknowledge the agreement between them, but she could not for the life of her think what. Guy grinned suddenly, then stepped forward and extended his hand. Relieved that he had found a way to cover the difficult moment, Rachel met him in the middle of the room and clasped his hand formally. A shock ran through her at the contact. "Magnus and Christine are dining out," she said, "but I need to go to the theater. Will you come with me?"

Guy's eyes narrowed, and Rachel knew he was thinking about his investigation. The theater was the obvious place to start. "With pleasure," he told her.

"Good. We should speak to Magnus before he leaves, but he'll be dressing now. If you don't mind, I'd like to tell the children at once. It's difficult to keep secrets in a house of this size, and I wouldn't want them to learn it from anyone but us. I told them you were back and I'd bring you up to see them." She hesitated, recalling the children's faces when she'd spoken with them late this afternoon. Guy had once been a great favorite, but a lot of things could change in two years. "I'm not sure how they'll react. This is going to be a great shock and—"

"Stepparents are not always greeted with unadulterated joy. I'm a playwright, remember. I know all about domestic drama."

In the years before he left England, Guy had been constantly in and out of Rachel and Cadogan's house. Alec and Jessica had always seemed to be underfoot, both there and at the Tavistock, but though Guy had been fond of them, they had rarely been at the center of his attention. He had been too busy changing the world and outwitting the state censor

71

and scraping up enough to pay the rent. And agonizing about Christine.

Guy pushed this last thought aside as they reached the third-floor landing and Rachel opened the door to a large apartment with white-painted walls and dark blue drapes which had been drawn against the fading light. An indignant cry greeted them as they stepped over the threshold. "You can't look at the cards, Jessie. There's no sense in playing if you're going to act like a baby."

Three people were grouped on the carpet, engrossed in a game of cards. One, a thin woman of indeterminate age wearing a dark print dress, Guy immediately recognized as Jenny Alsop, who had come to work for the Fords when her husband, a stagehand, left the Tavistock for a job at the Drury Lane and left his wife for a pretty young actress. The two children beside Jenny were so changed that it was a moment before Guy recognized them. Alec, a sturdy boy with a shock of straight brown hair, had grown a good deal in the past two years. He was making an elaborate attempt to shield his cards from his sister's view, but he looked round at the opening of the door and stared at Guy with an expression of wariness if not outright suspicion. Guy began to understand what Rachel had been trying to tell him. He remembered Alec as a quiet, observant child, but this was something more. In the past two years, Rachel and Cadogan's son had learned not to trust.

Unlike her brother, Jessica seemed more curious than suspicious. She too had grown, and her face was thinner and more defined. Her features were delicate, but the set of her mouth and chin showed a will every bit as strong as her mother's. Jessica was the age Rachel had been when Guy first met her and the resemblance between them brought back an unexpected flood of memories. He knew well what it was like to be young and confused and mistrustful of a world which has taken away one's father.

Jessica tossed back her thick red-gold hair. "You're our Uncle Guy. You wrote the play I was named after."

"That I did," Guy agreed, sweeping a bow he had perfected when playing a part in *The Country Wife*. "You must be Miss

Jessica Ford, though you look so grown up I'd never have known it. And you," he continued, turning to Alec who was still regarding him through narrowed eyes, "must be Master Alexander Ford." Guy advanced into the room and extended his hand to Rachel's son.

Alec made no move to take Guy's hand, echoing his Uncle Magnus's behavior on the previous evening. Guy let the hand fall to his side, as if that was what he had meant to do all along, and smiled at Jenny. "Miss Alsop, on the other hand, looks quite unchanged. Save that I believe she is even lovelier than I remembered."

Jenny laughed, looking quite ten years younger and much more pretty. "*You* haven't changed, Mr. Melchett, that's for certain. It's good to see you back in London."

"Are you going to live here?" Jessica asked, scrambling to her feet.

"Perhaps," Guy said. "I'm not yet sure."

Jessica considered this. "Alec says Uncle Magnus doesn't like you."

"Ah." Guy looked from Jessica to Alec. "You see, when we were children, Uncle Magnus and I were rather like brothers. Aren't there times when the two of you don't like each other?"

Alec made no response, but Jessica's eyes gleamed with understanding. "Lots of times." She thought a moment, then added, "If I had a house, I wouldn't want Alec to live in it."

Rachel decided it was time to intervene. "I, for one, am very glad Uncle Guy is back," she said, moving toward the children. "I've missed him, and I'd miss him even more if he went away again." She hesitated, searching for the right words. "It's been two years since your father died and I've been lonely."

"You have us." Jessica seemed to be stating a fact rather than expressing hurt.

Rachel smiled at her daughter. "Of course I do, darling. But I need friends my own age, just like you do. Uncle Guy is my very best friend. I decided it's silly for him to go off and live by himself when we have such a nice house. So I've asked him to stay here, and then come with us when we go back to

Ormond Street." Rachel drew a breath and decided she had better just say it. "Uncle Guy and I are going to be married."

Rachel's announcement was greeted by silence broken by warm congratulations from Jenny. Alec remained very still, his gaze fixed intently on Guy. "Why?" he demanded.

"Because," said Guy, putting an arm around Rachel, "your mother and I want to spend the rest of our lives together."

In a literal sense, the words might be true, but their implication was misleading, as was the gesture. Acutely aware of the feel of Guy's body against her own, Rachel decided she would have to be very careful. It would be all too easy to believe this marriage was more than the practical arrangement she and Guy had agreed upon.

"Do we have to call you Daddy?" Jessica demanded, a furrow between her level brows.

"Not unless you want to," Guy assured her. "Look," he said moving away from Rachel and crouching down before the children, "I know this is a bit of a shock, but it doesn't mean things have to change so very much. I'll be living in the house, of course, but I'll try not to make a nuisance of myself and you can tell me if I get in the way."

"Why?" Alec said again. "I mean, why would you care if we mind or not?"

"Well," said Guy, "all other considerations aside, it was your house first, wasn't it?"

Alec made no comment, but Rachel could tell this was not the response he had expected. Jessica wanted to know when the wedding was going to be and whether her mother was going to have a new dress — which meant that she wanted a new dress herself. Alec remained silent until Rachel and Guy were about to leave.

"Uncle Guy," he said suddenly, as Guy was opening the door for Rachel.

"Yes?" Guy turned to look at him with friendly interest.

"Where have you been?"

There was a slight pause, and it occurred to Rachel that she did not yet know where Guy had spent his two-year exile. "Seeking my fortune," Guy said lightly. "It's not as exciting as it sounds. By the time you're my age, you learn there's a lot to be said for home, Alec."

As she and Guy descended the stairs, Rachel considered asking him where he had been, but something warned her that he would not tell her either. "Thank you," she said instead. "You may not believe this, but it wasn't as bad as I expected."

Guy grinned. "I thought it might be nice if I asked them for your hand, but I suspect I would have been met with flat refusal and then where would we be?"

Now that she had spoken with Guy and told the children, Rachel found the coming interview with Magnus less daunting. But she had not reckoned on the scene which met them when they entered the first drawing room, where the family was accustomed to gather before dinner. Magnus was standing by the fireplace, but he was not alone. As Rachel stepped into the room, the first words that greeted her were uttered by her sister. "Tell me it isn't true," said Christine.

Chapter Five

Christine was in spectacularly good looks. She was wearing blue, a cold ice blue that exactly matched the color of the gown worn by Penelope Quentin, wife of the fourth marquis, in the portrait which hung over the mantel. Like Penelope's, her pale blond hair was threaded with pearls, and a tangle of ringlets framed the delicate oval of her face. But Christine was in an absolute fury.

What Guy felt, Rachel could not tell, and he gave her no time to wonder. He moved forward quickly, captured Christine's hands, and bent to kiss her on the cheek. "It's true, coz," he said, "and you are to wish me all happiness."

It was a typical Guy performance. He stood looking down at Christine as though he had just given her a great gift. It was not that he was unaware of her response, nor forgetful of what had been between them. Guy was sensitive to the smallest nuances of feeling, but as often as not he chose to ignore them, blundering through the most awkward situations, using his good humor as a shield. Nine times out of ten his seeming obtuseness was justified, for shallow complaints or wounded vanities or even petty tyrannies yielded before the onslaught of his high spirits.

Not so tonight. Christine pulled away from Guy abruptly, her face contorted with passion, and Rachel, who had seen her like this before, felt a familiar stab of envy. Even thus her sister was impossibly lovely.

"You can't," Christine said, her voice sharp with outrage. "You can't marry."

"Why not?" Guy was not in the least offended. "I thought you'd have reason to recommend the state."

Christine stared at him, frustrated by his unwillingness to understand her. "It's not the same," she whispered. She glanced at Rachel, a look compounded of anger and envy and bewilderment. "It's not the same at all."

There was a time when Rachel would have gone to her sister, when she would have sought to moderate her anger, to soothe her disappointment, to assuage her genuine if short-lived grief. But no more. Even before Edmund's death, Christine had gone her own way, making it clear she wanted none of Rachel's care; and Rachel, who had grown more clear-eyed about her sister but also more tolerant of her faults, had let her go. Tonight Rachel's tolerance was stretched beyond her own generous limits. Christine's behavior was wounding and outrageous. Even Magnus, who had his own reasons for disliking the marriage, recognized it.

Rachel would have given words to her anger had not Guy stepped back and put his arm around her. "Don't fret, Chrissie, we'll do the thing quietly," he said, refusing to acknowledge Christine's meaning. He gave Rachel a reassuring hug. He had often done so in the past when he came upon a quarrel between the sisters, but now Rachel found his touch unsettling. "It's a sorry thing, having a ramshackle fellow like me in the family, but I won't spoil your marriage, pretty one. Quiet as a mouse, that's what I'll be. You'll scarce know I'm about."

It was a speech directed as much at Magnus as Christine. Christine turned away, refusing to acknowledge it. Magnus turned to Rachel, his brows drawn together in a disapproving frown. "You're determined to go through with this?"

Rachel returned his look, aware that this was a contest between them. "I am."

Magnus held her gaze, then the trace of a smile crossed his face. "Yes, you would be," he murmured. "I think we should tell Christine the whole."

Christine whirled around. "Tell me what?"

"Tell you why your cousin has not yet been placed under arrest."

Christine caught her breath, as if only now realizing that more was at stake than the Arundels' approval of her marriage.

"They're still worried about what happened at the Tavistock," Guy said. "They'd like to question me—"

"They'd like to hang you," Magnus said.

"That too," Guy agreed cheerfully, "though they've precious little evidence to go on. But what worries them more is that I'm related to one of the most respected titles in the kingdom."

"You are, God help me, my heir." Magnus's frown was still in evidence. "At least till I get sons," he added under his breath. He turned to Christine. "Sir Nathaniel Conant called on me today. Guy has some ideas about what happened at the Tavistock, and he is to be allowed a few weeks of freedom to investigate them, provided I stand surety for his good behavior."

Christine's face showed sudden understanding. "And you didn't want to do so, did you, Magnus? You had to be persuaded, and Rachel found the only argument that would convince you." She turned on her sister. "That's it, isn't it, Rachel? That's what's behind this trumped-up marriage."

"I wouldn't count on that," Guy said quietly. It was a clear declaration that he was not marrying Rachel as a matter of expedience. It brought Christine up short, which it was intended to do. It surprised even Magnus. Rachel was grateful for Guy's defense, but she wished she could believe that he meant it.

Christine would have spoken again had Magnus not stepped forward and grasped her hand, forcing her to look up at him. "There may be something in what you say, little sister, but you haven't got the whole. Rachel has a mind of her own, and if she's set on this particular destiny, you'll not stop her. As for Guy, he knows which side his bread is buttered on." He loosed her hand and turned to his cousin. "I don't like this, Guy. I have no use for you nor how you choose to live, but for Rachel's sake I'll stand by you. But I warn you, cousin, be careful where you tread. It's five weeks to Christine's marriage, and nothing is to stand in its way. The

78

Arundels are an old family. They're steeped in bigotry and prejudice. They've accepted Christine because she's now a Parminter. They've agreed to overlook her wretched mother and her sister's connection with the theater and my own commercial bent. But even my name and my money will not be enough to see her through if there's any hint of scandal. Do you understand me, Guy? Do anything foolish and, Rachel or no, I will throw you to the dogs. You, too, Christine. Walk carefully."

The ghost of a smile crossed Guy's face, but Christine, furious now with her brother, flung herself on a sofa. "I will conduct myself as I please. This is my marriage, Magnus, and it is I who will see it through." She opened her fan, a frivolous affair of frosted blue crêpe, and wielded it vigorously. "Or is it your own marriage that has you so exercised? Little mousy Margaret, is it her loss you fear?"

"That's enough," Rachel said. Magnus's color was rising, and in truth they had given him the very devil these past few hours. "This has been sudden and a shock, but you're both capable of weathering it. I can't say the same for Lady Parminter, let alone the Arundels. It will be easier, Magnus, if the children and I go back to Ormond Street. Christine can manage very well without a chaperon."

"No," Magnus said with decision. "You'll stay, Rachel, till Christine's wedding, for my sake if not for her own. And Guy will stay, too. No matter how we feel about one another, there's to be no public breach of family unity."

No matter how we feel. That was no simple matter. Rachel looked at her sister, her pale blue skirt spread against the rose velvet of the sofa, a wary ice goddess. Dependent on Magnus's charity and good will, resentful of his high-handed ways, her younger sister had never ceased challenging his authority. Christine had her own weapons and she knew the points on which her brother was weak.

As for herself, Rachel knew that Christine had never considered her a threat. Not till tonight, when Rachel had acquired her sister's discarded toy. Christine was about to make a splendid marriage, but Guy was hers, irrevocably and for all time. Or that was what she had thought till Guy had made it clear, with a few simple words, that he was not. Christine's uncertainty, warring with her anger and resentment, could be read clear in her face.

Magnus's feelings were more straightforward. He didn't like Guy, and he never had. And Guy? As long as Rachel had known him, she still could not read his heart. Rachel suspected he saw something to admire in Magnus's energy and cleverness, though he made no secret of the fact that he disapproved of much that Magnus stood for. He had stubbornly refused to make an enemy of his cousin, yet he had never pretended to be his friend. Friendship had been reserved for herself, for they were of an age and, in different ways, lonely for companionship. As for Christine, he had been her protector, and then he had grown to love her. It was tragedy they were playing. Guy did not give his affections easily, but he gave them without reservation, and Christine was not for him.

Yet they were united, the four of them. They were one family, bound to each other by blood and memory. Rachel had never seen it more clearly than now, at the instant when the door opened and Justin Hever was ushered into the room, bringing with him that strain of difference that marks the outsider from one's own kind. There was the slightest pause while Justin took them in: Christine on the rose velvet sofa beneath the portrait of Penelope Quentin whom she so much resembled, though they were unrelated by blood; Magnus standing a little way apart, hands clasped behind him, his well-cut evening coat unable to disguise the fact that he was not at home in a drawing room; Guy in boots and buckskins, his cravat ill tied, resting his hands negligently on the back of a chair, at home wherever he chose to be.

How she herself appeared to Justin, Rachel did not know. He went straight to Christine and lifted her hand to his lips, murmuring, "You're exquisite tonight." The ice queen melted. Whatever the residue of Christine's feelings for Guy, she was not indifferent to Justin. For her own sake, Rachel hoped that the attachment was genuine.

Justin, who had beautiful manners, did not linger over his betrothed. He turned to Rachel, making her a friendly acknowledgement, offered his hand to Magnus, and only then addressed Guy. "Christine told me last night that you were back."

Guy smiled, but his eyes were wary. "I tired of foreign parts."

"Things have changed in the years you've been away."

"Yes, I understand I must address you as Lord Deaconfield."

Justin made a deprecating gesture. "I trust we're on better terms than that. I don't deny the title's welcome. I was able to give up my post as Lord Buckleigh's secretary, and I no longer live on Queer Street. And I suppose you've heard, I'm taking a wife."

"I've heard," Guy said. "I congratulate you. Chrissie, you are fortunate. You're marrying a clever man."

"I know my fortune well, Guy." Christine's voice was cool and bright. "I trust yours—"

"—will be every bit its equal. Thank you, cousin."

Christine left the sofa and put her arm possessively through Justin's. "Guy is to marry Rachel," she announced, looking straight at Guy and throwing the words out like a challenge.

"I am," Guy said. He looked at Justin. "Have I surprised you?"

"He's surprised us all," Magnus said. Rachel caught the faint trace of irony in his voice, but the others, intent on one another, seemed unaware of it. "I think, Christine, we should tell Lord Deaconfield what's occurred today. Beyond Rachel's betrothal," he added with a glance at his other sister, "though that is event enough."

"Allow me," Guy said. Wearied by the unspoken passions in the room, Rachel had sunk down in a chair and Guy now moved to stand behind her. "I left England because of what happened at the Tavistock," he told Justin. "You'll understand. You had your own griefs and I had mine." He put his hand on Rachel's shoulder. "I kept in touch through Rachel. I knew I was wanted for questioning, but somehow I had no inclination to talk."

Justin smiled. "How unlike you, Guy."

"How sensible, you mean," Rachel said. "It would have been madness to return at that time."

"And now?" Justin asked. "Is it madness still?"

"Oh, we've all grown very grand," Guy said. "I have a cousin who has some position in the world. It makes a difference, haven't you found? Does anyone care now, Justin, that you were once associated with the Levellers?"

"I've had nothing to do with them since that night." Justin's expression lightened. "Yes, it does make a difference. I do as I like, with no worries save displeasing my father. He's got both grander and more mean-spirited since he acquired the title. But my position isn't quite yours, Guy. Do they want you still?"

"They want to talk to me."

"They would like at least to close the book on this particular incident." Rachel twisted round in her seat to look up at Guy. "And if they must hang you to do so, they'll do it with pleasure."

Justin frowned. "Then you're free on sufferance?"

"On Magnus's good will," Guy said. "They've given me a month, and I intend to give them a culprit."

There was a brief silence while Justin took this in. "You're an arrogant madman," he murmured.

"Oh, I don't deny the arrogance," Guy said with an expression of the greatest good will.

Magnus, who had been consulting his watch, looked at the others. "The carriage has been waiting this quarter-hour. It's time we were off. Rachel, you'll see there's a room made ready for Guy." It was Magnus's admission that she had won, that he would stand by Guy at least for the present. But it was not all Magnus had to say. He took her arm and, indicating that Guy should follow, led her away from the others who were waiting by the door. "I won't pretend to know your reasons," he said, keeping his voice low, "either of you. But I won't be played for a fool. If this talk of marriage is a sham, tell me now."

"It's no sham," Guy said.

"Then if you're bent on it, let it be done and done soon. I'll arrange for a special license. The ceremony can take place here, in privacy and quiet. Do you understand me?"

"As you wish." Rachel smiled at her brother. "Trust me, Magnus. This will all come right."

She saw a flicker of acknowledgement in his eyes. "Good night," he said abruptly, and, walking quickly to the door, he followed Christine and Justin out of the room.

"He's thrown down the gauntlet," Guy said into the silence that came between them.

"He won't allow that what Christine said was true." It had been, of course, in the beginning, but now that she had talked Guy round and had told the children and had begun to get used to the idea herself, she knew without doubt that she wanted this marriage. But did Guy? She forced herself to meet his eyes, knowing that she had to give him a chance to escape the net Magnus was drawing all too quickly around them. "It's not too late," she said. "We can say we changed our minds. Or I can plead for time."

"You'll plead for nothing, Rachel, it's not your style. If you don't want to marry, tell me. If you fear I'm averse to the arrangement, that's not true. I've quite got used to the idea. Besides, I have some plays I want you to read."

She laughed. "I'd read them in any case."

"Ah, but not with that besotted blindness you'll reserve for your husband's work. Come, Rachel, we've agreed. Will you chance it after all?"

Her heart lightened. She could not imagine spending her life with anyone but Guy. "I'll chance it."

Guy gave her a crooked smile of delight and leaned down to kiss her, a clumsy brotherly kiss on her cheek that made her absurdly happy and brought tears to her eyes. She took refuge in making arrangements for his room, well away from Christine's or her own, and then they went down to the dinner she'd ordered hastily before he arrived. It was over dinner, when she'd dismissed the unnecessary footman and the butler whose attentions always made her uncomfortable, that she brought up the question that had bothered her for the past hour. "Is Justin still your chief suspect?"

"He was never my chief suspect. He's one of four."

Rachel laid down her fork and knife and looked directly at

Guy. "You've never liked him."

"No, but I'd hardly damn a man for that." Guy leaned forward, his elbows on the table. "Listen to me, Rachel. I won't interfere in Chrissie's marriage, not without proof that he's the man I'm after, but by all that's holy, proof I'm going to have."

Rachel twisted the stem of her glass, staring at the play of light through the rich red of the wine. Jealousy aside, she was fond of her sister and would not want to see her come to grief. She looked up and met Guy's eyes, aware that she had been uncommonly silent and that he had been watching her. "You have to understand Christine, Guy," she said, choosing her words carefully. "She wanted to marry Edmund because he was nephew to a duke, and now she wants to marry Justin because he's a duke's son and one day he'll make her a duchess. It's not the money she longs for, it's the position."

Guy continued to stare at her, but he would not acknowledge that what she said was true. Rachel lifted her glass and sipped the wine, savoring its slightly astringent taste. "I never minded being one of the outcast Melchetts," she said, staring into her glass. "I knew the Parminters were very grand and that our connection with them was very distant, but it didn't seem to matter much. We were happy enough, weren't we? And if we weren't, it wasn't because of the Parminters, it was because of us, who we were ourselves, as a family. At least that's the way it was with me."

Guy smiled. "And with me."

"But not with Magnus. I didn't realize it at first, but it was Magnus who really cared about what the Parminters thought of us. He saw them fairly often when he was older. Old Lord Parminter could never quite conceal his distaste for our father, nor for yours, and Lady Parminter was little better. Magnus hated it. I've always thought that's why he decided to ape them. If he couldn't have their lineage, he would have their money. He would become as wealthy as the Marquis of Parminter. No, wealthier. And he did."

"And now he has the title as well. What does he make of it?"

Rachel grinned. "He's cock-a-hoop. He revels in it. He

84

won't admit it, but he finds it enormously gratifying to be sought out by the people who used to consider him beyond the pale." Rachel paused, remembering that they had been speaking of Christine. "Magnus doesn't think much of Justin, who hasn't done a useful thing in his life, but he wants this marriage. He wants it as much as Christine and for the same reason. The Hevers are one of the oldest families in England."

"So Magnus will be vindicated."

"And Christine will. You wouldn't have thought she would have cared, not like Magnus. But she did, even in Hampshire where she had to make over her dresses and give way to the squire's daughter. Don't laugh, Guy. Magnus may always keep himself a handsbreadth apart, but Christine will belong to this world completely."

Guy looked at her a moment, then shrugged. His smile seemed enormously sweet. "How did you escape?"

"I don't know. I always felt complete enough in myself."

"Yes, you're a complete woman, Rachel." Guy had turned serious and she was not sure how to take it. "What will happen if I find that Justin is guilty?"

"Christine will never forgive you."

"And Magnus? Will he forgive me? Will you?"

"Magnus will wish you'd never looked under that particular stone. But he doesn't shrink from unpleasantness. Nor do I." Rachel suddenly felt very weary. "You'll do what you have to do, Guy. But you must be very, very sure."

The smile appeared again but did not reach his eyes. "No trumped-up stories because I want a happy ending?"

Rachel was torn between amusement and despair. "Oh, Guy, who's to know what makes for a happy end?"

Chapter Six

Guy followed Rachel into the carriage, giving the coachman the direction of the Tavistock. The barouche was new, Rachel told him, one of Magnus's recent purchases. It was a handsome carriage, dark and relatively unadorned, but it reeked of no money spared. Guy had no objection to luxury when it was offered, and he sank back against the soft leather seats and sighed in pleasure. His cousin sat close beside him, quiet now after her outburst over the dinner table. She had warned him, as she felt she must, but she had given him permission to go where he pleased. Rachel was a generous woman, and a fair one. If Justin proved the culprit, she would not flinch from the unpleasantness that would follow.

The carriage left High Holborn and turned down Drury Lane. Guy was in an odd mood he could not quite define, a mood compounded of anticipation and uncertainty and the challenge of the problem he had set himself. There was, too, he recognized, an unexpected feeling of exhilaration. It was partly his return to England and to the Tavistock. And it was partly Rachel, who would soon be his wife, a prospect at once welcome and terrifying. It seemed fitting that they make a life together. The house in Great Ormond Street had always been more a home to him than any other place in London, but he would be taking Cadogan's place there, and who knew what demons that would raise.

Rachel must have had the same thoughts, for she said, "If we're to go through with this, Guy —"

"You don't have to, you know," he said, as if it had been he and not Rachel who had proposed the bargain.

"Nor do you." She turned to him, a slight frown contracting her brows. "Guy, are we being utter fools?"

"Probably. But folly is good for the soul. Life's a hazard, cousin. I'm willing to chance it."

Her face broke into a warm smile. "And I." She turned thoughtful. "There will be some awkwardness. I should tell them tonight."

"The company? Yes, they'll wonder if it will make any difference. It won't, of course." Rachel had a sure instinct for what would draw people to the theater. She had, too, a talent for organization and a rare ability to combine firmness and tact that allowed her to fend off creditors and deal with the petty rivalries that plagued any company. Guy had no intention of entering her domain.

"Some of them won't mind," she said, "but the others— You'd think in a profession as precarious as ours, change would be the last thing they'd worry about, but they fear it above everything. It's the despair of my life. Alter a precedent, change the lighting or the set or someone's entrance and I've a rebellion on my hands." She laughed, a warm, familiar sound that more than anything else told Guy he had been wise to accept Rachel's proposal.

"It was hard, wasn't it, holding them together after the explosion." Only now did Guy realize how hard it must have been. Rachel's letters had made light of those months.

"Oddly enough they rallied round. We kept the company together with promises and pittances. Not much of the house was actually damaged, though backstage it was a disaster."

"Rachel." Guy laid his hand over hers.

She did not move her hand, but he could sense her slight withdrawal. "It's all right, Guy. It was two years ago, and it's in the past. But I'd rather not talk about Cadogan. He's in the past, too, and I'd like to leave him there."

Not understanding Rachel's rebuff, Guy removed his hand. "What do they think of me at the Tavistock?"

Rachel did not pretend to misunderstand him. "Everyone knew the explosion was no accident. It was set, and the police were questioning everyone in sight. Most of the company thought it was done by someone who objected to our doing

87

The Taking of Badajoz, probably one of the Levellers." Rachel was silent for a moment. "I know the police saw you as a plausible culprit, Guy, but there's scarcely a soul in the company who believed it. Even those who didn't care for your politics knew you'd never have destroyed something you loved so much."

"And my disappearance?"

She laughed. "They said Guy Melchett was always a canny man."

The carriage had left Drury Lane and turned into Little Russell Street. "I see they've finished it," Guy said as they passed the Drury Lane Theater. It had fallen to fire five years before and was still being rebuilt at the time he left London. "Is it as large as before?"

"Nearly. It holds over three thousand. Well beyond the capacity of the Tavistock."

"In the Tavistock you don't have to shout to be heard. That's an advantage."

"The receipts are smaller."

"And so are your expenses. What are you doing tonight?"

Rachel's face became animated. "I've revived *The Tempest.* Benjamin did it before, and this is my first chance to stage it. I've made it more magical and less of a farce. I've always thought it one of Shakespeare's darker plays. I cast Gerald Sneath as Prospero and he's magnificent. We're going to do very well with it." She gave a wry smile. "I'd like to think it's because of the cast, but I'm afraid people come because of the flying spirits. Ariel, of course, and a lot of fearsome unnamed figures that were my own idea. I told Bob Harper he had to construct a bridge across the stage that would be sturdy enough to support them. He grumbled and complained, and the expense nearly ruined us, but we'll make it all back. Audiences love it."

Rachel's enthusiasm was infectious. Guy would have continued the conversation, but they had reached the dirty but still handsome facade of the Theater Royal, Tavistock Street. The carriage turned into the dark alley that led to the stage entrance where a single lamp burned beside the door. The coachman, a small, elderly man named Collins who appeared accustomed to driving Rachel there, handed her down the steps as though she were a queen.

It was past ten o'clock. The drama would be over and the farce would be on. Guy followed Rachel up the steps to the stage door, nodded to the doorman, who was new since his time, and entered the theater. Guy had not been in the Tavistock since the explosion, and he found it virtually unchanged. He knew, because Rachel had told him in her letters, that they had added lamps on either side of the stage and had created additional slots for the scene panels. He could see that the walls had been repainted and had not yet acquired the dinginess he remembered, and that the newer portions of the floor were visibly lighter than those that had escaped the blaze. But here, a few feet beyond the stage door, he had the sense that the Tavistock, unlike himself, had stood still for the past two years.

As they moved into the theater, Guy heard a familiar babble of voices from the wings and from the stairs leading up to the dressing rooms, quickly muted as players and stagehands became aware of Rachel's arrival, then broken by a muffled "God almighty" from behind a nearby flat.

Guy moved toward the speaker, whom he recognized both by voice and choice of oath, and held out his hand. The voices from the stage, pitched artificially high to make the most of the lines of the farce, were drowned out by a burst of laughter from the house. "Yes, I'm back, Patrick," Guy said, leaning toward the other man and keeping his own voice low. "We can't talk now, or Rachel will have my head."

"I'll have both your heads," said Rachel, who had come up behind him. "Guy, I'm going to the office to check the receipts. Patrick, when the house empties, get everyone on stage. Players, crew, musicians, everyone. Tell them I won't keep them long." And with a smile directed impartially at both men, she vanished down the corridor that led to her office.

Patrick looked after her with admiration in his eyes, then turned to Guy. "It's you, is it. She's afraid people have forgot you."

"She's afraid they'll remember. Patrick, I want to talk to

you, but not tonight. Can you meet me at the Angel tomorrow? I'll buy anything you can drink."

Patrick grinned, revealing darkened teeth with a gap in them that Guy did not remember seeing before. "Two o'clock, and I'll hold you to it."

Guy left him standing in the wings, listening for the words that would signal the time for the next flat to be pushed into place. Patrick Reilly had been the Tavistock's stage manager for over thirty years and Guy had known him for ten of these. Patrick had boundless curiosity and knew everything that went on in the theater, but he did not take sides and he did not judge. Guy moved away from the wings, well-satisfied with the start he had made.

Patrick was not the only member of the company who knew that Guy Melchett had returned. By the time Guy reached the stairs he was surrounded by players and deluged with questions. I'm back, yes, I'm going to stay. Have I been writing? Yes, I've a trunkful of plays.

"Why did you go, Melchett?" This last was from a tall bearded man standing at the edge of the group. The beard was false, but the inquiry was genuine. Ralph Hemdale had not looked kindly on the Tavistock's favorite playwright, though he had had nothing but gratitude for the meaty parts Guy had given him the opportunity to play. It was from men like Hemdale, joined in their certainty that politics did not mix with art, that Guy could expect trouble.

"What was left for me here?"

"The police wanted you."

"They found me. I didn't care to be found again."

Hemdale persisted. "They'll want you still."

"I know. I saw them this morning." The assertion quieted Hemdale, who slipped away from the group, having no other bolts to hurl.

"Don't mind Hemdale," said a lean dark-haired man who had been standing on the fringe of the group. Gerald Sneath, whose customary air of cynicism hid a fanatical devotion to his craft, pushed his way through to Guy and held out his hand. "*I'm* glad you're back."

Guy clasped his hand and subdued a twinge of guilt.

Sneath was a former Leveller and an old friend. He was also one of the four men who might be the agent.

A young girl, barely more than a child by her height, turned impatiently to her neighbor. "Who is he, who is he?" she said, pointing to Guy.

"The devil," said the woman standing beside her. "Or an angel. Don't ask, you'll miss your cue."

Appalled by the near commission of an unforgivable sin, the young girl ran off, her short dancer's skirt revealing shapely but muscular legs. Her companion broke through the crowd and put her arms around Guy. "Welcome home, love. We've missed you."

Guy submitted to the fervent and prolonged embrace, then pushed the woman away so he could look at her. "Polly Eakin. You'd put a rose to shame."

Polly, who was old enough to be Guy's mother, gave him a gratified smile. "You always had a way with words, Guy Melchett. I never believe more than half of what you say."

Guy would have answered her in kind, but at that moment an irate man in a Harlequin costume strode out of the wings toward the group clustered at the foot of the stairs. "What kind of thundering bobbery is this?" he demanded, pulling off a cap and a coarse ginger wig. "I'll see you're all fined." He shoved through the crowd, then stopped short. "Damnation, it's Guy."

"In the flesh and breathing hellfire. Hullo, Ned." Guy moved forward to greet the agile comedian with the quizzical blue eyes. Ned Acorn was one of his favorites among the company, and Guy knew, from his pleasure in seeing him, that exposing the agent was not the only reason for his return.

With Ned's arrival, the group grew more boisterous, causing Patrick to emerge from the wings with threatening gestures. "Patrick, don't," said a petite woman with an elfin face and enormous dark eyes who had just run down the stairs. "I haven't had a chance to see Guy." She stood on tiptoe, flung her arms about Guy, and kissed him firmly on the mouth. Guy held her at arm's length and looked at her with pleasure. Cecily Summers, the Tavistock's leading actress, was a very pretty woman. Though she had three children, at the moment she looked little more than seventeen. Her flowing white gown and blond wig indicated she had been playing Miranda.

"Upstairs." Patrick had returned from the wings. "You're making a din to wake the dead out of eternity." He turned to leave, then looked back. "You're wanted on stage, all of you, after the performance. Mrs. Ford's orders."

Guy led the retreat to the floor above where they thought to take refuge in one of the dressing rooms, but as he reached the top of the stairs, a door opened and a man emerged who brought them all to a halt. It was Ned who found his voice first. "It's Guy, Brandon," he said, as though the other man might not understand. "He's back."

"I have eyes," Brandon said in a surly voice. A smear of greasepaint was visible beneath the angle of his jaw, and a faint smell of spirits came from his breath. He stared at Guy, his expression appraising rather than hostile. "You'd best come in," he said.

Guy smiled apologetically at the others and entered Brandon's dressing room. Brandon Ford was one of the principal members of the company, and it was not politic to deny him. He was also the son of Samuel Ford, who held a third interest in the theater, though to Brandon's credit he had earned his present position on his own merits. "A drink?" Brandon held out a flask.

Guy shook his head. "Not now. It's heady enough being back."

Brandon threw himself into the chair before the dressing table and motioned Guy to a nearby stool. "You're here to stay?"

"Here? Or London? Both, I think. Will you object?"

Brandon laughed, a harsh sound unlike his rich, sonorous voice. "Little use if I do. My father likes you. Rachel likes you. I don't."

"We were friends of a sort," Guy reminded him. They had known each other since they'd entered the University of Edinburgh thirteen years ago.

"You were Cadogan's friend." That was the rub. Brandon

92

was an uncommonly handsome man, with thick dark hair, well-marked features, and an unexpected grace of movement. But there was a lingering uncertainty in his manner, generally masked by truculence, that betrayed his knowledge that he would never match his cousin Cadogan's force or charm.

"I was. But I was never your enemy, Brandon. I thought you understood that."

Brandon shrugged and raised the flask to his lips. "No. Not my enemy. Not my friend."

It was, Guy supposed, a legitimate summing up of their relationship. Brandon had left Edinburgh early, knowing that even there he could not compete with his cousin, and had come back to London to inform his father that he had no intention of reading law and was interested neither in carrying a gun nor sitting behind a desk. He drifted into the theater by default and had an uncommon success, which left him cocky and a little bit wild. He drifted, too, into the group that coalesced around Cadogan at the Angel and became known as the Levellers.

Nothing could have better expressed Brandon's ambivalence toward his cousin than his association with this group. Cadogan was its leader, and Brandon knew he could not challenge him. But he could outdo him in the extremity of his positions, and so he caricatured his cousin. Guy had found it laughable and then pathetic, but he had sympathized with Brandon's frustration. Even Brandon's father seemed to prefer his brother's son to his own.

But in the end Brandon had proved to have some measure of Cadogan's talent for leadership. He gathered round him the more hotheaded of the Levellers and thus divided the group neatly into two quarrelsome factions. It had nearly killed him.

Brandon emptied the flask and set it down on the dressing table, overturning a basin of powder which scattered like snow over the scarred table top. "It was a filthy act, Guy."

"It was." Besides his cousin, Brandon had lost three friends to the explosion and the fire that followed. Guy was not surprised that Brandon seemed to have aged and to have lost the hectic gaiety that had been part of his charm.

And then Brandon turned on him, his dark eyes filled with such blazing hate that Guy blenched before it. "Oh, my soul," Guy whispered, "you think I did it."

Brandon's gaze wavered, and a look of uncertainty crossed his face.

"In the name of God, why?" Guy demanded. "Why would I destroy Ben and Samuel Ford's theater? They put my words on the stage. Why would I destroy what belonged to Cadogan and Rachel? They were closer to me than anyone in the world."

Brandon turned surly, a sign that he had no answer. "How would I know what goes on in your head, Guy Melchett. Perhaps you wanted to discredit us. Who else would it be? You were the one who disappeared."

"I left to save my skin. The police, it seems, were of your mind."

"With reason. I heard they found a man who saw you here that evening."

"He lied, Brandon. I was nowhere near the Tavistock that day."

With a gesture of frustration, Brandon swept a hand through the powder on the table, scattering it over his breeches and the floor. "It had to be you."

"It was not." Guy leaned forward, hands clasped between his knees. "Listen, Brandon. There are three possible reasons why someone went to the trouble of setting gunpowder in the Tavistock. He had a grudge against the theater. Likely? I think not. We've offended practically everybody, but not to that extent. Or he wanted to make a statement about *The Taking of Badajoz*. Who objected to the play? You did, for one. You and your friends. You nearly caused a mutiny in the company. You were meeting about it the night of the explosion."

Brandon stared at him with mounting anger. "Do you think I'm such a fool? Even if I were, would I hold a meeting in the storage room while a train of gunpowder was waiting to go off?"

Guy smiled. "Exactly. You wouldn't. That brings us to the

third possibility. Someone wanted to make it look as though one of the Levellers had taken action at last. It wouldn't matter which of them was blamed. The group would be discredited, and with luck some of its well-born members would be scared off."

Brandon frowned. "If I hadn't been there myself, I might have been blamed. Who would want that? Cadogan? Yourself?"

Guy shook his head. "You don't believe that of Cadogan."

"No, God help me, I don't." Brandon threw himself back in his chair and stared at his reflection in the mirror. "Jessop dead and Hinton and Hever. Cadogan, too. It worked, you know. It worked better than the perpetrator's dream. There's nothing left of the Levellers now." He turned abruptly, his dark eyes intense with unfocused anger. "Who could have done it?"

Guy's eyes did not waver. "I think we had a fox among the chickens."

Brandon drew a sharp breath. "The informer? My God. I can understand selling information, but to destroy the theater?"

"Why not? That's the role of an agent provocateur. To provoke."

Brandon was silent, considering the idea. "But if the informer was more than an informer . . . If he set the explosion . . ."

"He's one of four people. Gerald Sneath, Charles Pursglove, Alfred Billingham, Justin Hever."

Brandon's face grew hard. "Five. There's yourself."

Guy leaned forward. "Five. Agreed. Which of them knew you were meeting in the theater that night?"

"None of them," Brandon said quickly.

"Would Edmund have told Justin or Billingham?"

"Why should he? He hated Justin hanging on his sleeve, and he knew Billingham couldn't keep a secret."

Guy nodded. It was what he had expected to hear. "Did you hear anything that night, any of you? Or see anything out of the way?"

Brandon laughed, a short bitter sound. "There are only

two of us left. There's nothing more I can tell you. You can try Philip Weston. He lives at home still and doesn't get about much, but I doubt he'll welcome you. He blames you for making him a cripple." Brandon pushed himself up from the dressing table, leaving handprints in the whitened top. "It could be someone other than the informer, Guy. Think beyond our own little group. There must be a half-dozen of the Levellers who could be suspect. You might find your agent there. Talk to them."

"I will." Guy stood up too, grateful to stretch his legs after his cramped position on the stool. He had learned as much as he could from Brandon, at least for the moment.

Brandon considered him, a frown accenting the sweep of his brows. "If you suspected this from the beginning, why didn't you stay and see it through? If you were afraid to come back, why chance it now?"

Guy ignored the accusations behind the questions and smiled warmly at the man before him. They were not quite friends, but they had known each other too long to be anything else. "That's clear enough. I came back for Christine's wedding. And my own. I'm going to marry Rachel."

The words shocked Brandon into momentary silence. "So. This makes a difference."

"There'll be no difference," Guy assured him. "At least none beyond what two years have wrought. Rachel is announcing it to the company tonight. I hope you'll come to the wedding."

Brandon began to laugh, a high light sound that changed rapidly into uncontrollable spasms of mirth. "I would have seen you in hell, Guy Melchett. But I'll not miss this for the world."

Brandon insisted on seeing Rachel at once, a meeting Guy did not think fair to witness. When she joined Guy a half-hour later, she told him she had not asked Brandon to stay for the formal announcement. Brandon was in a strange mood and she feared he might confuse the others.

In this Rachel was probably right. The response of the company was everything they might have wished, had they wished to create a sensation. Reaction was divided among those who feared for their jobs, those who wished them well, and those who consigned the interloper to the devil. "About what I would have expected," Rachel said when they were once more in the carriage. "The worst of them will come round. They're always the first to do so. The others will find it a useful addition to their store of irritants. We couldn't survive without gossip, and even bad news is welcome."

Guy felt a pang of concern. "Am I going to make it hard for you?"

"I trust you are going to make it a good deal easier. Don't be a goose. Tell me what you've learned."

Rachel listened to Guy in silence. "I see Philip occasionally," she said when he had finished. "He was at the house last night. You missed him, Guy, and I'm glad you did. He knew you were there and he wasn't pleased. Perhaps I should call on him."

"No." Guy was firm on this point. "This is between Philip and me."

"I doubt he'll tell you much."

"It doesn't matter. I owe him something."

She rounded on him. "You owe him nothing. It was not your fault."

"I didn't stay to see it through."

"You didn't stay to be hanged."

It was an old argument between them, but Rachel's passion was undiminished. Guy found it reassuring. Rachel had never questioned his innocence. Trust would not be an issue between them. Still, there were bound to be things on which they would disagree. He smiled to soften his words. "I didn't stay, and I wasn't hanged, and I will see Philip Weston in the morning."

"You can see Philip in the afternoon," she said. "I believe he rises late. Tomorrow morning we're going to call on Samuel."

Samuel Ford, Brandon's father, was a respected solicitor with offices in Threadneedle Street. It was there that Rachel took Guy the following morning. He was Cadogan's uncle, and she owed him the courtesy of hearing of her forthcoming wedding from her own lips.

Though Samuel Ford had chosen the law well before his own father's death, he maintained a lively interest in the theater. Benjamin had always consulted his brother about major decisions concerning the company, and Rachel continued the practice. Samuel was therefore not surprised to see his niece, though he was obviously shaken by the appearance of Guy. "My stars," he said, wringing Guy's hand, "had I seen you in the street I would not have believed it. Are you all right, my boy? Are you safe?"

"Safe as Harlequin on a tightrope."

Samuel shook his head. "Not nearly safe enough."

Guy laughed. "I've always landed on my feet."

"Ah, you young ones. Sit down, sit down," he said, sweeping some books off one chair and a stack of files tied with buff-colored ribbon off another. "I suppose having your cousin elevated to the peerage does you no harm. Is that what brought you back?"

"He came back to marry me," Rachel said, deciding that this particular bit of news had best be delivered as quickly as possible. "I hope you won't think badly of me for it. It's been two years."

"Nonsense, of course you should marry again, a handsome woman like you. I've wondered you haven't been tempted before. You couldn't do better than Guy." He chuckled. "After Cadogan, I was afraid you'd select someone dull and safe. I should have known you'd have more courage."

Rachel jumped up and threw her arms around him. "Dear Samuel. You couldn't have dissuaded me, but I did want your blessing. You must come to the wedding, all of you. In four days time at Parminter House. It will be very quiet. Magnus does not quite approve of Guy. We'll have to ask Lady Parminter and the Arundels, and we'll need some friends on our own account."

"Of course we'll come," Samuel said, disentangling himself from Rachel and moving to the chair behind his cluttered desk. "Eleanor and I will be happy to give you any support you need. Cressida, too. And Dorinda and Charles." Cressida, the younger Ford daughter, was still unmarried and lived at home. Dorinda, the elder daughter, and her husband, Charles Pursglove, who held a living in Suffolk, were in London on a visit.

"We'd like Charles to perform the ceremony," Rachel said, glancing at Guy to see if he would object. He said nothing, which may have meant that he was not going to condemn any of the suspects out of hand. Or perhaps he merely thought the ceremony unimportant. Rachel returned to her chair and pulled off her gloves.

"I'm sure he'd be delighted." Samuel looked uncertainly at Guy. "Then there's Brandon."

"I've seen him," Guy said. "We've arranged a kind of truce."

"Young pup." Samuel's face grew disapproving. "He would blame you for it, of course."

"He had to blame someone. No one could go through an experience like that and be content to see it as divine intervention."

Samuel leaned back in his chair and regarded Guy thoughtfully over his spectacles. "And whom do you blame?"

"It could have been anyone," Guy said. "A ruffian hired off the streets to discredit the Levellers. Someone with a grudge against the Tavistock. But I think we were betrayed. There was an agent set among us, Samuel. One of us."

"I see." Samuel removed his spectacles and rubbed his eyes. It was a gesture of weariness, as though the follies of the world were more than he could contemplate. "I suppose it would not be unexpected. Cadogan had a blazing tongue, and you had a wicked pen. Between you, you were enough to cause fits in Whitehall. And you drew people, the kind of people who had no business listening to the things you had to say. Freedom's a dangerous word when you fear someone has his eye on your property." He replaced the spectacles. "Who is it you suspect? Not Brandon. He has an undisciplined mind, but he's too convinced of the rightness of his convictions to be a dissembler."

The anxiety behind Samuel's remark was evident. "No, not Brandon," Guy said. "He nearly lost his life. And for that reason, none of the others who were with him. But those apart—" He smiled, the smile that Rachel found so singularly sweet. "I suspect everyone."

Rachel found she had been holding her breath. She had been afraid he would name Charles, but he was showing uncharacteristic caution. Guy had set himself an impossible task. How was he to prove any man's guilt to Bow Street's satisfaction, let alone his own? Samuel saw the problem and offered Guy his help.

"Perhaps in time," Guy said. "But I have a few weeks grace, and after that they may question me as they please. Nothing will come of it. I'm Magnus's heir, did you know? It would be awkward to charge me. And the witness they claimed against me has disappeared."

"Convenient."

Guy grinned. "Divine retribution."

Samuel laughed, then turned serious once more. "You're a hopeless optimist, Guy. They'll proceed against you if it suits them, titled cousin Magnus or no. But I suppose you have to act as you see fit. If you're in trouble, you must call on me." He leaned back in his chair and folded his arms. "You relieve my mind on one score at least. I've always felt it was our insistence on producing *The Taking of Badajoz* that precipitated the whole affair. But if you're right, it would have happened in any event."

"The play made a convenient blind for the act. But they could have found another. It was not your fault."

Samuel's mouth twisted in a wry smile. "I urged doing the play. Cadogan put me up to it, but I thought it was a clever move."

"Cadogan?" Rachel was startled. "You never told me that."

"He was embarrassed to have it known, poor lad. I think even you failed to give him credit for his business sense, Rachel. He became concerned after the night the Duke of Cumberland walked out of the theater in disgust at what he heard on the stage—do you remember, Guy? It was one of your plays."

Guy looked unrepentant. "The publicity drew people to the house."

"But we fell out of royal favor. It seemed like a good idea to broaden our offerings. Brandon, of course, has never forgiven me."

"And Charles?" Charles Pursglove's desire to improve the lot of his parishioners, the inhabitants of an impoverished parish in Spitalfields, had led him to the Levellers where he found other men to share his disgust and desperation. But the Levellers relied too much on words for his taste, and in the frequent wrangling that marked their meetings, he had tended to side with Brandon and his followers.

"Charles does not want to offend his father-in-law. But he never talks of those days, perhaps because he left London not long after it all happened. He obtained a living in Suffolk — did you know? Not that I'm sorry, of course," Samuel added hastily. "Charles might have taken a vow of poverty, but I did not particularly like it for Dorinda. I'm very grateful to young Hever — what's he called now? Deaconfield? — for arranging the appointment. It was quite unexpected, and for Dorinda's sake I must avow myself happy, but I wish they were not quite so far away."

Samuel's clerk interrupted them at this point, and Rachel and Guy were forced to take their leave. It was a depressing conclusion to their morning visit. "Charles has turned cautious," Rachel said, taking Guy's arm as they crossed Threadneedle Street. "It's not that he doesn't remember Spitalfields, but he's got to think of his wealthier parishioners. When he first went to Suffolk, he frightened them with calls on their charity." Rachel pushed back a strand of hair loosened by a sudden breeze. "Why did everyone change so? Were they afraid? Or would they have changed anyway? Thrown off their youthful follies, or decided it was better to stand well with the world than to fight it."

"They haven't all changed." Guy pulled her back from a carriage that was making a sharp turn into Finch Lane. "Brandon hasn't."

"Brandon's half an outcast and can have the luxury of unpopular opinions. He doesn't count. But Charles does. And Alfred Billingham, who's terrified that people will remember his past association with the Levellers, and Philip Weston, who thinks all political acts are futile, and a dozen others I could name. That's of the men who were serious about it. Your agent provocateur doesn't have to be the informer, Guy. He could be any of the Levellers. Someone who's shown his true colors at last."

"Unlike Justin, who's shown them all along."

Rachel looked up sharply. There was a wicked smile on Guy's face, but she could not resist the challenge. "Justin never pretended to be anything but what he was. He only hung about the Angel to keep an eye on Edmund."

"He might have saved himself the trouble. Edmund was only after excitement and Christine." Guy stopped and pulled Rachel around to face him. "Come, Rachel, a truce. I won't be blinded by prejudice."

Rachel thought he was likely to be blinded by his passions, but she did not say so. Her own were making it difficult to think about Guy in the present. But she agreed readily enough, and they parted at the stage door of the Tavistock. Guy reminded her that he was going to call on Philip Weston.

Philip could barely be persuaded to receive Guy, and when he did, he proved less willing than Brandon to hear him out. Philip had been the youngest of the Levellers. An ardent disciple of Cadogan, he had transferred his allegiance to Brandon when Cadogan had refused to use his influence to stop the production of *The Taking of Badajoz*. A younger son of a wealthy East India Company merchant, Philip could not understand Cadogan's position which came down, in the end, to a matter of money. Philip never thought about money, save in a theoretical way as something that should be given to the poor, and to his mind Cadogan should not have thought about it either.

Now, at twenty-four, crippled by his injuries in the explosion, he considered his life ruined. He would have blamed Cadogan, save that he was dead, so he blamed Guy, who had been Cadogan's friend. It was not a rational position, but it was a firm one. Philip heard Guy out, said that his notion of an agent provocateur was fanciful, and refused to discuss it further. Under the circumstances, Guy did not tell him of his forthcoming marriage to Rachel.

Despite his conviction that the agent had to be the man they called the informer, Guy knew this was not a certainty. Brandon had pointed it out and so had Rachel. Over the next few days, when he was not rewriting *The Steward's Stratagem,* which Rachel had agreed to produce the following month, or talking with Patrick and others of the Tavistock company, Guy sought out the men who had been his companions in the Levellers. They had been a motley group, mostly young and as yet unsettled in life, the sons of solicitors and merchants. There were a few tradesmen among them, as well as journalists and actors, and a sizable group of well-born young men, some serious, some following a fashion they had acquired at university, some in search of novelty and excitement.

Rachel had been right. Few of them wished to be reminded of that particular time in their past. The act of violence at the Tavistock—even more, the unexpected deaths that it caused—had frightened some and sobered others. Those bred to work were now devoted to their occupations. Those bred to leisure had discovered other interests. Some had retained their convictions, but only a handful still put them to the test, and none among these was a son of the aristocracy. The agent had done his work well.

There was little point in asking them where they had been on the night of the explosion at the Tavistock. Gordon Murray, on Guy's behalf, had ploughed that ground before. But Guy told them his belief that the explosion had been the act of an agent provocateur, one of their own number, and asked them what they thought. If he was right, he said, who might it be?

It was not an entirely futile exercise. Most of the men he talked to gave credence to the idea of an agent, but only a few were willing to treat it as a problem that ought to be solved. Guy learned nothing that would point indisputably to Justin, nor to Charles Pursglove or Gerald Sneath or Alfred Billingham. He would have to confront these four directly.

But not one by one. There might be something to be gained by seeing them together, and that was why, two days after his fruitless meeting with Philip Weston, Guy was in a back corner of the Angel at four o'clock on a Friday afternoon. Charles, puzzled and uneasy, had arrived before him. Gerald Sneath came a few minutes later, the red scarf which he always wore at rehearsals around his throat, and called for beer. Justin came with Alfred Billingham. They were a half-hour late and refused to drink at all.

Guy let them wait and listened. Charles, worried about keeping his growing family; Sneath, who had turned cynical and lost his taste for politics; Billingham, who had acquired a titled wife and a seat in Parliament; and Justin, who was now heir to a dukedom. None of them would want to remember their time in the Levellers. They had once all been on friendly terms, but their lives had diverged and, save for Justin and his brother-in-law, they scarcely knew how to talk to each other.

It was Sneath who broke through their halting attempts at conversation. "You haven't told us the reason for this convivial gathering, Guy. Let me guess. The five of us haven't been together — aside from the meetings here in the Angel — since we met that night in Great Ormond Street. That's when you guessed there was an informer among us. It's the informer you're after, isn't it?"

"We were more than five." Billingham folded his arms as though to protect himself from contamination by the others.

"Yes, but Cadogan and Harry Jessop and Edmund Hever are dead."

"Brandon Ford was there," Billingham said, confirming that he remembered the occasion very well. "And Philip Weston."

"Ah, yes, Brandon and Philip. Why aren't they here as well?" Sneath looked at Guy with a mocking smile. "Were they invited?"

Guy shook his head. Things were going better than he had hoped. Charles was frowning, Justin looked serious, and Billingham was clearly worried. As for Sneath, he was cleverer than the lot of them.

"No, they wouldn't be, would they?" Sneath kept his eyes fixed on Guy. "They were in the Tavistock when hell broke loose and they nearly lost their lives. They wouldn't have set the explosion. But one of us might. One of us who informed the Home Office of an article Guy had written, who got Gordon Murray's paper shut down, who half-destroyed the Tavistock and destroyed the Levellers as well. One of five men, all seated round this table."

Billingham was on his feet. Sweat shimmered on his fleshy face and his heavy jaw trembled as he spoke. "That's a vile accusation. Is that what you believe, Melchett? Is that the story you're peddling to save your skin?"

"That's what I believe," Guy said in a deliberate voice.

"Guy, you can't." Charles begged him to deny it.

"I've learned to believe almost anything," Guy said levelly.

"I won't stay," Billingham said. "I won't stay to be vilified by a rogue like you. Keep away from me, Melchett. I have influence and I won't be afraid to use it." On these last words his voice rose to an undignified squeak. His face reddening, Billingham set his hat firmly on his head, picked up his stick, and threaded his way through the half-filled tables in the Angel's principal room, ignoring the laughter that followed him out the door.

"It's a plausible story, Guy," Justin said, breaking the silence after Billingham's departure, "but no one will believe it. Save perhaps about you. You count yourself a suspect, don't you?"

Guy's smile did not reach his eyes. "It seems I must."

"You're honest, I'll give you that." Justin got to his feet with deliberate care and looked down at Guy. "I didn't do it, you know. Beyond that I have nothing to tell you. If you're sensible, you'll give it up. You're getting married tomorrow. Think of Rachel."

"He's right," Charles said when Justin had left them. "But if you persist in going on with this fantastic theory, then I'll make my declaration now. I was never an informer and I had nothing to do with what happened at the Tavistock. I don't want to talk about it anymore," he added with such vehemence that Guy wondered what it was Charles didn't want to say. "I'll perform the ceremony tomorrow, but understand, Guy, this is all to be behind us."

Guy let him go. There was nothing more to be learned from Charles, and the passage between them had been painful. He watched Charles make a dignified exit, then turned and looked into Sneath's lean, mobile face. For once it was free of derision. "And you, Gerald," Guy said, letting his face relax into a smile. "You didn't do it either?"

For a moment Sneath didn't answer. Then he said, "I wish you well, Guy, but you're treading in treacherous waters."

"I'm a strong swimmer. Did you?"

"I know my own soul, Guy Melchett." Sneath got slowly to his feet and wrapped the red scarf more tightly about his throat. "I hope you know your own."

And that was all. They were gone, all of them, and he had learned nothing, save that Charles had something to hide and perhaps Gerald did as well. Everyone had his secrets. They could have nothing to do with what had happened at the Tavistock.

Five days of Guy's allotted month had gone by, and he was no nearer learning who had been Mountjoy's tool. And why. What had been the bait Mountjoy had used? Money? In those days, all four of them were short of it. Conviction? Justin perhaps, or Billingham. Even Gerald, who could have turned bitter. Or perhaps it was done for the pleasure of sheer deviltry. If that was the case, Gerald or Justin was his man.

Guy started for Parminter House on foot. Walking cleared the head and made it possible to think. It also made it possible, Guy decided a half-mile later, to learn that one was being followed. Guy had caught a glimpse of the man, a nondescript figure in a brown coat and shapeless hat. He thought of turning back and confronting him, then decided against it. He felt much more cheerful. Perhaps he was not at an impasse after all. Mountjoy was on his trail.

Chapter Seven

Rachel woke early on her wedding day, sat up against the pillows, and looked about the room she had occupied since they had removed to Parminter House a few short weeks ago. By the time she retired this evening, the servants would have discreetly transferred her things to the suite of rooms she and Guy would occupy as man and wife. Rachel slithered down and buried her face in the softness of the pillows. She was not at all sure she wanted to face the day that stretched before her.

It was a moment of cowardice, no more. The day would have to be faced, and it was no use worrying that Alec would make a scene or Brandon would blurt out his suspicions about Guy to the Arundels or Christine would—God knew what Christine might do, but Rachel could think of a number of things that would not be particularly pleasant. She was gathering together the remnants of her courage when she heard a light scratching at the door. Assuming it was the maid with her morning tea, she sat up again, pushed the hair from her eyes, and bade the girl come in. The door swung open and Rachel found herself looking at her sister.

"Hullo, Rachel. May I talk to you for a moment?" Christine's voice held an unexpected note of diffidence. Once she had made a habit of slipping into Rachel's room for an early morning talk, but Rachel could not remember the last time her sister had done so. Not since before Guy left. Not since long before that, when Christine had still been young enough to ask for her sister's advice and Rachel had still been under the illusion that the advice might be taken.

"Of course." Rachel regarded her sister with curiosity. She was wearing an elaborate apricot-colored dressing gown trimmed with a great deal of Mechlin lace, but her golden hair was unbound and tousled, making her appear younger than usual. Rachel remembered the morning of her first wedding, nearly eleven years ago, when Christine had bounded into her room, excited about the ceremony and saddened at the prospect of losing her sister. It was difficult to believe those were the same people who now faced each other in this luxurious bedchamber.

In the old days Christine would have plopped down on the edge of Rachel's bed, but now she moved to a delicate giltwood chair and seated herself with precise, controlled grace. "I'm sorry, Rachel." The words sounded carefully rehearsed. "I haven't been kind these past few days. I hope you will be very happy." She hesitated a moment, then added deliberately, "You and Guy."

Whatever Christine's motive, that speech had not been easy for her and she deserved to be met halfway. "Thank you, Chrissie." Rachel pushed back the silk coverlet and reached for the white muslin dressing gown which was laid out at the foot of the bed. Parminter House might be sumptuous, but on a May morning its vast, high-ceilinged rooms were even colder than those in Ormond Street. She shrugged the dressing gown onto her shoulders and swung her feet to the floor, grateful for the warmth of the thick Wilton carpet. "I know these past few days haven't been easy for any of us," she said, moving to a second chair. "But in a few more weeks you'll have your own establishment and I'll be back in Ormond Street. I'm sure we can all manage to tolerate each other until then."

Christine gave a strained smile. They sat in silence for a few moments and then, just as that silence became oppressive, Christine rose abruptly, glanced about the room as if seeking diversion, and wandered to the dressing table which stood at the foot of the bed. "These are very fine," she said, staring down at Magnus's wedding present, an exquisite, creamy set of pearls which lay, translucent and

108

glowing, against the black velvet of their open box.

"Yes, Magnus quite overwhelmed me. Whatever he thinks of this marriage, he's determined to do everything right."

"I think he's decided he likes being head of the family. If we aren't careful, he'll become quite insufferable." Christine continued to look at the dressing table. She started to say something, bit back the words, and began to rearrange the toilet articles which stood before the looking glass. "This is a very handsome room," she said suddenly. "Won't you mind leaving it?"

Rachel was taken aback. Then she realized what lay behind her sister's question. Christine was the only woman Guy had ever loved, but however passionate their feelings for each other, that love had never been consummated. In a few hours Guy would be Rachel's husband, and tonight, as far as Christine and the world were concerned, he would share Rachel's bed.

Rachel felt a crazy desire to laugh. For a moment she wondered if she should tell Christine she had no cause to be jealous on that score. Rachel had regretted the awkwardness of pretending that she and Guy would be married in fact as well as name, but now she realized she did not care to have anyone, especially Christine, know the true state of affairs between them.

"The rooms down the hall are larger," Rachel said. "You can have this room if you like," she added, with an impulse which dated back to childhood and was not particularly kind.

Christine shrugged. "I'm perfectly comfortable where I am. And I'll be leaving in a month anyway. Rachel," she continued in a different tone, toying with the stopper on the bottle which held the rose scent that was one of Rachel's few extravagances.

"Yes?"

Christine set down the scent bottle, rattling the crystal, and turned to face her sister in one abrupt, economical movement. "Do you love him? Really?"

Rachel answered wholly on impulse. Looking into Christine's blue eyes, darkened with an emotion that went beyond jealousy, she said simply, "Yes."

It was easy enough to say. She had loved Guy from child-hood, as a cousin and a friend. But when she heard the un-shakable conviction in her own voice and saw the realization in Christine's eyes, Rachel knew, with a wonder and delight she had thought never to experience again, that the feeling went far beyond that. She loved Guy as a woman, passion-ately, romantically, with an ardor she had thought was long past, with an intensity that was as dangerous as it was exhilarating. She had loved him for years, but she had not al-lowed herself to admit it until the morning of their wedding day.

"In that case, I'm sorry for you." Christine moved back to-ward her sister, her voice taking on the bright, artificial tone she used in company. "I've come to the conclusion that mar-riage is a great deal easier without love to muddy the waters." She paused, one hand on the gilded back of the chair she had occupied. "It's so unpredictable. Love, I mean. You think you're over it and then all of a sudden . . ."

Rachel stared at her sister, beginning to understand what this scene had been about. "It's all right, Rachel," Christine said with a silvery laugh. "I have no intention of disrupting your marriage. I'm sorry," she continued, gathering up the trailing folds of her dressing gown, "I've kept you too long. You have more important things to worry about this morn-ing."

Rachel watched her sister move to the door and wondered how much of the scene had been calculated, how much spon-taneous. With Christine, one could never be sure. When she reached the door, Christine paused again and turned back to her sister. Her gaze was level and direct, stripped of the arti-ficial veneer, and Rachel knew she was in for one of Chris-tine's rare flashes of total honesty. "As soon as I saw Guy again, I knew I hadn't got over him," Christine said. "I don't think I ever will. But you of all people should understand that, shouldn't you?"

Hermione Melchett, who had been Marchioness of Par-minter for the past thirty-five years and would continue to hold that title until Magnus took a wife, cast an appraising glance around the first drawing room. The pink roses massed in vases about the room blended with the rose velvet upholstery and brought out the softer tones in the carpet and painted ceiling, so that the room appeared unaccustomedly light and airy. Rachel Ford might have a willful streak, but she had excellent taste.

A number of smaller chairs had been arranged in rows before the windows. The sofas and larger chairs had been shifted to the near end of the room for the comfort of the guests before the ceremony began. Magnus, the only other occupant of the room at present, gestured toward a nearby armchair. "Won't you sit down, Lady Parminter?"

"Thank you, I prefer to stand," the marchioness told him, leaning heavily on her walking stick. "I had enough sitting in the carriage. The crowding in the streets is becoming quite insupportable." She glanced about the room again. "What's become of the bridegroom?"

"He's in the library, having a word with his groomsman."

"Ah." The question of whom Guy Melchett would choose to support him at the wedding had been troubling Lady Parminter. "I don't believe I've heard the groomsman's name," she said, fixing Magnus with a stare which brooked no evasion.

"I doubt it would mean anything to you," said Magnus easily. "He's a Mr. Murray, an old friend of my cousin's."

"One of his former associates I take it. I expected as much." Lady Parminter preferred not to mention the Levellers whose very name conjured up ideas which should lie decently buried.

"Murray's a radical, if that's what you mean." Magnus had a tendency toward plain speaking which Lady Parminter admired, provided it wasn't carried to excess. "But he wasn't one of the Levellers. He's considerably older than Guy. He publishes a small newspaper. I believe it's called the *Phoenix*. I doubt it's the sort of publication you'd have come across."

"I see." It was rather worse than Lady Parminter had feared. "It's going to be a difficult afternoon, there's no sense pretending otherwise," she said briskly. "I will keep the Arundels occupied. That should leave you free to attend to the younger guests."

Magnus gave an ironic smile. "I shall naturally see to the comfort of all my guests, Lady Parminter."

"Don't beat around the bush with me, Magnus Melchett, you know what I mean. If you let Lady Margaret slip through your fingers, you're worse than a fool. She may not be a beauty or an heiress, but there's no more eligible girl in England, and her bloodlines are good. She shouldn't have any trouble giving you sons."

Lady Parminter regarded Magnus with exasperation. He had a force and intelligence worthy of his ancestors, but he did not appreciate what it meant to be responsible for the Parminter legacy. For the past sixty years, that legacy had been the primary concern of Lady Parminter's life. Descended from a daughter of the fourth marquis, Lady Parminter had married her cousin, the sixth marquis, and united the two branches of the family. When she failed to produce a living son, she had felt her failure keenly. Under the terms of the entail, the estates would have gone to her daughter Penelope, while the title went to Penelope's cousin Robert. The obvious solution was for Penelope and Robert to marry, but with wanton disregard for her heritage, Penelope contracted a secret marriage to an improvident country gentleman. Faced with the possibility that the Parminter legacy would be broken in two, Lady Parminter had suppressed the evidence of Penelope's marriage and hidden away Fiona, the child it produced. The fact that Penelope's subsequent marriage to Robert was bigamous had seemed the lesser evil.

Fiona had grown up not even knowing her mother's name. Not until last year when Lady Parminter had seen the past unravel before her eyes. By that time Penelope's son and heir, Adrian, had proved to be a wastrel who wanted to sell off the family estates piece by piece. And so to preserve the Parminter legacy, the marchioness had seen Adrian and his siblings branded bastards. Most of the Parminter estates had gone to Fiona, and Magnus Melchett, the upstart banker, had become Marquis of Parminter.

Fiona and Magnus had provided handsomely for Penelope

and Robert's children. Adrian had gone out to India to visit his brother who was stationed there; Lydia, the only daughter, was in Paris with her husband; and Robin, the youngest boy, who was still at university, made his home with Fiona during vacations. Lady Parminter's attention was now focused on Fiona and Magnus.

If Lady Parminter had had her way, Magnus would have married Fiona. Now the best she could hope for was to see him make a good match. He was well past thirty, and it was imperative that he set up his nursery without delay. If his marriage failed to produce an heir, the title would pass to his cousin Guy. Knowing what she did of Guy Melchett, Lady Parminter could not look forward to this prospect with equanimity, but if both Guy and Magnus died without heirs, the title would revert to the Crown. Anything was better than that. Guy, like Magnus, must have sons to guarantee the succession.

The door opened quietly to admit Christine, who dropped Lady Parminter a pretty curtsy and greeted her in well-modulated accents. She wore a demure high dress of white jaconet with a triple ruff at the neck. Clever of the girl to have worn white on her sister's wedding day, when the widowed Rachel would naturally choose a different color. But there was a luster in Christine's eyes which could not be disguised by the pure simplicity of her dress and hairstyle. The girl appeared no more a virginal maiden than did her sister. Thinking of her own daughter, Lady Parminter decided it was a very good thing that Christine was to be married next month.

The weight of the day beginning to descend on her, Lady Parminter allowed Magnus to help her to a chair just as the footman stepped into the room to announce the Carne family. Lady Parminter settled her stiff bombazine skirts and turned to survey the product of her daughter's first marriage, now her only legitimate grandchild.

Fiona Carne inclined her head in the marchioness's direction. "Lady Parminter." Though she was now publicly acknowledged as Lady Parminter's granddaughter, Fiona continued to address her formally, not, Lady Parminter knew, out of deference but out of a reluctance to acknowledge a personal relationship between them. Like Magnus and his sisters, Fiona had the pride of her ancestors. Like them she also had a strong determination to go her own way. They were a willful lot, this generation of Melchetts, and from the sound of it, Guy, whom the marchioness had not seen since he was a child, was the worst of the lot.

Fiona and her husband and children were no sooner settled than the Fords arrived, followed shortly by the Arundels. When formal greetings were done, Lady Parminter seated herself beside the duchess, but long years in London society had taught her the art of carrying on a conversation and observing the rest of the company at the same time.

The only person in the room who looked really uncomfortable was Alfred Billingham. The duke, an opinionated man, was holding forth to Magnus and Samuel Ford, who were very sensibly remaining silent. Justin crossed to Christine's side and lifted her hand to his lips in a fulsome display of gallantry. They were soon joined by Justin's younger brother, Lord Bertram, who could not seem to keep his eyes off Christine—the girl was a positive menace where that family was concerned—and by his sister Lady Frances. Frances Billingham was a pretty, dark-haired young woman whom the duchess described as having "so much more animation than poor Margaret," but in Lady Parminter's view, it was Margaret who had more character. She turned to look at the younger Hever daughter and saw with satisfaction that Magnus had excused himself to the duke and was making his way toward Margaret's side.

Margaret, who had sought refuge in studying the paintings which lined the walls, observed the marquis's approach with the trepidation which always gripped her in Lord Parminter's presence. To her surprise she also felt a thrill of excitement. Margaret had no illusions that the marquis's interest in her was motivated by anything other than her position as the Duke of Arundel's daughter, but it was gratifying to be sought out by such a man. Keenly aware of his approach, she stared fixedly at a small still life on the wall before her.

"For a study of a bowl of fruit it's remarkably well done, isn't it?" Lord Parminter sounded amused. "Rachel charged me to tell you she's very glad you'll be among the guests at her wedding."

"She must be very happy." Margaret was curious about Rachel's sudden betrothal and even more curious about Guy Melchett. He had been Justin and Edmund's friend, but her parents did not approve of him, and Christine refused to discuss him at all.

"Do you know, I think she is," Parminter said in a thoughtful voice which only increased Margaret's curiosity about the marriage.

"I admire her very much," Margaret said, "no matter what my parents — That is," she continued, embarrassed but determined to get the thought out, "they're rather set in their ways, and they find the thought of a woman managing a theater rather odd, but I think it's splendid."

In her determination to make her point, Margaret had quite forgot her shyness. Lord Parminter regarded her with amusement, but Margaret did not feel he was laughing at her. "I quite agree with you," he said with a glint in his eyes which made him seem much more human. "Rachel's a thoroughly managing woman. Much better for her to manage the theater than turn her attention to her relatives."

Margaret had never heard a gentleman express such an opinion before. She wondered if Lord Parminter would feel the same if they were discussing his wife rather than his sister. That brought her back to Guy Melchett. "Does Mr. Melchett feel the same way?" she asked.

"You can be sure of it. My cousin prides himself on being a radical in every sense of the word." The marquis's mouth curled in a sardonic smile, but his eyes grew noticeably colder, and Margaret regretted the loss of the easy feeling between them. She was not sure what to say next and was relieved at the diversion which was created when a side door opened and two gentlemen stepped into the room.

"My cousin and his groomsman," Lord Parminter said in a voice which seemed studiedly pleasant. "Please excuse me, Lady Margaret. I must tell my sister we are ready to begin."

The minister, Mr. Pursglove, a serious-faced, fair-haired young man, had gone to speak with the two men. His wife Dorinda, a lively young woman with an enviable head of chestnut curls, was seating herself at the piano. The other guests were beginning to move toward the rows of chairs, and the servants were filing in quietly behind. Margaret slipped into a seat on the aisle beside her brother Bertram and turned her eyes toward Guy Melchett. Her first thought was that he did not look particularly out of the ordinary. Like Lord Parminter, Mr. Melchett was not handsome in the classical sense of the word, but he was not as powerfully built as the marquis and did not have the aura of force and power which Parminter projected. Though he was not dressed as elegantly as Justin or Bertram, his light gray coat and buff-colored breeches would be acceptable in any drawing room. There was nothing to mark him as a man of danger, a man to be spoken of in whispers.

Then Mr. Melchett glanced out over the room and Margaret found herself looking directly into his eyes. They were gray-green, like Lord Parminter's, but far less cold, and they held a razor-sharp awareness. This was a man who missed nothing, a man who was utterly self-assured and not in the least intimidated by Parminter House or the Parminter family. Or the Arundel family. Margaret began to understand why people had such violent opinions about Guy Melchett.

The man standing beside Mr. Melchett looked to be well past forty. Though he was short, everything about him seemed a trifle oversized, from his comfortable girth to his broad nose and generous mouth. His hair was gray, but his eyebrows, which shot up in wings over eyes bright with mischief, were a thick, bushy black. Margaret was sure she liked him and equally sure that her parents would not.

The murmur of voices in the room suddenly quieted as two footmen opened the tall beveled doors. Dorinda Pursglove began to play the wedding music from *The Marriage of Figaro,* and everyone rose and turned to the doorway as the bride stepped into the room on her brother's arm.

Rachel always looked elegant, but there was a glow about her today, the sort of glow brides were supposed to have but frequently did not. She wore a simply cut short-sleeved, rose-colored dress, unadorned save for the blond lace which fell in scallops from the low rounded neck. Her auburn hair was dressed in a loose knot and ringlets, ornamented only with a few pink roses, but she wore a necklace and earrings of exceptionally fine pearls, which Margaret knew her mother and sister would envy.

Lord Parminter walked beside his sister, sober and dignified in his light blue coat, looking rather more restrained than usual. Rachel's children followed them, Jessica in a dress of the same fabric as her mother's, Alec in a blue jacket and cream-colored breeches. Jessica seemed to be enjoying the attention. Alec did not look at all happy.

Mr. Melchett stood at the far end of the aisle, between two pedestals bearing vases of flowers. His eyes were fixed on Rachel with an expression Margaret could not describe. Surprise, or perhaps wonder. And something else which Margaret could not put into words, save that she knew she would give a great deal to have a man look at her in that way.

Moving down the aisle on Magnus's arm, Rachel did not look directly at Guy. As a child she had avoided meeting his gaze on solemn occasions for fear he would make her laugh. Now she was afraid of betraying far stronger emotions. Realizing she loved Guy seemed enough trauma for one day without having to go through the business of marrying him.

But as they reached the end of the seemingly interminable aisle, she could not help looking at her future husband. He gave her a brief, reassuring smile as he took his place at her side. Gordon Murray grinned, a welcome reminder that the formality of the occasion was little more than theatrical illusion.

A rustling of fabric indicated that the guests had resumed their seats. Charles Pursglove opened his prayer book. "Dearly beloved, we are gathered here in the sight of God and in the face of this congregation to join this man and this woman in Holy Matrimony; which is an honourable estate . . ."

They were the same words Rachel had heard eleven years ago, but then she had stood in the village church wearing a flounced white muslin dress. Magnus, already busy establishing himself in London, had arrived late and nearly missed the ceremony. It was her father who had walked her down the aisle. And it was Christine who had walked behind her. Christine, aged fourteen and as excited about her new dress as Jessica was today. Christine, who thought of Guy as no more than her cousin and Rachel as no less than her friend.

The local vicar had performed the ceremony. Charles Pursglove had not even been present — Dorinda, a pretty girl of fourteen unfairly cast into the shade by Christine, had not been acquainted with him yet — but the Ford family had been among the guests. Other than Magnus and Christine, they were the only link between her first wedding and her second.

Guy had not been there. After his mother's death, he had quarreled with Rachel's father and had not returned to England until his studies at Edinburgh were completed. Even in her joy Rachel had felt the ache of his absence. Had she loved him even then? She had first met Cadogan when he came down from Edinburgh and called on the Melchetts with messages from his younger friend who was still at university. Had she fallen in love with him because he was a link with her absent cousin? She had not thought so at the time. Perhaps she really had loved Cadogan, but it had been an ephemeral love, unable to survive the trials of their marriage.

That was the real difference between her first and second weddings. Then she had stood beside Cadogan, whom she had claimed to love with all the overblown passion of her nineteen years and whom she later found she did not love at all. Now she stood beside Guy whom she had loved for years and to whom she could not possibly admit her feelings.

Guy repeated his vows with quiet assurance. Rachel's throat felt dry, but she managed to keep her voice level. Then Murray reached inside his pocket for the ring and Guy took her hand. His fingers were warm but the metal of the ring felt cold as he slid it into place. It had been strange not to put on her old wedding band this morning. Rachel felt a pang of loss for the idealistic girl who had first worn it and a wave of relief at the thought that she was finally free of Cadogan.

"With this ring I thee wed; with my body I thee worship."
Guy's voice was clear and steady. The irony of the words
might have been funny, save that Rachel felt tears gathering
behind her eyes. It was a moment or two before she paid any
attention to the ring itself. She knew Guy's funds were limited, and only consideration for his pride had kept her from
offering to purchase the ring herself. But the ring he had
placed on her finger was of delicate, finely wrought gold with
a rosy sheen. Rachel felt a thrill of pride, not because of the
ring itself, though it was far handsomer than her first wedding band, but because Guy had chosen it.

". . . and have declared the same by giving and receiving
of a ring, and by joining of hands; I pronounce that they be
man and wife together. In the name of the Father, and of the
Son, and of the Holy Ghost. Amen."

They had reached the end of the ceremony. This was the
moment Rachel had been dreading for the past five days.
Dreading and anticipating. Guy took her lightly by the
shoulders and turned her to face him. The drawing room
seemed to have become unnaturally still. Rachel was acutely
aware of Alec and Jessica standing behind her. Jessica, she
was sure, was observing the proceedings with great interest.
Alec was more likely ready to take his fists to his mother's
new husband.

Guy was smiling, a faintly self-derisive smile clearly meant
to put her at her ease. But then his eyes darkened, and his
face grew more serious than Rachel had ever seen it. They
regarded each other for a moment that seemed to stretch in-
terminably, like a missed cue. As Guy lowered his head to her
own, Rachel closed her eyes, seeking safety in the illusion of
darkness. She felt the warmth of Guy's breath and then he
touched her lips lightly with his own.

Guy made no effort to deepen the kiss, but his hands
clenched on the fabric of her dress. With a shock of surprise,
Rachel realized that this was the kiss of a man who was trying
to hold his passion in check. Reality rushed away, replaced by
the feel of his hands and the surprising softness of his lips.
They both stood very still, suspended on the fine line between a chaste salute and a wanton embrace.

Just as Rachel felt herself well and truly lost, it was suddenly over. Guy was shaking hands with Charles, Magnus was giving her a brotherly kiss on the cheek, and Jessica was tugging at her hand. Feeling shockingly bereft, Rachel bent to hug her children, then rose to face the congratulations of the guests.

"Very well managed, my dear." Lady Parminter was the first to reach them. "I daresay you remember me," she continued, her gaze moving on to Guy. "You've changed more than I have in the last twenty years."

"You haven't changed at all." Guy gave her his most winning smile. "It's many years since I've visited Parminter House, but your son-in-law had me to dinner at his club once or twice before I left England. He was very kind, even when I told him he had no right to derive so much wealth and privilege from the accident of his birth."

"Robert was a very tolerant man." Lady Parminter's tone made this less than a compliment to her daughter's late husband.

"Quite so," said Guy equably. "I don't believe you are acquainted with my friend Mr. Murray. Gordon, Lady Parminter."

The sight of Murray shaking hands with Lady Parminter, neither of them the least bit intimidated by the other, might have been amusing, but Rachel was preoccupied with the other guests. Christine had gone to stand beside Magnus and avoided the farce of congratulating her sister and Guy. The duke and duchess spoke to the bride and groom with cool politeness, making no reference to Guy's friendship with their late son. Billingham greeted Guy as if he were a stranger, which was not at all surprising, considering the confrontation at the Angel the day before. Justin gave no sign that anything was out of the ordinary. Charles said everything that was proper, but Rachel could see the disquiet in his eyes. She felt a pang of guilt when Dorinda gave her a congratulatory hug. The guilt worsened when she saw Dorinda go to Charles's side, squeeze his arm, and smile up at him with obvious devotion.

When they finally adjourned to the garden, where the

120

wedding breakfast was to be served, the gathering took on a more informal air. The air was fragrant with the scent of lilac and hyacinth, the sun was fine, the champagne plentiful. The guests began to mingle more freely, some wandering off down the hedged walks, and the bride and groom were no longer the focus of attention. Rachel and Fiona saw the children settled at their own table with a pitcher of lemonade and a plate of biscuits to tide them over until the breakfast was served. To Rachel's relief, Alec and Jessica were on their best behavior. Whatever their feelings about their mother's marriage, they took their duties as hosts to the younger guests seriously.

"It was kind of you to invite them," Fiona said as she and Rachel rejoined the other guests.

"They're as much a part of the family as everyone else. Besides, it gives Alec and Jessica something to do." Rachel suppressed the urge to say more. The wedding breakfast was scarcely the time for confidences about the children's hostility to her marriage.

Fiona eyed her shrewdly. "Acquiring a stepparent can be quite a jolt. Gideon's children weren't at all pleased when he told them we were to be married, but I think they've adjusted admirably."

"More than admirably." Unlike Alec and Jessica, the young Carnes had seemed delighted with the arrangement by the time of their father's wedding. Rachel was silent for a moment, thinking back to that occasion, the first time she had met any of the Carnes. It had been far more informal than today's affair. It had also been far more genuine. Rachel had a sudden recollection of Gideon kissing Fiona with a hunger he scarcely tried to hide. That was a marriage of true minds. And hearts and bodies.

Suddenly it all seemed overwhelming. Magnus's dislike of Guy, Christine's jealousy, the Arundels' coldness, the strain of pretending this was a true marriage, all the time not letting Guy see how much she wished it really was. It was foolish to pretend things were other than they were. "You must realize a number of people are less than happy about this marriage," Rachel said when she and Fiona had accepted glasses of champagne from one of the footmen and sought refuge in the shade of a lime tree. "My brother has never liked Guy. Neither has Brandon, if it comes to that. And I think the Arundels only accepted the invitation because they wanted to see how disreputable Guy really is."

Rachel was surprised at the bitterness in her own voice, but Fiona regarded her with understanding. "Family gatherings are often a trial and our family is worse than most in that respect. But I shouldn't worry about the Arundels. Lady Parminter seems to have them well in hand."

"Yes," Rachel agreed, glancing at the marchioness who was holding court on a bench of white-painted metal set between two classical statues, "she's taken the marriage remarkably well. I thought she'd object to Guy more than anyone."

"On the contrary," Fiona said dryly. "I doubt my grandmother would object to the devil himself if he could help guarantee the Parminter succession."

For a moment, Rachel looked at Fiona in puzzlement. Then she choked on her champagne. Of course. Lady Parminter wanted Guy to have sons in case Magnus failed to produce an heir. "I'm sorry," Rachel said. "I hadn't thought of it in quite that way before."

"I'm not surprised," Fiona said with one of her warm smiles. "I saw your face during the ceremony. I imagine dynastic maneuvering was the furthest thing from your mind."

"Was it as transparent as all that?" Rachel asked, trying to make light of the question.

"To anyone familiar with the emotion."

Rachel took another sip of champagne. It was already beginning to go to her head, for she had eaten nothing that morning, but it helped to blur the hard edges of reality.

Guy was finding his wedding more of a trial than he had expected. He had been surprised at his own nervousness, surprised at the rush of emotion he felt when he saw Rachel walking down the aisle, surprised at how close he came to losing control when he took her in his arms. And then there was the strain of facing three of the four men he had confronted at the Angel the day before. He'd been prepared for Billingham's coldness, but it was difficult to meet Charles's eyes without feeling a qualm of conscience. Only Justin seemed genuinely sincere in his congratulations. He was delighted to see Christine's old love safely married. As for Christine herself, she had managed not to come near Guy for the entire afternoon. It was probably just as well, for all their sakes.

When they reached the garden, Guy was relieved to escape the babble of wedding talk and snatch a few moments' rational conversation with Gideon Carne. The two men had met once, some eight years before, for Carne had been a friend of Robert Melchett. Robert, a Whig politician with a liberal bent, had made a point of seeking out the young cousin who was making a name for himself by writing inflammatory plays and pamphlets. Over a dinner at Brooks's, Robert and Carne had listened patiently to Guy's diatribes against the way the world was arranged and then said that they quite agreed with him, but they found it difficult enough to pass a parliamentary bill, let alone change the world.

Even in his hotheaded youth, Guy had known there was a need for men like Robert Melchett and Gideon Carne who worked within the system, just as there was a need for men who attacked it from without. He was glad that Carne, who had spent some years in the army, had resumed his political career. He told him so and added, "I don't think much of your party, but it's better than the other one."

Carne grinned. "I feel much the same myself." He had aged a good deal since their last meeting and he walked with a slight limp, but to Guy's mind he appeared happier. He remembered Carne as a restless man with the cynicism found only in the disillusioned idealist. What had changed him? Marriage? Not likely. The transforming powers of wedlock were highly overrated. "Speaking of returns to England," Carne continued, "I'd like a word with you."

"Of course," Guy said promptly. The two men wandered down one of the flagstone paths, stopping before a pair of stone griffins which stood guard over a bed of primroses.

"I was out of England two years ago," Carne told him. "All

I know about what happened at the Tavistock is what I've been told, and I suspect most of it is far from the truth. But you should know that there's been talk since your return."

"What kind of talk?" Guy asked, scratching one of the griffins behind the ears. Bow Street's suspicions of him were not generally known, but people could well have made a link between the explosion and his disappearance.

"I haven't heard anyone accuse you directly, but your return has reminded people that no one was ever charged with the explosion at the Tavistock. At the time, Perceval's assassination pushed the matter from everyone's mind. Now they have more leisure for speculation."

"Nothing like an unsolved mystery to liven up the back benches."

"At the moment. Another week or so and it may reach the floor. It's already much talked of in the clubs. I wouldn't say you're seen as the only suspect, but a number of people on both sides of the aisle are less than pleased by your return. You have a wicked pen and an extraordinary talent for using humor to get your material past the censor."

Guy grinned. "I'll take that as a compliment."

"It was meant as one." Carne sobered abruptly. "If I can be of any assistance — I don't know what sort of terms you stand on with your brother-in-law. I know from experience that he can be a formidable ally, but I wouldn't care to have him as an opponent."

"At the moment," said Guy judiciously, "I'd say he's neutral. But I've got Rachel on my side and she's worth ten of Magnus."

"I'm inclined to agree with you," Carne said, glancing across the garden. "She's a remarkable woman. You're a lucky man, Melchett."

Following the direction of the other man's gaze, Guy saw Rachel and Fiona Carne standing beneath a lime tree which must have been as old as Parminter House itself. A slight breeze had come up, stirring the skirt of Rachel's rose gown and Fiona's green one, loosening strands of carefully coiffed hair, Rachel's auburn, Fiona's pale gold. Though the two women were only distant cousins, Guy realized there was a similarity between them. Not in their features but in the assurance with which they carried themselves, an innate elegance which was quite without artifice.

As he watched, Fiona turned, caught her husband's eye, and smiled. An answering smile broke across Carne's face, a smile of affection and tenderness and desire. Guy decided he had been wrong about the transforming powers of wedlock. Feeling a pang of envy for something he suspected he would never know, Guy looked at Rachel. My wife, he thought, with a mixture of pride and self-consciousness. He stared at her, willing her to glance in his direction, but she was speaking to one of the footmen and seemed unaware of his regard.

When the footman started back toward the house, Rachel and Fiona made their way toward the damask-covered tables where the sunlight glanced off highly polished silver and sparkling cut glass and exquisite creamy china. The Parminter House tableware would probably fetch a price that could feed the occupants of a poor house for years to come. The guests crowded together, arranging themselves at the tables. As he and Carne made their way toward their wives, Guy felt a light hand on his arm. He looked down to see Christine standing directly in front of him.

The suddenness of her appearance was unnerving. He found himself thinking that she was wearing a new scent, something heavier and more exotic than the vanilla and orange flower he remembered so well. Before he could order his thoughts, Christine's hand moved from his arm to his shoulder, and then she reached up and kissed him lightly on the lips. She stepped back and smiled at him with a parody of sweetness.

"Welcome to the family, brother."

Rachel and Guy spent the remainder of the afternoon taking Alec and Jessica on a drive to Richmond. It was less than an unqualified success—Alec was silent and withdrawn and Jessica, now that the excitement of the wedding was over, fell to watching Guy with appraising eyes—but at least it got them away from the house. By which,

Rachel acknowledged, she meant away from Christine.

That evening the Carnes gave a dinner for the bridal couple. It was a small party, and the carefully selected company acted as if they had never heard of the incident at the Tavistock. Rachel was congratulating herself on having got through the day when the carriage drew up at Parminter House and she realized that this was her wedding night and that as far as Magnus and Christine were concerned, it was a real one. She stole a look at Guy as he handed her down from the carriage. He looked completely unruffled. Ever since that moment at the breakfast when Christine had kissed him — a moment which had thrown Rachel's feelings into turmoil — he had been at his most charming, which meant it was even more difficult than usual to tell what he was thinking.

"I have some papers to look over," Magnus said briskly when they reached the entrance hall. He relinquished his hat to Thomas, the footman on duty, and strode down the hall without a backward glance. Coward, Rachel thought, though she did not see what Magnus could have done to improve the coming scene.

Christine pushed her blue velvet evening cloak back from her shoulders with an impatient gesture. "I'm not used to being home so early. Have some chocolate sent to my room, Thomas. No, have it sent to the library. I want to look for a new book."

Thomas inclined his head and moved toward the baize-covered door which led to the lower reaches of the house. Christine started for the library, but paused before an ornate silver-framed mirror and made a show of adjusting her hair and smoothing the folds of her cloak.

Guy gave a stifled yawn which sounded a bit too theatrical. "Getting married is strenuous business. Excuse us, Chrissie, we're not all as young as you." He took Rachel's arm and gave it a reassuring squeeze.

As if to prove she could do it, Christine turned from the mirror and smiled at them. "Good night," she said, with studied indifference.

Rachel smiled back. Then, without looking at each other, she and Guy made for the stairs. Up two flights and down the long, carpeted, candlelit corridor to what was now their suite. When they reached the door of her room, Rachel looked at Guy, her lips trembling with the words she was not quite brave enough to speak. *Stay with me. I know I'm not Christine, but you can't find me totally repulsive. We're married after all. What harm can it do?*

So easy to say, and so impossible. Guy's eyes were dark and unfathomable as they had been in the moment before he kissed her, but when he spoke his voice was light. "All things considered, I think it went remarkably well."

"And without a dress rehearsal."

Guy smiled, though his eyes were unchanged. He lifted his hand and hesitated, then flicked his fingers lightly against her cheek. "Good night. Wife," he added deliberately, before he turned and walked quickly to the door of his own room.

Chapter Eight

Rachel started at the knock on the door which connected her room to Guy's. They had been married for four days, and he had yet to set foot inside her bedchamber. "It's me," Guy said cheerfully. "Are you decent?"

"Almost." The rumpled dress she had worn that morning at the theater lay hastily discarded over a chair back, and she was in the midst of pulling on a clean frock without her maid's assistance. Rachel fumbled with the seemingly innumerable fastenings, aware that her fingers were trembling, then crossed to the door. It was ridiculous to be nervous. Guy had just returned from lunching with Gideon Carne and she wanted to hear what he had to report. He was bound to have come into her room sooner or later. Besides, it was early afternoon and the chamber was as large and formal as a small reception room. In the old days, before they were married, before she realized how she felt about him, it wouldn't have bothered her in the least.

"I'll say this for large houses," Guy remarked, sauntering into the room as if he were perfectly at home there, "they make it much easier to hold private conversations."

"What did you learn?" Rachel asked.

Guy stopped before the fireplace and stared at a handsome landscape showing Sundon, the Parminters' country estate, on a summer day, its sandstone walls washed with golden brilliance. "Carne says William Mountjoy is angling for an ambassadorial post."

128

Rachel was startled. "He wants to leave the Home Office?" she said, dropping into an armchair. "Why?"

"Ambition." Guy hitched himself up on the edge of a table bearing a gilt clock and set of Chinese vases. "There's no chance of advancement in his present position. As an ambassador he'd be more or less his own master. It's also possible that Mountjoy feels he'd be wise to absent himself from England for a time. And if that's true, it means there's at least a grain of truth to my suppositions."

Guy looked outrageously pleased with himself, which could have been a sign of trouble. "If your suppositions prove correct," Rachel told him, "Mountjoy will be lucky to keep his present post, let alone become an ambassador. The stakes are almost as high for him as they are for you."

"Exactly." Guy grinned. "Even intelligent men can make mistakes when they're frightened."

"Even intelligent men can become ruthless when they're desperate," Rachel countered, feeling a prickling of alarm. "I suppose it's no good telling you to be careful?"

"Me? I'm the soul of caution, my sweet," Guy said dryly. "I spent two years in hiding, remember? I know." He flung up a hand before she could protest. "I had the best of reasons. As I now have the best of reasons for learning the truth. Which brings us to my four suspects. Well, Rachel? You've seen all of them in the past week. What do you think?"

Rachel was silent for a moment. "I'd prefer it to be Billingham," she admitted, "but I wouldn't have thought he had the wit to carry on a deception for so long."

"Nor would I, though he's just the sort who could deceive his friends and tell himself it was all for the good of his country. Gerald is far more clever, but I think he'd have found it more difficult to betray the people who trusted him."

"And Justin?" Rachel asked, watching her husband carefully.

"Oh, Justin's undoubtedly clever enough. And since he was never really one of us, I don't think it would have troubled his conscience. Though you'd think a self-respecting agent would have made more of an effort to appear committed to our cause." Guy picked up one of the vases and studied the hand-painted porcelain with apparent interest. "Of course, no one appeared more committed than Charles."

Rachel shifted uncomfortably in her chair. "I can't believe Charles was pretending all the years he worked in Spitalfields."

"Someone was." Guy set the vase down with careful deliberation. "A penniless young clergyman from respectable country stock is just the sort of person Mountjoy might have employed."

"Do you seriously think Charles could have been working for Mountjoy when he married Dorinda?" Rachel demanded.

"There's nothing that says agent provocateurs can't fall in love," Guy pointed out, "even with the daughters of solicitors with radical views. Or he might have started courting Dorinda in an effort to gain Cadogan's confidence. I know it's a bit far-fetched, but anything's possible." Guy regarded Rachel for a moment, his gaze at once hard and sympathetic. " 'Truth is truth to the end of reckoning,' " he quoted softly. "This is all speculation, Rachel. I don't have any answers yet. But it's bound to be someone we know, someone we once thought of as a friend. Betrayal isn't easy to face."

Because she knew more about betrayal than she ever wanted Guy to realize, Rachel got to her feet and moved to the dressing-table bench where her hat and spencer were set out. "I must go. Fiona and I are taking the children to the Bayswater Tea Gardens." She put on the hat, a frivolous creation of white satin and straw, and said in a more moderate tone, "You're right, of course. It could be anyone. I wish we had more to go on."

"No need to panic; we've got over three weeks left." Guy jumped off the table and crossed the room to stand behind her, too close for comfort. "What a charming hat," he continued, the light, teasing note back in his voice. "You look every inch a marquis's sister. Save that you've missed a few buttons." Before Rachel could respond, he moved even closer and she felt the warmth of his hands through her thin cambric dress and muslin chemise. It was impossible not to imagine how it would feel if he were not fastening her dress but freeing her from it, running his hands over her skin, pulling her into his arms . . .

"There." Guy completed the task and stepped back at once. "I'll say this for fashionable dress, it must provide endless employment for ladies' maids."

Rachel drew on her spencer, her skin still tingling where she had felt his touch. Years of celibacy could badly upset one's equilibrium. Perhaps if she'd taken a lover she'd be better able to cope with Guy's nearness. She picked up her gloves and reticule and turned round, half fearing, half hoping to see the same tumult of feeling on Guy's face, but he was already walking briskly across the room. "You'll probably find me in the library when you get back," he said, opening the door for her. "I want to tinker with Act V some more."

Rehearsals for *The Steward's Stratagem* were to begin in three days, and Guy's investigation had not prevented him from preparing for the play with his usual single-minded enthusiasm. In truth, Rachel was excited about the production as well — it was, she judged, Guy's best work to date — but as she descended the stairs, her thoughts were not on the play or the investigation but on her son. At breakfast this morning, Alec had been more sullen and withdrawn than ever. Rachel hoped today's outing would serve as a distraction. Bayswater Tea Gardens, blessedly removed from the fashionable throng and with a pleasant air of country tranquillity, was one of he and Jessica's favorite excursions.

The day was fine, so Rachel told Collins to put the top down on the barouche and then directed him to the Carne house in Dover Street. When they removed to Parminter House, Rachel had decided to take Alec out of school for a time, and she had welcomed Fiona's invitation to Alec and Jessica to spend their mornings doing lessons with the Carne children. Jessica was in high spirits when Rachel arrived in Dover Street as were Teddy and Beth, the younger Carnes — Peter, their thirteen-year-old brother, was spending the afternoon with his father. Alec was quiet, but by the time they reached the gardens and were settled beneath a white-painted arbor overgrown with wild roses, his spirits had improved.

131

Teddy and Beth, who tended to be shy, were in a talkative mood, and tea was a merry meal until Beth turned to Fiona and said in her soft, lisping voice, "May I have another plum cake, Mama?"

As Fiona reached for the plate of cakes, Jessica said, in a tone Rachel knew was meant to provoke discussion, "We don't call Uncle Guy 'Daddy.' "

"Of course we don't." Alec set down his teacup, scowling. "He's not our father."

"Aunt Fiona isn't Teddy and Beth's mother," Jessica pointed out.

"Yes, she is," said Teddy between bites of apricot syllabub.

"She's our mother because we want her to be," Beth added with the unimpeachable logic of the very young.

Jessica turned to her mother. "Does that mean Uncle Guy will be our father when we decide we want him to be?" Rachel was not deceived by her daughter's guileless expression. Jessica was testing the waters.

"We don't need another father," Alec said firmly before Rachel could respond.

"I might," said Jessica in the tone she used to contradict her brother's categorical statements. "If I decide I want Uncle Guy to be my father, he will be." She considered a moment, then added, "You don't have to share him if you don't want to."

Alec gave a derisive snort. Beth ate her plum cake solemnly. Teddy, showing a surprising talent for diplomacy, asked if they could go for a walk when the meal was finished. Fiona refilled the cups and sent Rachel a look of sympathy. Rachel took a long sip of tea, letting the delicately-scented beverage sooth her nerves. The children's chatter and the clink of cups and forks were loud enough that she did not hear the footsteps approaching on the gravel walk beside the arbor, and she was startled to hear a voice say, "Lady Rachel. What a pleasant surprise."

The voice was unmistakable, but so out of place in this setting that it was not until she turned and met William Mountjoy's piercing dark gaze that Rachel accepted who it must be. He was the last person she would have expected to find in

132

Bayswater Tea Gardens, especially on a Wednesday afternoon. It occurred to her that this seemingly chance encounter might have been deliberately arranged. Perhaps Mountjoy wanted to talk to her without calling at Parminter House.

"I would hardly have expected this to be one of your haunts," she said, giving him her hand.

Mountjoy smiled but volunteered no explanation, and Rachel's only course was to introduce Fiona and the children. "I understand I am to congratulate you on your marriage," Mountjoy said to Rachel when the introductions were done. "I hope you and Melchett will be very happy."

Rachel was taken aback. Magnus had sent news of the marriage to the papers, but she would not have expected Mountjoy to peruse the marriage announcements anymore than she would have expected him to frequent tea gardens. Mountjoy saw her surprise, and this time he was quick to explain. "News travels almost as fast in Whitehall as it does in Mayfair drawing rooms. I learned of the marriage from Lord Sidmouth, who learned of it from his friend Lord Buckleigh, who is Lady Parminter's nephew."

It might have happened that way, Rachel thought as Mountjoy turned to say something to Fiona. But it was far more likely that Mountjoy knew of the marriage for the same reason that he had known she would be at the tea garden: he was having them followed. He was almost certainly having Guy followed and today, at least, he had followed her as well. Rachel felt a chill which had nothing to do with the slight breeze or the lengthening afternoon shadows.

"I'll take my leave then," Mountjoy was saying. He smiled at the group in general, but his gaze lingered on Rachel. "Convey my felicitations to your husband, Lady Rachel. At such a time, I'm sure you are both thinking of the future. Indeed, I begin to think it is high time we all laid the past to rest. If your husband does not agree, perhaps you can help to persuade him."

The implication behind these words was so astonishing that it was a moment before Rachel grasped it. So that was why Mountjoy had sought her out. To offer a warning. And an overture of peace. If Guy gave up his inquiries, the Home Office would let the incident at the Tavistock fade from memory. Had they learned of the witness's disappearance and decided it would be more trouble than it was worth to put Guy on trial? Or were Guy's inquiries getting uncomfortably close to the truth? Either way, safety was within Guy's grasp, and Rachel knew there was no way her husband would accept it. "I fear you sadly overestimate my talents," she said, smiling pleasantly at the undersecretary.

"Oh, I very much doubt that," Mountjoy returned with a smile that was every bit as pleasant. "And I know a wife can frequently have a calming influence. Think on it."

Rachel could not help but think a great deal on it, but she had no intention of saying so and was saved from further speech by her son. Alec had been staring fixedly at Mountjoy, but Rachel, used to her son's suspicion of strangers, had not paid much attention. Now Alec blurted out, "I know you."

Mountjoy, not a man who startled easily, appeared completely taken aback. "I'm afraid I haven't had the pleasure of meeting you or your sister before, Master Ford," he said, smiling at Alec. "Lady Rachel. Lady Carne. Children. I trust you will have a pleasant afternoon."

Alec watched Mountjoy's departure with a frown, but said nothing further. Fiona gave no sign that she had noticed anything out the ordinary, but when the last of the teacakes was finished and they had begun to stroll about the gardens, she turned to Rachel with a look of concern. "I hope that doesn't mean trouble."

"Quite honestly," said Rachel, watching the children who had run on ahead and seemed to be having some sort of race, "I'm not sure if it makes things better or worse."

Fiona smiled. "I've never met Mr. Mountjoy, but I know Gideon was making inquiries about him this past week. I believe Guy asked him to do so. Gideon described Mountjoy as a dangerous man to cross swords with, but I should say you took the honors in that encounter." She was silent for a moment. "I like your husband, Rachel, but he doesn't strike me as a man who takes help easily. If he finds himself in trouble, you mustn't hesitate to come to us. Gideon may be something of a gadfly, but he's not without influence."

"If Guy is in trouble, you may be sure I shall beg, borrow, or steal help from any possible quarter," Rachel assured her. "Gideon has been a great help already. I hope he knows how much I appreciate it. Just as I appreciate having you to talk to. If it weren't for the two of you, I'm not sure I'd have survived this past year."

"Gammon," Fiona said. "You've adjusted far better than I have."

They walked on for a few moments, the only sounds the crunch of gravel and the children's shouts and the scurrying of small animals in the bushes which lined the path. Fiona seemed about to speak, but she hesitated. Rachel could have sworn her friend was embarrassed, save that that seemed unlike the forthright Fiona. Suddenly Fiona stopped and turned to Rachel, a smile breaking across her face. "This is silly. It's just that I haven't any practice at this sort of revelation. I've only just become sure, and you're the first person I've told besides Gideon and the children. It looks as if there are going to be more changes in our family in about seven months or so."

"Oh, Fiona," Rachel exclaimed, embracing her friend. "You must be so happy. I expect Gideon is in transports." At the sight of Fiona's radiant face, Rachel felt an unexpected shock of recognition. There was a time when she too had felt joy and wonder at the life growing within her, and at the love that had produced it. Feelings she had thought long dead welled to the surface. For the first time in years she wanted another child. No, that wasn't quite right. She wanted Guy's child, with an urgency which took her breath away. "How have the children taken it?" Rachel asked as they began to walk again.

"Very well, so far. Ever since we were married, Beth's been saying she's tired of being the baby." Fiona fell silent, a frown creasing her smooth forehead. "I've wanted a child so badly. But when I found out I was finally going to have one, I realized — it means I can't hide anymore."

"Hide?" Rachel asked.

"From the past. And the future. From who my parents were and what they left me. From being the Marquis of Parminter's granddaughter. I didn't make a marriage settlement, you know. At the time of my wedding I'd scarcely accepted that Sundon and Parminter House and the rest of the inheritance would be mine. Now it looks as though I'll have to accept it, for the child's sake if not my own." Fiona tucked a lose strand of hair beneath her bonnet. "I knew the truth about my parents might not make me happy. What I didn't realize was that it might not allow me to put the past to rest."

Putting the past to rest had been so much in Rachel's thoughts in recent days that she was unsure of what to say. Fiona gave a rueful laugh. "Listen to me. You'd never guess I was a happily married woman who's had more good fortune than she knows what to do with. Tell me what you think about names. Gideon says if it's a boy we can't call it Gideon, and I say if it's a girl we can't call it Fiona. Beyond that we're quite at a standstill."

The conversation continued in this vein until they caught up with the children who had stopped to watch a pair of young gray squirrels chasing each other around a tree trunk. In contrast to the lively squirrels, the children were beginning to tire, and they made no objection when their mothers said it was time to go home. Though plainly exhausted from the fresh air and exercise, they seemed in good spirits on the drive back to town. Rachel had quite forgot her son's surprising exchange with Mountjoy, but as soon as they let the Carnes off in Dover Street, Alec said, "I did know that man, whatever he says."

Rachel turned to look at her son. His brows were drawn together with dogged determination, and she knew better than to contradict him. Besides, Alec was not one to make up stories. "Did you see him at home?" she asked. It was possible he had glimpsed Mountjoy when the undersecretary called in Great Ormond Street two years ago.

Alec shook his head and continued to scowl. Jessica yawned. The traffic was moving at a snail's pace and enforced confinement always made her restless. "You're making it up. He said he'd never met us. I don't remember him."

"You weren't there. It was in the park. I was with Daddy."

It was a long time since Rachel had heard that word on her son's lips. Alec went out of his way to avoid speaking of his father, and when he did mention Cadogan, it was in the most formal terms possible. It was a moment before the full import of his statement hit her. "When was this?" she asked.

Alec frowned again, this time in an effort of memory. "I think it was the summer before the explosion and everything. We were playing with my boat by the Serpentine and then that man came up and Daddy told me to stay where I was and they walked off by the trees and talked."

"You're sure it was the same man?"

Alec nodded vigorously. "He had the same name, too. I heard Daddy call him by it."

Rachel was not surprised that Cadogan had not told her of the meeting. In those last years, they had scarcely spoken a dozen words to each other in private. But why had Mountjoy sought Cadogan out? To offer him a warning?

Jessica wriggled on the seat. "He probably didn't remember you."

"I don't think so," Alec said. "I think he just didn't want to admit he'd ever met me. Or Daddy."

Those few words were like the chord which signals the entrance of the villain or heralds approaching doom. Alec and Jessica chattered on, but Rachel scarcely heard them. The truth was staring her in the face, so obvious and so unthinkable that she refused to put the pieces together. The words Guy had spoken that afternoon echoed in her head. *It's bound to be someone we know, someone we once thought of as a friend.* It had been Cadogan's idea to produce *The Taking of Badajoz.* Could it all have been part of a plan—?

No. Rachel clutched the side of the barouche as Collins pulled up abruptly, his way blocked by a pair of sporting curricles. Cadogan had betrayed his marriage vows, but to betray his friends, to betray the ideals which were not only his own but his father's . . . And yet . . . Rachel considered Benjamin Ford, that kindly, amiable man who had taught her the business of the theater and entrusted the Tavistock to her care. She had loved him dearly, but she could not deny that he had been singularly detached from anything that did not fall within his immediate sphere of interest. Cadogan, she knew, had chafed at his inability to get his father to notice him. Many of the Levellers had adopted radical views to spite their Tory fathers. It had more than once occurred to Rachel that Cadogan could well have become a staunch conservative for the same reason.

She had never really known Cadogan. She had accepted that years before his death. Now she saw his secretiveness in a different light. The subterfuges, the small lies, perhaps they had masked a more complex betrayal than she had dreamed possible. It had sounded wildly improbable when Guy said Charles Pursglove might have courted Dorinda in an effort to gain the confidence of her cousin, Cadogan; but Rachel found herself wondering if Cadogan had begun courting her in order to gain the confidence of *her* cousin, Guy.

Rachel drew a shaky breath as the barouche swung through the pedimented gateway into the forecourt of Parminter House. It was shocking, yet not nearly as shocking as it should have been. And that, more than anything, made her believe her suspicions were grounded in truth. Alec shot his mother a curious glance and Rachel smiled, wondering how much he could read in her face.

Jessica jumped to her feet before the carriage had come to a stop. "Come upstairs with us, Mama."

"Later, darling." As Collins reined in the horses and walked round to let down the steps, Rachel rose and shook out her skirt. "I have to talk to Uncle Guy first."

Guy stared across a walnut library table strewn with books at the woman he had married and felt as if he were looking at a stranger. "You can't be serious."

"Do you think I would make such an accusation if I weren't?" Rachel demanded. "You said it was bound to be someone we knew."

Her gaze was unwavering, her voice filled with implacable determination. Guy could not begin to understand her accusation, but he had to respond to it. "Christ, Rachel. All other

138

things aside, duplicity wasn't in Cadogan's nature. You know that as well as I do. He was incapable of betrayal."

"That's just it, Guy." Rachel's back was very straight, her hands clasped tightly in front of her. "I know he betrayed me."

A moment ago, Guy would have sworn Rachel could say nothing further to surprise him. Now he knew he had been wrong. He had spent more time in the Fords' house than in his own lodgings. He had even lived with them for a few months when he first came to London. And he had never doubted that their marriage was anything but happy. Yet looking at Rachel now, he knew that in this at least she spoke the truth. Behind her steady gaze lay a wealth of pain, pain he had been too blind to see. Guy, who prided himself on being a shrewd judge of his fellows, was shaken to the core.

"It was Faith Harker," Rachel said in a voice stripped of all emotion. "I learned of it three years before his death. We quarreled and he promised to give her up, but the promise was short-lived."

Faith Harker. Guy remembered her vaguely as a minor actress in the Tavistock company, but the identity of Cadogan's mistress was of little account beside the grief Rachel was obviously still suffering. "Rachel—" Two strides brought him around the table. He reached out to comfort her, but she recoiled from his touch.

"I don't want your pity, Guy," she said in a sharper voice than he had ever heard her use. "I only told you so you would see that Cadogan wasn't the man he appeared to be."

That much was clear. The revelation of Cadogan's infidelity helped Guy make sense of Rachel's first accusation, though not in the way she had intended. "Rachel—" Guy said again. She had retreated to the bookshelves on the opposite side of the room, and he was careful to make no move toward her. "You have every right to be angry. But—"

"But betraying one's marriage vows isn't the same as betraying one's principles."

Guy regarded her levelly. "To Cadogan, it wouldn't have been." He hesitated, searching for the right words. "I make no excuses for him. I certainly don't expect you to forgive him. Under the circumstances I don't see how you can think about him objectively."

"Don't try to humor me." Rachel had surrounded herself with a shell of bitterness, and Guy knew there was no reaching her. "You think I accused Cadogan out of spite?"

With Rachel it was always best to face things honestly. "You claimed I accused Justin for the same reason."

She made an impatient gesture. "It's entirely different. I've seen Cadogan's faults for years. You're still bewitched by Christine."

"Damn it, Rachel—" Guy checked himself. Rachel's persistent belief that he still loved Christine angered him out of all proportion, perhaps because he knew that where Christine was concerned, he was far less rational than he would like to believe. "That's a matter of debate," Guy said pleasantly.

"Then by all means let's debate it." Rachel fixed him with a hard stare. "I stopped loving Cadogan years ago. Can you honestly say the same about Christine?"

Guy gave a mirthless laugh. It was not a question he wished to face, even in the privacy of his own thoughts. "Love? Love is an illusion, Rachel. A thing of airy nothings and theatrical make believe. A—"

"Don't, Guy." Rachel sank into a high-backed chair, arms folded in front of her, as if to seek the comfort she had refused from him. The harshness was gone from her voice and she sounded exhausted. "You said you wanted to discover the truth. You can at least grant me the same courtesy you'd give Samuel or Brandon or anyone else who brought you information. Find out if there's any truth to my story."

"And how would you suggest I go about that?" Guy inquired in a more moderate tone.

Rachel gave a faint smile, though she did not appear particularly amused. "It's up to you, of course, but I'd suggest you begin by talking to Faith Harker."

Chapter Nine

It was Polly Eakin who told Guy what had become of Faith Harker. Guy remembered Faith as a slight pale girl with a vapid blond prettiness and a singing voice of extraordinary sweetness. She had been an indifferent dancer and a hopeless actress, but her voice had kept her a member of the company for the better part of two seasons, after which she slipped away without anyone remarking much on her departure.

Until last night Guy had not thought of the girl at all. Now, as his hackney moved up Tottenham Court Road to the small street near Fitzroy Square to which Polly had directed him, Guy wondered what had possessed him to raise old ghosts. He had scarce been able to credit it when Rachel named the girl as her husband's mistress.

But Guy was no fool. Marital infidelity was common enough, and he must accept that Cadogan had betrayed his wife. What he could not accept were the other things of which Rachel had accused him. Betrayal of his principles? of his friends? of everything that formed the basis for his life? That was not Cadogan. That was Rachel in her bitterness, seizing on the smallest of cues to turn her husband into a villain. Guy would have laughed at her accusation had he not understood the pain that led her to make it.

He dismissed the hackney at Grafton Street and proceeded on foot, ignoring the second hackney which pulled up a short distance behind his own and discharged its single passenger, the familiar nondescript man in shabby genteel clothes who moved after him down the street.

Grafton Street proved to be a quiet thoroughfare lined with respectable-looking houses whose inhabitants seemed to keep to themselves. The half-dozen people he encountered passed him without greeting or curiosity, and even the maid servants walked with downcast eyes. Number nine was near the end of the block, with nothing to distinguish it from its companions. Guy climbed the steps, turned and saluted the man who was trailing him, and rang the bell.

The door was opened at last by an elderly black-gowned woman with suspicious eyes. Miss Harker, she said, occupied the first floor, and he must see himself up. Her rheumatics forbade her the stairs. With that, she disappeared behind a stout oak door, leaving a deadening silence in her wake. Guy smiled as he climbed the stairs. Incuriosity in a landlady was a useful commodity for women who relied on the liberality of a protector.

In this case the protector was generous indeed. The door was answered by a smartly attired parlormaid with a frigid manner who left Guy to cool his heels in a small antechamber while she ascertained whether or not her mistress was at home. Guy, who acknowledged curiosity as a virtue, looked at the door she had closed behind her, then opened a second one. It led to a parlor, a large, light, airy room furnished with some pretension to elegance. A small piano covered with sheets of music stood in a corner near the windows which overlooked the street. Miss Harker must have retained her voice.

The sound of footsteps warned Guy to close the door. The maid returned, her manner somewhat thawed, and told him that her mistress would be with him directly. She led him into the parlor just as a door opened in the far end of that room and Faith Harker appeared, hands outstretched and a welcoming smile on her face. "Guy Melchett. I never thought to see you again."

She had put on weight and it was becoming. It occurred to Guy that Miss Harker's former fragility might have owed something to hunger. She had more color, too, and an assurance he had not remembered. But memory was deceptive. He had not seen her in four years, and he had never known her well.

Miss Harker remembered Guy with some fondness. He supposed he had been kind to her at the time when she was a new and little-regarded member of the company, but this hardly accounted for the warmth of her welcome. It was soon explained. "I'm no longer on the boards," she told him, "and I don't receive many visitors, being out of touch as it were. Please, sit down." She indicated a pair of gilt armchairs upholstered in a faded blue satin. "The gentleman who pays for my lodgings likes me to keep to myself," she went on when she was settled. "He does well by me, but a woman gets lonely. I often think of returning to the theater. I'm not too old, twenty-three next month, and I still have my voice. Not that it could fill Covent Garden or Drury Lane, but it would do nicely for the Tavistock." She leaned forward in sudden pleading. "Are you still with them, Mr. Melchett? Do you think there'd be a place for me there?"

Guy felt a moment of intense pity for the young woman, scarcely more than a girl, who sat before him. Her small talent had not taken her far, and though she had found a protector, her life was a precarious and lonely one. "I've only been back in London a few days," Guy said cautiously. "I've been abroad."

"Yes, ran away, they said." Her voice was cheerful. "I didn't believe a word of it, of course—I mean, that you had any cause to run. Save that they were after you, I suppose." Her cheerful expression vanished. "Still, I thought that now you'd come back, you'd be with the Tavistock, and—I don't like to go to Mrs. Ford."

So it was true. Guy had hoped, irrationally, that Miss Harker would absolve his friend from blame. Now he knew that he would have to confront the reality of what Cadogan had been. "Mrs. Ford is not one to bear a grudge."

"No. Even when she learned about her husband and me, she let me stay on with the company, though she must have fair hated the sight of me."

Guy was startled. "Then she didn't—"

143

"Throw me out? Oh, no. I stayed on for a year after she found out, and I was with Mr. Ford all of that time. I was a bit uncomfortable, of course, but when I left the Tavistock, it was to better myself. They took me on at the Drury Lane, but like I said, my voice wasn't big enough for them, and by the time I thought to go back to the Tavistock, Mr. Ford was dead."

There were tears in her eyes. Guy would swear they were genuine, and because of this he determined to stay. "Tell me about Cadogan," he said.

She dabbed at her eyes with a scrap of lace. "He was your friend, Guy Melchett. You tell me. You must have known him better than anyone."

Guy shook his head. "I begin to think I didn't know him at all."

"Because of me?" She looked surprised. "That's nothing; it's just the way of men. Not that Mr. Ford was like other men. Secretive, he was. I think that's why he stayed with me so long: he liked having another life."

Secretive? Faith Harker was spinning tales. Cadogan was the most open-hearted man Guy had ever known.

Miss Harker gave him a look of pity. "Perhaps you didn't know him so well after all. People have different sides, but mostly you only see one of them." She laughed. "Not that I'm setting myself up as having more wit than most. But Mr. Ford liked to talk to me, I suppose because there were so many things he couldn't say to anyone else."

Guy had the feeling that he was treading on sacred territory, but Miss Harker had opened the door and he had to go through it. "What kind of things?"

She did not answer at once. She smoothed out the handkerchief she had used to dry her tears and folded it carefully. "He talked some about his father," she said at last. She looked up at Guy. "He must have been a slippery one, old Mr. Ford. Never said a harsh word to his son and never said a kind one either. Detached, yes, that's the word, detached. His mother, too, from what I gather, though she died when he was still a boy, and he had to go stay with his uncle for a while. Mind you, I'm not saying he didn't like his father. Poor lad, he wanted to impress him, one way or another. I don't think it mattered whether it was for good or bad, as long as he got some kind of response." She shook her head. "I don't think he ever did."

It made no sense. Cadogan had never spoken of his father with other than respect. But if what Faith Harker said was true, he must have felt anger and bewilderment as well. Guy stirred in his chair, aware of a growing discomfort. Why had he failed to read what was in his friend's heart?

Miss Harker seemed to understand his confusion. "He learned to play games, that's how he did it. He had his secret self, the place no one knew and no one could touch. And then he learned to like the games for their own sake." Her lips curved in a rueful smile. "Not that he ever told me much, you understand. I just picked up glimmers of things."

Faith Harker was a surprisingly perceptive woman. Guy told her so, and she colored in pleasure at his compliment. "Did you like Cadogan?" he asked.

She laughed. "Liking wasn't in the way of it. I fair loved him in the beginning. He was my first, you see. I suppose that's one reason he stayed with me so long. He felt responsible." A faraway look appeared in her eyes, as though she were seeing again the man who had been her first lover. "I guess I loved him to the end. I felt sorry for him sometimes, but I never let him see it. He had no use for weakness. He despised it in himself. I control them, Faith, that's what he'd tell me. I control them all."

The artless telling told Guy that Faith Harker spoke the truth, at least the truth as she perceived it. It was not Guy's truth. That seemed to have been built on sand. How many more truths would he have to hear before he understood the man who had been Cadogan Ford?

Miss Harker was regarding him with a worried look on her face. "I didn't mean to upset you," she said. "You miss him, don't you? You loved him too."

"I loved him." Her pale blue eyes, round and slightly protuberant, were directed to him in sympathy. Guy noted their darkened lashes, then became aware of her rouged mouth and the brassy tone of her hair. Withal, she was pretty — not

145

as pretty as Christine, there could be no comparison there. She had none of Christine's passion either, but she showed a ready sensibility that served nearly as well.

Miss Harker became aware of the dampened handkerchief in her hand and returned it to her sleeve. "I wish I'd been able to say goodbye to him properly. If I'd been able to keep him with me . . ." She raised her eyes to Guy. "He was in a strange mood that day, and I couldn't talk him round. He was like that sometimes, but this was worse than most."

Guy felt a sudden hollowness in the pit of his stomach. "What day?"

Her eyes widened in surprise. "The last day, of course. The day he died. He was here for about an hour, and then he turned about and left. He said there was something he had to do. I asked him if it was to do with the theater, but he just laughed." She shook her head slowly, as though contemplating the vagaries of fate. "Funny, isn't it? He might have seen the man that set the explosion. Now we'll never know."

No, they would never know. Not really, not for sure. It was only the faintest corroboration of Rachel's story. "After his death—" Guy broke off, unwilling to ask how Miss Harker had found her next protector.

"Oh, there was no problem about that," she said, cheerful once more. "Mr. Mountjoy came to see if there was anything I needed, and by that time there was, for I'd scarce a farthing saved from what Mr. Ford gave me. Then with one thing and another . . ." She gave him a roguish smile. "You understand how it was."

Guy stared at her, dazed by this new revelation. Mountjoy, who should not have known Cadogan at all, had known that Cadogan kept a mistress. He had known the mistress's name. So Alec had been right, and Rachel had been right as well. Guy stood up, too shaken to speak.

Miss Harker rose, too, and put out her hand. "You won't forget me, Guy Melchett?"

Guy tried to bring her face into focus. "No, I won't forget you."

She would not let go of his hand. "What I said before, I mean. If you could put in a word for me. Not that I'm unhappy with Mr. Mountjoy, but who knows how long that will last. A gentleman likes variety, and a woman has to look out for herself."

Whatever her sensibility, Miss Harker kept an eye on the main chance, as the Miss Harkers of this world must do. Guy, a prey to pity and cowardice, gave her a vague promise to put her case to the management of the Tavistock. He did not tell her that he had become Rachel's husband. She would have expected more.

Guy walked quickly down the street where the inhabitants held their secrets and kept to themselves. He was more shaken than he had ever been in his life. Not the death of his father, not the death of his weak, irresolute mother, not even the moment when he realized that his love for Christine would come to naught had affected him like the knowledge of Cadogan's betrayal. God in heaven, what kind of man must he be who was so unseeing that he could not recognize his cousin's unhappiness nor his friend's duplicity. How could he have let it happen? For Guy Melchett must be held accountable, too. There was no excuse for his blindness and stupidity.

He turned down Tottenham Court Road, intending to walk to Parminter House. He could not bear his own company, and the activity would distract him. It would also lead his watcher a fine chase. The man had been idling against a railing near Miss Harker's home when Guy emerged, and his footsteps still echoed after Guy's own. What would he do if his quarry suddenly turned and said, "I'm not the man you're seeking. I know his name, and I can tell it to you."

Only Guy could not, not with any certainty. What did he know beyond the memory of an eight-year-old boy and the word of a kept woman who said that Cadogan had been acquainted with a man he had no business knowing. But it was enough for Guy. He would go to Burley with the story. Better, he would go directly to Lord Sidmouth, and if the Home Secretary would not give him a hearing, he would confront Mountjoy himself. Mountjoy must not be allowed to escape the consequences of what he had done.

When Guy reached Bloomsbury Square, his follower, seeing his destination, hesitated, then turned away. Guy noted with satisfaction that the man had acquired a limp. Guy entered the gate, circled round the immense fountain in the courtyard, and approached the broad imposing building that was now his home. Two wings were linked by colonnades to the massive central block. It was large enough to house a small village, and it had housed the Parminters for over a hundred years. He belonged to the house, in the distant way that he belonged to that proud family, but it was alien territory. His heart, if he could lay claim to such an organ, was alien too. Guy had thought Rachel happy in her marriage, and she had not been. He had thought Cadogan open and honorable, and his friend had been secretive and a cheat. Guy had thought he understood them both. He was beginning to learn he had understood nothing at all.

In this black, self-pitying mood Guy entered the house where he was told that Magnus desired his attendance. "Where is Mrs. Melchett?" Guy asked, denying Rachel her title as though this would distance her, too, from the Parminters.

"Lady Rachel is out," the footman said, making it clear that the accidents of birth were to be honored. "Lord Parminter is in the library. He's with the Duke of Arundel. He asked that you join them as soon as you arrived."

Guy hesitated. He had no wish to deal with Magnus's problems, but he had no reason to deny him. He made his way to the library where he found the two men on their feet, their anger hanging like a fetid vapor in the air between them. Magnus's heavy brows were drawn, and his face was white. The duke, rigid with indignation, turned his back at Guy's entrance. The insult did not pass unnoticed. Magnus's frown deepened, but he kept his voice under control. "Guy. I'm glad you're here."

Thank God you've come was the message Guy received, but he could have been mistaken. Magnus had never before welcomed his presence.

Magnus turned to Arundel. "I believe you know my cousin."

"I do, sir, and I devoutly wish I did not."

148

Magnus frowned. His tolerance was wearing thin. "You are in my house, sir."

"And I will leave it with pleasure. Let me say that I find your attitude toward your cousin incomprehensible, but on that count I have said all that I have to say."

The duke turned to leave the room and found Guy standing in his path. Guy stared evenly at the older man. "I have given you cause for offense, sir?"

For the first time the Duke of Arundel looked directly in Guy's face, his aversion scarcely masking the sorrow in his eyes. "You killed my son."

Guy felt some lessening of his bitterness. Cadogan, in a tragic miscalculation, had killed Edmund Hever and had lost his life in trying to save the young man and his friends. Whatever else he had done, Cadogan had not been willing to take another person's life. But Guy could say none of this to Edmund's anguished father. "I grieve for your son's death, your grace, but I was not responsible for it. I give you my word."

"Your word." Arundel's voice was suffused with contempt. "What good is the word of a mountebank, a purveyor of lies and filth, a seducer of young minds—"

"That's enough!" Magnus's voice cut across this litany.

Guy waved him off. "No, no. Let the duke have his say. We may disagree on matters of politics and social justice, but I have no reason to impugn the sincerity of his beliefs." Guy's mouth twisted in a wry smile. "Though I would remind him that his son's mind was no younger than my own and his education possibly better."

"You mock me, sir," Arundel said, "and I will not have it. I have heard stories of you, and I have talked with the Home Secretary. You were a suspect—the chief suspect, I believe—in the explosion and fire that took my son's life, and had you not fled the country you would have been hanged."

"I have no doubt of that," Guy said, "but it does not make me guilty. Nor are Bow Street, nor even the Home Office, convinced of my guilt. If they were, if they had irrefutable evidence that I had committed that outrage, I would not have the pleasure of this conversation."

Guy's words did not sit well with the older man. "I have heard of your infamous bargain, sir." He rounded on Magnus. "It was your doing. If you had not lent Melchett your support, it would never have been made."

"The duke is of the opinion that I should throw you out of the house," Magnus told Guy. "If I do not, he withdraws his consent to Justin's marriage to Christine. Not, as I reminded him, that Justin has any need of his father's consent. The duke has also forbidden me to address his daughter if I do not break with you. I have told him I would far rather give up his daughter, whom I have not yet thought of addressing, than my sister's husband, who is bound to me by ties of blood." He turned to Arundel. "I think that is the substance of our disagreement, sir. I understand your position and you understand mine. There is nothing further to be said."

Magnus walked to the bellpull, then waited in silence for an answer to his summons. "The duke is leaving," he told the footman who opened the door. "When Lady Rachel returns, please ask her to join us."

Arundel walked stiffly to the door and once more Guy intercepted him. "I would not want to have ill feeling marring my cousin's wedding. If it is my presence in this house that disturbs you—"

"Nothing disturbs me, sir, save your presence on this earth, and nothing will satisfy me save to see you under it. Good day." And with these words, the duke followed the footman out of the room.

As an exit, it was a splendid one. Guy would have applauded, had he not been conscious of a rising anger. The unfairness of Arundel's accusation was of less moment than the effect it would have on Christine. Justin might be free to marry where he chose, but Christine would feel the estrangement from her husband's family. Guy knew about estrangement. His own father had been disowned by his parents for marrying beneath him, and his mother had never recovered from the imputation of disgrace on her marriage. "Magnus," he said, "I shall leave."

"Don't be a fool. I will have neither you nor Arundel telling

150

me how to order my affairs. Nor will I have you publicly abandon my sister."

Guy kept his temper with what he considered admirable restraint. "I was planning to take her with me. It's a husband's perogative."

"No, Guy, I want you here, both of you. We stand together in this, or we fall together. I will not let this family come apart because of the words of a doddering jobbernowl."

"He will make life difficult for Christine."

"He will make life more difficult for her if you leave. Understand this, Guy. I intend to see you through, in these next few days and after your precious month is up. I do not like what you stand for, and I do not like what you have done, but you have committed no crime, and I will not stand by and see you falsely accused."

It was Magnus's first admission of his cousin's innocence. Guy recalled the years of resentment between them. They had had nothing in common save the house they lived in and the name they shared. They had different images of the world and the parts they were destined to play in it, and these differences had widened over the years, but Guy had had no quarrel with Magnus, save the one forced on him. In later years they had simply grown apart. But now, here, Magnus had told him that he honored that bit of blood between them. For a man like Magnus, a man who disavowed everything Guy believed in, it was generosity on a scale he would never have expected. Guy had no use for the way his cousin had chosen to live his life, but he could be no less generous. He smiled and held out his hand.

They were in this position when the door burst open and Christine entered the room, closely followed by Justin. "Magnus, how could you," she said, throwing gloves and reticule on a table near the door. "What did you say to Arundel? He's in a fury, and you've ruined everything." She tugged at the ribbons fastening her bonnet and sent it after her gloves. "Justin, tell him."

"He was incoherent with rage," Justin admitted, "but it's not an uncommon state for my father. He claims you threw him out of the house."

151

"I did." Magnus was in good humor, perhaps because he had bested both Arundel and Guy. "I'm glad he recognized the gesture."

Christine flung herself into a chair and glared at her brother. "You're a fool."

"Hardly," Guy said, looking at her with admiration. Christine was beautiful at all times, but a touch of temper made her more so, giving her added color and fire. "The duke asked Magnus to disown me."

Christine's eyes widened. "Disown you? Why?"

"There's been talk, my love," Justin said, coming to stand beside her. "It was bound to reach him." He turned to Guy. "That's so, isn't it? He heard you were suspected of complicity in the explosion."

"He thinks me responsible for Edmund's death."

"But that's monstrous," Christine said, apparently forgetting that she had made the same accusation two years ago. "Edmund's death was an accident, and no one could believe Guy would destroy the theater. It's his life."

Justin grimaced. "My father has a tenacious and irrational mind. He can believe anything he chooses. I'm sorry, Guy. Edmund was his favorite, and he's never got over it. But it doesn't matter what he believes."

Christine looked round sharply. "Not even to us?"

"What can he do? By law I am his heir, and he won't let me starve. He can't forbid our marriage, and no one is likely to take him seriously. Heaven knows, I don't."

Christine relaxed, but her eyes continued wary. "Magnus," she said, turning to her brother, "is Guy in any danger?"

"Guy will always be in danger. He's too obstinate to avoid it and too clever to be caught. But in this case" — Magnus was suddenly serious — "in this case, with the floundering idiots in the Home Office eager to save their skin and the self-important clodpates in Parliament urging them on, yes, Guy is in some danger. But nothing," Magnus added, "that we cannot handle. I don't fear Arundel. He lacks imagination. And he has held the title behind which he hides little longer than I have held my own. We're more than a match for his kind."

"And Arundel's daughter?" Guy said, recalling the second of the duke's threats.

"A pleasant child, but I had not thought to make her my wife. My apologies, Deaconfield."

"Not at all," Justin said. "Meg's a sweet mouse, but she's meant for a quiet life." He perched on the arm of Christine's chair and put his arm around her. Guy was aware of an irrational flare of anger. Then he reminded himself that there was no longer reason to suppose Justin unfit to be Christine's husband.

The silence that followed Justin's last words was broken by the appearance of Rachel, who had apparently just arrived, for she was still wearing her bonnet and pelisse. She closed the door behind her and looked directly at Guy. "James Burley is here. There's another officer with him. He wants to see you, Guy, and Magnus, too. What's happened?"

Guy crossed quickly to her side. "Arundel has been complaining to the Home Office. I doubt that it's serious. I'll go out to Burley."

"No, I shall see him as well." Magnus walked once more to the bellpull. "Rachel, you'd better stay. Christine, if you'll excuse us . . ."

Christine settled herself firmly in her chair. "No. If it's about Guy, I want to be here."

Magnus looked at Guy, who shrugged and nodded. "Very well," Magnus said. "You might as well stay, too, Deaconfield. You know the story, and you'll soon be one of us."

While they waited for the footman to bring the Bow Street officer into the library — "Burley only, not the other one," Magnus had told him — Guy drew Rachel apart from the others. She was worried but composed, her mind bent to the immediate problem, no sign in her face of their bitter quarrel of the day before. Guy took her hand and raised it to his lips. "You were right, lady."

Rachel's eyes widened. "You saw her?"

"It seems your husband was a man of many secrets." Guy grimaced. "I guessed none of them. You were closer to the mark."

"You mustn't fault yourself, Guy."

"I do. He was with her that day, in a strange mood, she said. He left her to go on an unnamed errand. Hardly damning in itself, but this is. After Cadogan's death Mountjoy called on her to learn if she was in want. He knew of her relationship with Cadogan. He's now her protector."

Rachel's face went white, and Guy knew that till that moment, she had not fully believed the accusations she had made against her first husband.

Guy would have said more, but at that moment James Burley was shown into the room. Burley hesitated, seeing the size of the group before him. But he was not a man to be intimidated by numbers nor by grandeur. "Mr. Melchett," he said, turning to Guy. "I have a message for you. I think you should hear it in private."

"My family prefers to stay," Guy said. "They know what has passed between us."

Burley drew a deep breath, as though preparing to perform an unpleasant duty. "I fear this has nothing to do with our earlier meeting, Mr. Melchett. I am required to take you into custody."

Rachel stiffened, but said nothing. It was Christine who sprang up and threw herself on Guy. "No," she cried, "you cannot." Her voice was passionate and it left no doubt that she was driven by something more than simple concern for her cousin's welfare. Justin moved toward her, but she seemed unconscious of his presence, and he drew back, baffled and furious.

Guy was aware of Justin's mood. He was aware, too, of Magnus's disapproval and Rachel's white face. He disentangled Christine's hands from his coat. "I suspect that Mr. Burley can."

"On what charge?" Rachel asked.

Burley reached inside his coat and brought forth a large sheet of paper which he unfolded and handed to Guy. "Mr. Melchett is charged with spying for the French against his own country."

"But that's absurd," Christine said, rounding on Burley. "He hasn't been in France since he was a little boy."

Magnus took the document from Guy's hand and perused

it quickly. "It's nothing but a tissue of lies. Not even lies— nothing but innuendo." He returned the document to Burley. "The charges won't stand."

The officer's face was impassive. "That's not for me to say, Lord Parminter. I have my orders."

"I could make a run for it," Guy said, giving Magnus a warning look, "but that might make it awkward for Burley, and I've taken a fancy to his company. I daresay we'll sort it out by tomorrow."

"I'll send my solicitor to you," Magnus said.

"Guy." Rachel put a hand on her husband's arm. "Who laid the charges against you?"

Guy smiled at her, a smile of pure delight. "Lord Sidmouth, who else? By William Mountjoy."

Chapter Ten

Rachel took a few steps into the hall and watched, stunned, as Guy and the man called Burley disappeared through the front door. Then with sudden resolution she ran to the door, nearly colliding with the nameless officer who had accompanied Burley, and caught up with Guy as he was about to enter the carriage waiting in the forecourt of Parminter House. "I'm going with you," she said, as much to Burley as to Guy.

"I wouldn't advise it, Lady Rachel." Burley glanced at his prisoner, who gave an expressive shrug. Apparently satisfied, Burley turned back to Rachel, tipped his hat, and gestured to the carriage.

Rachel had no idea what she intended to accomplish by staying at her husband's side, but she could not remain behind. It was a trumped-up charge, of course, like the one made two years earlier with the bribed witness whom Gordon Murray had managed to slip out of the country, but it was somehow more frightening. Treason was a vague charge that could cover a multitude of innocent activities. It would be harder for Guy to defend himself against an accusation of treasonable acts than against a charge of setting an explosion in a particular place at a particular time. Even now that they were at peace with France, people were quite irrational on the subject of spies.

Had they any evidence at all? What secrets could Guy have supposedly transmitted to the French? He corresponded with Frenchmen. He had done so for years. The Home Office would know about it if they were having his letters intercepted. But it was all quite innocent. There was Henri Berton, an innkeeper and a friend of his father's who had once visited Guy on a trip to England. Guy, hanging onto this link with his barely remembered parent, had corresponded with Berton ever since. And Madame Hébert, the concierge of the building where Guy's family had lodged, he had written to her, too. It was all quite open. Or was it? Perhaps Guy had been reduced to smuggling letters out of the country, a fact that in itself would rouse official suspicion.

Rachel glanced at her husband. He was watching Burley, seated across from him in the badly sprung carriage. Rachel knew they would have spoken had it not been for the presence of the third man, the officer who sat bolt upright by Burley's side, ready to take action should Guy make a move to escape. But it was Burley who appeared to be in charge, so it was to Burley that she spoke. "Where are you taking him?"

"Bow Street, Lady Rachel. The Chief Magistrate will want to question him."

"And then?"

"Newgate, I would think."

It was intolerable. How could they hope to justify it? A few letters abroad. No, perhaps there were more than a few. Guy, who hated the very thought of war, had been in touch with groups in both France and America who were working for peace. Lending aid and comfort to the enemy, that's what they would claim. And his flight abroad would be taken as evidence that he was trying to avoid discovery. They would say he'd gone to France, to his paymasters. It was absurd.

But then Rachel knew with sudden certainty that it was not. Of course Guy had gone to France. Where else would he go. It was the country of his birth and he spoke the language like a native. But what a fool, mad, dangerous thing to do. The French would have had every reason to take him for an *English* spy. Why hadn't he told her—oh, not in his letters, which would have been unsafe, but in the last few days since he had returned to England, since he had become her husband? She knew Guy better than she knew anyone else in the world, save Christine. He might have trusted her. Feeling

157

hurt—yes, it was irrational, but she was hurt nonetheless—Rachel turned away from the others and stared unseeing out of the window.

She came this way nearly every day, but today the journey through the familiar streets seemed interminable. When the carriage pulled up at last, Guy helped her down the steps and shepherded her through the crowd that milled about in front of the entrance to the Public Office. Rachel scarcely saw them. She was conscious above all of Guy, of the closeness of his body and the feel of his arm around her. Following Burley—the other man had disappeared—they passed through a room crowded with suppliants and noise and the smell of unwashed bodies and came at last to the comparative quiet of a corridor. Burley opened a door leading to a small, barely furnished room and left them with the information that he would inform Sir Nathaniel of Guy's arrival.

When they were alone, Rachel said, "If you tell me not to worry, I will never forgive you."

Guy grinned. "You may worry as much as you please. You may worry for us both. God knows it's a worrisome enough business. But Rachel"—his eyes gleamed with mischief—"we've got them on the run. They're afraid."

Rachel recalled Mountjoy's veiled threat when he accosted her in the tea garden. "They're dangerous. They won't need much evidence, Guy. You say seditious things—"

"Seditious? Never. I only complain."

"It's a fine line," Rachel said bitterly, "and they'll choose to ignore it. You write seditious things, too. You mock people who don't take kindly to mockery. You frighten them. And on top of that, you correspond with the enemies of your country."

"Poor little Madame Hébert?"

"Don't play the fool, Guy, you know what I mean. And when you go abroad, you take refuge in the country with which our own is at war." He did not protest the statement, and she knew she had been right. "What do you suppose they'll make of that?"

"What do you make of it?"

"Oh." She threw her arms wide and walked away from him.

"I don't know," she said, turning to face him. "That you were tempting fate. That you were reckless beyond belief. It doesn't matter really, only—"

He raised his eyebrows. "Only?"

"I wish you'd told me what you were about." She felt better now having said it. "What were you doing, Guy, all those months?"

"I told you in my letters. Don't you remember?"

"Yes, you were working in the theater. You wrote and shifted scenes and made yourself useful backstage and even took your place on the boards. But what else? How did you live? Did you pass for French? How did you manage with the authorities?"

"I passed," he said. "And avoided the authorities when I could. But if you want to know where I lived and with whom I supped and with whom I shared my bed—" He smiled, letting the words hang between them.

"It's none of my affair. No, of course it isn't." Rachel felt herself color. She knew he had not been celibate, not after Christine had rejected him out of hand. She had no right to ask him what he had done before their marriage. She would have no right to ask him in the future, not after she had told him he would be free to live as he pleased. Rachel found the thought of Guy with another woman inexpressibly painful and she pushed it aside. There was something else she had to know. "Guy, did you see my mother?"

"I did," he said, hesitating for the fraction of a moment. "Theater is a small world, even in Paris."

Rachel knew there were things he did not want to tell her, but in this she would not let him off. "And?" she said, forcing him to meet her eyes. "How did you happen to meet?"

"I sought her out," Guy said. "I know none of you has any use for her, but I confess I was curious. The mysterious Arlette. The woman whose name was never mentioned in the Melchett house. She was not pleased to be confronted by a hulking grown fellow who claimed to be her nephew, but she was cordial enough. I was able to tell her that she was a widow. Not that it mattered, she said. She had no intention of giving herself to a man again."

"I doubt that." Rachel's voice was tart.

Guy studied her face. "She didn't mean it that way. You don't know her, Rachel. She has pride, and she values her independence. I don't say she's a saint, but that's neither your business nor my own."

Rachel was conscious of a sudden constriction in her throat. "Then she doesn't regret" — she made a vague gesture — "she doesn't regret leaving us?"

"No," Guy said deliberately. "She's prepared to live with the consequences of her choices. Not that she's forgot — any of you. She wanted to know what had become of her children."

"And what did you tell her?"

"That Magnus has a strength his father never had. That Christine has her features and you have her character. Yes, it's true," he said as Rachel shook her head, "you're very like her."

Rachel turned away, filled with a pain she could not quite understand. She had loved her mother, she remembered that clearly, just as she remembered the shock of her abandonment. But what hurt her now was Guy's assessment. Christine, he said, had her mother's beauty, while she — He saw nothing in her but her mother's pride.

At least she should be grateful for that legacy. Pride had seen her through the years after her mother's flight. Pride had shielded her against Cadogan's infidelity. And pride was all she had to armor her against the knowledge that Guy preferred her sister to herself. And that he had made a friend of her mother. "Is she beautiful still?"

A reminiscent smile crossed his face. "She is. Women like that never age."

Nor will Christine, Rachel thought, conscious of the faint dryness of her skin and the incipient wrinkles about her eyes. Christine, my lovely selfish sister, will be beautiful forever. As will our mother, who could not bear the tedium of her life and the demands of her children. "She's on the stage still?" Arlette Aubert was past fifty. It would be some small comfort to know that she was reduced to playing character parts.

"She's still with the Comédie Française. She no longer plays ingénues, but all the principal parts, yes. Arlette will never leave the stage."

Arlette. They were on intimate terms then. No, not that kind of intimacy, but the closeness of people who saw each other every day. "Were you at the Comédie Française too?"

"Hardly. Arlette got me into one of the boulevard theaters, the Olympique. I counted myself fortunate," he added. "I would not have survived without her." Guy's tone was a rebuke for her jealousy, her anger, her sense of betrayal. What else should he have done, having decided to go to France. Who else should he have turned to, but the woman who reminded him of Christine.

Rachel knew she was being unreasonable. What did it matter now whom Guy had seen in France. France was in the past. The charge of treason was now, unprovable but fraught with peril. "Guy," she said, pushing her mother into the recesses of her memory, "if it helps, tell Sir Nathaniel about Cadogan."

"I don't think so," he said slowly. "Think, Rachel. Sir Nathaniel has no cause to believe me. He'll go to Sidmouth with the story, but Sidmouth will know nothing about it. He's only had the office for two years. It's Mountjoy's pigeon, and between his word and mine . . ." Guy gave an expressive shrug and smiled at her. "I'll have to find a way to get at Mountjoy directly."

Rachel acquiesced, though she was thinking furiously. They said no more till Burley reentered the room with the news that Sir Nathaniel was ready to see Guy. "Lady Rachel," Burley added with a long-suffering look, "with all respect—"

"I cannot accompany my husband. Yes, I understand." She had been going to insist on it, had been ready to follow Guy to whatever place of confinement they would take him, but she knew it would do little good. And there was something else she could do which might be of far more help. "If you will be so kind as to procure me a hackney."

It did not matter that Guy thought her defection abrupt, for she suspected he would not approve of what she was going to do. Nor would Officer Burley. He had given the driver the direction of Parminter House and she had not contradicted him, but once they were safely away from Bow Street, she rapped sharply on the roof of the carriage and told the driver to take her to Whitehall. Guy had hurt her immeasurably with his disclosures about her mother, but he was her cousin and her husband and, God help her, she loved him.

It was nearly three when the carriage pulled up at the Montagu lodgings on Whitehall and Rachel climbed the steps to the first floor of the unpretentious building which housed the Home Office, praying that William Mountjoy would be in.

An open door led her to a large room where some dozen clerks were gathered around a long table shuffling papers and preparing to leave for the day. They looked at her in surprise, but it was one of the senior clerks, who occupied a desk of his own, who came forward and asked how he might serve her, then volunteered to inform Mr. Mountjoy of her arrival. Rachel took a chair, folded her hands in her lap, and tried to give the appearance of a confidence she did not feel.

Mountjoy, emerging from another room, was all affability, though Rachel could see he was both surprised and disconcerted by her presence on his own ground. Nevertheless, he ushered her politely into his room, offered her a chair, and closed the curtains a fraction so the afternoon sun would not be in her eyes. "I have come about my husband," she said, wanting to make her position clear at the outset.

"Ah." Mountjoy seated himself behind his desk, an act that made her feel curiously diminished and was perhaps intended to do so. "I understand he has been taken for questioning. Forgive me, Lady Rachel, but this is not a matter on which I am at liberty to speak."

"Not my second husband, Mr. Mountjoy. I am talking about my first." Rachel felt a moment of satisfaction as she saw the look of consternation that passed across Mountjoy's face. Passed and was gone, to be replaced by polite inquiry. "My first husband, Cadogan Ford," she continued. "I believe you were acquainted with him."

"I believe not, Lady Rachel. Our paths would not have been likely to cross."

"No," she said, giving his answer due consideration, "I suppose you would have been careful to see that that was the

162

case. Tell me, Mr. Mountjoy, when did you first recruit him to your cause?"

Mountjoy's brows rose in polite inquiry. "I don't think I follow you, Lady Rachel. What is it that you accuse me of?"

She had lost the advantage of surprise, but he was nicely on the hook and she had no intention of letting him wriggle away. "Of employing my husband as your agent, Mr. Mountjoy. Of paying him to spy on his friends and tell you what they did. Of inciting him to set an explosion at the Tavistock Theater, for reasons you no doubt found good, and causing the deaths of Harry Jessop and George Hinton and the eldest son of the man who is now the Duke of Arundel. Of causing his own death, for my husband, though he was willing to betray his friends, was not willing to kill them." Rachel stopped, conscious of the quickening of her breath and the pounding of her heart.

Mountjoy regarded her thoughtfully with something akin to pity in his eyes. She saw that he had decided to treat her as an overwrought woman. "You will understand I can say nothing in answer to these allegations, Lady Rachel. They would be laughable, save for your obvious sincerity in making them. Do I detect the hand of your present husband in these charges? It would be in his interest to divert attention from his own behavior in the matter."

Rachel forced herself to smile. "My present husband knows rather less than I do, and he would never assent to accusing Mr. Ford. Cadogan was his friend."

"I see." Mountjoy put his palms together and held them before his lips, as though considering how to rid himself of this importunate woman. "Tell me, Lady Rachel, what has given you the idea that Mr. Ford had anything to do with this office?"

"Oh, that is simple, Mr. Mountjoy. He told me so himself." Rachel could not mention Faith Harker, who was dependent on Mountjoy's good will. "Cadogan, as you know, could keep a secret," she went on, "but there are no secrets between husband and wife."

There was a flicker of emotion in Mountjoy's eyes, but his voice continued calmly. "So you have known for some time."

"Since well before his death."

"And yet you have said nothing about it. Nothing, that is, until today. Why didn't you come forward when your cousin was first suspected?"

"Because my brother was not then Marquis of Parminter," Rachel said with her sweetest smile.

"Ah." Mountjoy leaned back in his chair and regarded her with satisfaction. Only the faint twitching of a muscle in his cheek gave any indication of unease. "So you would bargain." He leaned forward in a sudden movement. "Let me tell you this, Lady Rachel, so there will be no misunderstanding between us. You have come to me with a cock-and-bull story for which there is no shred of evidence. There is no evidence because the story is untrue. Nonetheless, you hope to frighten me into intervening on behalf of your husband—your present husband, Mr. Melchett, who is being held to answer on charges of treason. I will not intervene. I will do nothing whatsoever save escort you from this office. I give you the lie, Lady Rachel, though it is not a gentlemanly thing to do. You may give it me in turn, but who is to choose between us?" Mountjoy rose and rested his hands on the desk. "Believe me, I have nothing but sympathy for your position, Lady Rachel. But you have made a mistake in coming to me."

"I have made no mistake." Rachel looked up at the man looming above her, noted again the intelligent eyes, the disciplined mouth, the lines that ran from cheek to chin and gave character to his face. "Sit down, Mr. Mountjoy. I have not yet finished what I have to say. You would be wise to hear me out."

Mountjoy stared down at her. He was not a man used to have his authority challenged. And then, to Rachel's surprise and relief, he sat down. "Very well," he said, folding his arms. "What is it I would be wise to hear?"

Rachel studied her opponent. So much depended on how she phrased her argument, on how frightened he was and how well she could arouse his fear. "You are quite right, Mr. Mountjoy. It is a question of your word against mine. But I would remind you that I have a voice, and I do not hesitate to use it. My brother, the Marquis of Parminter, shares my conviction in this matter" — Magnus, she thought, forgive me, it is for Guy's sake — "and he can get Lord Sidmouth's ear, even if I cannot. I suspect that the Secretary, having come into office after Cadogan's death, knows little or nothing of your involvement with him. I can myself approach the Duke of Arundel — and I will — to tell him who was responsible for his son's death. The duke had little use for Cadogan and he has little use for Guy, but I can turn his anger against a servant of the Crown who connived in an act that took his son's life. You can be sure he, too, will have words with Lord Sidmouth. There are other men I will talk to, men of less consequence than Arundel but of some position nonetheless. Lord Carne, for instance, will raise questions in the Upper Chamber, and Lord Carne is always listened to." She paused to allow these threats to sink in. "At the best, it will be uncomfortable for you, Mr. Mountjoy. There will be awkward questions asked. Are you prepared to answer them?"

He could defy her and it could all come to naught. He could alert Lord Sidmouth who would then be prepared to deal with Arundel and the others. But she would not allow her doubt to show in her face. Chin raised, back erect, she held his eyes as though she were the Medusa.

There was a long silence. Mountjoy's face gave nothing away, but a faint twitching was once more evident in his cheek. Then he gave a great sigh. "You are a determined woman, Lady Rachel. What is it you are asking?"

"I want you to withdraw the charges of treason against Guy Melchett. They are groundless, and you know it. I want you to tell Bow Street to drop their investigation into the explosion at the Tavistock. The matter is solved and the culprit dead, and nothing is to be gained by pursuing it."

"And?"

"That is all, Mr. Mountjoy."

He gave her a wintry smile and shook his head. "You ask a great deal."

"A great deal is at stake, for both you and me."

"Agreed. And what will you do for me in turn?"

"I will allow you to present the matter to Lord Sidmouth in

whatever light you please. If you do not agree to my terms, I will go to him myself. I will tell him how you used Cadogan as your agent and what you required him to do. I will tell him how you have used Guy to cover up your grievous mistakes. Come, Mr. Mountjoy," she said, her voice cajoling, "you are in trouble in any event. Don't make more trouble than you need."

He studied her for a long moment. Two opponents, weighing odds, gauging chances. Rachel's heart was pounding with fear, but she kept her gaze steady and was rewarded at last with a faint flicker in his own.

"Well," he said. It was an admission of defeat. "I may tell you frankly that I consider Guy Melchett a dangerous man. A clever one, I grant you, but dangerous. Still, treason is hard to prove. As for the matter of the explosion, the witness against him has disappeared and our efforts to find him have been unavailing. Prosecution on either charge would be difficult."

"Then we have a bargain?"

Mountjoy hesitated, sat forward in his chair, then subsided with evident weariness. "Yes, Lady Rachel, we have a bargain."

Once the matter was concluded, Mountjoy proved very efficient. He penned a letter to Sir Nathaniel Conant, informing him that it was in the interest of the Home Office that the charges against Guy Melchett be dropped. Sir Nathaniel could apply to Lord Sidmouth for confirmation on the following day. "I will tell him myself tonight," Mountjoy said as Rachel, at her request, read through the document. The inquiry into the incident at the Tavistock was also to be dropped. It had been resolved to the Home Office's satisfaction, and again, Lord Sidmouth could be applied to in the matter. Mountjoy then sealed the letter and handed it to Rachel. She had insisted upon it. She would take it at once to Bow Street and place it in Sir Nathaniel's hands.

As she prepared to leave, Mountjoy made her a slight bow. "I trust you will not have cause to regret this day's work, Lady Rachel." But his voice held no threat.

Rachel despised him for what he had done, but she found

herself thinking of him with some charity. He had given her what she wanted, and one could not ask a man for more.

It was not until she had regained the street and procured a hackney and settled back against the seat that Rachel allowed herself to feel fully her exultation and relief. Guy would be free this afternoon and the future would be clear. She smiled. Clear at least until he got himself in more trouble. But the past was over and she could bury it at last, Cadogan and his double betrayal and the love she had once borne him. She would never think of it again. Not unless she looked in Alec's eyes. He would have to know about his father, and it would be a cruel blow, but one day, some day, he would come through it. He might even learn to love Guy. And if he did not, she had love enough for her husband.

It was in this state, feverish, apprehensive, triumphant, feeling for the thousandth time the reassuring crackle of paper in her reticule, that Rachel arrived at Bow Street and demanded to be taken to the Chief Magistrate.

He was still occupied with Guy. It seemed incredible, yet when Rachel glanced at her watch she found that less than two hours had passed. "Tell him," she said to the apologetic officer who told her the magistrate could not be disturbed, "that I have an urgent message for him from the Home Office." The officer blinked in surprise, hurried away, and as quickly came back to inform her that Sir Nathaniel would see her.

Rachel swept into the room, ignoring Guy's presence but conscious at every moment of his nearness. Sir Nathaniel waited till she was seated before he slit the seal and opened Mountjoy's letter. He read it quickly, then read it again, frowning and pursing his lips. Only when he had read it a third time did he look up and glance toward the corner of the room where an officer sat with a much-filled notebook on his knee. Conant shook his head, dismissed the officer, and turned to Guy with what Rachel strongly suspected was relief. "We have made little progress this afternoon, Mr. Melchett. You understand that I felt bound to inquire into the charges against you, for they are of a very serious nature. So serious that despite your answers to my questions and despite the evident probity of your bearing"—he did not say, "despite your being cousin to the Marquis of Parminter," but he may as well have done—"I would have been obliged to keep you in custody. But," he continued ponderously, tapping the paper before him, "I have been given to understand that the charges against you are being withdrawn. I cannot say that I am unhappy that it should be so. Indeed, I am quite relieved. I might also say that our little agreement, Mr. Melchett, is at an end. There is no longer any need for it." He gave a self-conscious laugh. "Not that I will expect any other than good behavior on your account." Sir Nathaniel rose from his chair and held out his hand.

Guy looked at him in astonishment, then quickly got to his feet, took the magistrate's hand, expressed his gratitude, and ushered his wife out of the room. He did not look at her directly until they reached the street where he turned her round to face him. "You wonder," he said, his eyes dancing with delight. "You wondrous woman. How did you do it?"

Rachel laughed for sheer joy. "I'll tell you when we're private," she said, drawing aside to avoid an old blind man led by a small child. And she did, all the way home in the hackney. Rachel had a good memory, and she replayed each one of her exchanges with Mountjoy, down to her final threats and his final capitulation, even to the moment of charity she had felt toward the man who had set Cadogan on a course of deceit and betrayal.

"Be careful, Rachel," Guy said, drawing her to him, "Mountjoy plays dangerous games and you might learn to enjoy them."

Rachel responded with some random nonsense and subsided into the cradle of his arm. She felt so safe, so happy, so secure. Her marriage was real, not a sham, and she would make it work. She wanted to tell Guy of her new born certainty, but the carriage was not the place. Nor was Parminter House. They had to go to Magnus and tell him everything that had occurred, then tell Christine, who was near hysterical with relief, and Justin who had remained with her since Guy had been taken. They also had to tell them about Cadogan, which was far more difficult and caused Rachel immeasurable pain. Then they had to spend time with the children, whom Rachel had ignored for most of that day, and then it was time to dine, and Rachel had to return to the theater. Guy accompanied her and they talked of the changes he had made in *The Steward's Stratagem.* It was nearly midnight when they at last returned to Parminter House, mounted the stairs, and entered their separate doors.

Her maid was waiting in her bedchamber, and Rachel submitted to being unbuttoned and unfastened and helped into her nightdress and dressing gown. Her hair she insisted on doing herself. She dismissed the maid, feeling a twinge of guilt for her abruptness, and sat down at her dressing table to pull the pins from her hair and run a brush through the thick curls. So much had happened. She could not sleep. She pulled the loose strands from the bristles with a vicious tug and attacked her hair again. It was not fair, married to a man she knew she loved, a man who had at least some fondness for her, a man—it was an unworthy thought—who would have some cause for gratitude.

Rachel put the brush down, pushed it out of the way, and sat regarding her reflection, her face propped in her hands. She was not Christine, but she was a desirable woman. Wasn't she? Hadn't Guy shown that he found her desirable? She had set the terms of their agreement, and therefore she had the right to break them. And break them she would. She wanted her husband, wanted him as a woman longs for a man, wanted him to hold her and caress her and bring her oblivion. She had sworn she would take no less than everything. What a fool she had been. She would take whatever she could get and be happy with it. It didn't matter. Nothing mattered, save being in Guy's arms again as she had been in the carriage that afternoon.

Dismayingly conscious of the heat spreading between her legs, Rachel pushed herself away from the table, walked across the room, and knocked at the door that separated Guy's bedchamber from her own.

"Come in," he called. She drew a breath and pushed open the door. Guy was in his shirt-sleeves, seated at the rolltop writing desk near the fireplace. "Is anything wrong?" he said, getting to his feet.

"No, nothing. That is . . ." Rachel's resolution faltered. This was not going at all as she had hoped. Perhaps he did not even want her. And then her passion swept all uncertainty away. "Guy," she said, "I want to sleep in your bed tonight."

Chapter Eleven

Rachel stood as if transfixed, heart hammering in her throat, scarcely able to believe she had said it. A vast expanse of Axminster carpet stretched between her and Guy, as great as the gulf between love and desire, between what she wanted from him and what he was able to give. This room with its ornate paneling and rich wall hangings of dark green damask seemed far too cold for passion, far too formal for surrender.

The only light came from the brace of candles on the desk. The white of Guy's shirt gleamed in the shadows, but it was impossible to read his expression. Just as she was ready to scream with frustration or flee from the room and pretend it had never happened, he finally spoke. "We've both had a number of shocks in the past twenty-four hours. Shock can affect people in strange ways. Sometimes they do things they later regret."

"There's no need to humor me, Guy. If you don't want to, you'd better just say so." Rachel's voice was raw with pain. She had been devastated five years ago when she learned she was not enough for Cadogan. She was not sure she could bear a second rejection.

Guy started to move toward her, then checked himself. "You're not a woman to treat passion lightly, Rachel. I don't want to take advantage of you."

"Take advantage of me." The words burst from her dry throat on a note of hysterical laughter. "Guy, I'm thirty years old and I have two children and I haven't—After Cadogan and

171

I quarreled we didn't — That is, I wouldn't, not if it meant sharing him. It's been five years, Guy. I thought I'd learn not to mind, but I must have been hopelessly naive and I don't think I can go on —"

She broke off and looked at him, need and longing sweeping away any last vestiges of pride. Guy drew in his breath. A moment passed and then another and then he strode forward again. This time he did not hold back. Without hesitation, he gathered her to him, his hands warm and sure, and then his mouth sought her own, assuring her in the most fundamental way possible that he had no intention of refusing what she had asked for.

At the touch of his lips, relief swept through Rachel, but the pressure of his mouth and the feel of his body against her own soon stirred something stronger. She had been starved for a man's touch for five years, but she had been starved for Guy's touch for far longer. She clung to him feverishly, returning his kisses with a hungry desperation she had never known and would not have thought herself capable of.

"Rachel." Guy lifted his head and captured her face between his hands, caressing her cheek with gentle fingers. There was a touch of amusement in his eyes and a tenderness which brought a lump to her throat. "It's all right, sweetheart. We have the whole night ahead of us. It's one of the advantages of being married."

Very slowly, with a fine-tuned care which sent shivers coursing through her, he traced the line of her jaw and the column of her throat. His eyes and the pulse beating in his throat and the hardness of his body, unmistakable despite the layers of fabric between them, all told Rachel he wanted her. It was heady knowledge, every bit as potent as his touch. But just beyond the intoxication and delight lay the bitter ache of sorrow. There was no doubt that Guy was aroused, but he was not taking her out of love or even desire, but out of kindness and generosity.

It doesn't matter, Rachel told herself, as Guy deftly undid the peach satin ribbon which held her dressing gown closed

172

at the neck. It was a lie and she knew it, but when he pushed the dressing gown back and let his hands drift over her shoulders and the swell of her breasts, it was seductively easy to pretend otherwise. Rachel pulled free of the heavy muslin folds and wrapped her arms around him, eager for more. He was kissing her again, or she was kissing him, tangling her fingers in his hair in an effort to get even closer.

"Oh, Rachel," Guy murmured against her cheek, his voice not quite steady, *"you have witchcraft in your lips."* With a leisurely grace which hinted at joys to come, he let his mouth follow the path he had earlier traced with his fingers, lingering in the hollow at the base of her throat. And then he lifted her off her feet and swung her into his arms.

Rachel, who hadn't been carried since she was a child, decided it was a delicious sensation. She would not have expected such a romantic gesture from Guy, but then she was fast learning that her husband was indecently practiced in such matters. Somehow he managed to push back the embroidered velvet coverlet without setting her down, and then he laid her against cool, pristine sheets which smelled of starch and lavender.

As Guy worked at the buttons on her nightdress, Rachel fumbled with the fastenings on his shirt. Her eagerness made her awkward and their arms got tangled up, and she started to laugh, but she was breathing too quickly and the laughter came out in strangled gasps. She raised her arms to help Guy pull the nightdress over her head, and it was only when he cast the garment aside that she suffered a pang of uncertainty. She was past her first youth, and two children had not failed to leave their mark. The candles suddenly seemed brighter than before and the air cooler. Rachel subdued an urge to wrap her arms over her chest. She wasn't a trembling virgin, and Guy wouldn't expect perfection. At least in this she did not have to worry about how she compared with Christine, for he had never seen her sister thus.

With the greatest care, Guy lifted her hair and pushed it

back over her shoulders, exposing her body to his view. "I'm a luckier man than I realized," he said softly. The words sent a tremor through her as did the admiration in his eyes. When he tugged off his shirt and drew back to remove his breeches, Rachel watched with frank curiosity. Then, feeling like a gaping schoolgirl, she hastily looked away. The flickering candlelight illuminated the gilt-framed picture which hung over the fireplace, a portrait of a long-dead Melchett in a starched ruff and doublet. There was a look of disapproval on his face, and he seemed to be staring at the bed, as if he knew exactly what they were up to.

"Guy," Rachel said as steadily as she could, "one of our ancestors is watching us."

"Let him watch," said Guy cheerfully. "I daresay we could teach him a thing or two."

Rachel smiled, her embarrassment momentarily forgot, but when she turned to look at him the smile froze on her lips. Save for his stockings, which he was holding in one hand, he was stark naked. The proof of his desire for her could not have been more apparent. Guy grinned, dropped the stockings, kicked aside his breeches, and caught her about the waist. "I've never bedded a married woman," he murmured into her hair. "They say it has a piquancy all its own."

Whatever she had felt before, it was twice as strong now, with naked flesh pressed against naked flesh. Rachel made an incoherent sound and then his mouth covered hers again and they fell back against crisp smooth linen embroidered with the Melchett coat of arms. The sheet was cold, he was warm. His lips were at once soft and firm, his touch by turns gentle and compelling. Cadogan had aroused her, but never like this. He had been far too determined to maintain control to show her such consideration. And he had never made her feel such wanton delight. Or such urgent desperation.

Unable to wait any longer, Rachel drew Guy to her, gasping in relief as his body at last slid into her own. As he came into her, Guy looked into her eyes and smiled. In that

174

moment he seemed so close and so far away that she wanted to weep. Then she found that their joining had only served to inflame her desire, and she moved impatiently against him, her need for physical release blotting out all else. Lowering his head to kiss her again, Guy began to move inside her, matching his thrusts to her rhythm. Rachel closed her eyes and let sensation take over. A storm was building within her, flowing between them, and even then they were not enough to contain it. She was desperate for the storm to break, yet sure that when it did she would shatter in pieces.

Suddenly she reached the peak toward which he had been driving her, sharper and sweeter than anything she'd known before. She cried out against his lips, clasping him to her. Guy let out a ragged breath, and his movements quickened. Then, with a muffled groan, he collapsed against the pillow and buried his face in her hair.

Rachel woke to the unaccustomed feeling of a man's arm around her and a man's naked body pressed against her own and a man's breath softly stirring her hair. Memories of the night before came flooding back, and she felt a moment of great joy, stronger than the languorous contentment which filled her body. Whatever else she could hope for from Guy, they had shared something special and intimate. Something uniquely their own. Something he had never known with Christine. A wholly unworthy thought, but no less true because of it. Rachel snuggled back against her husband, determined to enjoy the present.

She had thought Guy still asleep, but he propped himself up on one elbow and looked down at her with the crooked smile which would have disarmed her had she any defenses left. "Regrets, lady?"

Rachel rolled onto her back and smiled in return. "None. Save that we waited five days for our wedding night."

"A sad mistake, but I have every intention of making up for lost time." He slid his hand over her in a lazy caress, but when he reached her abdomen he stilled abruptly, the laughter gone from his eyes. "We didn't give much thought to consequences. Do you mind?"

"No," said Rachel truthfully, "I'd like another child." Your child, she added, but only to herself. What they had between them was too new and fragile to jeopardize by making demands Guy couldn't meet. "Do you?" she asked, studying his face with sudden concern. "Mind, I mean."

In answer, he moved his hand against her, as he might someday feel for the stirring of their child within her body. His touch was gentle, almost reverent. "Mind that in addition to everything else you've given me you might give me a child? You must think me an ungrateful wretch indeed." His expression was still serious, but as he watched her he began to smile. His hand slipped lower, parting her thighs, tangling in the hair still damp from their coupling. "We did talk about making up for lost time, didn't we?" he murmured. In answer, Rachel reached up and drew him down for a kiss which was a blatant invitation to more.

It was less frantic this time, with the early morning sun lighting the room and birds calling insistently outside the windows. But if her need was less desperate, that only meant she could savor the lovemaking more, and in the end it was no less intense and certainly no less pleasurable. Rachel hugged Guy to her, her gaze moving from the high canopy to the rumpled, sun-splotched bedclothes. Everything was softer and brighter this morning. Even the Melchett ancestor over the fireplace did not seem quite so disapproving. Rachel smiled at him, in perfect charity with the world. Then her eye fell on the ebony clock on the mantel. "Guy!" Rachel sat bolt upright, dislodging her husband from her chest. "The children. We're going to be late for breakfast."

Grinning, Guy swung his legs to the floor and retrieved her nightdress. "We've an excellent excuse. Pity we can't use it until they're a bit older."

Rachel went into her own room to dress, thinking how ridiculous it was for a husband and wife to occupy separate bedchambers. As soon as his own toilet was completed, Guy followed and helped do up her dress and pin up her hair, though this proved such an enjoyable process that it took more time than if she had dressed herself. They were laughing when they went into the corridor and still laughing when they reached the nursery.

"You're late," Alec informed them, looking up from a plate of poached eggs and ham.

One should not have to face one's children after one's wedding night. Rachel had never tried to hide such things from her children, and she suspected Alec had a fairly shrewd notion of what had delayed his mother and stepfather. Jenny almost certainly did. "I'm sorry," Rachel said, moving toward the table. She ruffled Jessica's hair but did not touch Alec who disliked such gestures. "It was quite unforgivable of us."

"It was my fault," said Guy with more chivalry than truth, "but I'll do my best to make amends. Suppose I collect you after your lessons and we go on an outing?"

Jessica broke off a piece of scone and spread it lavishly with strawberry jam. "Can we go to the Tower?"

"If you like," said Guy, pulling out a chair for Rachel.

Alec said nothing at all, but he didn't object to the plan. Rachel decided it was a sign of improvement. She said as much to Guy when they had finished breakfast and were on their way back downstairs. Guy grinned. "I'm inclined to agree, but then I've always tended toward optimism. I must see Burley this morning," he continued in a more serious tone. "He deserves to know the truth. And then I want to see Mountjoy."

Rachel nodded. She did not want to talk about Cadogan now. "You'll be at the theater by eleven?" They were to cast *The Steward's Stratagem* today.

Guy grinned. "Bow Street investigations are all very well in their place, but I never miss rehearsals."

They parted on the landing. Rachel continued on to her sitting room. Her fragile, ridiculously tiny writing table—so different from Benjamin Ford's commodious desk which she used in Great Ormond Street—was piled high with scripts to read, letters to answer, and bills to pay, but she found it difficult to concentrate. She had barely managed to pull out a sheet of writing paper and mend a pen when Guy appeared in the doorway, hat in hand. "I'm off," he said, crossing to her side.

Rachel smiled up at him, feeling utterly foolish and very happy. "Do you want one of the carriages?"

"No, I'll walk to Bow Street and the Tavistock, and we'll take a hackney to the Tower. Part of Alec and Jessica's education."

"Alec and Jessica are far more used to hackneys than to their Uncle Magnus's carriages," she assured him.

"Ah, but it's remarkably easy to forget," Guy said, bending down to kiss her goodbye. He probably intended it to be no more than a token of farewell, but the delights of intimacy were too new for them to do anything by halves. Lost in Guy's embrace, Rachel didn't hear the footsteps or the opening of the door until a familiar voice shattered her cocoon of happiness.

"Rachel, I—Oh. I'm so sorry," said Christine.

Guy straightened up without any apparent embarrassment. Rachel looked to the doorway and met her sister's gaze. Christine wore a simple cambric round robe and her hair was dressed in loose curls, but the springlike effect was spoiled by her stormy eyes. Rachel, who recognized jealousy when she saw it, felt a similar emotion lance through her.

"Good morning, Chrissie," Guy said, one hand still on Rachel's shoulder. "It's all right; I'm just on my way out." He spoke with great good will, but Rachel could feel the tension running through his arm.

"It was shockingly careless of me not to knock," Christine said in the sweet tone she always used when she was at her sharpest. "I keep forgetting that you're newlyweds."

"Yes, spending your honeymoon in the bosom of your family does create some problems," Guy agreed. "I trust you and Deaconfield will manage better."

Christine drew in her breath. "That isn't kind, Guy."

Rachel looked up at Guy. The mockery had fled from his expression but she could not say what had replaced it. Apology? Contrition? Tenderness? "It was meant as kindness," he said. "Or it should have been." He flicked his fingers against Rachel's cheek in a last caress, then walked briskly to the door. Christine moved aside, but only just, so that Guy brushed against her skirt as he passed. It was quite deliberate, and Rachel felt her chest constrict. She knew Guy too well to believe he had not been affected. He had shared a night of passion with her, but it was her sister who could stir him with the most casual touch.

Christine was watching Rachel with appraising eyes. She could not possibly know that Rachel and Guy had consummated their marriage the night before, but she seemed to sense that something in their relationship had changed. "Justin's dining with us tonight," Christine said shortly. "I wanted to be sure you knew."

"Thank you," said Rachel with the polite formality she would use with a stranger.

The sisters regarded each other in silence. "It's odd," Christine said suddenly. "Justin claims to love me and I think it may be true, but he knows I don't love him. You love Guy, and he—" She broke off, the pause crueler than anything she might have said. "Have a pleasant morning, Rachel. I'm sorry I intruded."

Christine walked quickly down the corridor. The sight of her sister and Guy embracing had shaken her more than she cared to admit. It had been bad enough knowing they were together behind the closed doors of their suite, but she had seen little indication of passion between them and had even allowed herself to hope that theirs was a marriage in name only. That clearly was not the case. Christine paused on the first-floor landing, her nails digging into the soft wood of the banister. Guy had always been able to do this, shake her to the core, upset her best-laid plans, make her forget what she wanted from life.

She glanced at the ranks of portraits which hung above the staircase and then at the plaster relief of the Melchett coat of arms in the ceiling, trying to remind herself of the things in life that really mattered, but it did little good. Guy was the most exciting man she had ever known. Beside him, all her other suitors had appeared foolish boys.

She couldn't have married him herself: it would have been madness. Even if Magnus had been willing to give her a dowry they could live on, she did not want to spend her life as the wife of a playwright who seemed determined to alienate and offend precisely the people whose acceptance she most craved. Yet that had nothing to do with the thrill she felt when he was near or the way her body responded to his touch or the awareness and longing which coursed through her whenever she looked into his eyes.

He should understand, damn him. Whatever she might say in the heat of the moment, whoever's wedding ring she wore, her heart would always be his. She had never doubted that it was the same for him. Not until she walked into the sitting room and saw him kissing her sister with such obvious passion. For the first time in her life, Christine was afraid that she might lose Guy. And she knew, with a certainty even stronger than her implacable determination to become Duchess of Arundel, that she would not allow that to happen.

Guy nodded to an errand boy scurrying across the forecourt, dodged round a cart laden with fresh produce for the Parminter House kitchens, and walked through the stone gateway into Bloomsbury Square, his thoughts filled with Rachel. In the past few days he had imagined taking her to bed often enough, but last night had exceeded his expectations. He hadn't realized how eagerly Rachel would respond to his touch or how much her response would stir him. Guy paused to look through the wrought-iron railing at the lush spring foliage in the square garden. He smiled involuntarily, seeing again the need in Rachel's eyes when he took her and the joy on her face when she lay in his arms afterward. For the first time in years he had made love to a woman without once seeing Christine's face before him, without once imagining it was Christine he held in his arms, without once sparing any thought for Christine whatsoever. He had woken this morning with a sense of peace and contentment he had not known since long before he left England.

And then Christine had walked into Rachel's sitting room. Swearing under his breath, Guy strode purposefully in the direction of Southampton Street. Christine was artificial, manipulative, calculating, and determined to get her own way. She was also his cousin, and he felt a brotherly need to protect her. But he would be lying if he pretended he didn't feel more than that. His illusions about her had ended the night she accused him of causing Edmund's death, but though the fire which had consumed him for so long had died, the embers of something remained.

He had loved Christine. He had loved her with a fervor he now saw as something approaching madness. He had loved her as he had never loved another woman, as he had no intention of ever loving again. Love was supposed to be an ennobling emotion, but Guy had found it quite the opposite. Looking back, he was appalled at his obsession, appalled at his jealousy, appalled at the way his feelings had destroyed the objectivity and detachment on which he so prided himself. He was appalled at the way they still threatened to do so. Though he might not be able to define what he felt for Christine, he feared he would never be completely free of her.

But that would not prevent him from getting on with his life. At last he could put the explosion and all that followed behind him. He looked forward to the rehearsals for *The Steward's Stratagem* with great anticipation. It seemed he had been away from the theater for months rather than weeks. After Christine's wedding, he and Rachel and the children would return to Great Ormond Street. Christine would be the Countess of Deaconfield and one day the Duchess of Arundel, and they would see little of her. He was older now, old enough to see love for the folly it was and to know he was a thousand times better off with what he had with Rachel—friendship, affection, and mutual passion. They'd have the theater and the children and very likely more children of their own. Rachel seemed to want them, and Guy found, rather to his surprise, that he wanted them as well.

Feeling the tension begin to ease from his shoulders, Guy took note of his surroundings for the first time since he had left Bloomsbury Square. He had made his way along High Holborn to Drury Lane and was nearing Covent Garden. It had probably been foolish to refuse Rachel's offer of a carriage, but he had an instinctive aversion to accepting Magnus's charity. It was damnably hard to get past childhood rivalries. Besides, he liked to walk. There was no better way to observe one's surroundings, to feel the pulse of the city. No place in London was as alive as the quarter-mile which enclosed the Covent Garden, the Drury Lane, and the Tavistock.

And few places were as depressing. Poverty had its own smell, sharp and sour, no different in London than it had been in Paris. The narrow side streets were cramped with dingy houses and with brothels and gin-mills which trafficked in one form of escape or another. Women sold themselves in these streets and husbands sold their wives and parents sold their children. Yet in these same streets children played, heedless of the squalor. Guy paused to watch a pair of grubby urchins laughing with glee over a game of marbles. So different from Alec and Jessica, yet fundamentally so much the same. They had not yet been beaten down by the bleak life around them. It made Guy angry, and it gave him hope.

He went directly to the Brown Bear and found Burley seated at the same table as before. Burley greeted him without surprise and made no objection when Guy suggested they walk to Somerset Place. When they were once again standing on the terrace which overlooked the Thames, Guy took a breath of the fresh cool air, leaned his arms on the balustrade, and looked out over the river. "How much do you know?"

Burley gave the trace of a smile. "This morning Sir Nathaniel informed me that the investigation into the business at the Tavistock was closed. He didn't volunteer any details."

Guy had suspected as much. He proceeded to tell Burley the whole: what Rachel had guessed, what Faith Harker had told him, what he had surmised on his own. "We'll never know the exact truth, but I'd stake my life that this is close to it." Guy paused for a moment, studying Burley's face. "Do you believe me?"

"Oh, yes, Mr. Melchett. It was clear to me from the first that Mr. Mountjoy had something to hide. I suspected that the witness against you had been bribed and there had to be a reason for it. This makes sense of a number of things. But it also creates some complications."

He spoke calmly, but there was a note in his voice which told Guy that these complications were going to prove far from insignificant. "What?" he asked sharply.

Burley was silent for a moment, his eyes on the water lapping against the wall below. "Edmund Hever didn't die in the explosion. He was already dead. Someone had made sure of it."

Chapter Twelve

Burley's eyes, piercing in their intensity, remained on Guy. Then, perhaps satisfied with what he saw there, he turned away and resumed their stroll along the terrace. It had been an extraordinary announcement. Edmund had been found in the Tavistock, along with the others who had not escaped from the burning theater. The backstage was a shambles. Walls had collapsed and beams had fallen. The floor was littered with lumber and props and bits of stage machinery. A man could panic, trying to escape the sound of the explosions and the terror of the fire. Could panic and fall and hit his head. That's what they had been told, that Edmund had died of an injury to his head.

Guy swung round in front of Burley and compelled the other man to stop. "How do you know? How can you be sure?"

Burley considered him a moment. "I've seen a great many men injured, Mr. Melchett. I've seen men die of their hurts. I know the look of a man whose skull has collapsed under a falling beam, and I know the look of a man who's been helped to his maker. I wasn't sure, mind you, but I was suspicious by the look of him, and I had the surgeon take a look as well. Hit twice, he was. I suspect the first one didn't do the trick. Or perhaps his assailant simply wanted to make sure."

Guy was sickened by the image, but he did not at first realize why it held such special horror. When he knew the reason, he spoke his thought aloud. "It was not Cadogan Ford."

"No, it couldn't have been." Burley regarded him thoughtfully. "A question of times, you understand. Mr. Ford was in the Angel from seven o'clock that evening, in clear view of a dozen people until they heard the explosion and the shouting and everyone ran outside. At seven o'clock, young Hever was taking his leave of Miss Melchett—Lady Christine that is now—in Great Ormond Street. We went into it very carefully at the time." Burley patted the pocket of the greatcoat which he wore even on the warm May morning. Guy knew it was the pocket in which he kept his Occurrence Book. The notes Burley had taken then would have been carefully preserved, pored over, thought about. The investigation would be as fresh in Burley's mind as if the destruction of the Tavistock had taken place two weeks and not two years ago.

It was not Cadogan. In his relief, it took Guy a moment to remember that the problem of Edmund's murder remained. If murder had occurred. Guy had conceived a great respect for Burley and was willing, on the officer's evidence, to believe it had. "You've done nothing about it, have you? Why not? Why haven't you spoken?"

Burley stopped and thrust his hands in his pockets. "Well now, Mr. Melchett. It seemed clear at the time what had happened. Our culprit had entered the theater with his gunpowder to do the deed. Mr. Hever must have surprised him at it. He seems to have arrived at the Tavistock well before the others. So what more natural than that our culprit panics and attacks him." Burley strolled to the edge of the terrace and leaned his arms on the balustrade, then turned to look at Guy who had come up beside him. "We thought it was you."

"Many thanks." Guy's words sounded harsh to his ears.

Burley turned back to the river. "You've posed me a pretty problem, Mr. Melchett. If your friend Ford was the culprit but couldn't have killed Mr. Hever, then it didn't happen as we thought. Mr. Hever must have been killed for quite another reason."

Guy had a sudden image of Edmund Hever and through the cries of the watermen and the horns of the tugs he heard the sound of Edmund's laughter. A tall, dark-haired young man, large of appetites, impulsive, selfish, quick to take whatever he wanted from life. Guy had had no cause to like Edmund, but he found it hard to believe that anyone could have hated or feared him enough to end his life. "He could have been followed to the theater," Guy said slowly, "in which case it might be almost anyone. But it's more likely, isn't it, that he was killed by someone who knew he would be at the Tavistock that evening."

"My thoughts, Mr. Melchett. My thoughts exactly. Brandon Ford, that would be. Philip Weston. Harry Jessop. George Hinton. That's the lot." Burley straightened, hands clasping the balustrade. "Of course, we have to wonder if Edmund Hever told anyone of his intentions. Lady Christine, for one, she knew he was bound for the Tavistock and might have told somebody of it." He gave Guy a sharp sidelong look. "I don't doubt that others could have known about it. Tell me, Mr. Melchett, who was in Edmund Hever's confidence?"

Guy hesitated. "I suppose he might have told his brother or his sister's husband, Alfred Billingham. But the meeting was to be held in secret."

"Ah, yes. Still . . ." Burley shook his head.

"You intend to pursue it then?"

"That's a question I cannot answer, Mr. Melchett. Mr. Read knew of our findings, but I have not communicated them to Sir Nathaniel. The case being temporarily dormant, as you might say, until your reappearance in England. And now the case is to be dropped. But you will understand that I cannot in justice let it drop without informing Sir Nathaniel of this new complication."

Burley's determination matched Guy's own. "It's motive you want, isn't it?" Guy said.

"Aye. If there was a reason, it can be learned. Of course,

Jessop and Hinton are dead, but they left kin and friends behind. The dead could have had reason to wish Hever dead as well as the living. Yes, Mr. Melchett, there will be a motive. Your own, for example."

Guy raised his brows in a look of polite inquiry.

"You had a row with Edmund Hever not a week before his death. Didn't care about keeping it quiet, I guess. More than one person heard the two of you and told me of it. About Lady Christine—forgive me, Mr. Melchett, if I raise a painful subject. I gather that young Hever had not been quite the gentleman."

There was no point in denying it. "As I recall," Guy said with a bitter smile, "I threatened to kill him. At that moment I would have too, but it would have been in a fair fight. I'm not a silent stalker, Mr. Burley."

"No, I can see that. But the matter was never settled, was it? Perhaps you followed Hever to the theater to renew your quarrel. In a passion a man is capable of things his dispassionate mind would reject." Burley smiled again, more broadly this time. "I'm not saying I hold you guilty, Mr. Melchett, but at the moment yours is the only motive I've got." He raised his hat. "I must get busy. Good day to you, sir."

Guy watched the long-legged officer stride across the terrace, his coat billowing out behind him. Burley was a fair man and would not accuse Guy until he had ruled out everyone else, but Burley would have difficulty finding out the kinds of things he would need to know. Not so Guy. These people were his friends, or if they were not his friends, he knew them well.

Guy remained standing by the balustrade till Burley was out of sight, thinking of everything that had been said between them. Then reluctantly he pushed himself away and began to walk toward The Strand. He intended to see William Mountjoy that morning. Rachel had bested him the day before, but Guy had questions of his own before he could lay Cadogan to rest.

A half-hour later he found himself in Whitehall. As he

entered the shabby building that housed the Home Office, he wondered if Mountjoy would still be there. Mountjoy was a clever man, but there was little way of disguising the folly of what he had done. He could be nothing but an embarrassment to the Home Secretary.

But when Guy entered the clerks' office, he learned that the undersecretary was at his desk. Mountjoy came to the door of his office, gave Guy a hard look, then with obvious reluctance invited him in. "I hardly expected to see you here," he said when Guy was seated. "Do you have some quarrel with the bargain your wife struck?"

Guy passed a hand over his forehead. He felt inexpressibly weary. "No quarrel. Not with you nor with the bargain. I have some questions, Mountjoy. You'll oblige me by giving me some answers."

"I hardly see why I need to oblige you, Melchett."

"You lose nothing by it." Guy made a gesture that encompassed his pain and uncertainty. "I would like to put a period to it."

Mountjoy raised his brows but said nothing. If he had been shaken by his interview with Rachel and by the difficult interview with Lord Sidmouth that must have followed, he gave no sign of it.

"How did it happen?" Guy said. "Where? When?"

Mountjoy did not pretend to misunderstand him. "At Edinburgh," he said calmly, "some fourteen years ago. I had gone to visit my younger brother who was at university there." He looked away as though seeing once again that long-ago time. "I had not been long in this position," he continued, "and I was an ambitious man. The universities were seething with ideas. You'll remember. All right within their walls, but ideas have a way of spreading beyond them. Educated men learn the words to breed discontent. We were a worried nation, Melchett. I had a duty to my government."

"You were ambitious," Guy reminded him.

"That too." Mountjoy sighed. "We needed to know what was being said and whom we had to fear. We needed information and were willing to pay for it."

Guy felt a moment of revulsion. "And that's why Cadogan—" He let the thought drop.

"Not entirely," Mountjoy said. "Cadogan Ford knew my brother. That's how I met him. We thought alike, he and I. He had a devious turn of mind and an inclination toward deceit. I think the money meant little to him. It was the game he enjoyed."

It was what Faith Harker had told him. Guy could not help but believe it now. "All those years."

"Yes, all those years," Mountjoy said. "He was useful to us, but by 1812 we knew it was time to bring the Levellers to an end. It was my idea to snare you in the process. I don't think Ford would have agreed to it had he known. He had some fondness for you."

It was a dismal gloss on Guy's friendship with Cadogan. "None of us knew," Guy said. "None of us guessed."

"None save his wife." Guy did not bother to correct Mountjoy. "And young Hever."

Guy looked up sharply. "Edmund? When?"

"Not a week before he died. He'd gone up to Newmarket to look at a horse and ran into my brother. They got to talking and he learned that Cadogan and I had met in Edinburgh. Hever knew there was a rumor of an informer among the Levellers. He came to me and asked me to confirm or deny it. I did neither."

So Edmund had guessed about Cadogan. "Hever didn't die in the fire," Guy said, trying to absorb this new information. "He was killed."

"Killed?" Mountjoy was so visibly shaken that Guy was sure he hadn't known. "I thought it was an accident," Mountjoy said. "Like the others. Neither Ford nor I knew anything of the meeting."

"James Burley told me this morning," Guy said. "Bow Street have known for the past two years. They assumed that Hever surprised the man who set the explosion, but Burley said Cadogan was out of the theater before Hever arrived."

Mountjoy stared at him, becoming aware of the enormity of what Guy had said.

"So it's not your problem," Guy told him.

"It's not my problem." A wintry smile crossed Mountjoy's face. "Ford might have had something to lose if his activities became known. I had none. His usefulness had come to an end." He pushed himself to his feet and looked down at Guy. "None of it is my problem, Melchett. I won't say that I've come out of this with a whole skin, but I'm not destroyed either. Lord Sidmouth has privately commended me for my zeal and publicly suggested that I pay an extended visit to my wife's relatives in Staffordshire. It may be some months before we meet again. If we meet again at all."

The interview was at an end. Guy rose to take his leave, eager to break his ties with the past. At least this particular battle was won. He must bury his dead and move on.

He left Whitehall and walked rapidly toward The Strand. He must be sure to be done at the Tavistock in time to collect the children for the promised visit to the Tower. He could not afford to disappoint them. And somehow he must find time to tell Rachel what he had learned.

It was this last thought that led Guy to quicken his pace toward the theater and to tell the people who waylaid him there that it was urgent that he speak with his wife. This brought forth some ribald comments and a spate of conflicting information. Rachel had been seen in her office, in the ladies' dressing room, at the back of the upper gallery, and somewhere in the pit. He ran her to earth at last in the carpenter shop. Wearing a linen smock to preserve her dress from the flying sawdust, she was in earnest consultation with Bob Harper, the chief carpenter, a lean, dour, heavily wrinkled man who had seen service with the Tavistock since the early days of Benjamin Ford's tenure. They were both on their knees, arguing about a set of drawings laid out on the floor, and neither turned round at his entrance. Guy, watching Rachel's rounded linen-covered rump, had some totally inappropriate thoughts. He pushed them aside. He had murder on his mind.

Five minutes later the matter between Rachel and Harper was resolved. In Guy's view Rachel had had the day, but Harper had the deeply satisfied look of a man whose point has been taken. He gathered the drawings, pushed himself to his feet with surprising agility, nodded at Guy, and returned to his workbench. Rachel looked up at Guy in surprise and got quickly to her feet. There was a faint sheen of sweat on her forehead, and tendrils of red-tinged hair clung to her face. Guy had an urgent desire to kiss her, but he knew Harper would not understand. He drew her quickly out of the room and proceeded to do it in the corridor outside.

"Guy," she said, laughing and pushing him away. "If we're seen like this, no one will ever take me seriously again." Her face sobered. "I told Brandon about Cadogan this morning. He wanted to break the news to his father, and I told him to go. I don't have the heart to face Samuel."

Guy released her. "Edmund knew about Cadogan. He found out shortly before his death. Mountjoy told me."

"Edmund? He knew and he said nothing?" Rachel shook her head in bewilderment. "Not that it matters now. Did you see Burley, Guy? Is it over?"

"It's not over, not for Burley and not for me. They've accepted Cadogan's guilt, but—It's Edmund. He was dead before the explosion."

Rachel stared at her husband with wide eyes. "He was killed? Someone killed him and left him here to—No," she said, her voice a bare whisper of sound. "No, it's not possible."

"It wasn't Cadogan," Guy said quickly. "It couldn't have been, Burley's convinced of that." Speaking quickly because the theater had an impatient life whose demands needed to be met, he told her of his talk with the Bow Street officer. "Burley wants to pursue it. He doesn't know what Conant or Sidmouth will say. It's possible they'll think the matter should be dropped."

"But they can't. They daren't. If the Duke of Arundel hears—"

"They'll find a plausible story to fob him off. But I can't let it go, Rachel. I had little use for Edmund Hever, but he was Christine's betrothed. For her sake we should know the truth."

Rachel stiffened. "Christine won't thank you for opening up this particular wound. You can't bring Edmund back, and she's committed to Justin now. She's about to be married, and Justin's parents are barely reconciled to the event. This may bring everything to a crashing halt."

"Nevertheless." His eyes were steady upon her.

Rachel threw up her hands in a gesture of defeat. "Yes, I know, you must. We must. We can't live with not knowing, though I would to God we could. Guy, it will be someone we know. Which of them could have wanted Edmund dead?"

Guy gave a crooked smile. "Besides myself, you mean. As of now, I'm the only person with a passable motive."

"I wouldn't count on it. Come, we'll talk of it later. We have work to do."

They took a few steps and found themselves looking into the mocking eyes of Gerald Sneath.

Sneath was seated on a box outside the lamp-lighting room, one knee drawn up, his dark hair falling over the brows which shadowed his deep-set eyes. He wore neither shoes nor coat, but his long red scarf was wrapped round his neck. Sneath had a sonorous flexible voice which he used to great advantage on the stage. It was his one vanity.

"Gerald," Rachel said, as though denying the possibility that he had overheard a great part of their conversation, "on stage. We want you for Captain Speedwell. Or Mr. Hayrake, we aren't sure. You're to read both."

Rachel's authority was generally unquestioned at the Tavistock, but Sneath did not move. "I heard. I won't tell anyone else if you don't want me to, but I have something to say. Now, before I lose my nerve."

It was so out of character for Sneath that Rachel, who

had begun to move off, turned and walked back to the actor. He was on his feet now, perhaps recollecting that some deference to Rachel's sex was in order. He brushed off the box and waved her to the seat. Rachel took it, her eyes wary. "Tell us."

Sneath tightened the scarf round his neck, folded his arms, and took a pose. It was not consciously done. Sneath had spent the best part of his near forty years on the stage, and stage and life had become inextricably entwined. "I was here," he said, "that night. In my dressing room. I didn't know there'd be others about, or I wouldn't have chosen it for—" He broke off, then gave them a self-deprecating smile. "It was a lady. We were trying to avoid her husband."

"Understandable," Guy murmured.

Sneath gave him a sharp look. Where his person was concerned, Sneath had a thin skin. "I may be an ugly bastard, but I've had my moments."

"That doesn't surprise me at all," Rachel said, quite as if she had given the matter much thought and was offering a considered opinion. "I've always thought you a very attractive man." There was no trace of mockery in her voice.

Sneath flushed and looked away. "You'll want to know if we heard anything," he continued when he had recovered his self-command. "We didn't, not while—" He glanced round to see that they were unobserved. "We weren't expecting anyone else to be here, and there were matters enough to occupy us. It was when we were leaving that I saw him. Edmund Hever."

He looked deliberately from Rachel to Guy, knowing he had his audience and nothing would drive them away. "We were coming down the stairs from the dressing room, not talking because, even if the theater was empty, it didn't seem right after what we'd been doing. We heard Hever first. You couldn't mistake his voice, loud and clear as if he owned the world." Sneath shook his head, his eyes focused on the long-ago scene. "I never liked that voice. I remember thinking, what right does he have to that kind of pride? He had nothing, he was nothing. Still, I never thought the

193

world would go any other way than his own. Funny. He must have been within an hour of his death, poor sod."

The term was wildly inappropriate for Edmund, but Sneath's meaning was clear enough. Guy felt a burst of impatience. If Edmund was talking, it was to someone. "Go on," he said.

Sneath would not be hurried. "Hever was near the proscenium door, stage right. We couldn't see him at first. I sent the lady back up the stairs till I'd scouted around. That was when I saw him. He was with Pursglove, and they were in a rare passion."

Rachel sat forward, astonishment on her face. "Pursglove? Charles Pursglove?"

Sneath grinned. "Meek and mild clergyman Pursglove, that's the one. He wasn't meek and mild that day, I tell you. I didn't stay to learn what they were brawling about. I fetched my lady down the stairs and got her out the stage door and down the alley as quick as might be."

No one spoke for a moment. Guy stirred. "Have you told anyone?"

"Why should I? It was a private quarrel. It was nothing to do with the explosion. Poor souls. Pursglove must have left well before that particular bit of hell erupted, while Hever stayed on for the meeting. If he was in any state to think about it." He glanced at Guy. "That's the point, isn't it? Hever's death. Pursglove could have had a hand in it." He turned to Rachel. "I'm sorry. I knew you'd have to know."

"Thank you, Gerald." Rachel stood up slowly, as though the movement brought her pain. Her face was drawn, but she managed a faint smile. "Don't say anything about it for the moment. There's nothing we can do now, and we're all needed on stage." She turned and made her way onto the cavernous stage where most of the company were waiting in attitudes of boredom or impatience.

Guy was not certain how Rachel got through the next two hours. She was fond of Charles Pursglove, whom she had known from the time Cadogan brought her to London.

Guy, who had seen Charles roused to wrath on behalf of the unfortunate, was not surprised by Gerald's story of the quarrel. Rachel was. He could see it in her posture, more erect than usual, in the way her hands lay clasped in her lap, in the stricken look in her eyes.

Rachel spoke briefly of *The Steward's Stratagem*. Guy talked of it at considerably greater length. He discussed his conception of the characters, heard preferences expressed by the members of the company, listened to readings of several scenes. Then there was a hasty discussion with Rachel and an announcement of the casting decisions, followed by stifled grumbling from those who were not given the part they chose or were given no part at all, and more open expressions of satisfaction from those who had had their way.

Rachel rose and dismissed the company. The first reading would take place tomorrow morning, and they would answer in all things to Guy.

Guy followed her back to the office. He would have comforted her, but by then she was in command of herself and had no need of comfort. "I'll talk to Charles," he said. "There'll be an explanation."

"Yes, of course." Rachel looked at the watch pinned to her dress. "You'll have to leave, Guy. Alec counts the times I'm late and adds them up in a ledger in his head to hold against me. He'll do the same for you."

Guy gave her a warm smile and was relieved to see that she could smile in return. "Then I won't give him the chance." He kissed her quickly and left the theater with far less confidence than he had shown to Rachel.

If truth be told, there were a dozen things he would rather do than face Jessica and Alec. But he had promised and promises must be honored and he was, he hoped, an honorable man. He hailed a hackney and sat impatiently in the carriage, clasping and unclasping his hands, wondering what on earth he would say to them. Incredible. Guy Melchett, a man who was never at a loss for words. By the time the hackney drew up at the Carne house in Dover Street, Guy had very sensibly decided to let them take the lead and speak only when he was spoken to. Feeling virtuous and full of good intentions, he told the driver to wait, climbed the steps to a simple porch set off by austere Doric columns, and rang for admittance.

In contrast to the severity of its exterior, the house was warm and inviting—far less grand than Parminter House—made for comfort rather than display. Parminter House belonged to Carne's wife, but Guy did not wonder that they chose to live in Dover Street instead.

The footman led him through the hall to a small garden at the back of the house where Guy found Fiona Carne. The children, both Rachel's and her own, were clustered about a metal table, playing a game of jackstraws. Fiona came forward at once with outstretched hands. "Mr. Melchett—no, may I call you Guy? It's much less formal, and we're some sort of cousins. Only you must call me Fiona. I'm still not used to my title." Guy murmured a confused assent as she drew him down the garden toward the table. "Miss Bentley," Fiona went on, addressing a tall young woman who had been sitting to one side of the table, "this is Mr. Melchett. Mr. Melchett, Miss Bentley, the children's governess and a treasure." Miss Bentley rose and shook hands with Guy. Alec and Jessica drew away from the table, their laughing faces drained of animation.

"I'll have to leave you now," Fiona said. "I'm taking Teddy and Beth out for the afternoon and I have to change my clothes. I won't be above ten minutes," she told her children.

Guy looked after her, wondering at her ease with her stepchildren. Teddy and Beth were watching him with wide-eyed curiosity. Alec was standing some distance apart, his face sober. Miss Bentley had crouched down to tie the ribbons of Jessica's bonnet. Jessica squirmed and turned her head so she could look up at Guy. "You're trying to come round us, aren't you?"

"Jessica." Miss Bentley could not allow this to pass.

"I don't mind," Jessica said, turning back to allow the

governess to complete her ministrations. "I want to go to the Tower."

"You should thank your stepfather for this treat," Miss Bentley said sharply.

Guy kept the smile from his face. "I don't think thanks are in order, at least until the excursion is over. Jessica may be dreadfully disappointed."

Jessica looked up at Guy again. "I won't be disappointed, but Alec may be." She turned her gaze to her brother. He was standing by the table looking fixedly at the discarded jackstraws, his shoulders hunched as though to ward off any physical contact.

Miss Bentley seemed to sense his mood, for she hugged Jessica and contented herself with a formal goodbye to Jessica's brother.

The children started in surprise when Guy led them to the waiting hackney. "I thought you'd bring one of the carriages," Alec said.

"Did you now." Guy opened the door and helped Jessica up the carriage steps. "But they're your Uncle Magnus's carriages, and I don't like to inconvenience him." He waited to indicate that Alec should mount by himself. "Hackneys are useful things, you'll find."

Alec climbed up and took the back-facing seat, making it clear that he did not intend to sit by Guy. "The Tower," Guy told the driver, then mounted himself and closed the door.

"Does that mean you're never going to have a carriage?" Alec's voice made this an accusation.

"I hope to have one someday," Guy said. "What would you say to a curricle and pair? You could stand up behind and be my tiger."

"I don't want to be your tiger."

"No, of course you don't. I was making a joke, but it wasn't very funny. What I would really like to do is have you on the seat beside me and let you take the ribbons now and then."

Alec looked at him with accusing eyes. "Is that a bribe?"

"Not at all," Guy said, realizing that this was going to be

more difficult than he had expected. "But you're going to have to learn sometime, and I doubt your mother has the experience to teach you."

"Do you know how? I thought you only took hackneys."

"Actually, I prefer to walk, but I've driven a bit in my time and I manage well enough, though I doubt I could handle a coach and six." This was not true, but Guy felt moderation was in order.

Jessica had been following this exchange with increasing indignation. "What about me? Why can't I take the ribbons?"

Guy tried to conceal his surprise. "Why, I suppose you can."

"She's too young," Alec said with evident scorn.

It was progress of sorts. In that remark Alec had clearly ranged himself on Guy's side. Still, it would do no good to appease Alec by slighting his sister. "Not too young," Guy said, "but perhaps with not yet enough strength in her hands. But that will soon be remedied. I daresay that in time Jessica will tool a carriage as well as any other lady in London."

There. He had avoided any invidious comparisons with her brother and saved her consequence all at the same time. Guy watched the children who, their quarrel honorably concluded, were looking out of their respective windows. Jessica was thoughtful, as though she were mulling over his last remark. Perhaps he had not been as clever as he thought. Jessica would want to tool a carriage quite as well as her brother, and he had relegated her to the female sex. She was much like her mother in this respect. Rachel was a formidable woman, but she had had to fight for the recognition that was now hers.

The carriage arrived at Tower Hill and pulled up before the westernmost gate of the fortress that had stood on the banks of the Thames for over seven hundred years.

"Have you been here before?" Jessica asked as they moved in through the crowd of people at the entrance.

"Yes, though not till I was grown. But my father used to

198

tell me about the Tower. It was his favorite place in all of London. He promised to take me when we came to England, but then he died." Guy had been six years old. He looked down and saw Alec's eyes fixed upon him. Alec had been six when Cadogan met his death. Remembering the pain of his own loss, Guy had a moment of intense compassion for the sullen boy at his side.

But children have the blessed capacity to live in the moment, and when Jessica demanded that they go immediately to see the lions, Alec echoed her with enthusiasm. The king's menagerie was just inside the gate, in the Lion Tower, built around a crescent that followed the tower wall. It consisted of a series of dens, with rooms above and below, in which the animals could be seen. The lions lay sleeping in the upper compartments, which let in the most light and air, or paced restlessly in the small confines of their cages. "Do you think they like it here?" Jessica asked.

"No," Guy said, "I don't think they like it at all."

Alec had walked as near the dens as he could get. "I'd let them go," he said, looking up at a sad-eyed lioness whose eyes seemed fixed on some faraway place. He turned back to Guy. "I want to see the armory." He didn't wait for an answer, but left the menagerie and ran across the causeway to the main body of the fortress.

Guy and Jessica caught up with him near the White Tower, but neither child had much thought to spare for that handsome building nor for the ravens stalking insects on the patches of lawn. The armories drew them, not the collections of arms and ordnance, but the horse armory with its life-size figures of the kings of England mounted on their chargers, some clad in the actual suits of armor they had worn into battle. From William the Conqueror to George II, they ranged the length of a long room lit by tall windows, lances or swords at the ready, their horses snorting with impatience or raising their hooves as though they could not wait to enter the coming fray. "That's William the Conqueror," said Alec, pointing to the first in line. "Who's the next one?"

"His son William, I would think." Guy had to tell them about this second William who was called Rufus and met his death by an arrow while out hunting. The children continued down the line of kings, demanding that Guy tell them the story of each one they saw, and since a few words never sufficed and stories were his stock in trade, Guy soon gathered a considerable crowd who followed them as they made their slow progress down the room. The children seemed to have forgot that they did not really like him.

After the armory Jessica and Alec were in high spirits and ready to be fed. As they returned to Tower Hill and sought a hackney, Jessica took Guy's hand. "You know a lot."

"I've read a lot."

"Would you tell us more stories sometime?"

"Nothing would give me more pleasure." Guy glanced down at Alec, now seated on his other side, and saw that he had turned sober again. By the time they had driven back toward the City and found a pastry shop and settled in a quiet corner, even Jessica had lost her desire to chatter. Guy ordered a quantity of cakes and let them be.

For a while eating filled the silence, but then they could eat no more and Guy knew it was time to put an end to the outing and take the children home. But he was curiously reluctant to do so. There was something between them that had to be addressed, and he did not know how to begin.

It was Alec who finally broke the silence. He looked up from the unfinished cake he had been crumbling to bits on his plate. "Why did you go away?"

"I had to," Guy said, and then knew it was no kind of answer. They were young for the truth, but only truth would serve him now. "The police were going to arrest me for the explosion at the Tavistock."

"Did you do it?"

"No, but they had a witness who claimed he saw me at the theater just before the gunpowder went off."

"He was lying?" Alec said in the incredulous tone of someone who has always been told to tell the truth.

"I'm afraid so. He admitted as much to my friend Gordon Murray. Then he disappeared so he wouldn't have to tell lies in court."

Alec thought about this for a bit. "If there was no witness, you'd be all right. So why did you have to go?"

"It was some time before he disappeared. And they could have found another witness."

Jessica leaned forward. "Were they going to put you in prison?"

"I suspect they were going to hang me." It was a brutal statement, but to Guy's surprise it elicited no response. Prison and hanging seemed equally incomprehensible in their eyes.

Alec frowned. "Where did you go?"

Guy told them—his two years in France, the friends who gave him shelter, the work he had done. He omitted telling them of his friendship with Arlette Aubert. She was their grandmother, but only Rachel had the right to speak of her.

Alec's frown deepened. "Some men from Bow Street came to the house and took you away. Was that about the explosion?"

"No. They decided I didn't have anything to do with the explosion, but they thought I might be a spy." Guy grinned. "I'm afraid I wouldn't make a very good spy, and after they talked to me they began to think so, too. They said they'd made a mistake and let me go."

Jessica put down her fork. "Then you aren't going to prison?"

"No."

"And you aren't going to be hanged?"

"Not that either."

"Then are you going back to France?"

The accusation in Jessica's question was echoed in her brother's eyes. Guy chose his words carefully. "I don't intend to leave your mother, Jessica. If I ever go to France again, it will be to visit, not to stay. And I'll only go if Rachel and you and Alec come with me." It was a firmer commitment than Guy had intended to make, and it shocked him. Parenthood, it seemed, brought responsibilities in its wake, and marriage involved more than taking Rachel to bed.

His statement did not ease the line of worry between Alec's eyes. His sister studied him dispassionately, then turned back to Guy. "Mama and Daddy used to fight. Alec's afraid you'll fight with Mama, too."

"I daresay we'll have our disagreements," Guy said, feeling his way. "But they won't last long. I'm a very agreeable fellow."

The joke fell flat. Alec looked him full in the face, all caution gone. "He made her unhappy. He made her cry. If you're going to make her cry, I don't want you to be my father. I don't want any father at all." Alec threw himself back in his chair, folded his arms, and glared at Guy through narrowed eyes.

"I see. You haven't much cause to like me, have you?"

Alec maintained a mulish silence.

"But your mother likes me. It was her idea that we get married. Did you know that?"

"She thinks we need a father. We don't."

"Perhaps not. But your mother needs a husband." Guy looked at the children. Alec would not bend. Jessica maintained a cautious neutrality. Guy leaned forward, his arms on the table, his hands clasped. "See here, both of you. I met your mother when I was six years old, and I like her better than anyone else I know. I wouldn't hurt her for the world, and if I do — I can't promise that I won't, for people's feelings sometimes get the better of them — but if I do, if I ever make her sad or unhappy, you must come to me at once and remind me of what I've said to you today."

The children stared at him, their faces without expression. Then Jessica climbed down from her chair and announced, "I need to be excused."

There was a flurry of activity while Guy, feeling rather a fool, fetched the woman who had served them, and Jessica was led behind a curtain into the back recesses of the shop. Guy sat down again, relieved to have managed that minor crisis, and looked at Alec. "Do you—?"

Alec shook his head. Something was bothering him, but it took him a while to put it into words. He continued to shred the crumbs of cake before him. "Why did they decide you had nothing to do with the explosion? Do they know who did?"

"Yes," Guy said cautiously, unsure how far he should go. "It was done by a man who was working for the Government. Their agent, a kind of spy. The idea was to discredit the Levellers. They didn't know there would be people in the theater when the gunpowder went off."

Guy stopped, hoping this would suffice, and for a moment it seemed it would. Then Alec, his eyes still fixed on the table, said, "The man who was working for the Government, it was my father, wasn't it?"

It was an astonishing leap for the boy to have made. He had nothing to go on, save that glimpse of his father with Mountjoy and perhaps the knowledge that Mountjoy was connected to the Government. Guy did not know how to respond. It should be up to Rachel to tell him, but the time was now. Alec raised his head and looked into Guy's eyes. "Wasn't it?"

Guy had no choice. "Yes, it was."

Alec's face crumpled. "Why did he do it?" he whispered.

"I don't know, Alec," Guy said, trying to keep the despair out of his voice. "Perhaps he believed it was right."

It would be easier if Alec would cry or grow angry or deny that it had ever happened. He did none of these. He sat in some kind of inward meditation as though preparing himself to assume the burden he would carry for the rest of his life.

"Alec," Guy said, "your father didn't want to hurt anyone. He died trying to save their lives."

Alec was silent. It was something, but it was not enough. Guy feared nothing would be enough, save time. That, and a willingness to listen whenever Alec was ready to talk.

"Don't tell Jessica," Alec said as his sister's voice could be heard chattering to the woman who had taken her away.

203

"No, I'll leave that to you. You might ask your mother. She'll know what to do."

Whatever the effects of this exchange, it did not totally suppress Alec's spirit. He was less taciturn than usual on the way home, and when Guy delivered them to Jenny's care, they parted with some measure of good will on all sides.

Guy came down the stairs in a thoughtful mood. If memory could not be trusted, what did one cling to? It was not enough to live only in the present, for without the past there was no future either. That was Rachel's problem and his own. It would be Alec's problem, too. It might be easier for Jessica, for Cadogan had been less of a presence in her life.

Guy reached the first floor and debated whether he should continue down and seek refuge in the library. Then he saw Christine ascending the stairs and felt a moment of such intense pleasure that everything else was driven from his mind. She was wearing a soft, light dress, the color of ripe peaches, and a confection of straw and feathers dangled from her hand. She looked up at him with an enchanting smile and for a moment she seemed the Christine he remembered, vibrant, alive, eager to live life to the full.

"Guy, I didn't expect you back at this hour."

"I've just brought the children home. We went to see the lions in the Tower."

She made a moue of distaste. "What an appalling way to spend an afternoon. I trust they enjoyed it."

"I think so," Guy said, realizing he had to tell her about Edmund. He wondered how upset she would be when she learned how her betrothed had died and where she would place the blame for his death. "Christine," he went on, his voice now sober, "there's something I have to tell you. Where can we talk?"

Chapter Thirteen

Christine made her way unerringly through the labyrinth of the first floor to a pair of double doors topped by a pediment. The doors opened onto a spacious cedar-paneled room with heavy drapes of blue and white damask and carved giltwood furniture upholstered in pale blue satin. The sort of room Christine loved and Rachel loathed. An exquisitely rendered medallion in the ceiling depicted Danaë under a glittering shower of gold. Guy wondered if the artist had had a sense of humor, and then he wondered how he could ever have thought he and Christine could build a life together.

Christine tossed her reticule and bonnet onto a marquetry side table and turned to face him. Her color was high and there was a smile playing about her lips. "Are you sure this is wise, Guy?"

It was going to be even worse than he had anticipated. Guy might find Christine's hostility painful, but it was far easier to deal with than her flirtatious moods. "It's about Edmund," he said.

Guy's words and tone were meant to disabuse her of the notion that there was anything personal about this interview. Christine seemed to take it as a personal affront. "Well?" she demanded, beginning to remove her gloves. "I thought we could put all that behind us now. It's a painful memory for me."

"I know. But I also know you have the strength to face what I'm going to tell you."

"What?" she asked impatiently, tugging off her second glove.

"The explosion didn't kill Edmund, Christine. He was murdered."

Christine went quite white. Then her color returned and she gave a nervous laugh. "That's not funny, Guy."

"I'm afraid it wasn't meant to be funny."

It was a moment before his words registered. Then Christine gave an exclamation of disbelief. The gloves fell from her fingers to lie disregarded on the Persian carpet at her feet. She swayed unsteadily and grasped hold of the table for support. Guy went to her at once and put an arm around her, an action which would have been unthinkable a few moments before. Christine seemed unaware of his touch save as a source of support. "Who?" she asked, when Guy had steered her to a nearby sofa. "Why? How can you be sure?"

Guy told her the substance of his talk with Burley. Christine seemed to have recovered enough to follow him, but she frowned in bewilderment. "Who would have wanted to kill Edmund? It doesn't make any sense. There's no one who could possibly have a motive, except—" She flushed.

"Except me," Guy concluded. "Burley said as much. I did threaten to kill Edmund, you know, quite publicly, scarcely above a week before his death."

"That was different." Christine made an impatient gesture. "You didn't mean it."

"No, but only because I'm not a man of violence. If I believed in duels I would have challenged him."

"You were very jealous." It was a statement, not a question.

"I was furious. Your betrothal didn't give Hever the right to take advantage of you."

"No?" Christine shot him a look full of mischief. "Wouldn't you have done the same if I'd given you the opportunity?"

Guy stood abruptly and crossed the room because he

wanted to distance himself from her smile and because he wasn't at all sure of the answer to her question. "You wouldn't have been fool enough to give yourself to me, Chrissie. I had nothing to offer you."

Christine gasped as if he had struck her. "I didn't realize you despised me."

"I don't." Guy bent to retrieve her gloves and placed them on the table beside her reticule. "I was crediting you with having at least a modicum of method in your madness."

This time his abrasive tone did not have the desired effect. He turned and found Christine watching him, her eyes bright with understanding. "You're still jealous," she said, a note of triumph in her voice.

"Don't flatter yourself, Chrissie. I would have felt the same if it had been Rachel."

Christine laughed. "Would you? Before or after she was your wife?"

Guy raked a hand through his hair. The discussion of the past had taken him back to a time when Rachel was merely his cousin and Cadogan's wife. Not only had circumstances changed, his feelings had as well. At the thought of Rachel with another man, Guy felt a wave of anger and jealousy every bit as strong as the anger and jealousy he had felt over Christine's affair with Edmund. "Whatever Burley thinks, I didn't kill Edmund," he said, seating himself in a chair which was far enough away to afford at least the illusion of safety. "Whether or not you believe me."

"Don't be absurd, Guy. Of course I believe you." Christine colored, as if only then recalling that she had once accused Guy of causing the explosion in order to bring about Edmund's death. "I was so upset two years ago. I didn't know what I was saying. You must know that I could never think such a thing of you. You do know it. You had no call to use it as an excuse to—"

"Run away? But I did that for a far less romantic reason. I did it to save my skin. Who else might have wanted Edmund dead, Chrissie?"

Christine seemed to realize it would be useless to try to

divert him. She began to fluff her curls. "No one. I told you: Edmund didn't have any enemies."

Guy settled back in his chair and crossed his legs. "Unless Edmund was followed, whoever killed him must have known he'd be at the Tavistock that night. You knew about the meeting. Did you mention it to anyone?"

"No, of course not. That is, I don't think so. Why should I?"

Why indeed, Guy wondered wryly. Christine had enjoyed the admiration of the Levellers, but she had had little interest in their activities. "You were with Edmund just before he went to the theater," Guy said. "He left earlier than necessary. Did he tell you why?"

"No, only that"—Christine frowned—"only that he had something to attend to. He didn't seem very happy about it," she added, as if the memory were coming back. "Do you think he was meeting someone at the theater?" Her eyes widened. "Then that must be—"

"Not necessarily." Guy did not want to introduce Charles Pursglove's name. Christine would leap to conclusions, and Guy doubted if he could persuade her to hold her tongue. "At least four other people knew Edmund would be at the Tavistock that night," he said. "Brandon, Philip Weston, Harry Jessop, George Hinton. For the sake of argument, let's add Billingham, who could have been in Edmund's confidence after all." He did not add that they could include Justin on the same grounds, for that would put an end to any hope of rational discussion. "What do you know about Edmund's relationship to the five of them?"

"They were his friends. More than—"

"More than Cadogan or I. Edmund is one of the few people who ever accused me of being staid. Could any of them have owed Edmund money? Was he in debt to one of them himself? He lived extravagantly enough."

Christine's chin shot up. "He lived like a gentleman."

"It's much the same thing. I take it you don't know if he had financial problems?"

She shook her head. "We never discussed money."

"Did Edmund ever quarrel with any of them?"

"Edmund was always quarreling with people—he had a hot temper—but he made up the quarrels just as quickly. And it was never serious. That is—" She hesitated a moment, her eyes darkening.

"What?" said Guy sharply.

Christine twisted her hands together. "It's Philip," she said at last. "He was fond of me. You know that. He never made advances but he—"

"Worshipped you," said Guy. "It's a common failing of young men with idealistic natures. Go on."

"It couldn't have been more than a fortnight before the explosion. Edmund got up a party to go to Vauxhall. There must have been nearly a dozen of us. Billingham and Fanny were there—though they quarreled and left early— and Brandon brought one of the actresses from the Tavistock. Philip didn't bring a girl and I'm afraid he felt rather left out. He must have wandered off on his own later in the evening and—" Christine hesitated, looking down at her clasped hands. "It was difficult for Edmund and me, you must understand that. We could never contrive to be alone together. There were always people under foot in Ormond Street and I couldn't go to his rooms, so—"

Christine broke off, but she had said more than enough. Guy felt a surge of anger at the thought of Edmund taking Christine in the Vauxhall shrubbery like a common whore. Had he been lost to sense as well as honor? Anyone could have stumbled upon them. "You're sure Philip saw you?" he asked evenly.

"Oh, yes. He seemed to think I was unwilling. Or perhaps he thought I needed to be saved from myself. It was all very embarrassing." Christine shivered, then looked up at her cousin. "Guy, you can't think that Philip—"

"He has a temper like the rest of us."

"It's all so ugly." Christine shivered again and rubbed her arms. "Why can't—"

"Why can't we let well enough alone? Someone has to ask questions."

"But why does it have to be you? Why can't you leave it to Bow Street?"

"Because I like puzzles," said Guy, getting to his feet. "Because at the moment I'm Burley's only suspect and I'd like to provide him with a few more." He hesitated, then added, "Because whatever I thought of Edmund, he was your betrothed."

"You mean you're doing this for me?" The hint of triumph was back in Christine's voice.

"Let's say I'm doing it for the family." Guy smiled. "After thirty years, I'm finally beginning to sound like a Melchett."

There was silence in the drawing room, the sort of tension-filled silence one strives to build on stage just before the denouement. Or before the interval, Rachel decided. They were nowhere near the denouement of this particular drama. The clock on the mantel, sounding preternaturally loud in the stillness, announced that it was a quarter to eight. At any moment Justin would arrive at Parminter House, and by tacit agreement they were all waiting for him to join them before they spoke of Edmund's murder.

Rachel had returned home from the theater to learn that Alec had guessed the truth about his father. She had meant to tell both the children in any event, and now that Alec knew the story, Jessica must be told as well. Rachel had spent two hours answering the children's questions. There had been no chance for private conversation with her husband nor with her brother or sister. Guy, who had already broken the news about Edmund's death to Christine, had talked to Magnus when he returned from the bank.

Magnus was now standing with one foot on the grate, staring into the unlit fireplace. His eyes were unusually hard, and there was a grim cast to his expression. Rachel, who would have expected the news to affect him the least of any of them, was puzzled by his reaction. He seemed almost as shaken as Christine. Rachel looked from her sister, sitting alone in a high-backed chair, her pallor emphasized by the rose velvet upholstery, to her husband, sitting beside her on the sofa, lost in his own thoughts. Not for the first time, she wondered what had passed between them during their tête-à-tête.

The silence ended abruptly when a footman threw open the double doors to announce Lord Deaconfield. One look at Justin's white face answered the question of how Conant and Sidmouth had reacted to the news of the murder. If Justin knew, his father must have been informed. An official investigation was now inevitable.

"Forgive me," Justin said after the most cursory of greetings, "but Sir Nathaniel Conant called on my father this afternoon with the most disturbing story."

"You'd best sit down, Deaconfield," Magnus said, dropping into a chair. "If your news concerns your brother, we heard it ourselves this afternoon."

"You did? How?" Justin's polished address had deserted him.

"I went to see Burley this morning," Guy explained. "He told me his suspicions and said he meant to go to Conant with the story."

"What were you doing talking to Burley?" Justin demanded, fixing Guy with a hard stare.

"Telling him what I knew about Cadogan," Guy said with a measured calm which was in marked contrast to the other man. "I thought he deserved to know."

"Oh, yes. Of course." Justin drew a breath and smiled apologetically. "I'm sorry, Guy, I haven't been able to think straight since I heard."

"It's been a terrible shock. For all of us," Christine said in a tremulous voice.

Justin at once went to Christine's side and put a protective hand on her shoulder. "Forgive me, my darling. I'd have given anything to have spared you this."

"I still can't believe it." Christine's eyes were bright and glassy. "It was bad enough losing him, but to find it was deliberate—"

"I know. It doesn't bear thinking of." Justin settled himself

211

on the arm of Christine's chair. He spoke gently, but his eyes darkened momentarily, and Rachel suspected he did not relish hearing Christine speak of her love for his brother.

"Unfortunately, we must all think of it." Magnus leaned forward in his chair and surveyed the others. "There are going to be a devil of a lot of questions asked."

Christine eyed her brother reproachfully. "Don't, Magnus."

"It's a simple statement of fact, Chrissie," Magnus told her. "When there's a murder, questions generally follow."

Christine gasped as if Magnus had made a remark of surpassing crudity. Rachel met her brother's gaze and, with a chill of surprise, suddenly understood. Magnus was afraid Guy might be guilty. And he was worried, more worried than she had ever seen him. Was it simply part of his newfound concern for the family name? Or was he genuinely worried about the safety of the cousin he had professed to hate for twenty-five years?

"We'll have to face it sooner or later," Justin said wearily. "And it's impossible not to wonder. Who could have done this to him?"

Guy, who had been almost unnaturally still throughout most of the conversation, shifted his position on the sofa. "For the record, I didn't."

Justin looked up from Christine and met the other man's gaze. The ghost of a smile crossed his face. "For the record, I didn't either."

"Don't be silly, Justin," Christine said. "Why on earth would you have wanted to kill Edmund?"

Justin's eyes softened and his hand moved against Christine's shoulder in a gentle caress. "My dear girl, you of all people shouldn't have to ask that. But Edmund was my brother. There are certain things I would never do. Even for you." He turned back to the others. "Conant assured my father that they'll keep the inquiries as quiet as possible, but I expect Burley will want to talk to all of us. He'll want to talk to everyone who was close to Edmund."

212

"It must be dreadful for your parents," Rachel said with genuine sympathy.

Justin grimaced. "Once he got over the initial shock, Father went into a rage. Bertram's swearing vengeance right and left. I sympathize with the sentiment, but it hasn't helped matters much. Mother and Fanny are quite prostrated. Meg's doing her best to look after them."

"And Billingham?" Guy asked with polite interest.

Justin regarded him for a moment. Rachel was sure her sister's betrothed knew perfectly well what lay behind Guy's question, but he merely said, "As shocked as the rest of us, though he's borne up rather better. He insisted on going to the House this evening. To own the truth, I wouldn't have thought he'd show such fortitude. But perhaps he was glad of an excuse to be free of Arundel House. Emotional crises are scarcely his forte." Justin paused for a moment, still looking at Guy. "Are you going to continue your investigation?"

"Oh, yes. The facts may have changed, but the mystery remains unsolved. And I continue to be under a cloud."

"Stop it, Guy," Christine said with sudden sharpness. "No one's going to arrest you."

"I don't think it likely," Guy agreed, "at least at present. But I mean to learn the truth."

Justin tightened his arm around Christine. "I want to know the truth as much as you. More perhaps. If there is anything I can do to help . . ."

"I'm much obliged." All the tension in the room was suddenly focused between the two men, like a wire about to snap. Knowing how little that tension had to do with Edmund's death, Rachel felt a flash of anger and sorrow. The mystery might have changed, but the underlying problems remained the same. Christine glanced from Justin to Guy. Rachel would have sworn there was a look of satisfaction on her face. Magnus remained impassive.

Justin broke the silence. "I believe my father intends to call on you tomorrow," he said to Magnus. "He's very sorry for the unpleasantness between you and wishes to make his apologies." He said nothing about the duke's unpleasantness to Guy. Guy might have been cleared of complicity in the explosion, but until the question of Edmund's death was settled, the most he could hope for was that Arundel would ignore him.

Dinner was a constrained meal. With the servants in and out of the room, it was impossible to discuss the murder, and to discuss anything else seemed callous and unfeeling. They had planned to attend a reception given by the Princess Sofia, a connection of the Russian imperial family now married to an English diplomat. The princess, who was a friend of Fiona's, had sent a note assuring Rachel that Guy would be welcome. Christine had been looking forward eagerly to the event, for the princess's cousin, the Grand Duchess of Oldenburg, sister of Emperor Alexander, was to be among the guests. Even Rachel had acknowledged a mild curiosity to meet the grand duchess, who had become the rage of London since her arrival in England at the end of March. But the events of the day had driven the engagement from her mind, and she was only reminded of it when Justin suggested they put in an appearance. It would help take Christine's mind off the tragedy. Magnus seconded the suggestion for more prosaic reasons. The investigation into Edmund's death was not generally known. It would look odd if they all stayed at home. "You'd better come with us, Guy," he added. "It's time we put an end to the talk about you once and for all."

Rather to Rachel's surprise, Guy made no demur. He attracted a good deal of interest in the princess's crowded reception rooms, but most of it seemed to be friendly. The grand duchess, a lively, fair-haired young woman, seemed quite taken with him. It was ridiculous to be jealous, Rachel told herself sternly, even if the grand duchess was four years her junior.

Rachel spent the evening listening to talk about the peace negotiations in Paris, Bonaparte's arrival on the island of Elba, and the forthcoming visit of the grand duchess's brother, the Emperor Alexander, and pretending to everyone, including Fiona, that nothing was out of the ordinary. Guy was a constant distraction. Even in the midst of the crowd, the sound of his voice or a glimpse of his gold-streaked hair were enough to blot out everything else.

Fortunately, none of them wished to stay at the party long, and they returned to Parminter House shortly after one o'clock. As she prepared for bed, Rachel tried to order her thoughts, and by the time she knocked at the door of Guy's chamber, she felt quite satisfactorily in command of herself. Guy would have murder on his mind, not lovemaking, and she intended to follow suit. But when she stepped into the room, Guy walked toward her with the familiar heart-stopping smile on his face and a glint in his eyes that had nothing to do with murder. He lifted the hair from her neck and let it fall, a simple gesture which was more eloquent than a passionate caress. "That's a very fetching dressing gown," he said, gathering her to him, "but one of these days you're going to have to let me undress you myself."

For all the teasing, the words offered the reassurance Rachel had been seeking. Guy had affirmed that their marriage had indeed become a true one, on his side as well as her own. She laughed in delight as he kissed her, and then he carried her to the bed where the magic of his hands and the seductive cadence of his voice and the warmth of his body soon banished all conscious thought. Even when the world settled back into place, Rachel was content to savor the moment and hold reality at bay.

"Christine told me Edmund had something to attend to before the meeting at the Tavistock," Guy said, quite as if they had not just shared the most intimate experience possible.

Such practicality in the face of what had just passed between them was so utterly like Guy that Rachel was disposed to smile, though she wished her sister's name had not been the first word he spoke. "He'd probably arranged to meet Charles before the others got to the theater," she said. "Which brings us back to the question of why he and

Charles quarreled."

"Yes." Guy gave Rachel an absent kiss. "My first guess would be money or a woman," he said, withdrawing from her and flopping back against the pillows. "But Pursglove was far too poor to have lent Edmund money, and if he needed assistance himself, I should think Edmund would have been the last person he'd have turned to. As for a woman, Pursglove always seemed a devoted husband—"

"You can never be certain," Rachel said, her voice expressionless.

"Quite so." Guy drew Rachel against him and settled her within the crook of his arm. "But Edmund was so besotted with Christine, I doubt he'd have taken anyone else to his bed in those last few weeks. I'll call on Pursglove before rehearsal tomorrow morning," he continued, his calm voice at odds with the way he was caressing her shoulder. "And then I'll have a word with Brandon at the theater. Do you think you might possibly find time to call on Philip? I'm not sure he'll agree to see me."

"Of course," Rachel said promptly. "Philip should know the truth about Cadogan."

Guy's caress stilled. "I'm afraid it's more complicated than that. It seems Philip stumbled upon Edmund and Christine in the shrubbery at Vauxhall about a fortnight before Edmund's death."

"Oh, poor Philip," Rachel exclaimed. "It must have been dreadful for him."

"Chrissie said he went into a rage. He thought Edmund was taking advantage of her. Which he was, though Christine was far from unwilling."

"You think Philip might have killed Edmund in revenge?" It was difficult for Rachel to take the suggestion seriously.

"I think Philip's just the sort who'd go to extravagant lengths in defense of his lady's honor. It must have been quite a blow for him. God knows it was for me."

There was a bitter undercurrent in Guy's voice. Rachel pulled away from him and sat up, hugging the covers about her. "You're still angry with me, aren't you?" she said, feeling as if they had been transported back to the day Guy had stormed into her office at the Tavistock and informed her that her sister was Edmund's mistress.

"Don't be ridiculous."

Rachel looked down at her husband and tried to read his expression in the flickering candlelight. "Christine was three-and-twenty, Guy, and I wasn't her keeper. I couldn't watch them every minute."

"I didn't say you should."

"Two years ago you did."

"I was furious," Guy acknowledged, "but at Edmund, not at you. Christine could have been ruined."

"They were betrothed."

"But they never married."

There was no answer to this. Rachel felt an irrational and quite overpowering desire to wound. "Can you honestly tell me you wouldn't have done the same if Christine had given you the chance?" she demanded.

Guy drew in his breath, then gave a shaky laugh. "Christine asked me that."

"What did you say?"

"I didn't answer."

He had been honest and Rachel found herself wishing he had lied. She couldn't think of what to say. She couldn't even turn away because that would have been a statement in itself. "Rachel." Guy put a hand on her shoulder and tried to draw her back down beside him. "It doesn't matter anymore."

It mattered more than he could possibly know, but she was not about to say so. "Did Christine tell you anything else?" she asked, pulling away from him.

"Very little." Guy pushed himself up against the pillows. "She doesn't remember telling anyone about the meeting at the Tavistock, but she can't be sure she didn't. And of course Edmund could have told someone himself."

"I thought Brandon was trying to make a great secret of it. He didn't want you and Cadogan to find out."

217

Guy folded his arms behind his head and stared thoughtfully at the canopy. "Edmund might have told Billingham. He might even have told Justin."

"Dear God, are you determined to suspect Justin of this too?" Rachel demanded.

"That depends on whether or not he has a motive. Edmund's death made Justin his father's heir. How much did he stand to inherit?"

"Almost nothing." Rachel was convinced Guy was letting his emotions cloud the issue, but it was difficult to say so when he sounded so rational and she felt so furious. "Two years ago there was no reason to believe Edmund and Justin's father would ever become Duke of Arundel. Their cousin, the fourth duke, died in an accident when he was cleaning his gun. He was scarcely forty, and he had a young wife and two small daughters. There was every reason to believe he would live for years and have sons to follow him. Edmund had a meager allowance, and he was constantly out of pocket. If you don't believe me, ask Magnus. I told him at the time that I was worried Edmund wouldn't be able to support Christine."

"I see no reason not to believe you," Guy said mildly.

"Then you don't think Justin killed Edmund?" Rachel asked, regarding him with suspicion.

"He doesn't seem to have much of a motive, does he? There's always Christine, of course, but Justin doesn't strike me as the sort to commit a crime of passion. Though, mind you, love can make people act in all sorts of irrational ways." Guy laughed suddenly and pulled Rachel to him, taking her by surprise so that they both fell back into the pillows. "We're lucky, Rachel. We should have a thoroughly successful marriage, as long as we manage not to fall in love."

Not trusting herself to speak, Rachel buried her face in the hollow of Guy's shoulder. One thing was certain. If they were going to have a successful marriage, she must never let her husband know she loved him.

218

Guy arrived at the Ford house in Bedford Row early the next morning only to be informed that Mr. Pursglove had already gone out. While he was still talking to the manservant, Dorinda came into the hall, her elder child, a curly-haired boy of three, hanging about her skirt. She was not sure precisely where Charles had gone, she said, but he was sure to be back by the afternoon as he'd promised to take the children to the park. Could she give him a message? Guy said he'd see Charles another time and declined an offer of refreshment. The sight of Dorinda and the child had given him a disgust of the investigation and all it might uncover, and he was aware of a craven desire to be gone from the house.

Besides, he was expected at the theater. As he pushed through the stage door and called a greeting to Patrick, Guy's preoccupation with the murder gave way to the combination of excitement and apprehension he always felt when he was about to hear his words read for the first time. He found his wife onstage, talking with Brandon and Cecily Summers. Rachel looked a little tired, but otherwise gave no sign that she remembered their quarrel of the night before. And the tiredness was probably owed less to the quarrel than to the highly enjoyable way in which they had made it up.

Brandon greeted Guy with a careless nod. He was an actor first and foremost and rarely allowed personal disagreements to interfere with his work. Cecily, wearing a thin muslin dress and a frivolous ivory satin bonnet which were woefully impractical in the dusty, draughty theater, crossed to Guy's side and squeezed his arm. "Corisande is positively the best part I've had in an age. Don't you dare leave England again until you've written me at least a dozen more."

Guy grinned. Though she persisted in dressing for rehearsals as if they were social events, Cecily was refreshingly free of pretension. She was also one of the most beguiling actresses on the London stage, with an uncanny ability to produce either laughter or tears from her audience. He felt lucky to have her. "I have no intention of leaving England again," he said. The words were directed to Rachel as much as Cecily, and Guy was rewarded by seeing a smile on his wife's face.

The rest of the cast soon began to assemble. Generally Rachel staged the Tavistock's productions herself, but she had given Guy a free hand with *The Steward's Stratagem*. Guy, who had learned long ago to focus on the immediate problem and push extraneous concerns aside, spoke briefly about the play, expanding on what he had said the day before, and then settled back to listen to the actors read it through.

Set in the Restoration, *The Steward's Stratagem* centered on Corisande, the eldest daughter of a minor gentry family, whose beauty won her the attentions of two suitors, Lord Rockingham, an aristocrat who had returned from exile with Charles II, and Mr. Newcombe, a merchant who had made a fortune during the Civil War by supplying both sides. Corisande's father favored Newcombe while her mother urged Rockingham's suit. But Corisande, with the help of her childhood friend, Nicholas, now the family's steward, schemed to avoid marriage to either, to the great disgust of her two younger sisters, each of whom was secretly in love with one of the suitors. The play ended with a masquerade—shamelessly borrowed from *The Merry Wives of Windsor*—in which Corisande's mother arranged for her to be married to Rockingham while her father arranged for her to be married to Newcombe. Corisande and Nicholas contrived for the suitors to marry the two sisters instead.

The conflict between Newcombe and Rockingham allowed Guy to make a number of points about the importance of money and birth—the Restoration setting would make it harder for the censor to object than if the play was set in the present day—but none of the characters was completely a figure of fun. For all the lightness of their scenes, there was genuine feeling in the awakening love between Corisande and Nicholas.

At least that had been Guy's vision of the play. Some

scenes he now listened to with genuine enthusiasm. Others he felt a strong desire to interrupt and rewrite then and there. The cast was excellent. Cecily was an enchanting Corisande and Ned Acorn was exactly right for the clever Nicholas. Brandon, who had an unexpected genius for character parts, was arrogant but not ridiculous as Rockingham. Ralph Hemdale had Newcombe's bluster but tended to play the part a little too broadly.

After the read-through, they broke for the midday meal. Some of the company unwrapped packets of sandwiches while others went out to buy meat pies or sausages from street vendors. Those more plump in the pocket took themselves off to nearby coffeehouses. Brandon was about to leave for the Angel with Ned and Gerald Sneath when Guy asked if he could have a word with him. Brandon gave a curt nod and told the others he'd catch up. When they'd climbed the stairs to his dressing room, it was he, not Guy, who spoke first. "I said it to Rachel, but I'd best say it to you as well. I'm sorry about Cadogan. I keep thinking I should have guessed."

Guy felt an unexpected moment of kinship with Cadogan's cousin. "That's what I've been telling myself ever since I learned the truth."

Brandon dropped into the chair in front of his dressing table. "Is that why you wanted to talk to me? So we could commiserate over what bloody fools we've both been?"

"Not exactly." Guy perched on the stool which was the only other seat in the room. After Cadogan's betrayal the news of Edmund's murder seemed hopeless excess, worthy of a Jacobean tragedy. There was no way to lead up to it gradually. "Edmund Hever was murdered."

Brandon stared at Guy in stupefaction. Guy thought he was going to treat it as a joke, but instead he tugged open a drawer, pulled out his brandy flask, and took a large swig. "Christ." Brandon ran a hand through his hair, swallowed another draught of brandy, and offered the flask to Guy. "There's no doubt?"

"Apparently not." Guy waved aside the proffered drink

and leaned forward. "Edmund told Christine he had something to attend to before he met you and the others at the theater. Do you have any idea what that might have been?"

"None at all. Why should I?"

"You were his friend."

Brandon gave a bark of bitter laughter. "You were Cadogan's friend. You knew damn' little about him."

"Fair enough." Guy studied the other man. For a moment, when they spoke about Cadogan, they had been on easier terms than they had in years. But with the revelation about Edmund's death, Brandon's mood had subtly changed. The wariness was back, and the faint but persistent note of hostility.

"So you've taken it upon yourself to find out the truth?" Brandon demanded.

"I set out to discover what happened at the Tavistock that night."

"And you'd like to find out the truth before Bow Street do, since there's a fair chance the murderer will turn out to be one of us."

"Perhaps."

"Whoever killed Edmund had to have known he'd be at the theater." Brandon reached for the flask again, then thought better of it. "Does Burley think Edmund was killed by one of the men at the meeting?" he asked abruptly.

"Not necessarily. He could have arranged to meet someone at the theater before the rest of you arrived."

"So he could." Brandon's eyes hardened. "Have you told Burley you had a rousing quarrel with Edmund not ten days before he died?"

"He already knew. I'm his first suspect."

"But not his last."

"Not if I have anything to say about it." Guy hesitated a moment. "I didn't kill him, Brandon."

Brandon gave a grunt which acknowledged the statement without making his own views clear. Then he pushed himself to his feet with sudden decision. "I suppose I can expect a visit from Bow Street myself. Is there more? I haven't eaten since last night. I won't be much good at rehearsal unless I get some food in me."

"Just one thing." Guy got to his feet as well. "Do you know if Charles had any reason to quarrel with Edmund?"

Brandon stared at Guy with the naked shock of a man taken completely unawares. "Good God." The exclamation seemed quite involuntary, but it held a note of bitter resignation. Then his face closed abruptly. "You'll have to ask Charles about that," Brandon said, his fine-toned voice devoid of inflection. He walked briskly to the door and held it open, indicating that Guy should precede him into the corridor. "If you'll excuse me, my friends are waiting."

They descended the stairs in silence. Brandon left by the stage door, and Guy went in search of Rachel whom he found in the wings, eating a sandwich and conferring with Patrick about a sandbag, part of the pulley system for *The Tempest*, which didn't seem to be weighted properly. She greeted Guy with an utterly bewitching smile and told him there was a hamper of food in her office. There was no chance for private conversation. Guy busied himself arranging battered chairs into a semblance of a set for the afternoon's rehearsal.

By the time Brandon returned from the Angel, he seemed to have recovered his self-command, but his thoughts were clearly elsewhere. They worked on a brief scene between Corisande and her suitors, then Guy told Brandon he wouldn't need him for the rest of the afternoon. Brandon took himself off with evident relief. Once again losing himself in the play, Guy called a halt to the rehearsal only when Cecily gently reminded him that some of them had a performance that evening. Rachel had left the theater early, planning to call on Philip on her way home. Guy gathered up his script and notes, shrugged on his coat, which he had taken off to demonstrate a piece of business, and made his way through the stage door to the narrow alley which ran alongside the theater. As he turned into Charles Street, he was assailed by the sights and sounds of Covent Garden as it came alive for the evening. Pleasure-seeking young bloods were already on the prowl, as were women and girls plying their wares in thin frocks and thick layers of rouge. The sky was still light, so all was revealed in garish detail without the muted glamour of twilight. Laughter and bawling voices and snatches of ribald song spilled out of coffeehouse and tavern doorways to blend with hawkers' cries and the clatter of wheels and the random noise of pedestrians. As Guy neared Russell Street, a young man lounging in a doorway gave a piercing whistle for no discernible reason. A gesture of defiance perhaps, or a shout of freedom at the end of a long day.

Guy reached the intersection, glanced carelessly to either side, and started across the street. Then, suddenly aware of the thunder of hooves, he looked round in time to see a dark blue carriage swing around the corner at full speed. The driver, a heavyset man in a caped coat, was staring straight ahead as though Guy did not exist. Guy realized that the man had no intention of stopping. Moreover, thanks to drink or absent-mindedness, he was veering dangerously close to the curb. Cursing under his breath, Guy flung himself back into a doorway. The carriage passed by, its body brushing the wall near where he stood. The driver was damnably careless. If the door hadn't been conveniently at hand, Guy would have found himself under the wheels.

Chapter Fourteen

Philip Weston stared at Rachel, his face white, his eyes wide with shock and disbelief. "No." The single word was barely a whisper but it was spoken with an intensity which seemed to echo through the walled garden.

For all that Philip was only six years her junior, Rachel felt very much as she had when she'd tried to answer Alec's and Jessica's questions about Cadogan. "Is it any easier to believe that Guy would cause such destruction to the theater he loved?" she asked.

"No, but—" Philip's face twisted as if even the memory brought pain. "I could understand Guy doing it because he was angry about the play. I felt the same myself. I suppose that's why—"

"Why you found it so easy to blame him?" Rachel asked gently.

"Yes." Philip met her gaze and his bitterness gave way to a moment of honesty. Then the pain returned. "But for Cadogan to have betrayed us all from the first—"

"It doesn't bear thinking of," Rachel agreed. "Unfortunately, it's the truth. Cadogan was—He was a very complicated man." It seemed a woefully inadequate summation of her late husband's character, but Rachel did not understand Cadogan enough herself to do him justice. "But you have to remember that he thought there wasn't anyone in the building. And when he realized he was wrong, he tried to save all of you."

"But it was lies." Philip looked so hurt and bewildered

225

that Rachel was tempted to put her arms around him. "It was all lies."

"No," Rachel said. "Not all. Guy believed every word of what he said. He still does. So do I."

Philip's face crumpled, and he dropped his head into his hands. There was nothing more Rachel could say. At least not yet. Philip would have to understand about Cadogan before she told him of Edmund's death. She sat quietly, listening to the muffled sound of carriages from the street and watching a small robin drink from an ornamental fountain in the center of the garden. When Philip at last raised his head, he seemed calmer and older somehow, as if accepting the flaws in a man he had once admired had made him more of an adult himself. "It's hard to believe Cadogan could have done it," he said, "but the funny thing is it doesn't hurt as much as suspecting Guy."

"I'm glad. For Guy's sake as well as yours. Philip, there's something else I have to tell you." Rachel leaned toward him. They were sitting on opposite sides of a wrought-iron table where Philip had been reading when she was shown into the garden.

Philip's eyes narrowed. "You mean about Edmund."

It was completely unexpected, like the night when Brandon had got foxed and begun spouting *She Stoops to Conquer* in the midst of *Much Ado About Nothing*. For a crazy moment, Rachel thought Philip was about to make a confession.

Her shock must have shown on her face, for Philip said, "Burley was here this morning. He told me."

"But not about Cadogan?"

"He just said Edmund had been killed and they were satisfied the murderer wasn't the person who planted the explosives. I was too startled to ask questions, and Burley didn't volunteer a great deal."

It made sense. Burley would have wanted to hear what Philip knew without telling him more than was absolutely necessary. But Rachel still found it odd that Philip had said nothing about Edmund's murder until she mentioned it. Perhaps the mystery was making her jump at shadows.

"I couldn't tell him much," Philip continued. "Everything seemed normal enough that night until all hell broke loose. After that I only remember bits and pieces. I didn't see Edmund at all. Not even after— Not even when he was dead."

Philip hunched his shoulders and seemed to shrink within his coat. It was cruel to make him remember that horror, yet it would have to be faced. "It can't have been easy for you in those last weeks," Rachel said quietly. "Knowing what you did about Edmund and keeping it to yourself. You might have told me, you know. Christine is my sister, and my sensibilities have never been particularly delicate."

Philip stared at her. "You know?"

"I've known about Christine and Edmund for some time. I only learned last night that you knew about it."

"I see." Philip's eyes hardened. "And I see why you came here today." He pushed back his chair, the metal grating against the gravel at their feet, and stood abruptly. "You want to know if I killed Edmund."

Rachel got to her feet as well. "I came because you deserved to know the truth about Cadogan. I would done so even if the questions about Edmund had never been raised. But yes, I also came because I wanted to talk to you about Edmund and Christine."

"You think I killed Edmund."

"I haven't the faintest idea who killed Edmund."

"But you think I might have killed him." The vulnerability was gone. Philip's voice fairly shook with anger. "Good God, Rachel, you think I'd be capable of—"

"Until this afternoon you thought Guy was capable of planting explosives in the Tavistock," Rachel said sharply.

"You mean we can't any of us trust each other." Philip sounded bitter but no longer quite so hostile. "I admired Edmund, you know. Oh, not like I admired Guy and

227

Cadogan. They were the ones with the vision. At least that's what I thought. But it was Edmund who always seemed to know what to do, how to act, how to"—he colored—"how to talk to women. I wanted to be like him. I suppose that's why I didn't mind so much when Christine chose him. I knew I could never win her myself. Then to discover—" He looked at Rachel with sudden sharpness. "You knew and you didn't stop it?"

"How could I? Christine was of age. She was quite willing, Philip," Rachel added gently.

"Willing." Philip fairly spat the word. "She gave Edmund her heart, and he treated her no better than a common doxy." Philip's eyes were bright with something like defiance. "I hated him when I found them together. And I went on hating him. But I didn't kill him. I didn't have the guts."

Magnus returned home from the bank shortly after five, divested himself of his hat and gloves, and was about to take himself off to the library for a whiskey when Thomas coughed in evident confusion. "Lady Margaret Hever is in the blue saloon, my lord. She's been waiting for nearly an hour. She asked for Lady Rachel, but I'm not sure—"

"Thank you, Thomas. I'll have a word with her. Tell Lady Rachel as soon as she returns home." Puzzled and intrigued, Magnus started up the stairs. He had reached the landing before it occurred to him to consider the propriety of receiving Margaret alone. That accounted for the footman's embarrassment. Magnus hesitated for a moment, then shook his head at his own folly. He took his new role seriously, but he was damned if he'd let himself be imprisoned by it. Besides, Margaret's visit probably had to do with her brother's death.

Margaret was sitting in a spindle-legged chair, hands clasped in her lap, back very straight, though she must have been sick to death of waiting. Magnus felt an unexpected flash of admiration for her fortitude. As he stepped into the room, Margaret turned round with an expression of relief which quickly changed to confusion. "Lord Parminter. I didn't expect—"

"I know. You were waiting for my sister. I'm afraid she still hasn't returned, so I thought I'd see if I could be of help." Magnus settled himself in another of the room's ridiculously fragile chairs.

"Thank you. That's very kind of you. I'm not sure—"

"Not sure it's any of my business?"

Margaret colored. "No, of course not, it's just—" She bit her lip and smiled reluctantly. "Yes, I'm afraid that's it exactly."

Magnus found himself smiling in return. He recalled their brief conversation at Rachel's wedding. He'd known then that Margaret had more spirit than he'd credited. Now it seemed she had a sense of humor as well. The smile lit up her eyes, and the blush brought color to her pale cheeks. She really wasn't at all bad looking when she showed some animation. It occurred to him that in all likelihood her parents knew nothing of her visit to Parminter House. Arundel had called on him this morning, and they had established an uneasy truce, but the harsh words they had exchanged could not be forgot. Nor could the fact that Guy was a suspect in the investigation of Edmund's murder. The sensible course would be to send Margaret home at once, but Magnus found himself reluctant to do so. "If what you have to say concerns your brother's death," he told her, "I'm afraid it's all of our affair."

Margaret's eyes grew serious. "I didn't know Edmund very well. He and Justin went away to school before I was out of the nursery, and when they were home they always seemed fearfully grand. But he was my brother and I can't—I want to know who did this to him."

"We all do," Magnus assured her, though he knew as he

229

spoke that this was not completely true. They all wanted the mystery solved, but they also wanted to protect themselves and those close to them. If he learned that Guy had been Edmund's killer, Magnus would do his utmost to keep the truth from going further. For Rachel's sake, but also because of something else, some vestige of childhood solidarity which he would not have believed existed until Arundel inadvertently tapped it by ordering him to throw Guy out of the house.

"I hate all this," Margaret said, clenching her hands. "I just want it to be over."

"It will be," Magnus said, more grimly than he intended. "One way or another."

Margaret looked at him, and for a moment differences in age and experience were stripped away. For the first time, Magnus admitted to himself just how afraid he was. Margaret's candid brown eyes told him that she understood. Unnerved by the thought that a slip of a girl could read him so well, Magnus was relieved to hear the well-oiled sound of the door opening. "Rachel," he said, getting to his feet. "Lady Margaret has something to tell you, but she's not sure it's fit for my ears."

"No, please don't go, Lord Parminter," Margaret said. "You're right. This is all of our affair." She stared at her clasped hands while Magnus and Rachel seated themselves. "It's Alfred, you see. Alfred Billingham," she added, as if they might not know of whom she spoke. "I heard him talking to Edmund one night, quite by accident. I'm not sure exactly when it was, but it couldn't have been more than a month before Edmund died. Mama and I were staying with Alfred and Fanny. They'd taken a house for the Season. Of course, they live with us now, but Papa wasn't the Duke of Arundel then, so we didn't have a town house of our own. Mama and Fanny and I had been to a reception at Arundel House. My cousin Henry lived there; he was the duke." Margaret twisted her hands together. "I rather dreaded going to Arundel House in those

230

days. Cousin Henry had a fearful temper, and it got worse as he got older, though I suppose he had some excuse. He suffered from migraines, you see, and then he developed gout when he was barely forty and had to use a cane, though he hated anyone to know it—I suppose he thought it made him look weak. At all events, that night he'd been in one of his moods and he said some dreadful things to Cousin Elizabeth—his wife—for no reason whatsoever. I was too upset to sleep when we got home, so I went down to the library for a book. But I didn't go in because I heard Edmund and Alfred arguing." She hesitated, her eyes troubled. "Alfred sounded angry, and I think underneath the anger he was frightened. He said, 'It's never going to end, is it?' And Edmund just laughed and said, 'What are friends for?' That's the last thing I heard before I went back upstairs."

Margaret looked from Rachel to Magnus as if pleading with them to tell her she had been imagining things. Magnus felt an impulse to do just that, but it was Rachel who spoke first. "You don't have any idea what the quarrel was about?"

Margaret's eyes widened, as if that simple question had confirmed her worst fears. "None at all. Edmund and Alfred had been friends for years. I thought about asking Fanny, but I decided to come to you first. Fanny's been quite overset by the whole business, and I don't want to make things worse for her unless I have to."

"Have you told anyone else about this?" Magnus asked, reminding himself that he, too, wanted to get to the truth of the matter and there was no room for sentimentality. "Does Burley know?"

"No, Mr. Burley hasn't questioned me. But I know your husband is investigating the murder as well, Rachel. He knew Edmund and Alfred, and I thought—"

"That he'd be safer than Burley?" Magnus said with a smile.

Margaret lifted her chin and her whole face suddenly

appeared stronger. "If Alfred killed Edmund, I won't try to protect him."

"No," said Magnus slowly, "I don't believe you would. You're a remarkable girl, Margaret."

Margaret did not seem to take exception to his inadvertent use of her given name. Rachel glanced at her brother in surprise, then spoke to Margaret. "This doesn't mean Billingham killed Edmund, Meg. They could have quarreled about any number of things. Friends often do."

"I know," Margaret said with a smile which was at once grateful and nervous. "But if by any chance there's more to it . . . I want to know the truth, Rachel. You mustn't keep it from me. Nor you, Lord Parminter."

Magnus grinned unexpectedly. "I can't answer for Rachel, but I'll tell you as soon as I know it myself." It was a reckless promise, and it surprised Magnus as much as anyone, but before he could give the matter any thought, the door opened and Guy stepped into the room.

Rachel smiled with the simple delight she always felt when her husband was near. Then she saw that Guy's coat was stained and rumpled and there was a tear in the shoulder. When he moved forward to greet Margaret, she noticed a nasty-looking scrape on the back of his hand.

"Guy, what happened?" Rachel's voice was sharp with worry.

Guy stared down at his hand in mild surprise as if he had forgot the injury. "I was a bit late jumping out of the way of a carriage. The driver was thundering along as if pedestrians didn't exist. I'm sorry, I'm scarcely fit for your drawing room, am I?"

Rachel kept her voice light. "Perhaps not, but this is the blue saloon, so we'll permit you to stay. Margaret has a story to tell you."

"If you don't mind, Rachel," Margaret said, rising from her chair, "I'll leave you to tell Mr. Melchett. I must be getting home."

Magnus moved to the door. "I'll take you to your carriage."

"Actually, I came in a hackney," Margaret confessed. "I didn't tell my parents I was coming here."

"Then I'll order one of our carriages made ready," said Magnus with perfect equanimity. "God knows we have enough of them."

He held the door open for her, but Margaret paused and turned back to Guy. "Justin told me you were trying to find out the truth about Edmund, Mr. Melchett. I want to help in any way I can."

"Thank you," Guy said politely. He hesitated for a fraction of a second then added in the same tone, "Purely as a matter of curiosity, Lady Margaret, you don't think I might have killed him myself?"

Margaret's eyes widened, but she gave the question honest consideration. "These past days have taught me that I can't be sure of anything. But I trust Rachel. And she trusts you."

"A refreshingly honest young woman," Guy said when Margaret and Magnus had left the room. "What's more," he added, perching on the arm of Rachel's chair, "Magnus seems to appreciate her."

"I think this may be the first time he's taken proper notice of her," Rachel said, remembering the way her brother had looked at Margaret.

"I could give him some advice on the delights of matrimony," Guy suggested with the smile which always sent a thrill of anticipation through Rachel, "but advice from me is likely to persuade him to do just the opposite. Do you know," he continued, gathering her to him and bending his head to her own, "I don't believe I've kissed you since this morning."

Rachel had no objection to being kissed, but as she emerged from a lingering embrace, her eye fell on his scratched hand and her earlier concern came flooding back. "Guy." She wondered if he would think her a fool, then decided it didn't matter. "The carriage that almost ran you down—are you quite certain it was an accident?"

Guy burst into laughter. "Rachel, my sweet. All other things aside, no one could have known I would be crossing Russell Street at that particular moment."

"Someone could have watched for you and signaled the coachman. Did you see anything out the ordinary before it happened? Don't laugh at me, Guy, this is serious."

"I'm sorry, it's just—" Guy broke off, frowning.

"What?" Rachel demanded.

"I didn't see anything," Guy said slowly, "but I did hear someone whistle shortly before it happened. Whistling, however, is not unknown on the streets of London."

His hand was resting on her shoulder. Rachel reached up and gripped it with her own. "Edmund was murdered, Guy. You're investigating his murder, and today you had a brush with danger."

Guy looked at her for a moment, his eyes serious. Then he shook his head. "There wouldn't have been time for any of them to arrange it."

"You told Brandon this afternoon, didn't you? And he left rehearsal early. He could have gone straight to Bedford Row and told Charles the whole. Burley talked to Philip this morning. And Billingham learned the story last night. Justin said he went out afterwards."

"All right," Guy conceded, "I'll grant you there was time, but only just. Besides, I don't know enough for anyone to go the trouble of getting rid of me." He grinned. "Unless it's a jealous lover of yours."

This suggestion was so patently ridiculous that it made her cross. "Don't, Guy."

"Don't what? Admit that I have a beautiful wife and many men would have cause to be jealous of me? All right then. Why don't you tell me Lady Margaret's story instead."

Knowing it would be little use to pursue the matter of the carriage accident, Rachel complied with this request.

Guy listened intently and was typically noncommittal when she had done. "Interesting," he said. "It's going to be difficult to talk to Billingham. I don't quite feel I can call at Arundel House. Perhaps I should take Justin up on his offer of help."

Rachel decided it would be best to let this pass without comment. She told Guy about her visit to Philip, and Guy told her about his talk with Brandon—which left her more than a little worried, on Brandon's account as well as Charles's—and then it was time to go up and see the children and dress for dinner. Rachel had considered going to the Tavistock that night, but the events of the afternoon had left her more tired than she realized, so she spent the evening curled up on the library sofa reading a script while Guy sat at a nearby writing table and worked on revisions of a scene between Corisande and her sisters which hadn't played well at rehearsal.

There was something comfortingly domestic about the scene. The library was an enormous room, but a series of Corinthian columns broke it into less daunting spaces. Comfortably ensconced on the soft leather sofa, Rachel could hear Guy muttering under his breath. She had only to glance up to see him scribbling furiously or biting his pen in frustration. Magnus, Christine, and Justin were out for the evening. Guy had spoken briefly with Justin before they left and had arranged to visit Billingham the day after tomorrow. But for the time being, all that could be ignored. Rachel knew instinctively that this peaceful interlude was as important to building a lasting relationship as the hours she and Guy spent in bed. And it was almost as pleasant. Almost, Rachel thought with a smile. She forced her attention back to the script. It had been written by Cecily's brother, a talented playwright, though he lacked Guy's brilliance. She made a note in the margin just as Thomas knocked at the door. Rachel, who had been half-lying on the sofa, swung her feet to the floor and hunted for her slippers. Guy continued to work as if there had been no interruption.

"Excuse me, my lady, sir," Thomas said, entering the room. "Mr. Pursglove has just called and he's asking for Mr. Melchett. Are you at home?"

Guy swung around from the writing table, instantly alert. "Show him in, Thomas," Rachel said. When the footman had left the room, she turned to Guy with a look of inquiry. "How much does Charles know?"

"I'm not sure. But I suspect Brandon warned him after our talk this afternoon." Guy moved to the sofa and squeezed Rachel's arm as if to bolster her spirits for whatever was to come, but there was no time for further conversation. Thomas opened the double doors again and announced Charles Pursglove.

Charles was thin and pale at the best of times. Tonight he looked gaunt and positively ashen, despite the warm glow of the candlelight. He waited until Thomas had withdrawn before he spoke, but otherwise he seemed lost to the most rudimentary rules of social conduct. Scarcely acknowledging Rachel's presence, he turned to Guy and spoke without preamble. "Tell me how much you know."

Guy very sensibly made no effort to pretend he didn't understand what Charles was talking about. "You and Edmund were heard quarreling in the Tavistock the night he died."

Rachel could see the pulse beating in Charles's temple. His normally pale blue eyes burned with intensity, but when he spoke his voice sounded strangely calm, like a rope pulled taut to the point of breaking. "I thought as much. I won't ask how you know. It scarcely matters. It's true, of course. I did meet Hever at the theater that night."

"By prior arrangement?" Guy asked.

Charles seemed surprised by such a matter-of-fact question. "Yes. It was Hever's idea to meet at the Tavistock. He knew I'd be able to get a key from Samuel. I didn't know about Brandon's meeting until later. After it was all

236

over."

"You and Edmund met and then you quarreled?"

"Yes."

"About what?" Guy asked in the same level voice.

Charles drew a long, shuddering breath. "I can't answer that, Guy. That's why I came here tonight. I didn't kill Edmund Hever. But if you want to know more about the night he died, you'll have to ask someone else. I have nothing more to say."

As Justin reined in his horses at the top of St. James's Street, Guy ran a critical eye over the building opposite: the first-floor balcony supporting a series of Ionic pillars, the neat railing at street level, the bow window on the ground floor. "So that's the sanctum sanctorum. I must say, it doesn't look nearly as daunting as Parminter House."

"Watch your tongue, Melchett," Justin said, relinquishing the reins to his groom. "I don't fancy finding myself the first Hever to be expelled from White's."

Justin led the way up the front steps, nodded carelessly to the porter, then glanced about the entrance hall. Save for a pair of elderly gentlemen talking earnestly about the peace negotiations as they made their way up the curving stairs to the coffee room, it was momentarily empty. "I imagine Billingham is in the morning room," Justin told Guy, "but if you don't mind, I'd like a word with you before we go in."

Not waiting for Guy to give his assent, Justin walked quickly to the back of the hall where, if they spoke quietly, they could expect not to be overheard. "I've been wanting to speak to you, and at Parminter House Christine always seems to be about." The drawl was gone from Justin's voice and the lazy mockery had vanished from his eyes. "I don't have to tell you that Christine is very fond of you, Melchett."

"We grew up together," said Guy mildly.

"Quite. And you know enough, I'm sure, never to imagine that that fondness means anything more."

Guy met Justin's gaze squarely. "I'm a married man," he pointed out.

Justin gave a brief laugh, but his eyes remained cold. "In our circles that's hardly cause for reassurance. How you and Rachel arrange your lives is your own affair. But understand this, Guy. Christine is mine and I won't brook any interference."

"Then you're going to have your hands full," Guy told him. "Men will always be trying to interfere with Christine. I wouldn't dream of adding to your troubles."

Justin drew in his breath as if to say more but he was interrupted by a voice from the other end of the hall. "Deaconfield, it's been an age since I've seen you." A young gentleman in sporting dress strode rapidly toward them. All traces of anger gone, Justin introduced Guy to Lord Winchester. Winchester's slight start and widened eyes told Guy that his fame had gone before him, but the viscount was too well-bred to betray any surprise. Winchester made some ribald remarks about Justin's approaching nuptials, said if his own parents had their way he would be trapped himself before the Season was out, and then continued upstairs to join some friends in the coffee room. Justin made no attempt to resume his earlier conversation with Guy, but led the way across the hall to the morning room.

They were greeted by that faint but distinctive aroma which unmistakably signifies wealth and status and quiet exclusivity. The room was crowded but not overly noisy. Some of the men were engaged in low-voiced conversation, but a number of others were engrossed in the *Morning Post* or the *Times* and looked as if they did not wish to be disturbed. Billingham, hunched in a leather armchair on the opposite side of the room, was among the latter. Justin made his way toward his brother-in-law, stopping occasionally to nod to an acquaintance.

Billingham glanced up from the paper. "Justin," he said, "didn't expect to see you here today. Have you—" He saw Guy and broke off with a shocked expression which would have been comical had it not been for the anger in his eyes. "What the devil?" he demanded, turning back to Justin with a look of accusation.

"Guy wants to talk to you," Justin said. "If you know him at all, you must realize that he'll contrive it sooner or later. I thought this would be better than having him run you to earth at Arundel House. If you want to argue about it, let's at least go somewhere more private first."

Billingham drew in his breath as if to protest, then stood abruptly and tossed the newspaper onto a nearby table. Without further speech and without once acknowledging Guy directly, he led the way to a small chamber at the back of the building. It was quite empty, but he glanced around suspiciously as if to be sure no one was lurking in the woodwork or hiding behind the curtains. Then he turned to confront Guy. "Well? I haven't got a great deal of time. Fanny and I are dining out."

"It's barely past five, Alfred," Justin said, disposing himself in a chair. "Why don't you sit down and be civilized."

Billingham glared at him. "There's nothing civilized about being questioned like a common criminal. I've already been through this with Burley. I don't see why you can't leave the questions to him, Guy."

"I could of course." Guy walked to a chair and rested his hands on its back. "I could go to Burley and tell him Lady Margaret overheard you and Edmund quarreling not more than a month before Edmund was killed. But I thought you might prefer that I discuss it with you first."

Billingham's face drained of color. His mouth worked rapidly, but no sound came out. Justin, who had not yet heard this piece of information, looked sharply at Guy. "How do you know?"

"Lady Margaret called on Rachel yesterday afternoon. I

hope neither of you will hold it against her. She and Rachel have become good friends and she needed to confide in someone."

"Yes, I suppose brothers don't make the best of confidants, do they?" Justin turned back to Billingham. "Well, Alfred? Meg's not one to make up stories. What was it she overheard?"

"How the devil should I know?" Billingham demanded.

"Presumably because you were in the room at the time," said Justin dryly.

"I mean," said Billingham, with a stony face, "how should I know what Margaret thinks she overheard. Edmund and I must have had words a score of times. I expect he was asking me for a loan. He was always hard up." Billingham flung himself into a chair. "I must say you have a lot of nerve asking all these questions, Melchett. You had as good a motive to kill Edmund as anyone. For that matter," he added, fixing Justin with a hard stare, "you weren't exactly the devoted brother, were you?"

Guy was conscious of the sudden tension between the two men, but Justin spoke in a colorless voice. "The feeling between brothers is rarely as simple as devotion."

Billingham continued to look fixedly at him. "You're a cold bastard, Deaconfield. But I know you, don't forget. Edmund could be damned difficult. And he was always your father's favorite. You wouldn't have been human if you hadn't resented him."

"Resented him?" Justin's quiet voice held a savage undertone. "My dear fellow, there were times when I hated him. Edmund could do no wrong, and if he did it was my fault for not looking after him properly. Our parents made that clear quite early. It was not conducive to brotherly feeling." Justin turned to Guy, a mocking light in his eyes. "Well, Melchett? Am I now one of your suspects, too?"

Guy had never realized how deep the rivalry between the two Hever brothers had gone. He thought of Magnus

240

and himself. If Justin had not killed Edmund for money or for Christine, could he have done it out of the pent-up jealousies of childhood? "At the moment," said Guy, meeting the other man's gaze, "I think we're all suspects."

"Yes, well, you both had better motives than I did," Billingham said in an aggrieved voice. "I wasn't anywhere near the theater that night. I didn't even know about Brandon's cursed meeting—" He broke off, a slow, satisfied smile spreading across his face. "You're wasting your time with me, Melchett. You ought to be talking to Brandon. Or Pursglove."

Guy was aware of a sick feeling in the pit of his stomach. "Why?" he asked.

Billingham looked from Guy to Justin with an expression of triumph and relief. "Edmund was bedding Dorinda Pursglove."

Chapter Fifteen

Brandon Ford had rooms in Panton Street, and it was here Guy sought him out the next morning. The Tavistock was not the place to discuss Dorinda's adultery.

If the story were true. Brandon's sister was a lively young woman, prettier than most, with a neat, rounded little body, bright blue eyes, a mop of curly brown hair, and a ready smile which showed a tantalizing dimple in her cheek. She could well have caught Edmund's eye, though she was no match for Christine. And Dorinda was known to be desperately in love with her husband. Or so the story went. Guy was ready to question every one of the assumptions by which he had lived for the past several years.

Still, it was true that Dorinda had made quite a point of marrying the penniless Charles Pursglove. She had coaxed and entreated and threatened and in the end Samuel Ford, a soft-hearted man where his children's happiness was concerned, had given way.

Brandon would know the truth. He was closer to Dorinda than to his younger sister, and he had been Charles's friend before the two became related by marriage.

Guy rapped sharply on the door of the narrow house in Panton Street, received no answer, knocked again without effect, then descended to the street and bellowed Brandon's name. Windows opened in nearby buildings and their occupants looked out, offering questions and advice.

Guy acknowledged these with a cheerful wave and shouted again. "Brandon! Brandon Ford!"

A moment longer, then Brandon's window was flung open. He hung on the sill, hair tousled, eyes not yet washed of sleep, and shook his head to clear it. His attention finally focused on Guy. "For the love of God, it's not yet nine."

"Come down and let me in," Guy called. "I want to talk to you."

Brandon moved back into the room, then returned to the window. "I can't. She's not awake."

"Then meet me at the Lion."

Brandon hesitated. He seemed on the point of slamming the window shut, but instead he called back, "Why should I?"

"It's important. I'll buy you whatever you like to break your fast."

Brandon groaned, a theatrical sound that gained the approval of the onlookers. "Ten minutes. Make it a heavy wet."

Guy grinned and made his way to Blue Cross Street and then into the doors of the Lion, a small dark public house which drew its customers from the immediate neighborhood. By the time Brandon joined him, Guy was seated at a table beside a grimy window which allowed him to watch the life in the street outside. A cup of coffee was before him, and at the place opposite, a tankard holding a pint of stout.

Brandon drew out a chair and drank gratefully. "You're a hellhound, Guy Melchett. If this is about the play, I'm going back to bed."

"It's not about the play. It's about Dorinda."

A wave of pain crossed Brandon's face, followed by a look of mulish obstinacy. It was as good as a confession. Feeling the meanest wretch alive, Guy pressed on. "Billingham said there was something between Dorinda and Edmund. Is that what the quarrel was about? What we talked about Saturday, Charles and Edmund."

"Guy, don't."

"We have to know, Brandon. Don't turn your back on it."

"In the name of heaven, why not? The man's dead, God rot his soul. It won't bring him back. It won't do anything but feed Guy Melchett's insatiable curiosity."

Guy winced. There was some truth in the charge. But more than curiosity was involved and he could not let Brandon divert him. "Edmund was killed. Someone decided to put an end to his life."

Brandon drained the tankard and leaned back in his chair. "No. It was most likely an accident. You know the kind of thing. A quarrel, a blow, the man falls and hits his head. It happens all the time. No intent involved. So why persist, Guy? Why rake it up?"

"The blow came from behind."

"Oh, God." Brandon put his elbows on the table and buried his head in his hands.

"Was it Charles?"

Brandon looked up with a ravaged face. "No. Not Charles. He wouldn't, not like that."

At an earlier time, Guy would have agreed with him. Now he would not trust his judgment of any man. Or woman either, he reminded himself, thinking of Dorinda and then, inconsequently, of Christine. "How did Charles find out about his wife and Hever?"

Brandon began to laugh. "She told him. It seems my honorable, truth-loving little sister has a jealous streak a yard wide. Edmund threw her over, and when she heard he was bedding Christine, she couldn't bear it." Brandon's laughter came to an abrupt end. "Don't be surprised, Guy, the story got about. I don't know why she listened to Hever in the first place. He flattered her, of course. And I suppose it was sometimes difficult to be married to a saint. She was furious when Edmund put a stop to it — she's never had a great liking for Christine — and she felt guilty as the devil. Cleansing her soul, that's what she was doing. She knew Charles would forgive her anything."

"But he wouldn't forgive Edmund."

Brandon raised his brows. "Would you?" He pushed the tankard away. "Guy, listen to me. I know Charles. He may have had words with Hever, he may have wanted to see him dead, but there's not a chance on God's green earth that he killed him."

"Even by accident?"

"You said it was no accident."

"So I did." Guy kept his eyes on Brandon who was now looking down at the table, tracing the marks carved in its top. He had confirmed Billingham's malicious bit of gossip. Charles might or might not have brought about Edmund's death, but Brandon feared that he had. Feared it and denied it. He would do anything to protect his sister, and that included protecting the man she had married.

It might also include avenging an insult to her honor. If that were so, Brandon's obvious concern about Charles's involvement was a clever blind, designed to draw attention away from his own guilt. "Did you see them?" Guy asked.

"You mean, did I hear them quarreling? No, Guy, I did not. When I learned about Dorinda, I was tempted to tell Edmund not to show his face at the meeting, but I didn't want to start any talk about my sister. I didn't know Charles had arranged to meet him that night. The last thing I remember before that inferno burst upon us was thinking that Hever, who never thought of anything but his own convenience, was late again." Brandon's laugh was harsh. "And when I staggered to the door and heard the crackling of the flames, I thought, 'Lucky devil.' It was one more sin to add to his account, not being there to help get the others out. Philip was pinned beneath a beam, and I had the devil of a time getting him free."

Brandon raised his eyes and looked directly into Guy's own, as though willing him to see the things he remembered. "Philip kept screaming all the time I was dragging him out. When I got up the stairs, I saw Cadogan, looking as though he were staring into the jaws of hell. Jessop had made it up ahead of me. I told Cadogan to get Hinton. But I didn't see Hever. I was in the Angel pouring blue ruin down Philip's throat while that butcher of a surgeon tried to set his leg when an officer came in and said it looked like Jessop wasn't going to make it. Cadogan was dead and Hinton and Hever. Hever? I thought there'd been a mistake. Poor bastard. He'd come to the meeting after all."

It was a compelling story. Guy had heard it before, but he had never heard it with the intensity and ring of truth that Brandon gave it now. Hear me, he seemed to be saying. Remember what I am remembering. Understand that I could not have killed Edmund Hever.

Guy felt a pricking of conscience at the thought. He liked Brandon. He would like to believe Brandon now, but he dared not. Brandon was a subtle and accomplished actor, and Brandon, for his sister's sake, would have been capable of killing Edmund Hever.

That same morning Rachel was in Bedford Row calling on Samuel Ford. It was her custom to breakfast with him every Tuesday, giving her a chance to review the Tavistock's expenditures and income for the past week and to tell him what decisions she had made with respect to staffing and the selection of manuscripts. This morning Samuel talked chiefly of *The Steward's Stratagem*, which he had finished reading the previous evening. His eyes were drawn, but he would not talk about Cadogan.

"He's a nimble-witted man, this husband of yours," Samuel said, passing the manuscript to her across the table. "Nothing quite actionable. Wit enough to keep them amused and action enough to claim their attention. They won't know what they've heard till they've left the theater. Would you mind giving me some more tea, my dear." He handed her his cup, waited for her to refill it, then stirred in his customary two spoons of sugar. "There are two scenes that may give you trouble. Scene Two in the third act, and the opening of the fourth."

"That's what the Examiner of Plays wrote," Rachel said. "We sent him the manuscript last week and had it back yesterday. The writing is Larpent's, not his wife's. I suppose we must be grateful that she wasn't acting for him in this instance. The scenes have been deleted, and Guy has written others to take their place."

"Already?"

Rachel leaned forward, elbows on the table, and rested her chin on her hands. "Actually, they were written at the same time as the originals."

"I see." A faint line appeared between Samuel's brows. "It was a feint. Oh, Rachel, Rachel, when will you learn to be careful. You must not play games with the censor."

"I had no intention of doing so. You know that plays must be rewritten as they get into rehearsal."

"If anyone objects, you may be forced to withdraw it."

Rachel smiled. "Then we will have had one splendid performance."

"Yes, that will be something." Samuel put down his napkin and got to his feet. "Now if you'll excuse me, I must get to my office. Would you mind staying on a bit? Dorinda should be down soon. She seems blue-deviled, but she won't say a word to me, and Eleanor and Cressida have already gone out." He hesitated, then added hurriedly, "I daresay Dorinda's upset by this business about Cadogan. It's distressed us more than I can say, and you must be distressed most of all. I'm sorry, Rachel, I can't bring myself to talk of it. You know what he meant to me. But I can't offer you the consolation you deserve, and I'm no good for Dorinda. Perhaps, if you can bear it . . ."

He turned away, but not before Rachel had seen the tears in his eyes. She rose quickly and put her arms around him, and they took what comfort they could from each other. When Samuel left the room, Rachel returned to the table and thought about what Guy had told her the night before. If Billingham was right, Dorinda would have other cause to be blue-deviled. Edmund was two years dead and the affair had stopped well before that time, but she would just have learned how he had died. The pain would begin afresh, as it had for her when Mountjoy confirmed the extent of Cadogan's treachery. And whether Dorinda mourned Edmund's loss or the loss of her own virtue, she must wonder at the role her husband might have played in his death.

Dorinda came into the breakfast parlor a quarter-hour later and started at seeing Rachel still at the table. "I thought you would be gone," she said, with some want of graciousness.

Rachel ignored the other woman's tone. "I was hoping to talk to you." She poured a cup of tea and set it down before Samuel's obviously unhappy daughter.

"I'm being beastly, aren't I?" Dorinda gave her an apologetic smile. "You've had this dreadful news about Cadogan, and I should tell you how sorry I am, but I'm not, really. I never liked Cadogan that well, and I can't understand what Papa saw in him, and you can't deny that he was a deplorable husband. Cadogan, I mean, not Papa. While Charles—"

Dorinda burst into tears and fumbled in her pocket for a handkerchief. Rachel handed her her own and waited till the storm had passed. "I'm sorry, Rachel," Dorinda said with a last gulp. "I'm sorry for everything." The tears had intensified the blue of her eyes, and she looked, despite her weeping, as pretty as ever.

Rachel leaned across the table and stretched out her hands. "Let's not talk about Cadogan. That's over. Let's talk about Edmund Hever."

Dorinda snatched her hands away as though Rachel's hands were fire. "What do you know?"

She was transparent. Impulsive and generous, Dorinda had never been able to hide her feelings. To keep a secret was a torment. To keep a secret from her husband—and Rachel was now sure there had been a secret to be kept—Dorinda must have suffered the pains of the damned.

Rachel knew she must be as direct as possible. "Charles

248

was heard quarreling with Edmund at the Tavistock not an hour before the explosion. Two days ago Charles came to Guy to admit the quarrel and to deny that it had anything to do with Edmund's death. He wouldn't tell Guy what the quarrel was about, and he wants Guy to stop asking questions." Rachel smiled. "Fruitless, of course. Guy doesn't mean to hurt anyone, but he's determined to get at the truth. Then Alfred Billingham told him that Edmund had seduced you. Was he right, Dorinda?"

Dorinda began to laugh. The laughter changed to hiccups, and when those had subsided, she looked directly at Rachel and said in a now calm voice, "Right and not right. I was mad as a hare. Edmund had only to crook his finger and I came. I thought I was in love with him. No, I was in love. It wasn't what I felt for Charles, even in the beginning. It was more a terrible thirst, and Edmund was the only one who could slake it. And all the time I went on loving Charles, too." She dabbed at her cheeks with the drenched handkerchief. "You'll think badly of me, I know. I deserve it. I treated Charles no better than Cadogan treated you. Worse even, for one expects those things of men."

"I don't think badly of you at all," Rachel said. "I like Charles, but I would think he'd be a rather daunting man to live with. All that earnest saintliness. And Edmund was enormously attractive. I might have been tempted myself, if he hadn't been so obviously smitten with Christine."

As soon as she saw the bitter look on Dorinda's face, Rachel knew she had made a mistake. That's what came from thinking of herself rather than Dorinda. "Is that why it ended?" she said bluntly. "Because of Christine?"

Dorinda nodded. "He didn't want me anymore. He didn't need me. Christine was giving him what he'd had from me." A stricken look crossed her face. "Forgive me, Rachel. But it was true."

"Yes, I know it," Rachel said. She pushed aside the painful memory of her quarrels with Christine and Guy. "Charles learned about you and Edmund, didn't he?

That's why he and Edmund had words."

"Yes, but Charles didn't kill him." Dorinda reached across the table and clasped Rachel's hand. "It was my fault. I told him."

"Charles?"

"Yes," Dorinda said impatiently. "I was furious with Edmund, and I wanted—No, I don't want to think about what I wanted. But Charles wouldn't have done it. He couldn't. He's incapable of hurting anyone."

"It's all right, Dorinda. I don't believe it either." Rachel gave Dorinda what she hoped was a smile of reassurance. "You don't need to worry. If Charles is innocent, he has nothing to fear."

The tears welled again in Dorinda's eyes. "It's not Charles I'm worried about. It's Brandon. Charles told him, right after he learned about me and Edmund, and Brandon went into an absolute rage. Charles forbade Brandon to interfere and said he would take care of Edmund himself. And then the next day Edmund died. I was devastated, but I was relieved, too, because that was the end of it. And then yesterday Brandon told us Edmund had been killed. Rachel, what was I to think? If it wasn't Charles—and it couldn't have been Charles—then it must have been Brandon."

"Not necessarily," Rachel said. "There could have been other men who had cause to think badly of Edmund Hever."

Dorinda looked at her in surprise. She did not seem to have considered that Edmund might have had a life that went beyond her own small circle. "Charles thinks it was Brandon," she said doubtfully.

"Then tell Charles to cast his net wider. Ask him who else might have wished Edmund out of the way and why. Dorinda, help us."

"I want to forget it." Dorinda's voice was suddenly passionate. "I want to go back to Suffolk and forget I ever had a life in London."

"You can. You will. But whatever Edmund was, whatever he did, his life did not deserve to end at the hands of a faceless killer. Help us find the truth, Dorinda."

Dorinda did not seem to hear. Wrapped up in her private pain, she could not attend to the wider story. Knowing it was useless to press her further, Rachel pushed herself away from the table. "Don't be so ready to blame your brother. I know Brandon. He'd start a mill, but he wouldn't hit a man when his back was turned."

"No, he wouldn't, would he?" Dorinda raised her eyes, now free of tears. "Thank you, Rachel. I'll tell Charles."

Rachel left the breakfast parlor doubting the wisdom of her behavior. She knew that either Brandon or Charles, blinded by rage, could have brought about Edmund's death. She should not have been so quick to assure Dorinda of their innocence, but the urge to comfort had been too great. Poor Dorinda, living with the knowledge of her betrayal. And poor Charles, living with it, too. Yet at her wedding, they had seemed as happy in each other as they had always been. Charles, dear man, had forgiven his wife. So fidelity was not an absolute thing. If it were shattered, it could be rebuilt. The notion was new to Rachel, for whom the betrayal of another's trust was the absolute sin.

Rachel let herself out of the door of the Ford house and walked down the steps to the barouche. "The Tavistock," she told Collins who was waiting to hand her into the carriage. "Then I won't need you for the rest of the day. Call for me at five."

Collins touched his hat, closed the door behind her, raised the steps, and mounted the box. As the horses were given their office, Rachel sank back against the soft leather seat. She felt unutterably weary, and it was not yet eleven in the morning. Moreover, she felt a faint throbbing in her temples, a sure sign of an impending headache. She rubbed them vigorously and sat up straighter on the carriage seat. It was useless to take on the burden of Dorinda's folly, and it was useless to fret about Charles and Brandon, who might have done nothing at all.

251

She wished she could forget Edmund's death. The horror of that night had passed, and no good would come of opening old wounds. But his death could not be ignored. Burley was worrying the problem like a dog at a rathole, and the Home Office would never let this particular puzzle rest. For one thing, Arundel would not let them, and for another, murder was not a crime to go unpunished. And Guy, she suspected, was again their chief suspect. Dear Heaven, would they never have done with him? Incendiarism, then treason, and now the most unforgivable crime of all.

Guy was still their favorite scapegoat—thank his wicked pen for that—but at least Mountjoy would not be using him to save his skin. Rachel allowed herself a small feeling of triumph. Lord Sidmouth, Magnus had told her that morning, was displeased with his undersecretary, and Mountjoy had left abruptly for the country. Poor William Mountjoy. He would never get his diplomatic post, his very future with the Government was in doubt, and he had brought it all on himself.

Feeling much cheered by these uncharitable reflections, Rachel turned her thoughts to the matters that needed her immediate attention. One of the stagehands was in hospital, and someone must be found to take his place. The housekeeper had complained of the condition of the curtains in the boxes. Worn to shreds, she had said. Rachel hoped she exaggerated. They could not afford to replace them. Their principal dancer was demanding an immediate increase in her already handsome salary, which Rachel had no intention of granting, and she must find some other way to keep her from carrying out her threat to leave the company.

They were rehearsing Act IV. Rachel could tell by the shouts and the clash of steel against steel. She moved into one of the wings to watch its progress. Cecily Summers, fashionably dressed in pink muslin, her dark curls covered by a long blond wig, was sitting on a chair that had been brought from one of the dressing rooms. The chair represented a rocky promontory overhung by trees—at least it would be overhung by trees when Prentice had finished painting the flat. Brandon and Guy were having at each other with a pair of Italian rapiers while Ralph Hemdale looked on. Brandon was an excellent swordsman, but Ralph was not. Guy was demonstrating the moves of the fight and shouting explanations to Ralph. Guy's face was damp with sweat. He had removed coat, waistcoat, and cravat and had opened his shirt and rolled up his sleeves. Rachel could see the golden hairs on his arms glinting in the flickering light from the rehearsal lamps. "Like this," he cried, "watch out for the feint."

The fools, they hadn't tipped the rapiers. Brandon lunged at Guy, the point of his rapier aimed straight at Guy's heart. At the last moment it veered, passing close under Guy's arm, so close that Rachel heard the tearing of his shirt. Guy, with a beautiful economy of movement, rose up in surprise, as though refusing to take the thrust that had already gone home, spun around once, and fell to the ground. "There," he said, tossing Hemdale his rapier. "Five minutes, then you try it."

He bounded to his feet and came toward Rachel, the joy he had taken in the fight still visible on his face. "It's going well," he said, giving her an absent-minded kiss.

Rachel felt a little frisson of delight and wished that her husband was not quite so preoccupied. Then she remembered her own cause for concern. "Guy, you mustn't let them fight with uncovered blades. Brandon is nimble enough, but Ralph doesn't have the skill and he tends to be clumsy."

Guy threw up his hands in mock surrender. "I promise. I can't afford to lose him." His face turned serious, and he pulled her farther away from the stage. "I saw Brandon early this morning," he said in a rapid whisper. "He's afraid Charles may have had a hand in Edmund's death."

"I saw Dorinda." Rachel kept her voice low as well. "Charles thinks Brandon may be guilty."

Guy groaned, then gave a short laugh. "Enough. We

have work to do." He squeezed her arm and strode off, leaving Rachel in a troubled frame of mind. She had turned away from the stage, intending to go to the house-keeper's room, when she was arrested by the sound of a familiar laugh. Christine. What the devil was she doing here? Rachel hesitated, wondering whether or not to join her sister who was obviously talking to Guy. She could hear the deeper tones of his response. And then she heard a drawling voice and knew that Justin was with them as well. Cursing herself for a jealous shrew, Rachel forced herself to think of curtains and proceeded at a brisk pace to the housekeeper's room.

Christine's visit was no surprise to Guy. In the days after her father's death, when she first came to live with Rachel and Cadogan, she had often accompanied Rachel to the theater. She took a keen interest in the progress of rehearsals and the designs for the stage settings and, Guy remembered with amusement, the younger actors as well. Rachel had had to give strict orders to the company that her younger sister was to be treated with the utmost respect. Then, during the time when Christine and Guy had fancied themselves in love, she had come to the Tavis-tock to be with him. Later Edmund had followed her here. And now Justin.

Guy always enjoyed having an audience at rehearsals. After calling the actors back to the stage, he joined Christine and Justin in the pit. "Act IV," he said, "the duel on the riverbank."

"I haven't read the play," Christine reminded him.

"You haven't? It's been lying about the house. Hemdale," Guy called, jumping up from the bench. "Start farther downstage or you'll end up in the river."

Ralph Hemdale looked aggrieved. "Where is the damned river?"

"Just beyond the chair where Cecily is sitting. Someone fetch a rope." Guy ran through the pit door and up onto the stage, dragging a long rope which he proceeded to lay in an irregular line from the front wing to a point far upstage on the opposite side. "Something like that," he said, leaving the stage once more. "Let's try it again," he called out when he reached the pit. He threw himself down on the bench next to Christine and for a few moments nothing could be heard save the muted sound of women's voices from the boxes above and the clash of metal against metal as Brandon and Ralph went through the movements of the duel.

"Brandon's quite splendid," Justin remarked.

"You should know," Christine said. "So should you, Guy. I remember watching both of you practice with him. A lovely accomplishment for a man. He shows off to much better advantage with a sword than with his fists."

"I'll remember that." Justin lifted Christine's hand and brought it to his lips. Guy ignored them. He was on his feet again, shouting instructions to the duelists. When they began once more and Guy was reseated, Justin asked, "Is that Corisande? She looks rather like Christine."

"That's the wig. Mrs. Summers wants to rehearse with it to be sure it stays on properly. Christine is far prettier."

Justin raised his brows. "Pretty? I thought you were good with words. That's a paltry one for the loveliest woman in London."

Guy turned to Justin and smiled. "Christine's beauty is beyond words." Justin gave him a sharp look. Christine, her eyes on the stage, seemed pleased by the exchange.

Guy was on his feet once more. "Hemdale, no. Five steps back, turn, duck, and thrust. Here, I'll show you." He left the pit once more and joined the sweating participants on stage. Taking Hemdale's rapier, he demonstrated the desired movements, then watched while Hemdale went through them a half-dozen times. "Good, good. Once more from the beginning. Then we'll take Corisande's scene," he called to Cecily who was waiting patiently on the chair by the river.

When Guy returned to the pit, Justin had gone. "He's wandering about backstage," Christine said. "He saw *The*

Tempest and he wants to know how you manage the flying spirits."

Guy grinned. "I don't. I'm more earthbound than the bard."

Christine was silent for a time as they watched the progress of the duel. Then she said, with a suddenness which startled Guy, "Why did you marry Rachel?"

"You might ask why Rachel married me."

She ignored his evasion. "You swore you'd never marry anyone."

"So I did." It had been after Christine became betrothed to Edmund. Still conscious of what was taking place on stage, Guy turned to his cousin. "I couldn't support a family then."

"And now?"

"My income is erratic. You know that. But Rachel needs no support."

"You mean you married her for her money?"

Guy felt unreasonably hurt. Christine was baiting him. "You know that's not true."

"No, of course not." She covered his hand with her own in an impulsive gesture. "I'm sorry, Guy." Christine was like that, brittle, gay, vengeful, generous. "Do you love her?" she said, meeting his eyes.

"Do you love Justin?"

She withdrew her hand abruptly. Then she laughed. "Oh, Guy, what happened to us?"

Guy studied her lovely, discontented face. "I think we grew up."

There were shouts from the duelists, followed by oaths and laughter, and Guy was forced to turn his attention to the stage. Then Justin returned and took Christine away. Guy stopped the rehearsal at four and took Brandon and Ralph off to the Angel where they continued to discuss the problems of the duel. Guy left them there and returned to the theater. Rachel had promised to go out that evening with her brother and sister, so Guy planned to stay on and see the first act of *The Heir at Law* in which

Hemdale was playing that night. He spent the next two hours in the paint shop talking to Prentice and trying not to think of his conversation with Christine.

Why hadn't he been able to tell Christine that he loved Rachel? Of course he loved her, but it had nothing to do with those heady feelings he'd known when he had been young and all the meaning in the world was reduced to one beloved person. He was fond of Rachel, he was happy with her, and Christine, who kept throwing the past in his face, was a dangerous woman. Dangerous to his peace of mind and thus to Rachel's as well. It would be a relief when she married Justin and they were all finally sorted out.

When Guy left the theater at the interval, it was nearly nine. There was an unaccustomed warmth and gentleness in the night air, and Guy decided to walk to Bloomsbury Square. His thoughts were on Hemdale's performance, about which he had a great deal to say to Rachel, and then they turned inevitably to Rachel's bed. Love or no, what they had between them was uncommonly pleasant.

The streets were crowded, but Guy gave little thought to the people jostling him as he turned into Charles Street. He was not a hundred yards from the Bow Street Public Office when a scruffy little man with an unsteady gait came up to him and took his arm. "See here, mate," he said in a thin reedy voice, "I've got a powerful thirst. Could you see your way clear—"

Guy shook him off with a good-natured smile, but the man returned, tightening the hold on his arm. Guy felt a flicker of alarm and turned around, pulling the scruffy man in front of him. The man would have a partner, and his partner would be coming up behind, ready to slit Guy's pocket and take his purse. The partner, a much larger man with a pockmarked face, was taken aback by this maneuver. Guy pushed the scruffy man toward his friend, thinking to gain a moment to allow him to escape, but the scruffy man dropped to his feet and the pockmarked man lunged toward Guy. Guy was aware of a glint of steel as the knife intended for his back was buried between his ribs.

His hand went to his chest, and he felt the hot stickiness of blood. His head was light, and he staggered to a doorway to keep himself from falling. Strange, he had never been knifed before. So this was how it felt. He was on the ground without knowing how he had got there, aware that he should call for help from the passersby, but he could not utter a sound and no one stopped. In his cups, that's what they would think. With a movement that cost him his last bit of strength, Guy untied his cravat and pressed it against the pain in his chest. After that he felt nothing at all.

Chapter Sixteen

Christine, who had been pacing restlessly ever since she and Rachel adjourned to the drawing room, stopped abruptly and broke the silence which had reigned between the sisters since they left the dinner table. "Shouldn't Guy be back by now?"

Rachel looked involuntarily at the clock on the intricately carved gray marble mantel. It was four minutes past ten, four minutes later than the last time she had checked. The first act should have ended well over an hour ago, and she had been watching the clock like a lovesick schoolgirl ever since. She was hoping for one of Guy's smiles before they went out. Or better yet one of his kisses. Now, looking into Christine's brilliant, glittering eyes, Rachel realized that her sister had been watching the time as closely. It was not a comforting thought. "I daresay he decided to stay on for the rest of the play," Rachel said.

"Of course." Christine moved to a gilt-framed pier glass on the opposite wall and made an elaborate show of adjusting her lace sleeves. Her gown, a frock of gossamer-thin India muslin beneath a robe of shimmering pink China crêpe, reminded Rachel of Cecily's masquerade costume in *The Steward's Stratagem,* just as Cecily's blond Corisande wig always made Rachel think of her sister. But then it was not merely in looks that Christine resembled the heroine of Guy's new play. Whether Guy knew it or not, Rachel was convinced that the mercurial, spirited Corisande was an idealized version of her sister. That had nothing to do with the fact that it was a splendid play. Rachel was determined not to let personal feelings cloud her professional judgment.

Or to let them cloud anything else. With a stab of pain, Rachel recalled how her jealousy had eaten away at her feelings for Cadogan. That was not going to happen in her second marriage. She glanced at the clock again. Ten past. There was still time for Guy to put in an appearance. But when the door opened, it was to admit not Guy but Magnus and Justin. Justin went directly to Christine's side and lifted her hand to his lips. Magnus walked toward the fireplace and offered his arm to Rachel. "I've rung for the carriage. Have I told you you look splendid tonight?"

Rachel smiled at her brother as she took his arm. She was grateful for the compliment, but she would have preferred that it come from her husband. Though she might not be a match for Christine, Rachel knew her new dress was becoming. The moss green satin clung to her figure admirably and brought out the green in her eyes, and the creamy lace drapery provided an effective contrast to her hair. It all seemed rather a waste if Guy was not going to see her in it.

Justin was holding open the drawing-room doors. As she followed Christine onto the gallery, Rachel became aware of voices in the hall below. Thomas, clearly agitated, and rougher accents which seemed out of place in Parminter House and yet were curiously familiar. Puzzled but not alarmed, Rachel moved to the gallery railing. She saw Christine freeze, one hand gripping the newel post, and heard her sister's quick gasp. Then she reached the railing and saw for herself.

Thomas, crisp and elegant in his red-and-black livery, was standing near the door. Opposite him was a burly man in dusty breeches and a well-worn coat. Patrick, Rachel realized, recognizing the Tavistock's stage manager with a start of surprise. Patrick was half-supporting, half-carrying a shorter, slighter man who was swathed in a blanket. The second man's head was lowered, but the tousled hair glinting in the candlelight identified him at once. It was Guy.

Rachel barely had time to take in the scene before it exploded into action. Patrick looked up at her but his words were drowned out by an incoherent cry from Christine. Before Rachel had reached the half-landing, Christine was running headlong across the marble-tiled floor, her skirt held indecently high, her golden ringlets flying out behind her. She reached out both arms, then sprang back with an exclamation of horror. Her gloved hand, which had touched Guy's chest a moment before, was stained bright red.

Rachel felt a chill run the length of her body, but years of motherhood had taught her to suppress her own feelings in times of crisis. Dimly aware that Magnus and Justin were following, she walked down the remaining stairs. "Thomas, have someone bring hot water and cloths to the library, then go directly to Dr. Grey in Brunswick Square. Tell him there's been an accident."

Magnus had gone to assist Patrick, and Justin was cradling Christine in his arms. Rachel hurried across the hall and flung open the library doors. Magnus and Patrick eased Guy onto a sofa, while Rachel took a tapestry cushion from one of the chairs and settled it beneath his head. It was the first time she got a good look at his face. Guy's skin was a pasty, bloodless white streaked with dirt, and the sweet, sickly smell of blood was overwhelmed by the more pungent odors of filth and decay. It must have happened in the streets, and he must have been left to lie there for some time. She didn't want to think about how much blood he had lost.

Guy's eyes were closed, but they flickered open as Rachel knelt beside him. "Sorry," he mumbled. "Making a damn' nuisance of myself."

"That's not very original and not in the least intelligent," Rachel told him, pushing back his coat and beginning to unfasten his waistcoat. "If you can't think of anything sensible to say, you'd best keep quiet."

"Not up to my usual standards." His voice was slurred, but his mouth curved in a faint smile.

After that, he lapsed into silence, which was just as well. Magnus appeared at Rachel's side with a cloth and a basin of hot water which one of the servants must have brought in while she was attending to Guy. Rachel dabbed at his torn and bloodstained shirt, then eased it back to reveal a jagged gash. To her untutored eye it appeared perilously close to his heart.

"I daresay it's not as bad as it looks," Magnus said quietly. "They seldom are."

Rachel spared her brother a brief smile, but before she could speak, they were interrupted by a cry from beyond the open library doors. "Let me go, Justin, I'm all right." Christine ran through the doorway. She had removed her gloves, her hair was disordered, and her gown crumpled, and she looked more beautiful than ever, the heroine of some great drama rushing to the side of her wounded lover. "Dear God," she breathed, staring down at Guy.

"If you're going to be squeamish, you'd best leave the room," Magnus told her, handing Rachel a fresh cloth.

"Leave?" Christine demanded. "How could I?"

"Christine." Justin appeared behind her and tried to draw her back into the circle of his arm, but Christine shook him off, her eyes riveted to Guy's face. "What happened? Who did this to him?"

"I don't know, Lady Christine." Patrick spoke up for the first time. "A pair of urchins showed up at the theater just after the interval. Their story was a bit garbled, but apparently they stumbled on Guy lying in a doorway. He was conscious enough to send them to the Tavistock for help. He wasn't able to talk much when I got to him."

Rachel gave Patrick a look of gratitude. She had cleansed Guy's wound as best she could and was now holding a clean towel against it in case the bleeding began again. With her other hand, she smoothed back Guy's tangled hair and felt his forehead. It was cold and clammy but at least there were no signs of fever. Guy stirred suddenly, moving his head restlessly against the pillow, though his eyes were still closed. Christine made a small sound of distress.

"Christine," Justin said again in a low, persuasive voice. "There's nothing you can do here, darling. Come upstairs and change your dress."

He tried to take her arm, but Christine rounded on him with fury. "Leave me alone, Justin. You don't understand.

You couldn't possibly understand."

This was the old passionate, willful Christine, stripped of the clever, brittle facade she had acquired in recent years. Justin went very white. Even Christine seemed to realize she had gone too far, but the words had been spoken and there was no taking them back.

In the wake of Christine's outburst, an uneasy silence descended over the library until Thomas at last ushered Dr. Grey into the room. Richard Grey, a well-favored, dark-haired man in his late thirties, was an old friend. He took charge of the scene with quiet competence. When he requested that everyone but the patient's wife leave the room, even Christine did not protest. Holding her questions at bay with a Herculean effort, Rachel stood by quietly while Grey examined the wound. He looked up at last with a smile which sent a wave of relief through her. "It looks as if you needn't fear to find yourself a widow again in the next day or so. But he's going to require stitches." Grey had stripped off his coat and now began rolling up his sleeves. "Could you ring for some more hot water? And you might want to change your dress. I'm going to need your help."

"I'll be all right," Rachel said, moving to the bellpull. During the long weeks of Benjamin Ford's last illness, she had frequently assisted Grey, as she had when Alec broke his arm and when Jessica cut her finger on a kitchen knife. She had welcomed occupation then as she did now. There was no opportunity to think about anything but the immediate task until the wound was stitched and dressed and Guy, who mercifully had remained unconscious throughout, was securely wrapped in the blanket Patrick had brought from the Tavistock.

"Your husband's a lucky man, Rachel," Grey said, doing up the buttons on his cuffs. "A few inches higher and there wouldn't have been much I could do for him. London's a dangerous city after dark."

Rachel nodded. She was certain this had been more than a chance attack, but there was no sense in trying to explain that to Richard now.

Grey put on his coat and packed up his bag. "A few days'

rest and he should be feeling himself again," he said as they reached the door. "You can move him upstairs—I daresay he'll sleep better in his own bed—but have a care he isn't badly jostled. I'll stop in tomorrow afternoon, but you'll let me know at once, of course, if there are any signs of suppuration."

"Of course. Thank you, Richard. This isn't the first time we've had cause to be grateful to you."

"Only doing my job." Grey hesitated a moment, then added, "This may sound odd in the circumstances, but it's good to see you looking so happy."

Rachel was taken by surprise. Was her love so obvious? If Richard had seen it, surely Guy would as well. Or did he have too much on his mind to notice something so trivial? Pushing these thoughts aside, Rachel opened the door to the hall. The others were still there. Magnus and Patrick were talking quietly together. Justin stood alone, his gaze fixed on a marble bust of the Emperor Augustus. Christine, still wearing her crumpled pink dress, had dropped down onto a high-backed mahogany bench, but she sprang to her feet as the door opened, her face a study in anxiety. "What's happened, Rachel? Is he—?"

"He's all right. At least Richard assures me that he will be in a few days."

"Thank God," Magnus said with a heartfelt relief which startled Rachel. She would not have expected her self-contained brother to be so openly emotional about anyone, let alone Guy.

When Grey had taken his leave, Patrick prepared to do so as well. "I left young Ted in charge," he told Rachel. "He's a clever lad and the experience will be good for him, but I'd as soon look in before he locks up for the night. Lord Parminter's kindly offered me the use of one of his carriages."

"It's the least we can do." Rachel pressed his hand and saw him to the door, then went to confer with Magnus about the best method of moving Guy upstairs. Justin joined them and suggested that they place Guy on a settee and carry it upstairs like a stretcher. Christine seemed to have disappeared, but Rachel did not give much thought to her sister's whereabouts until she went back into the library and saw Christine kneeling by the sofa, her disordered golden hair tumbling about her shoulders, one of Guy's hands clasped between both her own.

As the door opened, Christine looked up and smiled at her sister. "He's awake," she said.

Rachel forced herself to speak in a normal voice. "That's splendid." Christine showed no sign of abandoning her place beside Guy. Rachel walked around to the back of the couch and smiled down at her husband. If anything, he was even paler than before, but his eyes were clear and focused. That was the important thing, that he was awake and not delirious. Still, Rachel could not help hoping for some sign of affection, some words of endearment which would quiet the demons raised by the sight of Christine holding his hand.

"Rachel." Guy gave a pallid imitation of his crooked grin. "I'm afraid you're going to have to take rehearsal tomorrow." This said, he closed his eyes, but opened them long enough to add one final thought. "Don't let Hemdale overdo it in the second act."

Guy emerged from a fog of sleep, aware that something was not as it should be. Normally, he woke with Rachel in his arms, her hair spilling over his chest, her body curled against his own. Normally, his first action upon waking was to kiss whatever part of her was most available, and then they would make leisurely, delicious love. But this morning Rachel was not beside him. It was only when he had accepted this fact that he became aware of the pain in his chest. With that awareness, memory returned. The man with the pockmarked face, the knife, the two children who had discovered him, then finding himself in the hall at Parminter House with no clear awareness of how he had got there. Now that he recognized it, the pain was damnable. Still, as he was not dead yet, the odds that he would live seemed fairly good.

Moving gingerly, he tried to push himself up against the pillows. At once he heard a rustling of skirts and a light voice. "No, Guy, let me help you." Before Guy could respond, Christine had taken him by the shoulders and eased him into a sitting position. Her scent washed over him and her long hair brushed against his face. It was unbound, caught back with a blue ribbon which echoed the blue of her eyes. She looked very like she had at eighteen, and the sight stirred a longing for the past as her proximity stirred his senses.

"There," Christine said, fluffing the pillows. "I'm so glad you've finally woken up. I was beginning to worry. It's past noon, you know."

"Fashionably late." Guy glanced about the room, seeking some sign of his wife. "Where's Rachel?"

"At the theater, seeing to your rehearsal. I'm going to look after you." Christine smoothed the green velvet coverlet with a great show of seriousness. She had always been able to throw herself into activities with tremendous, if short-lived, enthusiasm. Guy had once found it endearing, but he suddenly felt an impatience which surprised him. Christine was no longer a girl, she was a woman of five-and-twenty. He was decidedly uncomfortable and in no mood to humor his cousin while she played ministering angel.

"My poor darling," Christine exclaimed, sensing his feelings but not their cause. "Does it hurt very much?"

"Fair to middling." Guy decided it would be best to ignore the endearment.

"Dr. Grey left you some laudanum." Christine gestured toward the bedside table where a bottle and spoon stood on a small tray. "Would you like some?"

"Not yet. I'm enjoying being conscious. It's quite a novelty."

"Then you must want breakfast. Cook's waiting to prepare it." Christine hurried from the room, but soon returned carrying his breakfast tray herself. "Boiled eggs and currant scones and some lovely strawberries," she said proudly. "And broiled mackerel. I made sure Cook knew it was your favorite."

The prospect of any food, let alone mackerel, made Guy rather ill, but a cup of strong, scalding coffee had a marvel-

266

ously revivifying effect. After a second cup he decided that perhaps he had an appetite after all. While he ate, Christine perched on the edge of the bed, nibbling one of the scones and keeping up a bright commentary about the impending arrival of the Emperor Alexander and the rumor that Queen Charlotte was trying to restrict Princess Caroline's presence at the next Drawing Room for fear of an embarrassing scene. Then she broke off and was silent for a moment. "Do you remember last night at all?"

"Vaguely." Guy cut off a small piece of the mackerel and chewed it experimentally. He had a sudden image of Christine running across the floor toward him, arms outstretched. "I made rather a mess of your gloves, didn't I? I'm sorry."

"It doesn't matter." Christine made an impatient gesture. "Guy—" She looked fixedly at him, her eyes wide and very dark. "I thought you were going to die. I've never been so frightened."

The words were spoken with a quiet intensity that was completely free of artifice. Guy felt a stab of guilt for his earlier impatience. For all her playacting, Christine was capable of real feeling. Involuntarily, he placed his hand over her own in a gesture of comfort. Too late, he felt the shock of response that ran through her and realized he had led them both into quicksand. Grateful for the unromantic presence of the breakfast dishes, he released Christine's hand and devoted himself to the mackerel, firmly ignoring any twinges of nausea.

When he had finished breakfasting, Guy said he'd try to get some rest. It was an excuse to distance himself from Christine, but the bed was soft and warm and he was asleep within minutes. He slept off and on for the remainder of the afternoon. Christine was always there when he woke, but other than offering him laudanum or asking if he was warm enough, she said little. Late in the afternoon—he knew it was late because of the shadows slanting through the windows—he awoke to find Dr. Grey conferring with Christine and Magnus. Grey, whom Guy had known in the days before he left England, told Guy it was good to see him again, congratulated him on his marriage, and added that he was mending remarkably well.

"It looks as if you're going to recover," Magnus said, when he had seen the doctor out and returned to the sickroom. "You gave us all quite a scare."

He was smiling, but there was an unusually serious look in his eyes. Guy was surprised and touched. "I'm sorry," he said. "It seems you aren't going to be rid of me for a while yet."

"Believe it or not," said Magnus, matching Guy's light tone, "I don't want to. For a troublemaking devil with a lot of starry-eyed ideas, you're not nearly as bad as you might be."

For the first time in the past twenty-four years, the two men regarded each other without rancor. It was a major turning point in their relationship, and like most such moments, Guy thought wryly, it slipped by almost unnoticed. "Do sit up, Guy, you've got the pillows all crumpled," Christine said. Guy complied with this request, and Christine bent over to fluff the pillows just as the door opened and Rachel walked into the room.

At the sight of his wife, Guy felt a surge of sheer happiness. She was wearing a spencer the color of wild roses and a bonnet ornamented with rose-colored ribbons and she looked—beautiful, Guy thought with faint surprise. If Christine stirred longings for the past, Rachel was the present, less idealized but far more real. Guy grinned at her. "You didn't let Hemdale overdo it in the second act?"

Rachel, who had been looking rather serious, gave a smile which lit her whole face. "I was wondering if you remembered any of last night."

"Only the important parts," Guy told her.

"He's doing splendidly, Rachel," Christine said, settling the last pillow. "I've been looking after him all day."

"Thank you, Chrissie. I knew I could count on you."

Guy was surprised by Rachel's tone. There was discord between her and Christine, as there was between all siblings, but it was unlike Rachel to speak so sharply. It occurred to Guy that this sharpness had less to do with the

268

fact that Christine was Rachel's sister than with the fact that he was Rachel's husband. Which was ridiculous. Rachel had no more cause to be jealous of Christine than he had cause to be jealous of what she had once felt for Cadogan. And yet, Guy realized, the memory of Rachel's love for his dead friend made him feel anything but tranquil.

"The children have been asking about you," Rachel was saying. "I've assured them that you're all right, but they don't seem to believe me. Could I bring them in to see you for a few minutes?"

"By all means," Guy told her. He felt a craven sense of relief when Magnus took Christine by the arm and escorted her from the room. A few minutes later Rachel appeared again with an unusually solemn-faced Alec and Jessica.

Jessica studied Guy intently. "You look green," she informed him. Then, in an accusing voice, "Are you going to die?"

"I don't think so," Guy said. "At least not for some time. Dr. Grey patched me up quite thoroughly."

"Dr. Grey took care of Grandpapa," Jessica said, "but he died anyway."

"Yes, I'm afraid even the best doctor can't always save lives," Guy conceded. "But your grandfather was an old man. I'm young and infernally stubborn."

"Our father was young." Alec was scowling furiously, not from anger, Guy realized, but from fear. The boy could not rid himself of the thought that Guy was going to leave them one way or another. Looking from Alec to Jessica, Guy felt a surprising wave of tenderness. He had always been fond of them, in a careless, avuncular sort of way. When he agreed to marry Rachel, he had been determined to do his best to be a father to them. But that had been an abstract thought, born of duty and obligation. Now he found it had become a reality. Alec and Jessica were a part of him and of the life he and Rachel were building together.

Guy considered any number of soothing answers and abandoned them. He couldn't promise not to get himself killed. Instead, he fixed his stepson with a level gaze. "I'm not like your father, Alec. I think you know that."

Alec made no reply but his brow lightened. Jessica tugged at Guy's sleeve. "Mama says we can come see your play if we promise to be very quiet. I'm good at being quiet. I saw *The Tempest* and I didn't talk the whole time."

"You squirmed though," Alec said, sounding much more like his normal self.

"I did not." Jessica was indignant. "Much," she added after a moment's reflection.

"It's hard to sit for four hours without squirming a bit." Guy was learning to play peacemaker between them. "But I'd be honored to have you there. It will be nice to have my family beside me."

At the word "family," Alec gave a brief but heartfelt smile. When Rachel said it was time to leave, Jessica stood on her toes and planted a kiss on Guy's forehead. "Goodbye. Daddy," she added, with the air of one bestowing a great privilege. Watching the children leave the room, Guy decided that that was exactly what it was.

"Well done," Rachel said when she returned to her husband's room.

"Yes, I think I'm beginning to develop a knack for it. Though considering I make my living dealing in words, I have a damnable talent for walking into pitfalls when I talk to them. Speaking of words, I want to hear what you've been doing to my play. Did I mention how grateful I am?"

"I think that was taken for granted." Rachel sat on the edge of the bed where Christine had perched earlier. She had removed her bonnet and a few tendrils of hair fell about her face. Guy felt an impulse to pull out the pins and set the whole fiery mass tumbling about her shoulders. If he was the least bit stronger — But he wasn't, so he was forced to content himself with watching the play of light and shadow on Rachel's face while he listened to her account of the rehearsal.

"I quite enjoyed myself," she told him. "It's a splendid play, Guy. I've been quite longing to get my hands on it. You're right about Ralph: he tends to play character parts too broadly. I think I've toned him down a bit. We spent most of the day on Act V. You may not like what I've done

270

with the last scene. I think Corisande is sharper than Cecily's been playing her."

Guy frowned in consideration. "You're probably right. Cecily's excessive sweetness is one of her few flaws."

"She was terribly worried about you," Rachel said. "They all were, even Brandon. Guy, what did Richard say?"

"That if I'm very careful I may be able to get back on my feet next week. Fortunately I have the best of incentives."

"Rescuing your play from my ministrations?" Rachel asked tartly.

"On the contrary," said Guy, reaching across the coverlet for her hand. "I wasn't talking about the play at all." He lifted her palm to his lips and held it there a moment. "I missed you last night."

"Gammon," said Rachel, coloring slightly. "You were barely conscious last night."

"This morning then." Guy retained hold of her hand and laced his fingers through her own.

Rachel smiled with a warmth which kindled an answering spark within him, then suddenly grew serious. "Will you tell me what happened last night?"

Guy had known the question was inevitable. While he doubted the attack had been accidental, he preferred not to dwell on the fact. Briefly and dispassionately, he told Rachel what he remembered. Rachel was not taken in by his tone. "They weren't after money, Guy," she said when he had finished. "They were trying to kill you. Just as the driver of that carriage was trying to kill you four days ago."

"Perhaps. But the brush with the carriage could have been accidental and the two men last night could have been merely bent on robbery."

Rachel regarded him with exasperation. "If it were only robbery, they wouldn't have drawn a knife on you." Her grip on his hand tightened. "Humor your overanxious wife and don't walk alone until this is settled."

"I have no intention of dying, Rachel," Guy assured her. "I'm enjoying life far too much."

"I'll never forgive you if you get yourself killed, Guy Melchett."

271

Guy grinned. "I'm not foolhardy. I'll even consent to travel in one of Magnus's crested barouches."

"Promise." Rachel continued to grip his hand and her eyes held his own.

"On the honor of the Melchetts."

"That's a dubious thing to swear by, but it will do." Rachel was silent for a moment, a faint line between her brows. "Would you recognize the men who attacked you?"

Guy had a vivid image of the scruffy little man and his taller companion with the pockmarked face. "I think so. But I doubt I'll see either of them again."

"They may be known to Bow Street," Rachel said with an air of brisk purpose. "I'm going to call on Burley tomorrow."

"He'll tell you such things happen in Covent Garden every day," Guy warned her.

"Murder isn't an everyday occurrence," Rachel retorted, "even in the worst of London's slums."

This was true and it brought Guy up short. Edmund's killer was either very frightened or very ruthless or possibly both. For all he had once feared hanging, Guy had never had as close a brush with death as last night. It was not an experience he cared to repeat, but he had no intention of allowing fear to curtail his investigation. He was used to running calculated risks. But the thought that Rachel might find herself in danger turned his blood to ice. "You made me give you a promise," he told her. "Now I want one from you. Be sure you have a footman or Collins or one of the grooms with you whenever you go out. Even in daylight, even in areas that seem safe."

"Now who's being overprotective?" Rachel asked with a smile.

"I mean it, Rachel. Perhaps we'd better send one of the footmen with Jenny when she takes Alec and Jessica to the Carnes' for lessons."

At the mention of the children, Rachel tensed. "You think they could be in danger?"

"I doubt it. But using children as pawns is an age-old ploy. I don't care to take a chance and find out I'm wrong." He settled back against the headboard. "About the fifth act.

Do you think the last scene between Corisande and Nicholas needs to be rewritten again?"

Rachel called on Burley on her way to the theater the next morning. He listened to her account of the carriage accident and the knife attack without comment, then, as Guy had predicted, pointed out that such incidents did not necessarily convey any sinister intent. Perhaps the man with the pockmarked face had panicked and thought Mr. Melchett meant to attack him. As for the descriptions, they could each fit any of a dozen men who had passed through the Public Office. He would, of course, keep Lady Rachel's story in mind. And, if he might say so, he hoped Mr. Melchett would have a speedy recovery.

Rachel left the Public Office seething with frustration. She could hardly expect Burley to reveal a great deal to the wife of a man who was a suspect in a murder investigation, but it was galling to be told not to worry when all her instincts screamed that danger was close at hand. Guy was philosophical when she told him of the interview. Short of asking to have a runner assigned to Parminter House—which would be a mixed blessing—there was little Burley could do. Rachel admitted this was true, but she could not be easy. If Edmund's murderer had risked two attacks, it seemed all too likely he would try again.

Rehearsals occupied Rachel's attention for the remainder of the week. Christine abandoned her usual round of activity and stayed by Guy's side. Unable to persuade his betrothed to drive out with him, Justin took to dropping by the sickroom and playing chess with the invalid. As far as Rachel knew, Christine once again treated her fiancé with at least a semblance of devotion, and an uneasy truce seemed to be in place between them.

Guy grew stronger each day and chafed increasingly at his confinement. By the end of the week, even Dr. Grey agreed that he might get up for a short time, though he probably did not have in mind spending the whole day at the theater, which was what Guy did. The entire cast, including Brandon, greeted their playwright's return with enthusiasm. If Brandon was behind the attacks, Rachel thought, watching him wring Guy's hand, he was putting on the performance of a lifetime. It was a comforting thought, save for the fact that Brandon's talents were extensive.

Guy spent the day watching a run-through, taking notes, and going over them with the actors. Rachel was able to persuade him to leave not much after four o'clock. "It's finally beginning to take shape," he told her in the carriage going home. "You were right about the last scene. Corisande's no ingénue; she's got far too much of your strength."

Rachel, who had been convinced Corisande was a pattern copy of Christine, was taken aback, but Guy went on talking about the play and did not seem to notice. Looking at him now, one would never guess it was only a week since he'd been wounded. Perhaps tonight . . . Rachel turned to the window, feeling her pulse quicken. She ought to be thinking about the play and Guy's health and the danger of another attack, but she could not help but wonder if Guy would visit her bed tonight and thought of how it would feel to lie in his arms for the first time in a week.

With that intuitive understanding of her thoughts which he so often displayed, Guy lifted her hand from the seat between them and carried it to his lips. "I did say I had the best of incentives to recover, didn't I?"

Rachel smiled, warmed by the promise in his eyes as much as by his touch. They sat thus, hands linked, until they reached Parminter House. Magnus pulled into the forecourt just behind them, and the three of them climbed the front steps together. As they stepped into the entrance hall, Christine, who must have been watching from an upstairs window, rushed onto the gallery and leaned over the rail. "Guy," she called, ignoring her brother and sister as well as Thomas who was in the act of closing the heavy front doors. "Didn't you listen when Dr. Grey told you not to overdo it? Do come up to the blue saloon and rest. I've ordered tea."

"Still playing at nurse, Chrissie?" There was a teasing note in Guy's voice, but he did not decline her offer. Rachel felt a wave of resentment at Christine and at Guy for playing along with her, and then told herself it was irrational. They had had a long day and she was hungry as well. Magnus, who normally adjourned to his study as soon as he returned home, accompanied them to the blue saloon where a delicate porcelain tea service was laid out along with a plate of scones and another of bread and butter.

Christine poured the tea, playing the role of lady of the house to the hilt. "I spent the morning at Madame Dessart's," she said, handing the plate of scones to Magnus, who was sitting nearest to her. "My wedding dress is nearly finished."

It was, Rachel felt certain, a remark calculated to draw a reaction from Guy. Guy gave no sign that he was affected, which did not necessarily mean that he was not.

"Madame Dessart wants to start on the bridesmaids' dresses now," Christine continued. "Can you bring Jessica in next week, Rachel?"

Rachel took a sip of the soothing, fragrant tea. "Of course," she said, and got no farther, for the conversation was brought to an end by the appearance of Thomas.

An expression of discomfort on his face, the footman looked from Magnus to Rachel and cleared his throat. Then he spoke in the stentorian voice he used to announce visitors. "Mademoiselle Aubert."

Mademoiselle Aubert. Arlette Aubert, a name that belonged to the past. A name that conjured up pain and loss and betrayal. A name that should have nothing to do with life now, in London, in 1814. Rachel's fingers went suddenly nerveless, and she was vaguely aware of her teacup rattling against its saucer. She heard Magnus draw in his breath and Christine make an involuntary exclamation, but there was scarcely time to think before Thomas stepped aside and the mother whom none of the three Melchetts had seen since she abandoned them nearly twenty-five years before stepped into the room.

Chapter Seventeen

The woman announced as Arlette Aubert paused while the doors were shut quietly behind her and her three children watched her with expressions of frank disbelief. Guy bounded to his feet and crossed the room in rapid strides. "Arlette," he murmured, raising her hand to his lips, "I didn't think you'd come."

He'd expected her. Rachel took in that fact with growing anger and dismay. She could not see his face, but the quickness of his response, the tone of his voice, the curve of his body as he bent over Arlette's hand all spoke of his gladness in welcoming her to London. Rachel felt twice betrayed. Guy had expected Arlette to come and hadn't thought fit to tell his wife about it. Nor had he thought fit to tell her how close he was with the woman who had borne her.

Guy was bringing Arlette toward them and would have led her to a seat, but as they reached the cluster of sofas and chairs, she stayed him. "Not so fast, *mon Guy*. I have not been asked into this house, and I do not know if I am welcome to stay."

Magnus had risen at Arlette's entrance but had made no move toward her. At her words, the frozen expression left his face. "I remember you," he said, his voice harsh with ill-defined emotion. "Why the devil did you come?"

She studied his face a moment. "I remember you, too, Magnus. Those brows. You would draw them together so, even as a child. You have not changed. May I sit down?"

Magnus made an ungracious gesture of assent, and

Arlette selected a chair, close enough for conversation, too far for a declaration of intimacy. She settled the skirt of a French cambric high dress, very plain and outrageously becoming, and proceeded to remove her gloves, tugging thoughtfully as she loosened each finger. When they were laid in her lap, she looked up at her children. "I remember you, too, Rachel, with your large reproachful eyes. But Christine, I do not remember you at all. You are quite exquisite. I have come to London for your wedding."

Rachel glanced at her sister. Christine should have taken pleasure in the compliment, but she was watching their mother with wary eyes. Christine, who made heads turn whenever she entered a room, seemed less vivid than usual. Rachel turned her eyes back to Arlette and thought she understood why. Arlette drew attention like a magnet. Guy was hovering near her chair, as if ready to do her the slightest service. Magnus did not take his eyes off her face. Arlette was well past fifty, and she had perhaps never had Christine's beauty. Her features were not as finely drawn, but her wide-spaced eyes rivaled Christine's in size and expressiveness. No, it was not a matter of face or form, though her figure was shapely and her ample breasts drew the eye. Arlette had a presence that would not be overlooked, a presence compounded of physical grace and charm of manner and something more that Rachel could not quite define.

This was not the woman she remembered. Rachel felt a pang of loss so sharp she wanted to cry out with despair. She had had a mother once, an evanescent creature who came and went with capricious suddenness. Rachel could recall her vividly but in no detail. She remembered her warmth and her particular smell, like a field of spring flowers, and her casual generosity. And the feeling of impatience and discontent always hovering round her mother that Rachel had taken as a sign of her own shortcomings. She closed her eyes for a moment. Dear God, why did you leave? Why did you come back?

Arlette's last statement was met by a silence which grew to embarrassing proportions. Guy looked as though he

277

would say something, anything, to blot out their want of courtesy to a visitor, but he was forestalled by Arlette. She raised her brows and pursed her lips in a little grimace of self-mockery. "Of course, I will perhaps not be wanted at your wedding. I should have thought of that. I am something of an embarrassment, *n'est pas?* You are not certain you wish to acknowledge me."

"Christine," Guy said, a note of appeal in his voice.

Christine swung round to her sister. "Rachel, what are we to do?"

"I suggest we do nothing at all," Arlette said before Rachel could gather her wits. She had a beautiful voice, low-pitched but with a wide range. It would carry well, Rachel thought. It would fill a theater larger than the Tavistock and silence an entire house. She was with the Comédie Française, the pinnacle of an actress's ambition. Guy had been ardent in his praise of her performance. Well, why not. She had been only a minor member of an obscure French touring company when their father had married her, but she had had twenty-five years in which to hone her craft.

"I need not come to Christine's wedding," Arlette went on. "I would like to stay and become a little acquainted, but I will not remain long." She did not add that they need not see her again, though the words hovered in the air. Arlette Aubert was not a woman to beg for favors.

"What kind of acquaintance, madam?" Magnus had refused to sit in her presence, and he stood now, feet somewhat apart, hands clasped behind his back, the deep frown still marring his heavy face. "Would you like a catalogue of our activities over the past twenty-five years?"

"No, no," she said, ignoring the challenge in his voice, "that would be fatiguing for you, and for me as well." Her carefully spoken English was without the trace of an accent and only her choice of words occasionally betrayed that it was not her native tongue. "Besides, Guy has told me much of those years. You have made a success of yourself, Magnus. I admire that. Art, money, it does not matter, you have worked hard for what you have achieved. As have I."

She smiled, an enchanting smile that made her look like a young girl. "And now you are the Marquis of Parminter. It is a fitting reward, is it not? Had it come to him, your father would have been beside himself with joy, but I must confess he would not have filled the position well. You do. You are a man of uncommon strength, and I am proud that you are mine, though I can claim no hand in it."

It was outrageous flattery. Magnus saw through it, Rachel was sure of that, but his frown lifted and the ghost of a smile passed across his face.

Arlette turned her attention to her elder daughter. "And you, Rachel, I can see that you are strong, too. Guy tells me that you own most of the Tavistock Theater and that you manage it as well. That is uncommon work for a woman, but it is work a woman can do uncommonly well. I am pleased you have chosen the theater—" She laughed and gave an expressive shrug. "No, you did not choose it, did you, it was thrust upon you, but that is the way of the world. It is to your credit that you have made so much of what you were given. And with the burden of widowhood besides."

Guy laid a hand on her arm. "Rachel and I are married," he said. "Two weeks since."

"But that is enchanting," Arlette exclaimed. She turned from Guy to Rachel, her eyes appraising, and then looked again at Guy. "Yes, and it is a sensible match. You should suit."

Rachel felt a flare of annoyance, though Arlette's comment was no more than an echo of her own thoughts. A sensible match, that was what they had made, a suitable one. Guy continued to smile at Arlette, and if he felt any distress at this unromantic appraisal of his marriage, his face did not show it. "We do," he said, squeezing Arlette's arm.

"But Christine," Arlette continued, turning to her younger daughter, "you I do not know at all. I cannot see the child in the woman you have become. You are excessively pretty and you are to make a splendid marriage, but beyond that I can tell nothing about you."

Perhaps it was the demeaning adjective—Christine was used to hearing herself described as a great beauty—that caused Christine to flare up at these words. Or perhaps it was that she did not know how to think about her mother. Magnus and Rachel had been nourished by their anger, but Christine had nothing to which she could cling. "There is no reason for you to know me," she said with unexpected bitterness. "You have no right to ask questions. It is we who have that right, and you who owe us an accounting."

Rachel was startled by Christine's words. She ought to have spoken them herself, save that she felt strangely awkward in her mother's presence, particularly with Guy seated close beside Arlette, her avowed champion and thereby Rachel's enemy. But Christine's anger was Rachel's own, and she waited for Arlette to speak, knowing that nothing could explain, nothing could condone what their mother had done.

Her three children were ranged in a semicircle facing her, Magnus still standing between his sisters. Arlette remained quiet, looking at each of them in turn. It was an unnatural stillness, as though she had imposed it on herself against her will. Rachel remembered that her mother had never been a quiet woman. For her, movement and gesture were as natural as breathing. Only her eyes betrayed an inner disquiet. Long and perfectly shaped, of a familiar deep blue, they mirrored some emotion that Rachel could not define. Anger perhaps, or amusement or pity. Rachel raised her chin. She did not want her mother's pity.

"An accounting," Arlette said at last, "is that what you want? A tale of my life? No, I do not think so. You want abject apology, do you not? You want me to throw myself at your feet and declare that I have been miserable every day of my life since I last saw this stodgy, tedious country. Well, you cannot have it. What I did twenty-five years ago was not good, I grant you that, at least not good in your eyes. But I make no apology for my behavior and I make no apology for my life." She stopped abruptly. Her breathing had quickened, but she was still in command of herself and her audience. Then a faint smile appeared on her face.

"As I trust you will never have cause to apologize for yours."

It was an audacious speech, delivered with impeccable timing and great good humor. Rachel was outraged, but her brother merely nodded, as though his judgment had been confirmed. "So," Magnus said, "we understand each other, madam—What am I to call you? Mrs. Melchett?"

"Mademoiselle Aubert. It is my professional name. But I would prefer that you call me Arlette. I doubt that you could bring yourself to call me 'Mother.' "

"Just so." Magnus walked forward and took a chair that placed him nearer to Arlette. "You have the advantage of us. You know a great deal about our lives, but we know nothing of yours. As a matter of curiosity, how did it happen?"

Arlette did not have to ask him what he meant. "Shall I say it was a sudden caprice?" She leaned forward, her attention on her son, but her eyes encompassed her daughters as well. She ignored Guy who had left her side to stand behind his wife. Rachel refused to acknowledge his presence. "I had not intended to leave," Arlette went on, "not then, but there were few days when I did not dream of doing so. It was on one of those occasions when I went to London to see my friend Mrs. Roslin. I went to London often, perhaps you remember. I detested the country, and your father and I did not always agree. It was a foolish match, on both our parts, though in the early days of our marriage I fancied I was in love with John Melchett. And he with me, though his love was possessive and self-seeking. Rachel, you are fortunate, for Guy has a generous disposition. I pray that your husband will be the same, Christine. Jealousy is a sure receipt for disaster."

Jealousy is inevitable, Rachel thought, feeling a moment of resentment at Arlette's easy familiarity with Guy. But she had to acknowledge that Arlette was right about her father. He had been a charming, self-indulgent man in his younger years. As a child she had recognized the charm, but it had taken her many years to realize that he cared for nothing but his own comfort. He had given his children little enough, and he had been positively unkind to Guy's mother, who had tried so hard to take Arlette's place. After Aunt Julia's death he grew querulous with disappointment and made increasing demands on his daughters. No wonder she had been eager to accept Cadogan's proposal. No wonder that Christine, released at last from that prison, had come to London eager to drown herself in pleasure. No wonder that Arlette had left him — No, that could not be right. It was one thing to leave a husband. It was another to abandon one's children. Rachel felt her face grow tight and her body rigid. She would never be able to hear her mother with an unprejudiced ear.

If Arlette was conscious of the struggle going on within her elder daughter, she gave no sign. She had turned once more to Magnus. "But I wander," she said with a charming smile. "I had once again gone to London. As was our custom, Mrs. Roslin and I went to the theater — it was a farce, I cannot recall the name, by George Colman — and in the interval a man with whom she was acquainted came to our box. He brought with him a Frenchman who was then visiting London, a man of middle years and no visible distinction. But I was delighted to meet a countryman, and we talked until the interval was over. He proved to be a man of understanding and wit, and to my joy I found he was the director of a small company in Lyons. His name was Denis Forêt, and no, he did not become my lover, not then or ever, though I returned with him to France to take a position with his company."

"And that was all?" Christine demanded. "He asked and you went? Did you have no thought for us?"

Arlette lifted her hand in a graceful gesture of futility. "I did, but not for long. Magnus was growing too old to have need of a mother, and you were dependent only on your nurse. I thought of taking Rachel with me, but her father would never have allowed it. And in the end I was glad I had not. It was no life for a child, and I wanted no encumbrances."

"You stayed in Lyons?" Magnus asked.

"Not for long. The provinces were not for me. I will not fatigue you with the story of my progress. It was not an

282

easy one. But I have now achieved what I desire. As you have done, Magnus." She leaned forward with a conspiratorial smile. "You will acknowledge that feeling of triumph, will you not? That lovely moment of knowing you have vanquished those who would stand in your way?"

Magnus returned her gaze, no trace of censure on his face.

Rachel could not bear it. "You did not write."

"I wrote your father," Arlette said calmly. "I told him what to say to you on my behalf."

He told us nothing, Rachel thought, remembering her father's fury on the day the letter had arrived. "And later? You made no inquiry."

"Would you have welcomed it? Would you have wanted to hear from a mother who had no intention of returning to her motherly duties? Your father asked me to return and I would not. He then severed all connection between us, for you as well as for himself. Believe me, Rachel, it was better that way."

"Better for you."

"Yes, and I trust it was better for you as well. You would not have liked it in France. I had no time for you." Arlette rose in a sudden and fluid movement. "Now I have overstayed my welcome, and in a few moments we will be unkind. I did not wish to stir unpleasant memories, but perhaps there is now some honesty between us. You know who and what I am." She drew on her gloves, smoothing the fine leather over each finger. "As for me, I have nothing but admiration for what I have seen. Now, if someone will see me to the door . . ."

Magnus was on his feet, but it was Guy who hurried forward to escort her from the room. At the door Arletté hesitated, then turned and walked back a few steps. "You have children, do you not?" she said to Rachel. "Alexander—he is now eight?—and Jessica. Do they take after you?"

Guy answered for her. "Jessica is the image of Rachel when she was a child. Alec looks like his father, a handsome brute, but his character is his mother's. Perhaps you would like to see them."

Rachel came forward quickly, conscious of a sudden constriction in her throat. "They are at supper," she said, daring Guy to say otherwise.

Arlette understood the message. The color rose in her face, but she said merely, "Of course, it is not a good time. I wish you well, Rachel, and your children. They are more fortunate in their mother than you were in yours." And with these words she turned and left the room.

Rachel stared at the closed door through which Arlette and Guy had just passed, trembling with the surge of feelings the interview had aroused. She whirled round to face her brother and sister. Magnus was standing by his chair, his face giving nothing away. Christine, white with dismay, had drawn back into a corner of the sofa. "She's monstrous," Rachel said. She flung out her arms in a wild gesture. "She is lost to all sense of honor. She flatters without shame and makes a virtue of parading her iniquity. There is nothing to which she would not stoop—"

"Even the truth," Magnus said.

Rachel turned on him with revulsion. "Dear God, you like the woman."

"I do not," he said evenly. "Nor am I in danger of forgetting what she has done. But I acknowledge what she is, and there are things in her I can admire. She has strength and singleness of purpose and a kind of crude honesty. It would have cost her little to put up a pretense of remorse, but I would not think better of her for having done it."

"And you forgive her?" Rachel demanded.

A look of intense pain crossed her brother's face. Rachel had not seen it since the first days of their abandonment, after which Magnus's face had ceased to show any expression at all. "I cannot." His voice was ragged, but he soon brought it under control. "Vengefulness is a draining emotion, Rachel. I've come to see that in recent weeks. I advise you to put it aside as well."

"Never!" To her dismay, Rachel burst into tears. She flung herself on the sofa and buried her face against its back, abandoning herself to her weeping. Christine put an arm around her and pressed a handkerchief into her hand.

The storm seemed to last a long time, but when it was over, Rachel felt much refreshed. Dabbing at her face, she turned round to face her brother and sister. "I'm a ninny," she said. "She's not worth the candle. We'll forget her." Rachel glanced at the abandoned tea table and thought inconsequently that they had not offered their mother tea.

"You can't forget her, Rachel. She's part of your life and you have to live with her." Magnus's voice was rough, but his eyes were filled with an unexpected concern.

"Is that what you do, Magnus?"

He had the grace to smile. "It's what I should do. I knew that when she walked into the room this afternoon. It wasn't the fact of her coming. It was the discord between memory and the reality of who she is."

Discord, yes. Rachel knew that Magnus was right. Discord was at the root of the wrenching feeling that had pulled at her belly and tightened her throat throughout the whole of that long interview. She could not reconcile that demon image, an object of both hatred and desire which loomed in the recesses of her memory, with the prosaic woman who had sat in the blue satin chair a few feet away and told her that possession was not the same as love. Not that she had found Arlette prosaic, but in the end she was no more than a woman as Rachel was herself and Christine and countless others. It was an unsettling thought.

"I don't remember her at all," Christine said with a touch of petulance, "and I didn't like what I saw of her today. She puts on airs, and she has no call to. She's years old, and she's no more than a common actress."

"An uncommon one, I suspect." Magnus dragged a chair forward and sat down facing them. "But she's also a Melchett."

Christine sat up in alarm. "What are you saying?"

"I think he's telling us that we must acknowledge her presence in London." Rachel turned on her brother. "Why? Why must we have anything to do with her at all?"

"Because there will be talk," Magnus said in an infuriatingly reasonable voice. "And the talk will only call attention to the irregularity of her departure."

"Then she must depart again," Christine said, "and at once. Now that she's seen us, she has no more reason to stay in England."

"Who knows what reasons drive her," Rachel said, thinking with bitterness of Arlette's obvious friendship with Guy. "Do you think she'll go meekly away simply because we ask her?"

"She might." Christine met Rachel's eyes. "She might if Guy asks her. They seem to be on terms of some intimacy."

Rachel could not trust herself to speak. She turned to Magnus and saw that he, too, had been aware of the relationship between her mother and her husband. He could hardly avoid it. They had flaunted it from the moment Arlette entered the room. But there was something more in Magnus's face, something bleak and shuttered that took her back to the days when they had first known their mother would not return.

"If she leaves, there's no problem. If she does not, then we must recognize the relationship." Magnus's voice showed no trace of the emotion Rachel had just seen so clearly in his face. Her brother kept his passions under tight rein, and their dark side he would not admit even to himself. As for his sisters, Magnus demanded that they, too, keep their passions in check. "Listen to me, both of you," he went on as they began to stir in protest. "Our private domestic tragedy was of little interest when our branch of the Melchetts lived in obscurity. But we are no longer obscure, and the story will surface. The surest way to prevent disagreeable talk is to demonstrate that we are on the best of terms with our French mother."

Rachel was silent, trying to find a logical way around her brother's argument. Christine made no such attempt. "I will not have her at my wedding."

"Why not?" Magnus said. "Because she's an actress, and foreign into the bargain? The Arundels won't care. They already know who your mother is, and though they may not like it, they have given their consent to your marriage."

"But it'll be worse if she's actually there."

"It will be worse if she's in London and she's not. Arlette

Aubert is not a common little slut who tramps the boards and whores on the side. She's a reigning actress with the leading theater in France, and if I judge her rightly, her life has been discreet. As discreet as that of half the women in London. Arlette is a lady, or has the appearance of one, and she'll charm both the duke and his wife. They'll find the reality far more palatable than the rumor."

Christine made a futile protest. "I won't have it, Magnus."

"Then take your case to Lady Parminter. If she agrees that we need not acknowledge our mother, I will abide by her decision."

"And if she does not?"

"Then if Arlette intends to remain in London for more than a day or two, I think we must ask her to remove to Parminter House."

Rachel knew that nothing would move her brother. Worse, she suspected he was right. But to have that woman here under their roof, to meet her in the corridors and sit with her at meals, to watch her play the coquette with Guy, no, she could not bear it. Choked with feeling, afraid of what she might say, Rachel murmured some hasty words of apology and fled the room.

She made her way upstairs, intending to go to her room, but found herself, without thinking, climbing the next flight to the third floor. She was aware of a strong desire to see her children, as though to make sure that the corruption induced by Arlette's presence in the house had not somehow permeated to the nursery. Or perhaps merely to assure herself that she, Rachel, was a mother unlike her own.

In either case, the visit was not a success. Rachel's face was beaded with moisture and her palms were sweaty. The children noted her distress and did not believe her denial that anything was amiss. They asked after Guy. Alec had begun to show a cautious fondness for his stepfather, and Jessica, always ready to outdo her brother, spoke of him openly as Daddy. Rachel couldn't help but be grateful to Guy for gaining their trust though all the while her heart was screaming *traitor, traitor, traitor.*

She did not prolong the visit which seemed to make her children as uneasy as she was herself. She pleaded some problems at the Tavistock which were causing her a frenzy of worry, then hugged them rather longer than was her custom and bestowed a kiss on each. Alec advised her to seek counsel with Guy.

God have mercy, what was she to do? Guy had betrayed her from the moment he crossed into France. Yes, he had told her he had met her mother, but that was only an evasion of the truth. He had told her nothing of the relationship that had developed between them during his years of exile. He had known that Arlette planned to come to England and he had said nothing, not a word of warning or explanation. The visit may even have been his own idea, some crazy scheme for reconciling Arlette with the children he knew looked on her with nothing but scorn. What a sweet, tender picture he must have envisioned, what an excuse to exploit their emotions to the full. Perhaps he meant to build a play around that particular scene. But he must have known it would play false. If he knew Arlette, if he were not blinded by her charm, he knew she had no intention of reconciling with anyone. She had told them so. Here I am. Take me on my own terms or do not take me at all, and I don't care a fig which course you choose.

Rachel had somehow stumbled down the stairs to the second floor, and she moved down the corridor to the sanctuary of her own room. She knew she was being irrational, but her pain was irrational, too, and only her anger could keep it at bay. She would close the door of her room behind her and throw herself on the bed and weep until she could weep no more. And then, perhaps then, she would be able to sit calmly and sort through what had happened this afternoon.

When she opened the door, she saw Guy.

He was standing by the bed, blocking the way to her refuge. Rachel felt a burst of rage stronger than she had ever known, stronger than her anger with Cadogan when she learned that he had broken his marriage vows. But Cadogan had betrayed her with Faith Harker.

288

Guy had betrayed her with her mother.

"You lied to me." Rachel's voice was ragged and hoarse with unshed tears. "You played me false."

"Rachel." Guy stretched out a hand to her, and his eyes filled with concern.

"Don't touch me. Don't come near me."

Guy did not pretend to misunderstand the reason for her anger. "You knew that we had met."

"Met? Is that what you call it? The eyes, the hands, the particular voice? There is more than simple meeting between you. You like her, don't you, you admire her, you are her intimate friend. Are you her lover as well? Or does she merely keep you in her pocket to take out when she is bored and in want of amusement?"

All trace of concern had vanished from Guy's face. He was furious. "Stop it. You're distraught —"

"Hah!"

"— and you're unreasonable. I would have told you more, but you refused to hear me. When your mother is named, you close eyes and ears and heart and mind. How could I tell you? You would not listen." Guy's breathing had quickened, but he brought it under control, and when he spoke again, his voice was quieter. "Yes, I like and admire Arlette. Yes, we have become friends. I daresay good friends. Even so, I did not take her to bed, nor did she give me a sign that she wished me to do so. Despite the difference in our ages — and that would not have stopped me if I'd been so inclined — there is the matter of our relationship. We are nephew and aunt, by marriage I grant you, but related nonetheless. And if that were not important, there is the fact that she is Christine's mother and your own."

Unaware that she had moved, Rachel found herself standing behind a chair, gripping its back for support lest her legs give way beneath her. Christine's mother, that was what had mattered. He could not bed the mother when he still hoped, against all reasonable hope, to bed the daughter. Rachel closed her eyes. Oh, Guy, Guy, one more betrayal. I cannot bear it.

The floor felt unstable beneath her. She would have fallen had Guy not appeared at her side and swept her up in his arms and carried her to the bed where she lay against the pillows, stunned and drained of all emotion.

"Rachel." Guy sat beside her and reached for her hand.

She let it lie limp in his grasp, then pulled it away. The ring he had given her gleamed dully on her finger. It was an old ring. Looking at it now, it seemed strangely familiar. Rachel had a sudden image of her mother's dressing table. Strange, but then her mother's visit had unleashed a flood of memories. The image would not go away. And then she knew where she had seen the ring before. She sat up abruptly and held her hand out before him. "You got this from Arlette."

Guy did not seem surprised by her accusation. "She wore it sometimes. It had belonged to her mother. When she knew I was returning to England, she gave it to me to give to you. She didn't want me to tell you that, but she wanted you to have it. Grandmother to mother to daughter. It seemed fitting."

Fitting. Rachel tugged at the ring as though she would tear it from her finger, but Guy's hand closed around her own. "No, Rachel. It's your ring now. It's the ring with which we were married. Don't be a prisoner of the past."

Rachel pulled her hand free but made no further effort to remove the ring. She would not look at him. "You don't understand." Her voice sounded like Jessica's when she was fretful and feverish. Rachel knew it was an aberration, but her senses were heightened and abnormally sensitive. Strange, when her blood seemed to have stopped its flow and she could not feel the beating of her heart.

"No, perhaps I don't." Guy sounded puzzled, and Rachel turned her head to look at him. "I always thought we had this in common. When I came to you, I'd just lost my father."

"It's not the same."

"Isn't it? I suspect it feels much the same. When my father died, I thought it was my fault. If I'd been a better child, he wouldn't have left me. Was it like that for you?"

"Yes." Rachel felt the sting of tears in her eyes. "No, it was different, don't you see? Death is forever. Your father couldn't come back. Even a child learns that, Guy. Alec and Jessica understand, and Cadogan's been dead only two years. It was different for me. Mama could have come back, she could have come back any time, but she didn't want to. She left us thinking we were worth nothing, nothing at all."

There was a kind of shocked sympathy in Guy's eyes. "She didn't leave because of you, Rachel. I doubt that her children figured very much in her calculations."

"But that's just it, don't you see?" Rachel leaned toward him as though by her nearness she could bridge this willful gulf in understanding.

"I don't know. I don't know if I can see what you see. But I know this, Rachel. You are no longer a child, and you are separate from the woman who bore you. Your worth has nothing to do with anything your mother may have said or done. Arlette is no more than a fellow creature, selfish and erring as most of us are. She has her own demons to face and her own dreams to follow. Separate yourself. Stand back. Above all, let go of your anger. It's destroying you."

Rachel sank back against the pillows. Magnus had said much the same. What was it? Vengefulness is a draining emotion. She felt drained enough at this moment. Her tears were spent. She could no longer fight or plead her case with Guy. "I'm tired," she said. "I'd like to be left alone."

"Of course." Guy too seemed to have retreated. He leaned forward as though he would kiss her, then apparently thought better of it. He rose and left the room without once glancing back at his wife.

Rachel watched the door close behind him. The subdued click as it latched reverberated throughout the room. She could feel its echo on her skin, she could hear the silence he left behind him. Her husband, her enemy. No, not her enemy, she was not so far lost to reason she could not understand what had happened this afternoon. She would have to think about it, but not now. She would have to make some kind of peace with Magnus and with Guy and even, God help her, with her mother.

Everything had changed. They had been shaken up and tossed about and had come to rest in a new pattern under a new light. Even her marriage, her fragile, newly built marriage, had changed. Feeling desolate and betrayed, Rachel turned and buried her face in the pillow.

Chapter Eighteen

Rachel woke the next morning after a brief and troubled sleep, conscious that Guy was not beside her. It had been a week since he had been to her bed, an endless week marked by the attempt on his life and her fears for his recovery. But he had recovered. Yesterday he had gone to the theater, and last night she should have lain in his arms. Remembering why she had not, Rachel sat up abruptly, her head throbbing. Arlette had come and turned her world upside down. She had quarreled with Guy, quarreled bitterly, and the rift between them seemed irreparable. Rachel fought an impulse to burrow beneath the covers and forced herself to get out of bed. The day was bleak, but it had to be faced.

She came downstairs after her morning visit with the children to learn that Lady Parminter was in the blue saloon waiting to be attended by Magnus and his sisters. It was a peremptory message, but it reminded Rachel that this had been Lady Parminter's home for nearly fifty years, and it was not surprising that she still exercised her authority here. "Magnus has gone to the bank," Rachel said when she had entered the room and made her greeting, "and Christine, I fear, is still abed. I can send word to her if you like."

"No, that is not necessary. It's you and Magnus I wish to see, but I will make do with you. I suppose you know why I have come."

Rachel thought it must be something to do with the wedding, and she felt a moment of alarm. Lady Parminter would not have asked for Magnus if the problem was something as trivial as the guest list.

"Your mother is in London," Lady Parminter went on. "She was seen last night at the Covent Garden, and she seems to have no intention of maintaining a decent reticence about her presence in London. This is an awkward time for her to make an appearance."

Rachel answered with a faint "Yes." She was profoundly shocked by Lady Parminter's statement. Arlette was their private cross, and it had not occurred to her that her mother was a public figure and so well-known that even Lady Parminter, who was nearly eighty and led a retiring life, would have had intelligence of her arrival. "She called on us yesterday afternoon," Rachel added, wanting to waste no time in misunderstanding. "It was a difficult interview."

Lady Parminter's pale blue eyes, clear despite her age, watched her shrewdly. "Yes, you would take it harder than the others. You're less well-armored than your brother."

It was an all-too-accurate description, and Rachel refused to acknowledge it. "Christine fears Mademoiselle Aubert will disrupt her marriage. She refuses to have her at the wedding."

"A mistake. You realize that, don't you?" Lady Parminter was seated with her back to the light, her hat obscuring the fine network of wrinkles on her face. Her hands, clasped around the handle of a frivolous parasol, were deeply veined, but other signs of age were hidden by the high neck and long sleeves of her dove gray gown. Her back was straight, and her posture made no concession to comfort. She had been trained in a stern school and retained the authority she must have had as a much younger woman. At the moment, Rachel found it rather a comfort.

"I would prefer that she return to France at once."

Lady Parminter frowned in evident disapproval. "Of course you would prefer it, but you are not likely to be so accommodated. What is it you propose to do?"

"Magnus says that we must acknowledge her. To fail to do so will only call attention to what has gone before."

"A sensible man, your brother. But a distant acknowledgement will do no good. The world must see that you are on terms of amity with your mother and that there is nothing in the story of her past life worth the smallest *on-dit*. I think it best that you bring her here."

It was what Rachel feared. Magnus had told Christine to seek Lady Parminter's judgment, and now the judgment had been given. It would be wise; it would be politic; it would be as helpful to Magnus's future as Christine's. She, Rachel, could scarcely wish to put those futures in jeopardy, no matter that the sight of Arlette was enough to tear her apart. Feeling dangerously close to self-pity, Rachel clasped her hands and forced herself to speak calmly. "Magnus has already proposed it."

Lady Parminter made a small sound of satisfaction. "You must not take it so much to heart, Rachel. What your mother did is twenty-five years in the past, and you have no business turning it into a melodrama. What *is* your business is your family's reputation. The Arundels have accepted the fact that Christine's mother was not of their class and that she left her family to return to her native land. Much must be forgiven foreigners. It would have been far harder for them had she been English. Christine will do herself no good with them if she pretends to a horror of the connection. Family is to be honored, and if Christine cannot honor her own, the Arundels will doubt that she can honor Justin's."

Rachel knew it was sensible advice, worldly advice, but she could not stifle a feeling of revulsion at the pretense Lady Parminter demanded. "This marriage is important to you, isn't it?"

"As it should be to you. Listen to me, Rachel. Christine is twenty-five. She must have a husband, and she has chosen one who will be a credit to the Melchett name. I don't deny that this is important to me. It is important to Christine as well. Ask her. She's an ambitious young woman. It is even more important that Magnus make a good marriage. I had hoped that you—But you have married a Melchett and that is satisfactory enough. I never expected you to please anyone but yourself."

Rachel felt a wild desire to laugh. She had pleased no one at all, least of all herself. "Yes, I know the marriage is important," Rachel said. "We will do what we can to overcome any new reservations the Arundels may have about the connection, but we cannot answer for our mother."

"You expect her to make a vulgar scene? No, Rachel, I know Arlette. You will not remember, but I saw her several times during her years in England. She was a disreputable little actress in an equally disreputable provincial company when your father plucked her out of obscurity. She was not a great beauty, but even then she had an air about her that was far out of the ordinary. I found her restless and shallow, but she had a splendid talent for mimicry, and she learned quickly how to conduct herself in the fashionable world. Now Arlette is no longer disreputable. She is a reigning actress with the finest company in France and she has acquired powerful friends. Don't be surprised. I have a wide circle of acquaintances and I know these things. Arlette will not disgrace you. If you do not quarrel, if you do not humiliate her, she will play her part and play it very well."

Lady Parminter paused to see that her point was taken. "Now," she continued, "here is what you must do. Magnus must invite your mother to make Parminter House her residence while she remains in London. Then you must introduce her to your friends. A small dinner, I think. The Arundels must be there. I will come, and I suggest you ask the Carnes and the Buckleighs as well. Our family should be well-represented."

"In that case I shall also ask the Fords."

Lady Parminter raised her brows at this open challenge. "As you wish. I will suggest some other names. Not too many: it's hard to manage more than forty at table with any degree of success. Arlette must also accompany you on some of your social engagements. There will be no difficulty about invitations. People will be curious to see the exotic creature who is mother to the Marquis of Parminter."

Rachel saw a look of distaste cross Lady Parminter's face. "You hate this, don't you?"

"Of course I hate it. But the old values are gone and I move, if I must, with the times. Sometimes it is better to bend than to stand rigid against the tide."

Rachel felt a moment of pity for this stubborn old woman who wore her pride like a second skin. "Oh, why don't you give us up? Surely we are not worth the pain."

Lady Parminter gave her a glance that was close to contempt. "You understand nothing. Magnus is the eighth in the Parminter line, and that line must endure. For that I will do anything." Then, giving Rachel a forgiving smile, she suggested they adjourn to the writing room where they could make plans for the dinner.

The following day Arlette Aubert took up residence in Parminter House. She brought with her a maid, a footman, four trunks, a good deal of hand luggage, and an emanation of a complex and expensive perfume. Without seeming to make any effort to do so, Arlette quickly became the lodestar around which their lives revolved. The servants were similarly affected, from the footmen who waited in the hall to the cook and undercooks in the kitchen.

By this time Rachel had become reconciled to the necessity of her mother's presence. She maintained a polite neutrality in her conversations with Arlette and talked only of the present. This served until the day after Arlette's arrival when, stopping by the breakfast parlor after taking her morning meal with the children, Rachel found her mother alone at the table, breaking her fast on coffee and toast. Feeling obliged to stay for a few minutes of conversation, Rachel poured herself a cup of coffee and sat down. And then Arlette asked her what she thought of Sheridan.

A half-hour later they had covered the major plays and playwrights of the past half century, as well as innovations in staging and the problems of theater management in both France and England. Arlette had strong opinions, which she expressed with both discernment and wit, and a wide experience of theater. She was fascinated with the English stage and eager to hear what Rachel had to say. It was only at a pause in the conversation, caused by the entrance of the butler with a pot of fresh coffee, that Rachel realized what her mother had done. They had conversed as two women with common interests and problems and training. Not as mother, not as daughter. Rachel was totally disarmed. And because her guard was down, she was unable to ward off Arlette when she asked to see her grandchildren.

They left the breakfast parlor together and climbed the first two flights of stairs side by side. At the narrower third-floor stairs Rachel went ahead. She was angry with her mother for forcing the issue and with herself for being unable to deny her mother's request. She knew that her anger was unreasonable as was the fear that lay behind it. Arlette was not going to contaminate the children. Besides, Alec and Jessica had a right to know their grandmother, no matter how badly she had behaved.

Still, she would much prefer that this meeting did not take place. At the nursery door she hesitated, then grasped the handle firmly and pushed open the door, allowing Arlette to precede her into the room. Jessica was seated at a low table, her brow furrowed in concentration as her finger moved over the page of a book. Alec was curled up in the window seat with a book of his own. They raised startled faces to the stranger, then got quickly to their feet. "I've brought you a visitor," Rachel said in the most cheerful voice she could manage. She turned to Arlette. "Jessica and Alec. And this is Jenny Alsop, their nurse and companion." Jenny, who had also risen on their entrance, made a quick curtsy. "This is my mother, Arlette Melchett, who has come from France to pay us a visit. She goes now by the name of Arlette Aubert."

"You're our grandmother, aren't you?" Alec said in his customary blunt tone. "I was wondering if you would come to see us."

Arlette took the complaint in stride. "But of course I would come to see you. I only arrived yesterday afternoon and your mother had no time to bring me. And I had already made an engagement for the evening."

Jenny pulled forward a chair for Arlette, then at a signal from Rachel quietly left the room. Alec came forward with apparent reluctance and stood by his sister. Arlette showed no sign of discomposure at the lack of warmth in her reception. "Come here," she said, "let me look at you. I can see you're much like your mother, Jessica. You have her hair and her eyes. And you, Alec, you have her eyes as well, and a little of her stubborn chin. I am very glad to make your acquaintance at last."

"Why did you go away?" Jessica asked. The children knew the bare outlines of the story, though nothing of its wrenching impact on their mother.

Arlette seemed to find the question quite natural. "I was homesick. I was born and raised in France, and I was lonely for it."

"You stayed away," Alec pointed out.

"Ah." Arlette gave a graceful shrug. "There were terrible things happening in my country. Revolution, and then war. War with your own country, too."

Alec was persistent. "Not at first. You could have come back. Did you really mean to stay away?"

Rachel held her breath. The children would see through lies and evasion. But Arlette chose to be honest. "Yes, I did. I was not happy in England, and I was not a very good wife and mother. In France I had a chance to resume my life on the stage. There I have had some success."

Jessica gave her mother an anxious glance. Noting it, Arlette went on, "You must not be surprised, Jessica. Many mothers choose to see little or nothing of their children. But your mother is different. She would not leave you, even if she were unhappy in her marriage. I suspect much of her happiness comes from you."

Alec looked both wary and confused. "We don't want her to be unhappy."

"No, of course you do not. But you must not try too hard to make her happy. Be yourself and your mother will be content."

It was an oppressive conversation. Arlette must have recognized as much, for she said, "Now that is quite enough talk about mothers and children. You must tell me what you like to see in London. I have not been here for so many years that I feel quite a stranger to the city."

They passed a tolerable quarter-hour in this way, and then Arlette rose and said she would not keep the children any longer. "I did not want to outstay my welcome," she told Rachel when they were outside the nursery door. "You need not come down with me. You will want to go back and answer Alec and Jessica's questions about this strange creature who claims to be their grandmother. Grandmother, foh! It is not a title I relish. But I am glad you let me see them. They are appealing children, and you have not allowed them to be stifled. That is to your credit."

Rachel watched Arlette as she moved down the corridor. Her walk was graceful and elegant, as were all her movements. She wore her age lightly, this aging actress. Under other circumstances, Rachel would have admired her. As it was, she could only wonder at the effortless charm her mother had shown with Jessica and Alec. Perhaps it was merely the charm she displayed automatically to everyone. Perhaps it was a form of condescension, a pretense of interest in the commonplace affairs of commonplace people. Or perhaps it was genuine, born of a desire to please or a need to assuage her loneliness. This last was a novel idea, and it caused Rachel to hesitate once more before opening the nursery door and rejoining her children.

They were waiting for her as she knew they would be. "She didn't come back for years and years," Alec said as she entered the door. "Why did she come back now?"

"For Christine's wedding."

"Aunt Christine was a baby when she left. She doesn't even know her. Why would she want to come now? She didn't come to your wedding."

"She didn't know I was getting married," Rachel said, turning aside Alec's question. Perhaps Arlette had come to see Guy, hoping to take him back to France with her. Perhaps she had come because Magnus was now a marquis. Perhaps the news of Christine's marriage had triggered some crazy impulse to find out what had become of her children. "I don't know," Rachel said at last. "I don't know why she came."

"You don't like her, do you?"

"I scarcely know her anymore." It was an evasive answer and Alec knew it.

"I like her," Jessica said before Rachel could say more. "I like the way she smells."

Alec scowled. "How long will she stay?"

"Not long I think. Through the wedding at least." Rachel reached out a hand to her son and then drew it back. "She may not come to England again. You must get to know her while she's here. She's not only your grandmother, she's a leading actress with the Comédie Française, and that means she's a very good actress indeed."

Alec threw himself on the window seat. "I don't see what difference that makes. We'll never see her act."

Rachel stifled a burst of laughter. Oh, Alec, she thought, you already have.

Rachel did not see Arlette alone for the rest of the week. Guy brought her once to the theater, a reasonable act which Rachel, unreasonably, felt as a great intrusion. She let Guy show her mother about, pleading the press of last evening's accounts, and as she left them, she saw Arlette move onto the stage quite as though she owned the entire space. Rachel reminded herself that it was a perfectly natural thing to do. Arlette was that kind of actress.

That afternoon Rachel called on Fiona Carne to consult her about the dinner for her mother. As they sat drinking tea in a sunny and comfortable parlor, Rachel told Fiona about Arlette's arrival and Lady Parminter's subsequent visit. "It was a dreadful shock, having our mother arrive without warning after all those years. After she left, our father refused to have her name spoken, so we didn't talk about her at all." Rachel attempted a smile, then gave it up. "We were so confused and angry. We couldn't understand it."

Fiona's eyes were filled with sympathy. "How confused and angry you must still be. And you've felt obliged to bring her into your house, which must make it infinitely worse."

"Magnus proposed it and Lady Parminter concurred." Rachel picked up her cup, hoping the familiar ritual would calm her. Her heart was beating much more rapidly than it should.

"Families are the very devil at the best of times," Fiona said. "And parents and children are the worst of all. I don't think we ever outgrow the child we were."

"But that's just it," Rachel said with a shock of recognition. "I feel just like a child again, a child whose mother didn't want her." She found the cup was shaking in her hand and she set it down with care. "When I look at my mother, I see nothing but a stranger. What she did to us was wicked, but the memory of it slides off her like water. I can't touch her. I can't reach her. And I can't forgive her." Rachel's hands were now clenched in her lap. She forced herself to loosen them, wondering that she could still control their movement. "And the odd thing is," she went on, catching her breath on something between a laugh and a sob, "I can almost understand what drove her to it."

"I think I know how you feel," Fiona said, "though our situations are quite different. You've lived most of your life with the memory of what your mother did. It was only last year that I learned my mother had found me inconvenient and abandoned me to my father."

"Who refused to acknowledge your legitimacy." Wrapped up in her own anger, Rachel had forgot that Fiona had every bit as much reason to be angry at her parent.

Fiona smiled. "Yes, being a bastard was my particular cross." The smile vanished and she grew thoughtful. "Yet I think our feelings must be much the same. When I was young I knew I was different from other children and that the difference was bad. It's shame, I suppose, the sense that you're worth less than other people. The anger came later, when I learned the full story. My mother was dead and beyond my reach, but my grandmother was alive. It was Lady Parminter who set the course of my life."

"However do you manage it?" Rachel asked, remembering that Fiona and Lady Parminter occupied the same drawing room with no apparent evidence of discord.

Fiona stared into her cup, then set it down carefully on the small table that stood between them. "As for my mother, I never knew her. One cannot hate what one can scarcely imagine. As for my grandmother . . . I don't suppose I will ever forgive Lady Parminter. I understand her, I think. I even pity her for what she has lost by her wrongheadedness, though I doubt I will ever think of her without anger. I'm not that much of a saint." Fiona smiled. "But she no longer seems very important. Gideon is a blessing, as Guy must be for you. My life is too full for hate."

Rachel forced herself to smile in return. She had not told Fiona about Guy's friendship with Arlette nor could she bear to do so now. But the visit brought her a good deal of comfort and she was able to return to Parminter House with the conviction that neither Arlette nor Guy would be allowed to damage her newly found confidence. She would no longer feel a child in her mother's presence. They were two women residing for the moment under the same roof, with some interests in common and some degree of mutual respect. From now on she would be able to meet Arlette with perfect equanimity.

On the day of the dinner party, Guy returned from the theater early and went to the library to make some changes in Act III which was not playing as well as he had expected. He tossed his copy of the play on a writing table, took off his coat, sat down, and picked up a pen. But his thoughts refused to stay with *The Steward's Stratagem.* The last few days had not healed the rift with Rachel. It was his own fault. His efforts to bridge the gulf between Arlette and her children had been a disaster. No, not entirely his fault, for Arlette, now that it was safe to travel between France and England, would have come anyway, driven by curiosity about what had happened to her family. But Guy had encouraged her, thinking that it was time to heal the past, knowing it would be difficult for them all. More difficult than he had dreamed. He feared he had lost Rachel's trust.

He sighed and dipped his pen in the inkpot. But before he could set it to paper, he heard the door open and turned to see his stepson coming toward him. "You told me to tell you," Alec said without preliminaries.

Guy put down his pen and gestured to a chair near the writing table. "Tell me what?"

"My mother," Alec said. "You told me to tell you when she was unhappy."

303

"Ah." Guy leaned forward and clasped his hands between his knees. "What makes you think she's unhappy?"

"I can tell," Alec said. "You made her cry. You weren't supposed to do that."

"No, I wasn't," Guy admitted. It would be Arlette who had brought her to tears, but it would be his own behavior as well, the secrets he had kept because he feared Rachel would never receive her mother if she knew she were coming to England and because he wasn't sure that Arlette would actually come. "I'm sorry, Alec. I'm truly sorry. I didn't want to make her cry. I would give anything to see her happy again." He thought of the painful passage between them after Arlette's arrival. "I've talked to her, you know. I've tried to stop her tears."

"Then you've got to do something else."

"Sometimes these things take a while to work out."

Alec looked at him in silence for what seemed to Guy a very long time. "I don't think you should wait any longer," he said at last and without a backward look got down from the chair and walked out of the library.

Guy watched till the door was closed behind him. He had felt sympathy for Rachel, but impatience as well, for he thought she was creating a hell she had no need to inhabit. Not so with Alec. He had made an uncomplicated demand on his stepfather, and Guy feared he would be unable to meet his stepson's request. And if he did not, he risked losing Alec's trust as well.

That evening as Rachel was going upstairs to dress, Guy intercepted her and asked her what was wrong. Rachel felt a twinge of guilt. Since their quarrel about Arlette, she had not trusted herself alone with her husband. Now she merely said that nothing was wrong and if she seemed preoccupied, it was because she had a great deal to do. Guy stared at her as though searching for someone he had once known, then turned away in frustration. Rachel did not know how to call him back. He had not come to her bed since the night of their quarrel, and she missed him dreadfully. But her longing for him could not wipe out the memory of his deceit. If she had to confront her present feelings toward her husband, she did not know how she would get through the evening, let alone the rest of her life.

They were thirty-six at dinner. The company included three of the suspects in the murder of Edmund Hever: Brandon and Charles, who came with the Fords, and Alfred Billingham, who came with the Arundels. It also included four couples who were acquainted with the Arundels and two others who were friends of Magnus. The aristocracy, the City, and the stage. It was a motley group, but Lady Parminter, setting the tone for the evening, behaved as though these ill-assorted people were no different than those she was accustomed to meeting in the best drawing rooms of London.

Rachel had dressed with care, for she did not intend to be outshone by either her mother or her sister. She had chosen a robe of dark red crêpe over a white satin slip. She wore the pearls Magnus had given her, and her jeweled combs held back the profusion of ringlets in which she had instructed her maid to dress her hair. Guy paid her a surprised compliment, and Brandon, who was accustomed to seeing her in plain garb with a harried expression on her face, expressed his delight at her transformation.

In the half-hour before dinner was announced, Rachel moved through the drawing room, talking with guests and making discreet introductions. Her mother, seated on a rose velvet sofa, accepted these with a modest show of pleasure. However, it was not in her nature to be modest, and her presence shone like a beacon throughout the drawing room. Clad in a celestial blue silk that clung to her still high bosom with perfection, her pale gold hair piled high upon her head, an exceptionally fine set of diamonds glinting at her throat and ears, Arlette was not a woman to be ignored. The candlelight was flattering to her face, and she held her head high, which hid the softening of the skin beneath her chin. Lady Parminter, dressed in the pale lavender that was her preference for evening, sat beside her on the sofa, her presence heightening the impression of Arlette's youthfulness.

The Arundels accepted the introduction with some reluctance, but the duke was quickly charmed. He took a chair near Arlette, whom he addressed as Mademoiselle Aubert, claiming that Mrs. Melchett was much too prosaic a title for such a captivating woman, and proceeded to ask her what had become of Paris, a city he had visited in his youth. Lady Parminter watched the exchange with evident satisfaction.

Guy, standing on the other side of the room, found nothing surprising in the duke's capitulation. He had been captivated himself in the early days of his acquaintance with Arlette, and though he saw her now with clearer eyes, his affection and admiration had not lessened. This was the Arlette he had wished Rachel to know, not the childhood ogre who had turned her back on her daughter. Rachel should know the difference, but she persisted in seeing with the eyes of the past.

Short of denouncing Arlette, which in honor he would not do, there seemed no way to bridge the chasm that had opened between them with Arlette's arrival. Guy could not remember ever feeling so helpless. He missed the easy companionship he had had with Rachel. He also missed her in bed, with an urgency he would not have expected.

Preoccupied with the problem of his wife, Guy did not notice that Christine was by his side until she said, "Rachel's clever with people, isn't she?" Guy turned his attention back to the room and saw that Rachel, with a good deal of tact, had removed the duchess and the other women in the ducal party from the tête-à-tête between the duke and Arlette. "I hope Lady Parminter is satisfied," Christine went on. "She's managed every bit of this evening and she's managing my wedding, too. It does seem unfair that the bride isn't even consulted on the choice of guests."

"Arlette is your mother," Guy reminded her.

Christine shrugged. "That means nothing to me. I don't know her, and I won't have her spoiling my wedding."

"I hardly see how she can do that, Chrissie." Guy looked at her with admiration. She was wearing something soft and clinging in a pale shade of pink that heightened the radiance of her skin. "No one who sees you will have eyes for anyone else."

The compliment pleased her. She leaned toward him a little. He was aware of the delicate scent of her skin, and then, irrationally, he had an image of Rachel lying soft and open beneath him. Guy drew back, breaking the contact between them, and in that moment Justin appeared and laid a proprietary arm around Christine's shoulders. Justin made some comment about Arlette's success with his father, but there was jealousy in his dark eyes as he looked at Guy.

Jealousy, it seemed, was inextricably entwined with love. Guy remembered the depths of his own feelings for Christine and the rages that had consumed him. It was then, terrified by his inability to govern his passions, that he had sworn to never be mastered by love again.

His gaze sought out Rachel as a talisman of safety. She was standing beside Brandon, her hand on his arm, laughing at something he had said. Guy had seen them together so a score of times before and thought nothing of it. Now, with Justin's jealous gaze on him, Guy felt a stirring of the same emotion. Jealous of Brandon's attentions to Rachel? It was so unlikely, so unexpected that Guy replied at random to an inquiry from Christine. Her surprised laughter recalled him to the present and he made some apology for his inattention. But the awareness of these disturbing new feelings for his wife stayed at the edge of his consciousness, and it was with relief that he saw the butler enter the room to announce that dinner was ready.

Rachel found the meal interminable, though she had to admit that the food was exceptionally good, as was the wine, which Magnus chose himself; and the pairing of guests, constrained by issues of rank and precedence and family relationships, was more successful than she had dared hope. Conversation seemed less stilted than usual, and there was a good deal of laughter on the part of the younger members of the party. Rachel longed to be among them, but she was partnered by the duke, who plied her with unwelcome questions about her mother which she answered with as good grace as she could muster. He was drinking more wine than was his custom, and his attentions strayed frequently to the livelier part of the table which was centered around Arlette.

Rachel had sent her mother down to dinner with Samuel Ford, a pairing that she thought quite inspired, for it aroused neither jealousy nor comment on the part of the more exalted guests. Magnus was less fortunate, for he was companioned by the duchess, a proud woman who had little but inconsequential chitchat at her command. She kept a disapproving eye on her husband throughout the meal. Her disapproval extended to her youngest daughter. As a rule, Margaret was hopelessly shy in company, but Rachel had sent her down with Brandon and her diffidence was rapidly vanishing under his attentions. The duchess's tolerance was being severely strained this evening, but fortunately it was the duke's opinion that would matter in the end.

When the ladies rose and returned to the drawing room, Rachel turned her attention to the duchess's niece, whom she had met for the first time that evening. Elizabeth Hever, Dowager Duchess of Arundel and widow of the fourth duke, had only recently come to London. It was her first season after her period of mourning for her husband. She was a pretty woman with intense dark eyes and a pale, discontented face, younger than Rachel by three or four years. She should have been a good companion for Christine, but oddly she seemed to have taken Christine in dislike. Like Rachel, the dowager duchess—a ridiculous title for one so young—had been left a widow with two young children while still in her twenties.

"I meant to be in London sooner," she told Rachel, "but my youngest daughter came down with a rash. Fortunately, it turned out to be nothing but chickenpox."

Rachel, recalling the nightmare fortnight she had spent nursing Alec and Jessica through the disease, was surprised by Elizabeth Hever's choice of words. They spoke of their children for a few minutes; then Elizabeth went on to talk of the delights to be wrung from the remainder of the season.

When Justin joined them, Rachel excused herself and crossed the room to sit by Fiona. "I was so hoping we'd have a few minutes together," Fiona said, making room for Rachel on a small settee. "I find your mother charming, but I know that you do not, so I'll not urge my prejudice upon you. Still,

I fear I must talk about her. I called on the Princess Sofia today, and she could speak of nothing but her dear cousin Sacha. She hasn't seen him in years, but they've corresponded frequently. And now here he is arriving in England, the Emperor of Russia, and she's in transports."

Rachel nodded. The Emperor Alexander's visit might be the event of the Season, but it was the least of her concerns. She was surprised to find Fiona, who had little taste for gossip, paying it such attention.

Fiona adjusted a handsome gold bracelet, a recent gift from her husband. "The thing I must tell you is that dear Sacha saw Mademoiselle Aubert perform in Paris and was quite entranced. When he heard she was bound for London, he wrote the princess, saying that he must see her perform again and praying that she was not here on a private visit."

Rachel felt a sinking feeling in the pit of her stomach. "Oh, no, Fiona, I value your friendship, but you must not ask me that."

"Why not? Well, no, I will not urge it on you. But think, Rachel. Think not as a daughter but as the manager of a small and splendid little theater. It would be quite a coup to have the Emperor attend a performance at the Tavistock."

It *would* be a coup. Rachel was breathless at the audacity of the idea. "Could you guarantee that he would come?" she asked, her practical instincts aroused.

"Yes. Well, almost certainly yes. The princess finds your story very affecting and romantic, and she was charmed by Guy when he came to her reception. She is a woman who can arrange nearly anything."

It was almost too tempting to resist. She need do nothing but decide, then broach the question to Arlette, who would jump at the chance to perform upon an English stage. "I'll think about it," Rachel said, and they went on to talk of other things.

When the gentlemen returned to the drawing room, Rachel excused herself and sought out Samuel Ford. But she knew as soon as he had given an enthusiastic endorsement of the idea that her decision was already made. No matter what Samuel said—and she valued his opinion highly—she had every intention of asking Arlette to perform at the Tavistock.

Rachel felt strangely buoyant, and it took her a minute to realize that she had taken Fiona's words to heart. She looked toward the fireplace where Arlette was seated among a group of the duke's friends and saw not her mother but a woman of obvious charm whose talents might prove useful to the enterprise around which Rachel had centered her life. She felt, in that moment, the equal of Arlette Aubert. She would use Arlette for her own ends, as Arlette would undoubtedly use her. She was a match for the woman who had borne her, and she would never feel unworthy again.

It was in this spirit that she approached her mother and detached her from her admirers with the excuse that Lady Carne had something of moment to tell her. Arlette did not hide her pleasure at Fiona's report of the Emperor's admiration. The Emperor had sent her a charming note after his visit to the Comédie Française, but she had not expected that his regard would extend to a wish to see her perform again. It was a pretty and modest speech, which she made without once looking at Rachel. Rachel did not miss her cue. Her offer was made quickly and quickly accepted, so quickly that she was sure Arlette had had it in mind. Was this Guy's doing, too? Rachel felt a stab of resentment, but it quickly passed. Whether Guy had wished it or not, it was she who had made the decision. She had come to terms with her mother on her own.

Guy, watching the tête-à-tête between the three women, could not be but pleased. Yet bringing Rachel and her mother together no longer seemed as important as it had when Arlette first broached the idea of attending her youngest daughter's wedding. Something had happened to Rachel tonight. For the past few days she had wrapped herself in a cloak of self-sufficiency that kept everyone at bay, but tonight she was different. Self-sufficient, yes, but added to this was a radiant confidence that marked her as someone out of the ordinary. Brandon had noticed it, as had the duke and several of the other men in the company. Guy felt a surge of pride in his wife, accompanied by a return of the jealousy he had felt while watching her with Brandon before dinner. Jealousy had no place in their companionable marriage, nor did the grosser stupidities of love, though in truth they were happy enough in bed. Happy? The word seemed wholly inadequate to describe what was between them there. Guy was conscious of a vague unease. He was on a ship that had lost its course, a dangerous place for a man who always knew where he was going.

As he did whenever his feelings threatened, Guy took refuge in the affairs of others. The first person to hand was Frances Billingham, who was seated some distance from the group surrounding Arlette with no one nearby to talk to. She welcomed him with a warmth that could only be accounted for by her temporary isolation. Guy had been no particular friend of Billingham, and Frances had deplored her husband's association with the Levellers. But Guy was now a Parminter, or at least a Parminter cousin, and Frances had apparently decided that he was respectable.

Lady Frances was a pretty woman, resembling her younger sister Margaret in features and coloring, but unlike Margaret she had given her mother no cause for concern. She had been only eighteen when she married Billingham, and the match had been seen as quite acceptable for a girl of limited dowry, even if her father was uncle to a duke. But since her father's accession to the title, Frances had become very conscious of her position and of the lack of progress in her husband's career. "He should be given a place," she told Guy, her voice holding a touch of petulance. "He has been absolutely loyal to the party, and though his family lack a title, they are beyond reproach."

"And then there is his connection to your own family," Guy said, unable to resist teasing her a little.

She took him quite seriously. "Of course, and that should count for something. I've asked Papa repeatedly to do something for Alfred, but he keeps putting me off. He's exercised by Justin's wedding and now, with the investigation into Edmund's—" She broke off. "Then there's the matter of Christine's mother," she went on quickly, "though it does not seem that will count for anything. Mama's quite upset about it, but she does whatever Papa says. And as if that weren't enough, there's this idiotic fuss about Alfred's ward."

Guy raised his brows. "Alfred seems scarcely old enough to have a ward. Is it a boy or girl?"

"A young man, and just come of age. Alfred's father originally had him in charge, and I'm sure he managed his estate very well, just as Alfred has done. I know that he's spent an inordinate amount of time on the affair, and it's quite ungrateful of the young man to claim that—" She threw up her hands in a gesture of helplessness.

"I suppose it's about money."

"Of course it's about money, what else do such people have to think about? It's very tiresome. Alfred says it's all a misunderstanding and it's bound to come right, but it seems dreadfully unfair that he should be plagued so."

Guy murmured some soothing words, hoping she could be persuaded to say more on the subject, but she had exhausted this particular grievance. He turned the conversation to more agreeable topics, all the while thinking of what she had said. It made sense of the quarrel that Lady Margaret had overheard between her brother-in-law and Edmund. Alfred Billingham was a man of ambition and his wife wished to cut a great figure in society. They must have gone into debt. What more natural than that Alfred should borrow or speculate with his ward's money. If Edmund had got wind of it, Guy doubted he would have had any qualms about using the information to get money from his brother-in-law.

Guy continued to make polite conversation with Lady Frances until she was carried away to make up a fourth at a whist table requested by Lady Parminter. This left him free to think about the murder and to wish fervently that the guests would take a decently early departure. He needed to talk to Rachel.

But Rachel was occupied with her guests, and Guy did not see her alone until she left the drawing room to go to bed. It was natural for him to follow her. He had done so often enough, but that was before Arlette's arrival had changed everything between them. Rachel climbed the stairs a little ahead of him, reserved and elusive. Guy said nothing until

312

they reached her bedroom door. "I've learned something. I need to talk to you."

Rachel looked up at him as if seeking the message behind his words. Guy would have told her he intended no more than what he said, but the words caught in his throat. Whatever his intentions, he wanted far more, and as on their wedding night, he could not allow himself to reach out and take it.

Apparently satisfied, Rachel nodded and opened the door, and for the first time since their quarrel on the day Arlette arrived, Guy stepped into his wife's room. Rachel dismissed her maid, then turned and looked directly at her husband, her face without expression. He wondered if she saw the longing in his eyes, but her gaze held nothing but a mild curiosity. "I'm exhausted," she said, "but it must be important. What is it you've learned?"

Chapter Nineteen

Rachel was standing before the white plaster fireplace, her dark red gown falling in regal folds about her, her jeweled combs glittering coldly in the candlelight. Guy had a sudden image of sinking his fingers into her elaborate coiffure, tearing the elegant gown from her body, and taking her there on the Savonnerie carpet.

"I had a long talk with Frances Billingham." Pleased to discover that his voice was still his to command, Guy leaned against the back of a chair which created a barrier between them and hid his arousal from her view. "She's a talkative young woman and not nearly as sensible as Lady Margaret. I learned any number of details of the Billingham family, including some about a young ward of Billingham's who recently came of age." Guy sketched the story as he had had it from Lady Frances, leaving Rachel to draw her own conclusions.

Rachel's eyes widened. "Blackmail," she said softly.

"It seems likely. Edmund rarely thought of anyone but himself. If he needed money badly enough, I doubt he'd have caviled at threatening his brother-in-law to get it."

"The question is," Rachel said, "would Billingham have caviled at murdering Edmund to ensure his safety?"

"If he was angry enough or desperate enough—Oh, yes, I don't doubt that he might. Whether or not he did is another matter."

Rachel rubbed her gloved arms and Guy knew the chill she felt was emotional as much as physical. He longed to comfort her, but when she spoke her voice was brittle, holding him at bay. "In other words, we're still at a standstill." She moved to her dressing table and stripped off her pearl necklace and earrings. The candles in the crystal candelabra which stood on either side of the looking glass burnished her hair like a flame, just as the sunlight had that afternoon in her sitting room when she asked him to marry her. It was then he had first known he desired her. Dear God, how could he have been so blind for so long? Desire was far too paltry a name for what he felt now. He was consumed by a need stronger than anything he had known before and he could give it only one name. Rachel.

"I made an interesting discovery tonight," Rachel said, deliberately laying her wedding band beside her other jewelry. "The Princess Sofia told Fiona that her cousin, the Emperor Alexander, saw Arlette when he was in Paris and that he was quite captivated by her."

"That's hardly surprising. She captivated half the men in the city." Guy spoke at random, his thoughts a league away. Even as one part of his mind screamed he should leave at once for both their sakes, another said it was already too late.

Rachel looked over her shoulder at Guy, something like challenge in her eyes. "I asked Arlette to perform a piece after *The Steward's Stratagem*. I hope you don't mind."

Her words would have shocked him in any circumstances. In his present state Guy could merely gape at her in astonishment.

"Oh, dear," Rachel said, pulling off her gloves, "*do* you mind? I think the play is quite good enough to stand on its own. You needn't fear it will be overshadowed."

"No, I confess I'm far too arrogant." Guy managed to smile while he gathered his scattered wits. "It will do wonders for the Tavistock if the Emperor attends the performance. I congratulate you. And I'm delighted you and Arlette have reached some sort of accommodation."

Rachel's eyes hardened and her generous mouth drew into a thin line. "I haven't made an accommodation about anything. I've learned to make the best of the circumstances in which I find myself."

315

This ice-cold bitterness was worse than her anger on the day Arlette arrived. Guy wanted to stride across the room and break the barrier between them with his kisses, but he knew that was no kind of answer. "You aren't going to forgive me, are you?" His grip on the marquetry chair back tightened, but he kept his voice soft.

"It's not a question of forgiving, Guy." Rachel's voice held an undercurrent as fine and implacable as a steel rapier. "I used to think I knew you better than anyone on earth. I'll never feel that way again."

"God in heaven, Rachel," Guy exclaimed, the words wrung from him, "don't you know I'd never hurt you?"

Rachel lifted her chin, accentuating the proud line of her throat. "There's no telling what any of us might do, given the right provocation."

"True enough," Guy said, holding his voice steady. "We can only try not to hurt each other. But if we don't try, we'll lose everything we have."

Something snapped in the smoky depths of Rachel's eyes. "What we have is one part illusion and two parts convenience, Guy. Don't pretend otherwise."

For some reason this hurt him more than anything she had said thus far. "Just what is it you're accusing me of, Rachel? Making a friend of Arlette Aubert?"

"You have the right to make a friend of whomever you choose. In fact, you have the right to do a good deal more. It's no business of mine whom you take to bed. You said so yourself."

Guy winced. "I was talking about the time before our marriage."

"But our marriage wasn't supposed to change anything." Rachel's voice was bright, artificial, and razor sharp. "We agreed on that the day you accepted my proposal. You're quite free to sleep with whomever you choose. You must be sure to remind me if I ever forget." She turned and moved toward the fireplace as if she had just delivered a curtain line.

Guy reacted on pure instinct. In three strides he breached the distance between them and seized her by the arm. "God damn it, Rachel, I won't let this happen to us."

316

Rachel's eyes flew to his face, no longer cold but filled with a turmoil which echoed his own. Guy heard her quick gasp, felt the warmth of her breath, drank in the subtle, sweet fragrance of her scent. Honor, trust, fidelity, betrayal. They all faded to nothing beside his consuming need of her. He breathed her name, a last gasp of sanity, an entreaty for permission, a plea for forgiveness. Then he sank his fingers into her hair and covered her mouth with his own.

He was parched and she was water. He was drowning and she was land. Her hair was silk in his fingers, her lips warm and willing beneath his own. Hunger coursed through his veins, sharper than lust, sweeping aside all reason. Or almost all. It was the very knowledge of his loss of control which dragged him back from the verge of madness. God in heaven, he was behaving like a mindless, rutting animal, no better than Edmund Hever. It took every ounce of willpower he possessed, but Guy raised his head and drew back.

Rachel's hair fell about her face in glorious disarray. Her lips were wet from the kiss, her eyes dark with intensity, her skin flushed with desire. Guy tore his gaze away from her face and saw one of her combs glowing against the carpet where it had fallen during their embrace. He drew a shaky, painful breath and tried to speak, but Rachel forestalled him. "For God's sake, don't talk," she said, laying her hand over his lips. "Not now."

"Rachel." If he continued looking over her shoulder, he could manage to speak. "Dear heart, I don't think I can—"

"I don't want you to." Her voice was as harsh as her breathing. "I don't want to talk, I don't want to think. We need each other. That's all that matters."

One look at her face and he was lost. With a groan, he crushed her to him, kissing her lips, her eyes, her hair, fumbling frantically with her clothes. He vaguely recalled that there was an art to undressing a woman, so that each article of clothing was effortlessly smoothed away, so that each loosened ribbon and clasp became a prelude to the act of love. Any such skill had quite deserted him. Without knowing quite how he had done it, he managed to unfasten her robe. He tried to loosen her underdress and found himself cupping her breasts, taut with desire beneath the thin fabric.

More nimble than he, Rachel had already stripped off his cravat and unbuttoned his coat and waistcoat. She tugged at his sleeves and they stumbled toward the bed together, shedding her robe and his coat in the process, and collapsed upon the coverlet. Her breasts were pressed against his chest, her legs were parted beneath him. He pulled at her underdress, hearing the fabric give way. Soft as the satin was, her skin was softer. He covered her breasts with his hands and then his lips, lost in the sensation, aware that it was not enough for either of them. Rachel gave a sob of mingled pleasure and need as he pushed up her skirt and touched the burning flesh of her inner thighs.

Overwhelmed by his own need, Guy drew back and fumbled with his breeches. His hands were shaking, but when Rachel tried to help, her touch enflamed him almost beyond endurance. At last she lifted her hips and guided him into her, and the last fragments of his reason shattered to bits. He tried to move in some sort of rhythm, but his body was beyond his control. Rachel arched against him and he thrust into her, filled with a desperate longing for something more potent and powerful than physical release. He heard Rachel's sharp cry and felt her convulse around him, and then he was shuddering, straining her to him, gasping her name, lost in intensity as his own body exploded, yet never more aware of the woman he held in his arms.

For a long time after, Guy was conscious of nothing but the warmth of Rachel's body, the ragged movement of her chest, and the uneven sound of her breathing. His own breath was muffled by her hair and by the pillow beneath it. Their bodies were still joined and he could feel every inch of her, save that they were both wearing their stockings and his breeches were tangled around his ankles. And there seemed to be something wrapped around Rachel's waist. Something too soft and slippery to be a sheet. Her underdress. Consciousness returned in a sickening flood. Christ, he hadn't even taken the trouble to undress her properly. Never before had he lost control like that, not even in his distant youth when his enthusiasm had far outweighed his skill.

318

Guy pushed himself up on his elbows and looked down at his wife. Her head was turned a little to one side, and though she was not smiling, she looked serene and peaceful. Her eyes were closed but as he watched her they flickered open.

"I'm sorry," Guy said softly. "No," he amended, smiling in spite of himself, "that sounds ridiculous. I'm not sorry it happened. But I'm sorry if you'd rather it hadn't."

"As I recall," said Rachel, echoing his smile, "I was the one who insisted. You certainly didn't force me."

"No, I may be a bit mad, but I'm not"—Guy hesitated, wondering for an appalled moment just how far that madness could drive him—"I don't think I'd be capable of that."

"I know you wouldn't be." Rachel reached up and smoothed the hair off his forehead. "I don't think I could have waited much longer."

"But it doesn't change anything, does it?" Guy asked, studying her gravely.

Rachel smiled again, but this time the smile was without mirth. "Lovemaking has little to do with solving problems. I learned that when I was married to Cadogan."

It was bad enough that she mentioned Cadogan at all. To have her compare their present difficulties with the hell her first marriage had been was as stinging as any blow. Hurt and jealous and angry at himself for it, Guy pulled away from her and rolled onto his side.

Rachel turned to look at him. "We need to talk," she said. "I've put it off for too long."

Her eyes were wide and concerned, and they seemed to see far too much. Guy felt a moment of panic. Talk? Now when he was shaken and cast adrift in an uncharted sea? When a simple reference to the man who had once been his friend could stir a torrent of jealousy? When his feelings for Rachel, which had always seemed so blessedly clear, had become so inexplicably complex and overwhelming?

"You're right," he said, sitting up. "But for that sort of talk we'll both require clear heads. If I stay tonight, I fear it's not talking we'll be doing."

Rachel pushed herself up on her elbow and tossed back her

hair, unashamed of her nakedness. "Perhaps," she suggested, "we need to do that, too."

Her eyes filled with an irresistible invitation, she reached up to pull him down beside her. Guy laughed in capitulation and relief and fell back against the bed, pressing her into the pillows. Conscious thought could wait till morning. There was something to be said for madness.

Rachel woke to find herself alone in the vast, silk-draped bed. For the first time Guy had come to her bed and not stayed the whole night. She sat up and saw that her robe, underdress, and stockings lay neatly folded at the foot of the bed. Thoughtful of him, but she would have preferred to have him here beside her. Rachel reached out to touch the imprint of his head in the pillow, savoring her memories of the night before. They had resolved nothing, but for the first time Guy's hunger had matched her own. He might not love her, but he had wanted her with an intensity which went beyond generosity or pleasure. It was more than she had ever thought to have.

When she dressed and went up to the nursery for breakfast, Rachel learned that Guy had already looked in on the children but had left early for the theater. For an alarmed moment Rachel feared he had been foolish enough to return to his old practice of walking to the Tavistock, but Jessica told her he had been going to drive with Uncle Magnus. It was nice that Guy and Magnus were on friendly enough terms to share a carriage, but somewhat daunting that her husband felt easier in her brother's company than in her own.

When she arrived at the Tavistock, Rachel found Guy on stage, deep in conversation with Harper. Deciding she would prefer not to know what the problem was, Rachel went into her office to look over the receipts from the evening before. By the time she returned to the wings half an hour later, the murky light of the rehearsal lamps revealed a scene of furious activity. Patrick was bawling orders to two of the younger stagehands who were trying to position an elaborate arrangement of papier-mâché, painted to represent the rocks where

Corisande stood during the fight. One of the seamstresses bustled by, her mouth full of pins and her arms full of Brandon's first-act costume. Three young dancers who performed in the masquerade scene were doing pliés on the opposite side of the stage, their white skirts standing out in the dim light. Gerald Sneath and young Sally Lewis, who played Corisande's youngest sister, were perched on the edge of the stage running through a scene. Ned Acorn and Polly Eakin were doing the same up stage right, half-hidden behind a canvas flat and a rack of costumes. Guy stood in the midst of the chaos talking earnestly to Ralph Hemdale. He took no notice of his wife's arrival, but Brandon, who was leaning against the proscenium arch, holding a rapier and looking rather bored, smiled at her. Cecily got up from her chair — a much-used set piece recently given a new coat of gilt paint — and joined Rachel in the wings. "It may not look it," she said, "but it really is coming along quite splendidly."

"Ralph still can't get the hang of the fight." Brandon strolled over to the women, the rapier held negligently in one hand. "The fellow's just not a born swordsman. Remember *Romeo and Juliet?* One night he was standing in the wrong place, so I got him in the arm instead of the chest. It's the first time Tybalt's ever died from a wound to the elbow."

Cecily gave him one of her enchanting smiles. "If you think that's going to happen this time, you're underestimating Guy. I vow, your husband could manage anything, Rachel."

"Yes, he's quite damnably efficient," Brandon said, flexing the rapier idly.

Cecily looked sharply at him, then turned to Rachel. "Guy's decided I don't have to wear the wig, which is a great relief."

The thought that Corisande would not be quite as much a replica of Christine was absurdly satisfying, but before Rachel could speak, there was a sharp gasp from upstage and a roar of "Look out!" in Patrick's unmistakable accents. Rachel spun round in time to see Guy fall headlong to the floorboards, pulling Ralph down beside him. At the same moment there was a deafening crash as a dark object hit the stage exactly where Guy had been standing.

It happened so fast that Rachel scarcely had a chance to be frightened. By the time she realized that her husband had narrowly escaped being crushed under a hundred-pound bag of sand, Guy had scrambled to his feet and was offering a hand to Ralph. As she hurried toward him, his eyes met her own, warning her against saying anything which might further upset the company. "Thank goodness you have quick reflexes," Rachel said in the brisk voice she used when she didn't want Alec and Jessica to realize she was alarmed. "Are you all right, Ralph?"

Brushing the dust from his coat, the normally swaggering Ralph gave a shaky nod. Now that the first shock was over, there was a medley of questions and explanations as everyone within earshot rushed across the stage or out of the wings. "Bloody hell," Patrick said, surveying the sandbag, which had broken on impact, scattering coarse sand on the recently scrubbed boards. "I told them to check the ropes every night. Jem," he barked to the nearest of the stage-hands, "go up and be sure none of the rest are likely to fall on our heads."

Jem nodded and raced off through the crowd. Cecily gave a dramatic shiver and glanced up into the darkness toward the bridge. "I never did like that horrid contraption. This settles it, Rachel. I don't want to play Titania next season."

"Not a pleasant way to go," Brandon agreed. He looked at Guy. "Better you than me, old fellow."

"Thank you, Brandon," Guy said pleasantly. "I'm sure we all share the sentiment. What a lucky thing it didn't fall on the rocks. Prentice has done us proud. I want to rehearse the fight with them."

"Not until we've made sure of the rest of the sandbags." Rachel urged the milling crowd downstage and out of harm's way. Harper and his assistant had just emerged from the carpenter shop, and the questions were beginning all over again.

"See anything, Jem?" Patrick called as the others clustered together on the proscenium.

"No, sir." Jem's voice floated down out of the darkness, thin and ghostly in the high-ceilinged building. "Unless—Oh, Lord."

"What is it?" Rachel asked, moving upstage to stand beside Patrick.

Jem's voice seemed to deepen with the gravity of the situation. "That rope didn't fray. It was cut."

Christine unfurled a parasol of primrose-colored sarcenet, settled back against the squabs of Justin's luxuriously fitted curricle, and tried to recapture the glow of being the Marquis of Parminter's sister, the Earl of Deaconfield's betrothed, and the future Duchess of Arundel. Justin was a superlative whip, and his matched grays were as fine as any pair in the park. It was of course very pleasant to be seated beside him at the fashionable hour of five o'clock and to know that any number of people were watching them simply because of who they were. But today the sun seemed exceptionally hot, the path exceptionally dusty, and the idea of driving about a prescribed area at precisely the time when it was bound to be most crowded more than a little absurd. Nor did she view the prospect of Lady Windham's rout this evening with any more enthusiasm. With the Emperor Alexander's arrival, she ought to find the London social whirl more exhilarating than ever, but the novelty was losing its edge. Her mother's disconcerting reappearance had only made matters worse. While it was a great relief that Arlette's arrival had not caused a rift with the Arundels, it was not at all pleasant to find herself competing for attention with a woman who was nearly thirty years her senior.

And then there was Guy. Christine nodded and smiled automatically at Francesca Warwick, who drove her own phaeton and was considered rather dashing, and then murmured a polite greeting to a sporting acquaintance of Justin's who had pulled up his horse to discuss the Ascot races. Guy was the real problem, the core of her discontent. The night he was wounded she had been genuinely terrified. For a few crazy minutes nothing had seemed as important as her feeling for him. Even when it was clear he would recover, it had not been the same, not for her and not for Justin. Though he had said nothing, Christine knew her betrothed had not forgot the harsh words she had uttered in her distress.

In the wake of the incident, Guy seemed more distant than ever. There was a time when she had known instinctively that he followed her about with his eyes whenever she was in the room. But last night he had been looking not at her but at her sister. His wife.

"Are you feeling all right, my dear?" As his friend rode off, Justin set the horses in motion again.

"Of course. Why shouldn't I be?"

"You're unusually quiet. Oh, Lord, there's Lady Buckleigh with that insipid sister of hers. Don't let her catch your eye. She may be your cousin, but I'm in no mood to humor family."

Justin steered an expert path through the maze of carriages and horses, his eyes fixed straight ahead until they were almost level with Lady Buckleigh's landaulet. Then he turned with a nod of acknowledgement which was perfectly civil but allowed no opportunity for conversation. It was a masterful performance and at one time Christine would have found it diverting. Now it seemed rather silly. Guy would not waste his energies on such games.

Justin would expect her to say something clever but her head was beginning to throb and she could not think. Seeking diversion, she scanned the path ahead. "Oh look, Justin, there's Philip Weston. Do stop. I haven't talked to him in an age."

"As you wish."

Despite his injury, Philip still sat a horse admirably. Christine extended her hand, delighted to see someone from her old life.

"Lady Christine." Philip reined in his horse and tipped his hat. "Deaconfield."

Justin inclined his head. "Your servant, Weston."

The formality of this exchange made Christine smile. "Don't be stuffy," she said, tapping Philip on the wrist. "I own I quite like being called Lady Christine but not by an old friend."

Philip's serious face relaxed into a smile. "When you look so grand it's hard to think of you as anything else."

"Dear Philip," Christine said, feeling her spirits lighten. "I can always rely on you to pay me the nicest compliments. You must call at Parminter House sometime soon. We don't see nearly enough of you."

Philip seemed surprised by the invitation. "That's kind of you, Christine. I wasn't sure—Thank you. At any event," he continued, making an effort to recover himself, "I shall see you both Saturday night. My parents have taken a box at the Tavistock."

Justin raised his brows. "Decided to forgive Guy, have you?" he inquired.

Philip flushed but regarded Justin steadily. "I was wrong about a number of things."

"Yes, you can hardly blame him for the explosion now, can you?" Justin said in a voice of detached interest. "As for my brother's death, I suppose we all share the honor of being suspects."

"Justin." Christine looked sharply at her betrothed. She knew Bow Street had an investigation underway, but she refused to believe that it could lead to anyone of her acquaintance.

"He's right, Christine," Philip said quietly. "I'd give the world for this to be over. I hate to think it might cause you pain."

"Thank you, Philip." Christine pressed his hand and held it for a moment. "It's at times like this one really needs one's friends. You must come to Parminter House after the performance on Saturday," she continued, determined not to dwell on any unpleasantness. "Rachel's invited the company over, and we're asking a few close friends as well. We shall be very informal."

"I'd be delighted." Philip reined in his horse which had grown restive. "Give my regards to Rachel. And to Guy."

Christine smiled happily as he said his farewells and rode off. Despite the disquieting reminder of Edmund's death, the conversation had put her in better spirits. She adjusted her parasol to a more flattering angle and smiled at a young officer on a splendid bay. She could not quite remember his name but she had danced with him at the Davenports' two nights before.

Justin flicked the whip and set the horses in motion again. His expression was set and rather cold, but Christine did not pay it particular attention until she realized he was turning the curricle toward the Grosvenor Gate. "Where are we going?" she asked, though in truth it was a relief to be away from the churning dust and the incessant clop of hooves.

In answer, Justin pulled the horses up and addressed his groom. "Walk back to Arundel House and wait for me, Miles."

"Very good, my lord." Miles's voice conveyed no expression whatsoever. When the groom had dismounted, Justin drove on to the seclusion of a grove of trees near the reservoir. It occurred to Christine that he was very likely going to kiss her, which was a pity as she was not at all in the mood for it, but when he finally turned to her, his eyes were blazing not with passion but with fury.

"Must you flirt outrageously with every man who comes within a mile of you?" he demanded in a harsh voice she had never heard him use before.

Christine stared at him. "Justin, you can't possibly be jealous of Philip." The idea was so absurd she could not help but laugh.

"Don't play the innocent with me, Christine," Justin said, his eyes hard. "The man's been in love with you for years."

Christine had learned long since that her betrothed was no stranger to passion, but he had never spoken to her with anything but tenderness and solicitude. The anger in his eyes and the tension in his shoulders revealed a side of him she had never seen. "For heaven's sake, Philip's only a boy," she protested. "And he's an old friend. If you sent Miles off just to tell me that—"

"I sent Miles off because I think it past time we reached an understanding, Christine."

Such serious words in response to something as trifling as her talk with Philip struck Christine as rather funny. "I thought we already had an understanding," she retorted.

"We're to be married a week from tomorrow."

"We are indeed." Justin regarded her in silence, but there was a watchful intensity in his gaze that made her shiver despite the warmth of the sun. "If you believe you can continue to go on as you are after we are married, you are very much mistaken."

"Meaning that after we're married you don't want me to talk to Philip in Hyde Park?" Christine no longer found the conversation humorous, but she kept her voice deliberately light.

"Meaning that after we are married you will conduct yourself in a manner befitting the future Duchess of Arundel."

"Oh, that." Christine was stung by the imputation that she might not know how to conduct herself. "Then you're merely asking me to be discreet."

Justin seized hold of her wrist with a lightning quickness that took her by surprise. "Look at me, Christine, and believe what I say. You won't only be the future Duchess of Arundel, you will be my wife. And I'll kill any man who dares touch you. I may never have your love, but by God I intend to have your fidelity."

Too stunned and angry to speak, Christine could only stare pointedly at Justin's hand which was crushing the delicate yellow fabric of her spencer. At length, Justin removed his hand and it was he who finally ventured to speak. "Christine—"

"I would like to go home, Justin," Christine said, staring straight in front of her. "If you won't drive me at once, I shall walk."

"As you wish." Justin's voice was impassive, but Christine could hear the tension beneath it. He turned the horses around and they drove off in silence, the only sound the crunch of the wheels and the clop of the horses' hooves. Christine adjusted the sleeve of her spencer with care, not once risking a glance at her betrothed's face. Justin had always been possessive. She had found it flattering and rather exciting. But this irrational jealousy and highhanded belief that he could order her life were something very different. Her amusing betrothed suddenly seemed about to turn into

327

an insufferable husband. Did he think to order who she might and might not have as a friend? Would he forbid her to see Philip? Would he forbid her to see Guy?

At this last thought Christine went cold. As on the night Guy had been wounded, all the extraneous details of her life faded into insignificance. With sudden, shattering clarity she saw the mistake she had come perilously near to making, and she knew, beyond doubt, what mattered most.

Neither she nor Justin spoke until he turned into the forecourt of Parminter House. Christine murmured the hastiest of farewells, sprang down from the curricle without assistance, and hurried up the front steps. Scarce thinking of the impression she created, she demanded that Thomas tell her Mr. Melchett's whereabouts. Learning he was in the library, she crossed the hall and threw open the doors. Guy, who was seated at the desk where he frequently worked, turned round at her entrance. The sight of his face reinforced Christine's conviction of the rightness of her action. "Oh, my darling," she said without preamble. "I have so very nearly ruined everything. Can you ever forgive me?"

Guy, who had been working on some last-minute adjustments to the fifth act and thinking about the incident with the sandbag, stared at Christine in astonishment. Her color was high, her eyes brilliant. Her words could not mean what they seemed to imply, yet no other explanation was credible. "Hullo, Chrissie," he said, getting to his feet and playing for time. "I didn't expect you back so soon."

"Don't fence with me, Guy. Not now. This is too important." With a swish of silk, Christine was at his side, holding his hands, looking up into his face with wide, determined, incredibly blue eyes. "We belong together. I see that now. I was blind to ever deny it."

They were the words Guy had once longed to hear. Christine was here before him, looking into his face, asking to be kissed, as he had imagined her countless times in the past. For a moment, the pull of that old vision was so strong that he actually tightened his clasp on her hands. Guy drew a breath. He was going to have to move very carefully. "You've quarreled with Justin," he said in a matter-of-fact voice.

"Justin is a jealous, possessive beast," Christine said with feeling. "He has no right to order my life. And to get angry at Philip Weston of all people. Dear, sweet Philip. As soon as I saw him, I knew how much I longed for the old life. Thank God I came to my senses before the wedding."

Whatever she and Justin had quarreled about, it must have been serious. She would get over it, of course. And even if she did not, there was only one course of action possible. "You're forgetting something, aren't you?" Guy said gently. "All other considerations aside, I'm a married man."

Christine's eyes darkened momentarily, then she gave an impatient shake of her head. "You don't love Rachel. She knows that. We can go away together. Back to Paris. Or to America. I don't care as long as I'm with you."

Guy disengaged his hands from her clasp and took her by the shoulders. "This is madness, Christine. You'd hate such a life and you know it."

"I wouldn't," she said with a violence which reminded him of a much younger Christine. "If I have to spend another day seeing the same people and doing the same things, I shall go mad. I want to live among real people again. We can even stay in London. I thought none of your friends believed in marriage anyway."

"I believe in it," Guy said quietly. "I made promises to your sister and nothing on earth will make me go back on them."

Something in his tone must have got through to Christine. She stared at him for a long moment and then her face crumpled. "You can't," she insisted. "You can't make us both suffer just because I was too foolish to see how much you meant to me. You're the only man who's ever understood me. Oh, God, Guy, what am I going to do?"

The sight of her tear-streaked face undid him. This was not an act. Christine's sobs were real and heartfelt, and they brought all Guy's protective instincts to the fore. "All right, Chrissie," he said, gathering her to him and stroking her hair. "It's never quite as bad as it seems."

Christine made no response and for a long time they stood without moving. Guy refused to let himself think, refused to let himself consider that Christine's offer had been anything more than a reaction to a quarrel with Justin. The only way to get through a moment like this was to hold all feeling at bay. At length, when her sobs had quieted, he raised his head, intending to put her from him. But as he looked across the room, he went completely still. Christine had not closed the doors behind her, and standing in the doorway, her face wiped free of emotion, was the woman for whom he had sworn to forsake all others.

Chapter Twenty

Rachel went at once to her room, unable to face either her husband or her sister. She knew she should not be surprised. Christine had grown more and more indiscreet in her attentions to Guy, and Guy—Guy still loved Christine, no matter what he claimed or believed. The sight of them together, the way his head had bent to hers, the way his arms had encircled her body told Rachel it was true. She knew it, she had always known it, and she could not believe how much it hurt.

She looked at her bed and imagined flinging herself upon it and giving way to her grief, but it wasn't grief she felt. She turned instead toward the window where the afternoon sun was making patterns of light on the carpet and pressed her face against the glass, hoping its warmth would drive the chill from her body. She remembered the words her sister had spoken. Christine was ready to break her engagement and run off with Guy. It had been a wild, impulsive declaration. Christine might change her mind before the hour was up. But then she might not. Rachel had been wrong. She had sworn to Guy that it would not happen, that Christine would never be his. And then she had trapped him so that it could never come to pass. Guy would not leave her now, but he would spend every day of his life wishing their marriage had never taken place.

Rachel pushed herself away from the window. Her face was overheated despite the chill in her body, and her head was throbbing. She was not even angry. Guy could no more help loving Christine than Rachel could help loving him. She was terrified of losing him. His last brush with death had washed away the final traces of the resentment Arlette's visit had aroused. Rachel loved him, and she could not bear to see him unhappy.

We'll get an annulment, she thought, pacing the room. No, we can't, we've slept together. We were together last night. Even the servants must know. A divorce? Guy would have to charge me with adultery, and I will not go through that. She came to a halt by the bedpost and clung to it, hoping to still her raging thoughts. There was no way out for them. Or none that her unquiet mind could see.

She was still standing there when she heard the knock. "Come in," she called, turning to the door that led to her husband's room. She did not want to see him, but she was glad that he had come.

Guy closed the door and came toward her, not too close, but close enough that she could see the light glinting in his eyes. "I'm sorry you had to witness that scene."

"Why?" she asked, her voice steady. "It happened. Would you keep it a secret?"

"I would have told you. You know that I would." When Rachel made no response, he went on, "Christine quarreled with Justin. She was in a passion. She came looking for someone to tell about it and found me. I think anyone else would have done as well."

Guy was being naive. Rachel was sure that Christine had sought him out, that he had been in her thoughts from the moment she entered the house. She said nothing and waited for him to continue.

"She swore she would not go through with the marriage." Guy smiled, a tight ironic grimace. "Justin is a jealous possessive beast and she cannot bear to spend her life with him. She's tired of the people she sees and tired of the life she leads. She wants to live among real people again. I gather the quarrel began when they stopped to talk to Philip Weston. Christine said that Philip is real. Justin is not, and he took exception to the comparison."

Rachel waited for him to tell her what else Christine had

said. Perhaps he didn't intend to tell her everything. He wouldn't know how much she had overheard.

To her relief, Guy was honest. "You know how Chrissie is in these storms. She talked wildly. She reminded me that I'd loved her once. I was the only man who understood her. She wanted me to run away with her."

Rachel waited for the disclaimer, but it did not come. "Do you want to, Guy?"

Rachel thought it was a reasonable thing to ask, but Guy looked immeasurably hurt. "I have a wife. How in honor could I listen to Christine's proposal?"

Rachel felt a surge of grief. Oh, Guy, we're not talking about honor. And you haven't answered my question. "It doesn't matter," she said, forcing a smile to her lips. "Christine says whatever comes into her head at the moment. She'll think better of it by evening."

Guy returned her smile with perceptible relief. "You're probably right." He hesitated, as though uncertain how to bring the conversation to an end. "I'll leave you now. I have to finish the rewrite of Act Five." Guy ran his fingers through his hair, a familiar gesture that made Rachel's heart turn over. "The last thing I want to deal with is Christine's sense of drama."

By this time he was near the door. Rachel crossed the room swiftly, remembering what else was at stake. "Guy, you've got to go to Burley." The carriage and the knifing could have been accidents, but not the sandbag. That had been meant to kill him.

"And ask for protection? Rachel, the streets are full of peril."

Guy was the stubbornest man alive. "This wasn't the streets," Rachel said, anger warming her voice, "it was the theater. My theater. You weren't a target chosen at random. Someone wants you dead. Guy, you can't play at this investigation any longer. There's no time. You've got to tell Burley what happened today. You've got to tell him what you've learned."

"Including Dorinda? No."

Rachel had not thought that telling Burley would mean soiling the name of Samuel's daughter. But it was Guy's life that was at stake. "Stop this stupid chivalry. Suppose it's Brandon? Or Charles?"

Guy stared at her. "Do you believe that?"

She returned his gaze calmly. "After Cadogan, there's nothing I can't believe."

Guy flicked his finger across her cheek. "All right, Rachel. I'll see Burley this afternoon. The fifth act will have to wait."

After Guy left the room, Rachel remained by the door, still feeling his touch upon her face. Guy would not leave her, no matter how much he might regret his second loss of Christine. He had not denied that he loved her sister, and therefore it must be true. Guy knew that Christine would make his life a turbulence. It might be more than honor that bound him to the woman he had married. But there would always be a part of him that longed for the woman he had first loved.

Rachel moved to the window again. The sun had shifted and the glass had lost its warmth. Nothing has changed, she told herself. I knew this when I asked Guy to marry me. I knew it when we stood before Charles and said our vows. I knew it when I went to his bed. I thought I could make do with what was real between us. I thought friendship would be enough, and it's not. I want everything, or nothing. Dear God, what am I going to do?

Rachel stood by the window a long time, the tears running unheeded down her face. Life was a cheat, a trap, a farce. What had she expected, happiness everlasting? Happiness did not exist, save on the stage, and often not even there.

She turned from the window and walked to her dressing table to repair the ravages to her face. It was time to join the children for their supper, and a heavy heart was no reason to disappoint them. She studied her reflection in the glass. Her face was pale, but her eyes were dry. She tried a smile and was relieved to see that it did not seem forced. The children might see behind the smile, but they would be too polite to say so. It seemed her life had not come to an end after all. But she was no nearer knowing how she was going to live it.

After his talk with Rachel, Guy left the house and once more sought Officer Burley at the Brown Bear. The landlord told him that Burley was not there, though he usually made an appearance at this hour. If the gentleman would care to wait . . .

Guy ordered a glass of ale and retired to a table in the corner. He looked about the room, curious as always, but the hostile eyes that met his gaze told him that curiosity was unwelcome at the Bear, and he quickly looked away. In truth, he had enough to occupy his thoughts. He had been badly shaken by his encounter with Christine, and he was even more troubled by his feelings toward Rachel. Guy knew that he had hurt her, and he had not intended to. God help him, he had no intention of running off with Christine, but he could not deny that she roused him still. For a moment — it had been only a moment, but it had been filled with danger — he had wanted to take her, there, in the library.

Guy raised the glass to his lips, then set it down untasted. He leaned back in his chair, feeling sober and something of a fool. He did not want to love any woman, and now, it seemed, he was in love with two.

No, that was wrong. His affection for Rachel was genuine, as was his desire for her lovely body, but he could not put a name to the terrifying feelings she had aroused in him these past few days. As for Christine, that was momentary madness. Still, that madness could destroy his marriage. Rachel was a generous woman, but she demanded fidelity from those to whom she gave her trust.

It was not only Rachel to whom Guy owed his fidelity, it was Alec and Jessica as well. He could no more walk away from his stepchildren than he could walk away from Rachel. Guy had a vivid image of Alec's face when they had talked in the library. Children were vulnerable, as Rachel had been when her mother left her. Guy thought of Rachel's anger toward Arlette, which had always seemed so unreasonable, and for the first time fully felt the pain and devastation that her mother's departure had wrought.

"You're a troubled man, Mr. Melchett." Guy came back to the present with a start. James Burley was standing before him.

"Not troubled, Mr. Burley. Contemplating the sins of my past."

"A mistake, I always think." Burley pulled out a chair and sat down across from Guy. "One should be contemplating the sins one is about to commit."

The man was damnably close to the mark. "That too." Guy glanced quickly around the room. There were a dozen men there, all looking curiously at the stranger and the Bow Street officer. The landlord's gaze was curious, too. "I have some things to say to you," Guy said, "but I'd like to be private."

"That can be managed." Burley had a word with the landlord, then led the way up a narrow flight of stairs to a small room at the back of the house. A bed, a chair, a table, a washstand. An anonymous room, used by anonymous people who had no wish to leave their mark upon it. Burley motioned Guy to the chair and seated himself upon the bed. "Has something happened, Mr. Melchett?"

Guy folded his arms and stretched his legs out before him. The chair rocked on the uneven floor. "Another accident," he said. "My wife is concerned."

"And you are not?"

"No, this time I am concerned, too. It was at the Tavistock. A bag of sand weighting a pulley dropped from a bridge above the stage. There were a number of people on stage, including myself, but it dropped exactly where I was standing. I avoided it by a hairsbreadth."

"Ah." Burley's fingers drummed on the coarse gray blanket that covered the bed. "The rope was frayed? Badly tied?"

"It was cut. There's no mistake about that. A knife was found on the bridge. The most likely culprit is a boy who'd been taken on two days ago to replace one of the stagehands. A ferret-faced youngster, small and wiry. I'd put his age at fourteen, but he might be older. He was clever enough and he learned quickly. He was seen leaving the theater just after the sandbag fell."

Burley rose and walked to the window. There was little to be seen save a dilapidated yard, but he did not seem distressed by the view. "I wonder why you are a danger, Mr. Melchett. I wonder what it is you know, or what it is you are likely to find out."

The faces flashed quickly before Guy's eyes. Brandon, Charles, Philip. They were all friends or had been once. Billingham. A cold man and a timid one. Justin. He had resented Edmund, but he had had little to gain by his death. "You'd like to know what I've learned."

Burley turned round and looked sharply at Guy. "Why, yes, Mr. Melchett. I think it's time we pooled our resources. To put us on an even footing, let me tell you what I've found myself. Nothing conclusive, mind you, but that would be too much to expect in a case like this." At these last words, Burley's voice took on a touch of bitterness. "Young Weston, for one," he went on, his voice dispassionate once more. "He took a great and sudden dislike to Edmund Hever. He did not tell me why, but I would guess his reasons were much the same as your own. He is an admirer of Lady Christine."

Guy was silent. No need to mention the scene at Vauxhall. Burley had the essence of the situation.

"Then there's Mr. Brandon Ford," Burley went on. "He puzzled me, that one, till I learned of Mr. Hever's interest in Mrs. Pursglove. You weren't going to tell me that, were you, Mr. Melchett? I can see your reasons, but it would have been a mistake. Alfred Billingham told me. Mr. Ford had reason to think badly of Mr. Hever, and Mr. Pursglove did as well."

Burley was a tenacious man. He had learned nearly everything Guy had intended to tell him, and some things he'd had no intention of telling him at all. He did not know of Charles's meeting with Edmund, and Guy could not bring himself to disclose it.

"Mr. Billingham, now," Burley continued. "He has his secrets, I daresay, but I haven't learned what they are. In any case, his wife gives him an alibi for that evening."

"Which may be worth nothing." Guy was furious at Billingham for having brought up Dorinda's name.

337

Burley nodded. "True. But his reasons?"

"It's possible he was being blackmailed by Hever." Guy told him of the conversation Margaret had overheard and Frances's indiscretion about her husband's relations with his ward.

"Four suspects," Burley said with evident satisfaction. "All with reason to hate Edmund Hever. Any one of them could have done it. Perhaps five. The elder Mr. Ford might have taken it on himself to avenge his daughter's honor."

Guy frowned. The thought had occurred to him, but there was no reason to believe Samuel knew of Dorinda's adultery.

"There's Harry Jessop and George Hinton," Burley continued. "They were at the theater that night, but as far as I've been able to learn, neither had any reason to hate Edmund Hever." He raised his brows in inquiry. Guy shook his head.

"Then there's Lord Deaconfield," Burley went on. "His brother's death left him his father's heir, but his father was not yet the duke and there was only a modest inheritance. Men have killed for less, of course, but Deaconfield strikes me as a man who thinks on a grand scale. His brother's legacy would have been a paltry reward for something as consequential as murder. On the other hand," Burley continued with a sharp look at Guy, "there's the Lady Christine. He wouldn't be the first man to commit a crime for a beautiful woman." Burley returned to the bed. "What about it, Mr. Melchett? Do you know anything that could lead me to shorten that list?"

"Nothing," Guy said, "save my own instincts, and I've learned not to trust those. Five suspects you said. Six with Deaconfield. Am I no longer on your list?"

There was a slight movement at the corner of Burley's mouth that might have been a smile. "I'm not sure, Mr. Melchett. You could have staged your three accidents. You're a clever man, and I would not put it past you. But I spoke to Dr. Grey after you were knifed. You could have been dead as well as not. You might have chanced it, but I'm inclined to think you didn't. You're a man to take risks, but they'd be calculated ones."

Guy was at a standstill. He wondered if Burley was as well. "There's no proof, is there?"

"None. Nor likely to be." Burley seemed unperturbed.

"Do you give it up then?"

"I never give up, Mr. Melchett. We'll make an arrest."

"Because the Home Office say you must? Or because you know?"

Burley considered him a moment, then rose and walked to the door. "I'm glad we've had this talk, Mr. Melchett. You've been very helpful."

The last Guy saw of Burley, he was running down the narrow stairs of the Brown Bear. He had not answered Guy's question, but Guy could guess the answer easily enough. The Duke of Arundel was putting pressure on Lord Sidmouth, and Lord Sidmouth was demanding action. God help them all, there was going to be an arrest.

The next few days left scant time to think of Edmund Hever's murder. Guy did not waste time on things he could not help, and he was in any case far too busy with the final rehearsals for *The Steward's Stratagem*. The most he would do was promise Rachel to be careful.

From Rachel's point of view, the promise was a futile one. She talked to Patrick, who said he would keep an eye on Guy and so would every one of the stagehands he could trust.

Burley came by the theater the morning after his talk with Guy. He spoke at length to Patrick, who had found no trace of the ferret-faced boy, and to the members of the company who had been present at the time the sandbag fell. Rachel doubted that he learned anything of use, though she was comforted by his presence and by his obvious concern for what had happened.

But the everyday demands of the theater pushed the question of Guy's safety to the back of her mind, and there it stayed, an insistent nagging reminder that life was unsettled and full of danger. Playbills announcing that Mademoiselle Aubert of the Comédie Française would appear on Saturday night following the performance of *The Steward's Stratagem* had been printed and distributed. The announcement brought a modest but gratifying increase in the requests for tickets. Then, the day after Burley had visited the theater, Rachel went to her office to sort through the morning mail and found a crested letter which informed her that His Imperial Majesty, Emperor Alexander of Russia, would be attending the performance and a box was required. No, more than one, for the Emperor was coming with the Regent, some of his ministers, the King of Prussia, and a good part of the retinue that had followed him from Paris.

Rachel felt a moment of elation, then realized there was a great deal to do. She marched to the stage, called a halt to the rehearsal, and informed Guy and the company that they were having exalted guests in Saturday's audience and that nothing, absolutely nothing must go wrong. Then she sent a message to Burley saying that she wished to hire him to keep watch at the theater on Saturday night. And then she went to the carpenter shop to tell Bob Harper that it would be necessary to remove the partition between two of the boxes.

Word of the Emperor's intentions must have got out, for by the next day every one of the available boxes had been taken and the pit was oversubscribed. Rachel sent a second message to Burley. She would need additional men to help in maintaining order. Since his arrival in London, the Emperor had been mobbed by well-wishers and curiosity-seekers wherever he went, and the Tavistock was likely to be no exception.

There was no respite at home. Christine said nothing to Rachel of what had happened in the library and avoided being alone with her sister. She and Justin had again established an uneasy truce that did not bode well for their future. The wedding was less than a week away, but Christine had lost all interest in its details. Rachel and Lady Parminter must manage things as they pleased.

When Guy was around, Christine looked hurt and confused. When that failed to get his attention, she took refuge in a brittle gaiety. Guy seemed uncomfortable in her pres-

340

ence and devoted himself to Arlette, to whom he talked of nothing but the theater. He was gentle with Rachel. After his interview with Burley, he had gone to her bedchamber to tell her what had passed and had asked to stay the night. Rachel ached with longing for her husband, but the memory of Christine in his arms stood between them. Wanting him to be free to choose, she told him she needed to be alone. Guy seemed puzzled and hurt, and since then had made no further move to come to her room.

Alec and Jessica were excited by the prospect of the play. Fiona had invited them to share the Carne box, as their own children would attend, as well as the Princess Sofia's children, Simon and Alessandra. The children sensed that their mother was upset but did not talk about it. They were worried about leaving Parminter House, which they equated with leaving their new friends, the Carnes. Jessica, who had grown very comfortable in Bloomsbury Square, asked her mother if they must really return to Great Ormond Street.

Ormond Street, that had been the plan. As soon as Christine was married, Rachel's obligation would be at an end and she could resume her old life. After her own marriage she had assumed that Guy would come to Ormond Street, too. Now she did not know if she wanted him there. She was too uneasy and too harassed by the multitude of things that must be attended to—the wedding not the least of these—to talk to him. Please God, let the play go well, let Christine be safely married, let Arlette return to France, and then, perhaps then she could face what she was to do with the rest of her life.

On Saturday, Rachel left the theater at four and returned home to dress for the evening. She made a brief visit to the nursery to see Alec and Jessica, who were going to dine with the Carnes, and then went to her dressing room where she forced herself to remain patient while her maid attended to her hair. As she relaxed under the girl's ministrations, Rachel realized that it was a luxury she would miss. She would miss a number of things about Parminter House—the room to move, which she had found so oppressive when she first arrived; the housekeeper, who relieved her of the domestic duties that used to take so much of her time; the opulent carriages, available whenever she wished to drive. Even Jessica realized how different life would be in Great Ormond Street.

Rachel selected the dress she had worn on the night of Christine's betrothal ball, a tunic of dark red striped gauze, cut low in front and back, worn over a satin slip in the same color. The slip was finished with a flounce of blond lace, as were the sleeves which were cut full and gathered at four points along the arm. It was a dramatic and elegant dress. Rachel had had nothing like it before she came to Parminter House. She loved the opulence of the heavy satin and the lightness of the gauze on her arms. It will do, she thought as she clasped Magnus's pearls about her neck. She would be meeting royalty, and she need not be ashamed.

Shortly before six she was back at the theater. Burley was already there, along with three beefy men who looked nothing like police officers. Rachel thought it wiser to not ask where he had found them. Guy was still on stage, his hair tousled and his face smudged with dirt. She stopped to speak to him and saw his eyes lighten with surprise and admiration. "You look magnificent," he said.

Given the state of their marriage, it was a bittersweet compliment. "You don't," she said in a deliberately cheerful voice. "I've brought you some proper clothes. I'll leave them in the office. See that you put them on and don't forget to wash your face." Guy grinned, and Rachel knew she had spoken those words before. She had a sudden image of the boy he had been, coming home dirty and excited and not fit to be seen by her father, and felt a moment of great tenderness for him.

Two stagehands pushed by them with a freshly gilded coach. Rachel stepped back, pronounced it splendid, and left Guy to deal with its placement. She moved to the far side of the stage and looked up at the enlarged royal box which adjoined the stage. Curtains of crimson velvet, an expense they could ill afford, were drawn across the front. The top of the box was ornamented with crowns, cut out of a thin wood, flanking two large eagles and the Regent's plume. Like the coach, these were heavily gilded, tawdry when seen up close but splendid at a distance.

Rachel left the stage and climbed the stairs to the box. Three armchairs, newly covered in the crimson velvet of the curtains, stood in readiness for the three royal guests. The interior of the box had been left alone. There had been no time to improve it, but the paper on its walls, red flocked in gold, was still in passable condition. Rachel pushed aside the curtains and surveyed the house. No one was there but Burley, standing quietly in the pit. Rachel liked this moment. Swept and orderly, the house waited expectantly to be filled while on stage there was frantic activity and an air of suppressed hysteria. The thin notes of a musician tuning his violin rose over the tense voices of the stagehands and the anguished cries of the actors. As Rachel watched, the stage curtain was dropped, cutting off the sound and blocking the view of the stage from the house. At that same moment she heard the opening of the doors of the theater. Six o'clock. In the next hour, the house would begin to fill, though few of the box-holders would be present when the curtain rose at seven.

Rachel returned backstage and did not venture into the house again until a quarter of seven. Her first thought at seeing the seething, shouting mob in the pit was that she had been wise to ask Burley to get help. Her second was that even Burley and his men would not be enough. There was no way to move through the crowd in the pit. Rachel turned, climbed the stairs to the second tier of boxes, then went downstairs to the lobby. Two of Burley's men were trying to impose some order on the people struggling to enter. One of the interior doors, pulled loose from its hinges, stood at a drunken angle. She heard a man curse as his coat ripped when he pushed by it.

There was nothing she could do. She retraced her steps and returned backstage where she found Guy talking to the half-dozen actors in the first scene. "It's madness out there," she said to the group. "They may not listen to a word you say."

Guy's face took on a stubborn look. "They'll listen," he

said. "We'll think of something."

Rachel nodded and turned away. If anyone could manage the unruly mob that was their audience tonight, Guy could. She walked back to the second tier of boxes and found the one occupied by the Ford family. When they came to the theater, they were always on time.

Samuel was standing at the front of the box, hands behind his back, shaking his head in disbelief. "Look at that," he said to Rachel as she came up beside him. "There's no room in the pit and they're climbing into the lower boxes. They'd be staying there, too, if it weren't for Burley. He's doing a splendid job. Are those his men at the doors? If they hadn't been there, I doubt we'd have got in at all."

"It was dreadful," Dorinda said. "I saw one woman with her pelisse pulled right off her back and several with their hats squashed all over their heads."

"It will be fine," said her mother, who avoided unpleasantness whenever she could. "I'm sure Rachel has it under control."

Rachel doubted it, but she smiled and moved on to the Carnes' box. The princess and her family had not yet arrived, but Fiona and Gideon had brought the children well in time. They were excited by the disorder in the house which they saw as part of the performance they were going to witness. Fiona shrugged her shoulders and laughed. "It can't be helped," she said. "They might as well enjoy it."

The words did much to restore Rachel's sense of proportion, though she could not still a nagging worry about the damage being done to the house. She moved on to her own box, expecting to find it empty, but Christine and Magnus were already there. Justin was there as well, which Rachel had expected, as was his sister Margaret, which Rachel had not. "Christine insisted we be here for the first act," Justin said with mock despair, "and we haven't even dined."

"I hope you don't mind my coming," Margaret said. She was dressed simply in cream muslin, which flattered her sallow complexion, and her hair was pulled high on her head, which gave more definition to her oval face. Her eyes shone

344

with anticipation, and she looked far prettier than usual. "My parents are sharing Lady Parminter's box," Margaret went on, "but they'll be hours late, and I do want to hear all of Mr. Melchett's play."

"I told her you wouldn't mind," Magnus said.

"Of course I don't mind. I'm delighted you came." Rachel took a seat beside her, covered the girl's hand with her own, and gave her brother an approving look. "Though I'm not sure how much you'll be able to hear. I doubt anything will quiet this crowd until they've had a chance to see the Emperor."

Rachel had underestimated Guy. The curtain rose abruptly, revealing the entire company drawn up across the stage. They stood quietly, waiting till the audience was aware of their presence, and the players' silence, puzzling and unexpected, diminished the noise in the house. Then the musicians took up their instruments and played a familiar chord. With enthusiasm and creditable volume, the company broke into the opening line of "God Save the King."

Rachel stifled a burst of laughter. Englishmen, bless them, were sentimental about their sovereign, whether they liked him or not. The crowd stood and looked expectantly at the royal box, whose closed curtains showed no sign of parting. Then, apparently realizing that royalty would not give up its dinner to attend a performance at the time it began, they joined in the anthem, giving a good-natured cheer at its close. While they were scrambling back into their seats, the players quickly dispersed, leaving only the actors disposed for the first scene. Cecily, a great favorite with the Tavistock audiences, entered, and some sort of quiet settled over the house. Not the quiet one might wish for an unfamiliar play, but one little worse than that obtaining at most performances. Almost all the lines could be heard.

Rachel's attention, as usual, was on the audience. She was familiar with the production, but not with how it would be received. There was laughter, that was good, particularly the surprised laughter of an audience taken unawares, and there were hoots of recognition when Guy skewered some familiar pretensions. There were also occasional sounds of scuffling and cries of protest, quickly muffled, from the pit and from the gallery above, a sign that Burley and his men were still earning their pay. Rachel vowed to double it.

At the interval she slipped out of the box. There was a set of dances accompanied by songs, a divertissement designed to amuse the crowd while waiting for the play to continue, but Rachel doubted it would command much attention. It was nearly nine, and the royal party could be expected any time within the next hour.

Backstage there was an air of suppressed hilarity. The players had faced a challenge and had met it. Their gaiety was reflected on Guy's face. Normally he viewed the performance from the pit, but on this occasion he had remained in the wings. Shortly before ten Rachel was brought word that the royals had arrived. She found Patrick and went with him to the box entrance, leaving behind a suddenly sobered company.

Patrick was looking unaccustomedly grand in evening dress, and Rachel's own dress would pass muster in any drawing room in London. The Tavistock, unfortunately, was rather shabby. She would have to hold the royal party's attention until they reached their box and hope that it, at least, would live up to their expectations of what they were due.

It was much simpler than Rachel had expected. Despite the grandeur of their uniforms, the visitors proved to be no more than men, and men not above taking notice of a personable woman. The Emperor, a tall, round-faced man of courtly bearing, gave her a benevolent smile as she made her speech of welcome. His sister, he said, was desolated that she was unable to come. Frederick William, King of Prussia, nodded to her gravely. The Prince Regent stood beside them, irritable, impatient, impossibly fat. He smiled at Rachel and made some remark about the unfortunate incident that had prevented his visiting the Tavistock two years before. Rachel answered him with suitable gravity.

She led the way up the stairs to the royal box, opened the door, made another deep reverence, and motioned them inside. The curtains had already been drawn and the noise from those crowded above and below assaulted their ears. The three monarchs entered and moved to the front of the box, the Regent in the center, the Emperor on his left, nearest the stage, and the King of Prussia on his right. As the spectators caught sight of the royal trio, they rose to their feet and burst into vigorous applause, punctuated by noisy cheers which the royals acknowledged with graceful bows. Some of their party entered the box and stood waiting behind the state chairs till the acknowledgment ended. Rachel recognized Lord Liverpool, the Prime Minister, and Lord Castlereagh, the Foreign Secretary, but the other faces were unknown to her.

Rachel closed the door of the box and smiled at Patrick, who had shown the other members of the royal party to the adjoining box. The royals, along with the young blond Prussian princes and the attending ministers, marshals, and generals had all been properly disposed. Patrick sighed, gave her a mock bow, and made for the stairs. Rachel walked toward her own box to rejoin her family.

They were standing as well. Magnus made room for her at the front and squeezed her arm. "Alec is wild with enthusiasm," he said, leaning close so she could hear him. "He'll never forget this night." Rachel looked along the row of boxes to see her son leaning dangerously far over the railing, his face a study in pure joy. Gideon hauled him back, and Rachel could then see Jessica as well, jumping up and down as she clapped for the Emperor.

It might have gone on forever had not the curtain risen to reveal the company again drawn up upon the stage. The familiar chord, and then once more they sang "God Save the King." The crowd gave a laugh of recognition and then quieted in compliment to the three rulers. At the end of the anthem, the three royals bowed again and for the first time took their chairs.

But before the play could resume, Rachel heard a great commotion in the box directly opposite the royal one. She looked across the theater and felt a moment of alarm as she

347

recognized its occupant. Beside her, Margaret gasped. From somewhere in the audience an excited voice cried out, "The Princess of Wales." The Regent's estranged wife, Princess Caroline, dumpy and cheerful, wearing a glittering dress, her face painted and her hair a mass of yellow curls, walked to the front of the box.

Magnus leaned toward his sister. "Did you know she was coming?" he asked over the tumult.

Rachel shook her head, torn between dismay and a desire to laugh. "She must have borrowed the box."

The audience was standing and applauding once more, the applause directed now to the princess. People said she was used cruelly by her husband, a sentiment with which Rachel was inclined to agree. The husband, his face set in a mask of geniality, stood up and bowed in the direction of the princess. His two guests did the same, and Caroline bowed gracefully in return. Rachel could not tell whether the princess had bowed to her husband or to his foreign guests. Nor could she tell whether the Regent had bowed to the princess or had simply appropriated the applause intended for his wife. It was a surpassingly awkward moment. Whatever his intention, Rachel had to admit that he carried it off well. The threatened crisis had been averted.

The play continued. Guy had turned Ralph into a reasonable swordsman. Rachel could not help stealing glances at the royals and was relieved to see that they seemed absorbed by the events on stage and talked to each other rarely. But that may have been because the Prince of Wales and his guests were said to not be on the best of terms.

The final curtain descended to tumultuous applause, then rose again to show the company still positioned in the final attitudes of the play. Rachel looked toward the royal box. The Emperor was leaning on the railing, leading the applause for Cecily who walked toward his box and made a deep curtsy. Rachel smiled. The Emperor was said to have an eye for pretty women. King Frederick was applauding, too, a faint smile upon his sober face. The Regent looked pleased. Perhaps he had forgot his wife and the two monarchs whose popularity with the mob made it clear how low he stood in their affections.

It was over. It was a success. Rachel expected the royal party to take their departure, but they showed no sign of doing so. And then she remembered. Arlette. Since her first glimpse of the unruly crowd struggling to enter the theater, she had given no thought at all to the performance she herself had requested. It was not Guy's play that had brought the royals to the Tavistock.

The curtain rose once more to reveal Arlette alone on the stage. Behind her was a backcloth painted to show a turbulent ocean. She stood absolutely still, and in that moment Rachel understood something of her art. Without words, without movement, she commanded the house to be still, and they obeyed.

Rachel had expected Arlette to choose something from the French repertory. The audience must have expected it, too, for there was a thrill of surprise and recognition when the words she spoke were Shakespeare's. " 'O, never was there queen so mightily betray'd!' " Arlette was an unlikely Cleopatra, yet dressed in a gauze of deep blue shot with silver, her arms bare, her golden hair falling in artful disarray about her face, there was no doubt that she was a queen.

Arlette used the full range of her remarkable voice. The crowd, even those in the critical gallery seats at the top of the house, followed the melange of speeches with absolute attention. " 'Ah, women, women! Come; we have no friend/ But resolution and the briefest end.' " After these final words a collective sigh rose from the house, followed by furious applause led by the Emperor who was now on his feet. Arlette waited just long enough, then held up a hand to indicate that she wished it to come to an end. Her performance was not yet over. She moved toward the royal box and in the course of a few steps Cleopatra had vanished and a passionate and vulnerable woman had taken her place. Her words were directed to the Emperor. " 'Les moments me sont chers, écoutez-moi, Thésée.' " Rachel recognized the lines. *Phèdre,* the play in which the Emperor had seen her in Paris. She had chosen Phèdre's last speech, ending, like Cleopatra's, with her death.

When it was over, Rachel turned to look at her brother and sister. Christine had a look of pure envy on her face, but Magnus was visibly shaken. "Was it worth it?" he murmured. He meant, was it worth their pain.

"No," Rachel said, wondering if her mother could have found a way to not make a choice. Rachel had not done so herself. She had her children and her work besides, but in this matter Cadogan had been more complaisant than her father. "No," she said again, thinking that the world was not always kind to women.

The performance closed with a ballet, but Rachel did not wait to see it. She left the box once more and went backstage. Guy was in a cluster of people milling about the foot of the stairs to the dressing rooms. He was burning with excitement, and for a moment Rachel felt his exhilaration. "It was wonderful," she told him. Guy laughed and put his arm around her, drawing her into the group, and for the next few minutes she answered a torrent of questions about the performance and how it had been received.

When the questions subsided, she looked around. "Where is Arlette? I want to congratulate her."

"You'll have to wait your turn," Ned Acorn said. "She's with the Emperor."

"A summons. From an equerry in a uniform dripping with gold." Polly Eakin's voice was happy. They were not used to such attentions at the Tavistock.

The group drifted upstairs, and Guy drew Rachel aside. "Are you satisfied?" he asked.

His face was now serious. "Yes," she said with complete honesty. "With Arlette, too. She was magnificent."

Guy smiled but said nothing more. Perhaps he knew how much the admission had cost her.

They moved to the wings to watch the dancers. The monarchs were apparently remaining for the ballet. Rachel had intended to leave the theater early, so as to be ready to receive her guests, but she wondered about the etiquette of leaving before the royal visitors. The question was decided when Arlette came up to her in a whisper of gauze and heavy scent. "Rachel," she said, "we must talk."

They moved away from the wings. Arlette's face wore a rueful look, as though she had done something of which Rachel might not approve. "I have been with the Emperor," she said.

"Yes, I know. A great compliment, and well-deserved."

Arlette looked at her in surprise. "Thank you, but that is not what I wished to say. I was asked to take supper with the Emperor and his party—"

"But of course you must go," Rachel said, wondering that Arlette would think it necessary to ask her approval.

"I told him there was an entertainment for the company at Parminter House to which I was committed. And then—oh, Rachel, I hope I did not do wrong, but it will be so good for Magnus—I invited him and his party to come as well." She shook her head as though only now realizing the enormity of what she had done. "My dear child, they accepted."

Rachel felt a moment of pure panic, followed by a welling of anger. Then her good sense reasserted itself. It was done, it could not be helped, and no hostess worth her salt would hesitate at the opportunity to entertain guests of this distinction. "Listen to me," she said with more authority than she had ever used with her mother. "I must go home at once to make sure we are ready to receive them. I cannot stay to see our visitors out. Tell Patrick, he will have to do it. He must also pay Mr. Burley and his men—twice what we agreed. Then go to Magnus and tell him what to expect. He will want to invite Lady Parminter and the Arundels. The Fords and the Carnes have already been invited. And tell Guy as well."

"Trust me," said Arlette, quite as though the problem had not been of her own making. "I will arrange it all."

Arlette went off and Rachel started toward her office to collect her cloak. She did not reach it. James Burley intercepted her as she crossed the corridor. "It's under control, Lady Rachel, but there's some damage to the building. Nothing very serious."

"I'm enormously grateful. Mr. Burley, can you come to Parminter House after the performance? It seems we are entertaining the royal party, and I'd find your presence reassuring."

"Ah. That changes things a bit." Burley chewed his lip as though wondering how much more he could say. "The thing is, Lady Rachel, we have been moving along in the case of the murder of Edmund Hever, and I am ready to make an arrest. I wanted to wait until Mr. Melchett's play was over. I could wait a few hours more, but then I would have to do it at Parminter House."

Rachel felt the breath catch in her throat. "Guy?" She could hardly speak.

"Oh, no, not Mr. Melchett. I'm afraid I have to arrest Mr. Ford. Not the older gentleman. I considered him, but I was able to rule him out. It's his son. Mr. Brandon Ford."

Chapter Twenty-one

Once again Rachel stood at the head of the cedar staircase, smiling and shaking hands and directing guests to the second drawing room. It was strikingly like the night of Christine's betrothal ball little more than a month ago, save that Magnus and Christine were in the drawing room seeing to the comfort of the guests instead of standing beside her. And that if she had thought her life complicated then, it was nothing compared to the web in which she was now ensnared.

Rachel had thought she'd accepted the fact that Edmund's murderer was bound to be someone close to her, but Brandon's arrest had been an unexpected and staggering blow. Though an hour before she would have claimed she could not be certain of his innocence, the moment Burley made his announcement she was convinced Brandon could not be guilty. An irrational and unwarranted belief, perhaps, but Rachel was determined to do all she could for him nonetheless. She was not sure if Guy agreed with her, though he had insisted on accompanying Brandon to Bow Street. Brandon had been furious and in no mood to accept help, but he had calmed down when he realized it was Billingham, not Guy, who had betrayed Dorinda's adultery to Burley.

Despite objections from Brandon, who wanted his family kept out of the matter, Rachel had sent one of the stagehands to summon Samuel. Hiding his shock and dismay behind the mask of his profession, Samuel, too, had insisted on accompanying his son to the Public Office. Mercifully, in the backstage chaos few of the company saw them leave and those who did could be relied upon to keep quiet. Samuel had asked Rachel not to say anything to his family, but Rachel, knowing they would have to field questions, had quietly explained the situation to Magnus, Christine, and Justin when they reached Parminter House. Magnus handled the revelation well, as she had known he would. Christine took it better than Rachel expected, perhaps because she was beyond thinking much about anything but Guy. Justin looked genuinely shocked but said nothing about his opinion of Brandon's guilt or innocence.

With the entire Tavistock company, not to mention the entire royal party, expected at Parminter House within the hour, there had been little opportunity for discussion. Or for worrying about the evening ahead. It was not until she stood at the head of the stairs, greeting Ned Acorn and his wife and listening to the faint scuffling sounds below which indicated the frantic adjustments being made to the supper rooms to accommodate the royal guests, that Rachel fully faced the fact that her two worlds were about to collide.

By then she was beyond worrying about anything as trivial as the opinions of a prince, a king, and an emperor. The royal party arrived early, insisted that she not stand on ceremony, and progressed to the drawing room where Rachel profoundly hoped Magnus and Arlette would keep them occupied. Word of the royal presence at the reception had got round backstage. Some of the company were subdued by the formality of the occasion while others were frankly curious. But neither the unfamiliar setting nor the unexpected guests could take away the boyant afterglow of a successful performance. Despite everything, Rachel caught a whiff of the feeling. She could not say she was happy, but she was reminded that there were reasons it was good to be alive.

When most of the guests had assembled, Rachel drew a breath and followed the others to the drawing room, uncertain of the scene she would face. There were no colored lanterns tonight, but there were plenty of flowers, and the candlelight brought out the warm, golden tones in the carpets and tapestries. As Rachel surveyed the scene, she was assailed by delicate strains of Mozart. Giles Newton, the Tavistock's pianist, was providing expert, effortless entertainment, just as he would have done in her crowded drawing room in Great Ormond Street. In addition to being a skilled musician, Giles was young, dark-haired, and indecently handsome. A number of the younger actresses and dancers were clustered around the piano. In thin dresses of white or pale pastel, they looked indistinguishable from the well-born young women who had thronged the room at Christine's ball. Rachel realized that Princess Sofia's daughter, Lady Alessandra, was among them.

Despite the size of the room, the crowd was such that it was difficult to pick out the royal party. Rachel scanned the throng, then froze in astonishment. Not a dozen feet off, the Emperor of Russia and the Prince Regent stood side by side, laughing immoderately at something Gerald Sneath had said while Arlette looked on with great satisfaction. Magnus was standing near the fireplace, conversing with Lord Liverpool and King Frederick. Rachel caught his eye, and they exchanged a brief smile of acknowledgement. Then she began to move about the room. Gordon Murray, an excellent storyteller, had collected a small crowd around him. He greeted Rachel cheerfully but had the tact not to ask after Guy. So did Philip, whom Rachel found talking with Cecily, an unaccustomed smile on his face. The children were not so circumspect. Gideon and Fiona and Jenny were keeping them entertained at the far end of the room, but when Rachel approached, Alec and Jessica immediately asked after their stepfather. They looked unconvinced by her story that he had had to stay on at the theater.

Most of the company seemed to have taken the royal guests in stride, but a few, chiefly stagehands, were hanging about the periphery of the crowd. Rachel stopped to speak with them, made some introductions, encouraged the young men to join the group clustered about the piano. She wondered how the Arundels were faring, but the duchess was sitting with Lady Parminter and the duke was conversing with Lord Castlereagh. Rachel glimpsed Mrs. Ford talking to Polly Eakin and was relieved to see her occupied. She had managed to fend off the company's questions about the absence of Guy and Brandon, but she did not want to face Brandon's family.

Rachel dreaded supper, for as host and hostess she and Magnus would be expected to sit at the royal table, but she found that in some ways this made the meal easier. In the company of her friends, it would have been much more difficult to conceal her fears. The food must have been excellent, for the Emperor complimented her on her chef with every appearance of sincerity, but to Rachel the béchamel sauce tasted too rich, the pigeon pie too heavy, the jellies and tartlets too sweet. Even the champagne made her queasy.

She expected the royal party to depart after supper, for they must have had other engagements that evening, but instead they returned to the drawing room and seemed content to linger into the small hours. Fortunately, Giles was happy to continue his musical accompaniment. Faith Harker, whom Rachel had taken back at the Tavistock, joined him and entertained the company with songs. By the time Rachel and Fiona returned to the drawing room after seeing the children settled in the nursery, the atmosphere had grown even more convivial. Perhaps it was the lateness of the hour or the profusion of fine wine. Rachel caught sight of Magnus standing beside Margaret, his face lit with unforced amusement. The Emperor and the Regent, seated on either side of Arlette, were laughing as well. "Castlereagh ought to recruit your mother into the diplomatic corps," Gideon said, joining his wife and Rachel. "I think tonight is the first time the Emperor and the Regent have actually been heard laughing at the same time."

Rachel smiled and for a moment felt unadulterated admiration for what her mother had accomplished. She could not forget the cloud of disaster which hung over them, but she was able to hold it at bay. She was actually laughing when she felt her arm seized in a viselike grip.

"I'm sorry, Rachel, but I must speak with you," Dorinda said, not even acknowledging the presence of the others.

Rachel took one look at Dorinda's stricken face, murmured her apologies to the Carnes, and steered Dorinda into a shallow alcove. "Where are they?" Dorinda demanded, seizing hold of Rachel's other arm as well. "Papa wouldn't have business at this time of night and Brandon would never stay away so long. Mama won't admit anything is out of the ordinary and Charles won't talk about it at all, but I'm sure something is wrong. You must tell me."

"I know no more than you," Rachel said, sympathy warring with the certainty that she could not afford to have a scene on her hands.

"Don't lie to me, Rachel. You talked to Papa, you must know. Oh, God." Dorinda drew back and covered her face with her hands. "Brandon's been arrested, hasn't he? He killed Edmund because of me. I think I've always known, but—"

"Stop it." Rachel took Dorinda by the shoulders and shook her. "Try to have a little faith in your brother."

Dorinda drew a long, shuddering breath. "I'm sorry," she said, dragging her hands away from her face. She still looked frightened, but she no longer seemed on the verge of hysteria. "You're right, of course. It's just that I find it hard to have faith in much of anything anymore. And Brandon—" Her blue eyes, so like her brother's, darkened. "He has been arrested, hasn't he?"

"He's being questioned," Rachel admitted. "But—"

"But they haven't got round to charging him yet. I see."

"It may only be a ploy."

"A ploy?" Dorinda asked, her voice expressionless, her eyes dark with fear.

All at once Rachel understood. Dorinda had claimed that Charles could not have killed Edmund, but now, terrified as she was of Brandon's arrest, she was even more terrified that the arrest would force Charles to confess to his own guilt. Whatever the outcome of the investigation, Rachel wondered if any fragments of trust would be able to survive it. She was searching for some reply when Dorinda gasped. Following the direction of her gaze, Rachel saw Samuel standing just beyond the main doorway beside Officer Burley.

Dorinda moved at once, cutting her way through the throng with little heed to the impression she created. Rachel followed, doing her best to dispel any curiosity Dorinda had roused among the guests. Samuel looked drawn but in command of himself. When Dorinda seized his hands and said, "Tell me," he put an arm around her, at once offering comfort and shielding her from the company, and murmured, "Of course, my dear." Then, with an apologetic glance at Rachel, he steered his daughter out the door and toward one of the empty rooms down the hall.

Grateful that Samuel had taken Dorinda off her hands, Rachel turned to Burley. "I'm delighted you could join us, Mr. Burley. You must be tired and hungry. There are some refreshments laid out in the next room, but perhaps you could spare me a few minutes first."

"By all means, Lady Rachel."

Rachel led the way to the anteroom where she had spoken with Guy on the night of Christine's ball. After the hectic noise of the drawing room, the cool quiet was a welcome relief. Despite her impatience, Rachel seated herself so that Burley would be able to do so as well. He sank into a chair and regarded her with what might have been sympathy. "Your husband asked me to give you a message, Lady Rachel. He needed a bit of time to think, so he's gone back to the theater. He'll be along in an hour or so." Burley paused for a moment. "We've taken Mr. Ford into custody."

Though she had known it was likely, Rachel felt a

tightening in her gut. "You can't be certain he's guilty."

Burley's face became impassive. "He had the means and he had as good a motive as anyone."

"But no better than any of the others. Is this a stratagem, Mr. Burley? Or an act of desperation? You can't have enough evidence to convict him."

"Then you may comfort yourself with the thought that your cousin will be acquitted when he comes to trial." Burley got to his feet and looked down at her. "It was the magistrate, not I, who bound him over."

"I'm sorry." Rachel had not intended to speak with such emotion. She got to her feet as well and managed to smile. "And I don't believe I've thanked you for what you and your men did earlier this evening. We never would have managed without you."

Burley gave a faint smile. "I was merely doing my job, Lady Rachel. As I was when I arrested Mr. Ford. If it's any comfort, I believe your husband shares your belief in his innocence."

Rachel found it absurdly comforting to realize that in this at least she and Guy were in agreement, though it would not do Brandon much good in a court of law. She had a fairly shrewd idea of Burley's reasoning. Brandon and Charles had the strongest motives. If Brandon were guilty, his arrest might lead to a confession. If Charles were guilty, Brandon's arrest would almost certainly cause him to confess to his own guilt, just as Dorinda feared. Guy had not told Burley that Charles has been in the theater the night of Edmund's death. Rachel wondered if he would do so now. In fairness to Brandon, how could he keep silent? As she directed Burley to the refreshment room and made her way back to the drawing room, it occurred to Rachel that for all her conviction of Brandon's innocence, she still had no idea who might be guilty. Perhaps she would have been equally shocked if any of them had been arrested. No, she would not have felt so if it had been Billingham, but that had more to do with her feelings toward Billingham than with any rational ideas about the murder.

As Rachel entered the drawing room, Christine rushed toward her, Justin hovering close behind. "Rachel, Samuel's back and Dorinda looks perfectly ashen. Where's Guy?"

Rachel felt a flash of anger at Christine's preoccupation with Guy. She glanced at Justin, but his face was expressionless. Since his quarrel with Christine, he had seemed more controlled than ever. "He's at the theater," Rachel told her sister. "He'll be along presently. Have our guests shown any signs of leaving?"

"None." Justin moved to stand beside Christine. "They appear quite entranced with their company. You're going to be the envy of every hostess in London tomorrow, Rachel."

"I'd prefer to be the envy of every manager," Rachel said truthfully. She was prevented from further speech by the approach of Alfred Billingham. Frances had a headache and had gone upstairs to the ladies' retiring room. Did Rachel by any chance have a headache powder? Christine at once offered to fetch one, seeming relieved at the excuse to escape the drawing room. Or perhaps to escape Justin. Rachel excused herself as well and began to move about the periphery of the room, looking for strays who still felt ill at ease. But other than Peter Carne and his friend Simon di Tassio, who were perched on a settee near the wall talking happily together, most of the guests were mingling freely. Rachel persuaded one shy young dancer to join a group of the younger people, then saw Margaret sitting alone on a sofa in an alcove partially concealed by a screen of Corinthian columns. Her shoulders were hunched and her head bent, and the confidence Rachel had glimpsed scarcely half an hour before had quite vanished.

As Rachel slipped between the gray marble columns, Margaret looked up with an abashed expression. "I know, I'm hiding again. I'm sorry, I shan't stay long."

"You can stay as long as you like," Rachel assured the younger girl, dropping down on the bronze velvet sofa beside her. "But I thought you might want to tell me about whatever happened."

"Nothing," Margaret said quickly. "That is, nothing important. Please, Rachel, I don't want to take you away from your guests."

"My guests are doing very well without me. The Regent and Emperor have eyes for no one but my mother, and the last I saw of King Frederick he was happily discussing hunting with your father."

"Not anymore. Papa—Papa just spoke with me."

Rachel wondered what could have provoked the duke to speak sharply to his daughter in the midst of a royal reception. Had he learned of Brandon's arrest? That might have jolted him into an outburst, but not one directed at Margaret. Then Rachel had an image of Magnus and Margaret laughing together, and all at once she understood. "Your father objected to seeing you on such familiar terms with my brother?"

Margaret nodded, not meeting Rachel's eyes. "It was silly. But before I left Arundel House he told me—" Margaret drew a breath and spoke in a rush. "Papa called me into his study this afternoon. He said Lord Winchester means to offer for me and he and Mama want me to accept. And then he said that I might sit in the box with all of you tonight, but I wasn't to encourage Lord Parminter in any way. Not that I would, of course, but—"

"But your parents have decided that the Parminter title can't make up for Magnus's origins."

Margaret flushed bright scarlet. "He's never really forgiven Lord Parminter for speaking to him so harshly when they quarreled about Mr. Melchett. When Lord Parminter and I were talking just now—we may have been standing a little apart but we'd hardly slipped off by ourselves—Papa came up and said he had to speak to me privately. Then he read me a quite thundering scold. And I hadn't done anything."

"Fathers can be very trying." Rachel squeezed Margaret's hand, neglecting to mention that her own father had rarely paid enough attention to her to know with whom she was speaking, let alone to take exception to him. She studied her young friend. "I'll speak to Magnus. When he understands the circumstances, I'm sure he'll take care not to put you in a difficult situation again."

"Oh, no." Margaret looked up at Rachel, her eyes filled with alarm. "That's just it, Rachel. I wanted to talk to him. I used to be afraid of him, but now — He's one of the few gentlemen who talks to me like I'm a real person. Do you understand?"

"I think so." In truth, Rachel understood a good deal more than Margaret had admitted. While the investigation into Edmund's murder had thrown the Hevers and the Melchetts into turmoil, Margaret had been quietly falling in love with Magnus. Rachel wondered if Margaret's feelings were reciprocated. Whether or not he realized it, marriage to Margaret might be the making of her brother. "Meg," she said gently, "have you accepted Lord Winchester?"

"No," Margaret returned with unnecessary firmness. "That is, he hasn't spoken to me yet, but when he does — I used to think I'd be happy if any personable gentleman offered for me. And then for a while, when I thought Lord Parminter might — I knew he wasn't in love with me, but I thought we might be happy together. Not like you and Mr. Melchett, of course."

Rachel nearly laughed at the irony of this statement. Margaret, usually so perceptive, had quite misread the relationship between herself and Guy. "Marriage should be more than an arrangement of mutual convenience," she said with a vehemence she had not intended.

"But even that doesn't always assure happiness, does it?" Margaret's gaze held a worldly understanding which made her suddenly seem years older. "Fanny loves Alfred and it seems to make her miserable more often than not. And Justin and Christine — Well, I can see things aren't well between them. It's all very confusing. Marriage,

I mean and—and everything."

"Especially everything," Rachel said with a smile.

Margaret smiled in return. "I'm sorry, Rachel, I didn't mean to babble on like this. It's just that there's no one else I can talk to. Mama wouldn't understand, and Fanny's been so upset about Edmund that I haven't wanted to bother her. Cousin Elizabeth tried to offer me advice when I told her about Lord Winchester. It was very nice of her, though I must say it wasn't particularly comforting. She kept going on about how gentlemen claim it isn't any of our concern how they amuse themselves, but they can do unspeakable harm to their wives and children." Margaret shook her head in bewilderment. "It wasn't at all the sort of talk I'd have expected from Elizabeth. I know Cousin Henry wasn't a model husband, but I always assumed he and Elizabeth must have had some sort of understanding." She flushed again but did not look away. "Well, it's silly to pretend I'm blind, Rachel. Elizabeth was always discreet, but I could hardly fail to notice when my own brother—"

As Margaret broke off, Rachel stared at her. "Edmund had an affair with the dowager duchess?" she asked, delicacy fading to nothing before the need to learn the truth about Edmund Hever.

"No," Margaret said, her natural honesty overcoming her embarrassment, "it was Justin. But it was years ago, long before he was betrothed to Christine. I'm sure there's nothing between them now." Her eyes darkened with concern. "You don't think that could be the trouble between Christine and Justin, do you? Perhaps I should tell Christine she has no cause to be uneasy on that score."

"I don't think that will be necessary." Rachel stared between two columns at the shimmering, candlelit throng. Something was tugging at the recesses of her mind, some piece which, if fitted into place, would turn the fragments into a coherent picture. Justin's love affair with his cousin's wife was hardly more than an interesting bit of gossip. Unless—

The plaintive strains of "Barbara Allen" were an incongruous counterpoint to the chaos of her thoughts. Rachel sat immobile, suspended by shock, as realization washed over her. The pattern which had driven the events of the last two years was suddenly spread before her in all its intricate detail. For a moment she was too stunned to think, let alone act. Then the music came to an end and released her from her paralysis.

"I must talk to Justin, Meg," Rachel said, getting to her feet. "Have you seen him?"

"Not since supper. Rachel, what's the matter?"

Rachel managed to keep her voice under control. "Very likely nothing at all, but I'll feel better when I've talked to him." It was not quite a lie, she told herself. There was always a chance that she was wrong.

Margaret followed Rachel out of the alcove and stayed with her as she searched the crowd for Justin. Rachel thought she saw him in the first drawing room with Christine, but when she approached them she realized it was not Justin but his brother Bertram who stood beside her sister. Like Margaret, Bertram had not seen Justin since supper. Christine, looking bored, said she'd seen nothing of her betrothed since she left him to fetch the headache powder for Fanny. Then, with sudden sharpness, she asked her sister what was wrong.

Her unease coalescing into tightly coiled alarm, Rachel repeated the assurances she had given Margaret, then quickly made her way downstairs to the hall, vaguely aware that Margaret was still at her side. Yes, Thomas said, in response to her question, Lord Deaconfield had gone out about a quarter-hour ago.

It should have terrified her more than it did. Perhaps she was too numb to feel terror. "Thank you, Thomas," Rachel said in a level voice. "I want the barouche sent round. Please tell Lord Parminter that I was obliged to go out and will return as soon as possible."

Even Thomas could not remain impassive at the news

364

that his mistress meant to leave the house in the midst of a reception for royalty. Heaven knew what stories would be spread belowstairs, but that was the least of Rachel's concerns. Magnus would be furious, but he could be counted on to cover her absence. Beside Guy's safety, nothing else seemed of any importance.

"Rachel." As Rachel turned back to the stairs, Margaret tugged at her sleeve. "If this has anything to do with Justin, I'm coming with you."

Rachel started to protest, then realized that Margaret's presence might prove a tremendous help. At the moment, she was ready to accept help from any quarter. She nodded briefly and made for the stairs, intent on her next objective. If she concentrated on one thing at a time, she would be able to get through this.

Light refreshments had been laid out in the small saloon for those guests unable to survive without sustenance the interval before or after supper. Burley was still there, a plate of sandwiches in one hand. Rachel went to him and spoke without preamble. "I have reason to believe my husband is in danger. Lady Margaret and I are leaving for the Tavistock at once. Can you come with us?"

Burley set his plate down on an occasional table. The sudden alertness in his eyes was the only visible change in his demeanor. "I am at your service, Lady Rachel."

It was done, or very nearly. They had only to make their way downstairs and out into the waiting carriage and within a quarter-hour they would be at the Tavistock. But as Rachel led the way across the gallery, she found Christine standing in front of her. "You're leaving?"

"I have to go back to the theater," Rachel said. "I'll explain later. You and Magnus and Arlette can manage things here."

Christine looked from Rachel to Margaret and Burley who were standing just behind her. "Magnus and Arlette can manage. I'm coming with you."

"Don't be ridiculous, Chrissie. This isn't a game."

"I know it isn't." Christine's face was very pale, and her eyes were bright and hard. "Guy's in trouble. Nothing else would have you so overset. I won't be left behind."

For a moment, Rachel faced her sister, but she already knew it was useless. Without another word, the four of them descended the stairs to confront whatever awaited them at the Tavistock.

Chapter Twenty-two

Guy climbed the steps to the stage door. The theater was locked, but he carried a key. He swung the door open and stepped inside. Lamps and candles had been extinguished, and the building was in total darkness. Using the moonlight streaming through the open door, he found the candle that was kept on a shelf just inside and lit it. He picked up the candle, pushed the door closed with his foot, and made his way to the stage.

He lit two lamps which made small pools of radiance, intensifying the surrounding darkness. Then he set the candle on a table and walked toward the ropes that raised the curtain. It was two men's work, and Guy strained with the effort, grateful for the chance of action. The curtain raised, he walked to the very edge of the proscenium and looked out over the house. He could see nothing, but the theater was as clear to him as though it were brightly lit.

"Why?" he cried, his voice spilling out into the empty house. "Why?" The last was to himself, a mere whisper of sound.

Brandon's arrest had shaken him badly. Never close, not quite friends, they had lived in the same closed little world. Brandon was almost family. Guy had been willing to consider him a suspect, but now he could not believe in his guilt.

He turned away from the house and walked upstage. He had thought himself clever, coming back to England to outwit Mountjoy and unmask his agent, but it was Rachel who had first understood Cadogan's guilt. Then the first puzzle was overlaid by a second. Who had killed Edmund Hever? Guy had thought to be clever here, too, but he had learned little that Burley had not also uncovered, and what he had learned had taken him no nearer a solution of the problem. He was in check. And then Burley had declared the game to be over. Guy would not allow it, but he did not know where to turn. He had a ferocious impulse to beat it out of the other suspects. But which one? Gentle little Philip? Saintly Charles? Pompous, frightened Billingham? Envious, mocking Justin? It made no sense. He couldn't pick a murderer among them, yet one of them thought he knew too much and was trying to kill him.

Guy paced back and forth, in and out of the pools of light. He should leave, return to Parminter House, face the agony and questions in Samuel's eyes, comfort Rachel. But Rachel would be on the edge of exhaustion, occupied with her ill-assorted guests. There would be no time to talk of what had happened to Brandon.

A few minutes more, Guy promised himself. A few minutes more and he would leave. He did no good here. He stumbled in the dark and fell against a table just beyond the playing area. The table fell with a clatter and a ring of metal. Guy dropped to his knees and felt for the fallen objects. A prop table, of course. He remembered now where it had stood. Here were the Italian rapiers used in the duel. And here the dagger carried by Corisande. And a brass candleholder. There should be two, but Guy saw no need to continue his search. He carried what he had found to the table where the candle was still burning.

The candlelight flickered on the polished metal of the rapiers. They had not been tipped. Ralph had learned to protect himself, and Brandon had insisted the fight would look better with the naked blades. Perhaps he was right, though the artifice of the stage now seemed supremely unimportant next to the gritty reality of Bow Street.

Guy picked up one of the rapiers, tested its balance in his hand, whipped it quickly back and forth, listening to the singing of its blade. They had chosen the rapiers to suit the period of the play. Guy was more familiar with the foil and the épée, whose study had given him keen pleasure during his exile in Paris. He swung the blade again and was about to put it down when the sound of footsteps arrested his movement.

"Guy?" It was Justin's voice, coming from the edge of the blackness. "It's devilish dark in here."

"I'm in a mood for darkness," Guy said.

Justin moved forward with evident caution and appeared suddenly in the light from one of the lamps. His deep-set eyes were pools of blackness. Dark shadows heightened the leanness of his face, giving him a cadaverous look. His light voice, with its faint undertone of mockery, destroyed the illusion. "Why? Brandon was no particular friend to you."

"We were close."

"As brothers? Yes, I can understand that." Justin moved toward the table and stared as if hypnotized at the light playing on the glittering metal of the rapier and dagger lying there. Then he looked up suddenly, seeking Guy's eyes. "Did he do it? That's why I came. I have to talk to someone; I have to know. There's got to be an end to it. I can live with anything but uncertainty."

Guy felt a moment of pity for the other man. "Bow Street don't know. He'll go to trial and the jury who hear the case won't know either. Nor will the judge who sentences him to hang. I have my own private conviction, for what it's worth."

Justin waited. "And?" he said when it was clear Guy would say no more.

"He didn't do it."

"Did he have cause?"

"He had cause to dislike Edmund, but that doesn't make him a killer. I won't believe he's guilty. And by all that's holy, I'll spend the rest of my life finding out who is."

Guy's voice shook a little on these words. He was surprised by the intensity of his conviction. He was surprised by his own determination. It was liberating, this call to

369

action, and he raised the blade he was still holding and slashed it down to the floor.

"It will never be over, will it? We'll never know." Justin gave a great sigh. "So we learn to live with uncertainty." He picked up the second rapier and weighed it in his hand. "Life's like that, isn't it? A thrust, a parry, a riposte. And nothing but skill and chance to fend off mortal injury." He threw the blade in the air and caught it firmly. "What about it, Guy? A passage at arms to seal this unhappy day? *En garde.*"

Without thinking, Guy moved into a defensive position, his blade raised to parry the first pass. Justin was in an odd mood, but for that matter, so was Guy. And it felt good to move, to stretch, to focus one's senses on a single point, a single instant. They played for a while, getting the feel of the blades and the floor and the other's strengths and weaknesses. Guy became aware of Justin's breathing and the tightness in his own chest.

Justin stepped back out of Guy's range and laughed. "By God, this feels good. Lights. We must have more lights."

Guy dropped his weapon, took the candle, and lit several of the footlights that ran across the front of the stage. They could see better now. Justin had removed his coat and Guy did the same. It was madness, this mock duel in a darkened theater, but it had been a day that could end only in madness. Guy picked up his rapier and turned to confront Justin, who was moving rapidly across the stage, a look of pure joy on his face. Guy laughed and held his ground, parried the thrust that extended Justin to his complete reach, then ducked and swung round to avoid the inevitable riposte. "My point," Guy said as his blade found the sleeve of Justin's shirt. He drew it back before it could draw blood.

"Your point," Justin conceded, and came at him again. By this time they were both laughing. Then the laughter stilled because they needed all their breath. They were well-matched. Justin had strength and intensity. Guy was devious and able to see several moves ahead.

Some minutes later, sweat dripping down his face, Guy's passion cooled. The passage had helped, but it was time for them to put up their weapons and return to the world of Parminter House. "Enough," he said and pulled up his blade. Justin did not seem to hear him. He lunged forward, eyes intent on his target, a fixed smile on his face. Guy quickly lowered his blade and parried the thrust aimed at his heart, then leaped out of the way. "Enough!" he said again. Justin laughed and came at him with renewed ferocity. It took Guy by surprise, and he was driven to the edge of the stage.

They closed, their sweating faces inches apart, their hard breathing merged as though they were a single creature warring with itself. Guy broke away and retreated upstage. He was out of practice, exhausted, and annoyed. Justin was taking the bout seriously. It had become some crazy test of worth, a challenge for the right to win Christine.

Christine. Didn't Justin know that was over? Long over. With a shock of surprise, Guy realized he had been clinging to the past to escape the present. The present was Rachel. Beside her Christine meant nothing. It was Rachel who was the center of his life. It was Rachel he loved, and he was terrified by his need for her. Guy let himself be driven further upstage, using his blade only for defense. He had no wish to be victor in such a bout.

But Justin had no intention of ending it. His blade was subtle and quick, probing each point of weakness. Guy parried a thrust, not quite soon enough, and the blade slashed across his shirt, tearing the fabric and meeting his skin. It was a scratch, no more, but it should have stopped the bout. Guy felt a mounting anger and then a moment of horrified recognition. It was more than Christine. Justin was going to bring him down. Justin was trying to kill him.

The carriage that had nearly caught him under its wheels. The man who had put a knife in him. The ferret-faced boy and the cut rope that would have brought death from above. And now, face-to-face. "Why?" Guy said. He felt a new surge of strength and renewed his attack, driving Justin back toward the footlights.

Justin laughed. "You're in my way, Guy Mulchett." He stretched his long body out with a thrust that should have found its mark.

"Christine?" Guy jumped back out of reach. "I'm no danger there."

Justin came toward him, blade extended. "You're a danger while you live."

Guy feinted and drew a thrust which he parried with such force that Justin's blade was torn from his hand. It spun round and slithered across the floor, coming to rest several feet away. Guy moved quickly to retrieve the weapon.

Justin threw himself across the floor and grasped the handle of the rapier. Guy's foot held it to the floor. "It's Edmund, isn't it? You killed him."

"Perhaps I did," Justin said, struggling to free the weapon. "And perhaps I didn't."

Guy dropped to his knees, pinned Justin's arm with his hand, and brought his face close to the other man's. Justin's face was glistening with sweat and his eyes were lit with fury, but his mouth had not lost its mocking look. "What difference does it make? He's dead now."

"But I don't choose to be." Guy tightened his grip on Justin's arm. Justin was coiling himself for one last effort to free the rapier. Guy brought down his other hand in a vicious blow to Justin's elbow. Startled by the pain, Justin loosened his grip. Guy seized the rapier and flung it across the stage into the darkness of the wings, then threw his own after it. The clang of the falling blades rang through the theater, silent save for their harsh breathing.

Justin rose slowly, first to his knees and then to his feet, never taking his eyes off Guy. Guy matched each move. "You knew Edmund was coming to the meeting," Guy said as they stood some feet apart, watching each other warily, poised for attack and counterattack. "It was a dangerous place to try it. Why not the street, as you did with me?"

Justin laughed and stepped back toward the table with

372

the candle, the brass candlestick, and the very serviceable dagger. Guy moved round to head him off. "No one would have questioned a knife in the belly in a dark alley," Guy went on. "Accidents are safer than murder."

Justin made a sideward move that kept his path to the table open. "The explosion should have made it an accident."

Guy stopped, stunned by the unwitting revelation. "You knew what Cadogan planned," Guy said, trying to piece it together. "How? From Cadogan? Or from Mountjoy?"

"Mountjoy?" Justin laughed. He, too, had stopped moving. They faced each other, taut, wary, waiting for the other's mistake. "I heard it from Cadogan. Why not?" he added, watching Guy's face. "I knew what he was. Edmund told me. He was outraged by the duplicity. But I was inclined to sympathize with Cadogan. I persuaded Edmund to keep his mouth shut, and then I warned Cadogan, who told me the whole story. He must have tired of keeping it all to himself."

"You knew Edmund would be here. You knew about the meeting."

Justin did not trouble to deny it. God in heaven, he had known what Cadogan had planned to do, and he had known the theater would not be empty. A feud between brothers, this Guy could accept. But not the horror of letting men go unknowing to their death. He had never hated Justin till now, never felt the urge to rip life from the throat of another human being. Guy forced himself to relax, to be prepared. "Why?" he asked again. The word was torn from his straining throat. "Was it worth it? Did you have so much to gain?"

"A dukedom." It was Rachel's voice, coming improbably from the wings behind him. Guy spun round. Rachel emerged from the darkness, a slim, erect figure walking purposefully into the light. "You can't kill Guy, Justin. I heard you. You'd have to kill me, too."

Guy heard the long intake of Justin's breath. He did not look at Justin, but he turned slightly and took a backward step toward the table. Rachel had not come alone. He could see two shadowy forms behind her. Justin was not likely to risk an attack before witnesses, but Justin's life was at stake and it was as well to be prepared.

"I won't kill your precious husband, Rachel. We were fencing, that's all." There was the familiar tone of derision in Justin's voice. He had himself under control.

"Fencing?" Rachel's eyes widened. "It was more than that. I saw you. I heard you."

"You don't understand men's games, my dear."

"I understand this," Rachel said with sudden passion. "Brandon may hang for a crime you committed."

"Brandon may rot in hell for all I care. He must take his chances like the rest of us."

"Yours are over," Guy said. "Justice can be bought, but your stinking crime may prove too much for it. You're not too high to be brought down."

Justin's face darkened with anger. "You're a fool, Guy Melchett. There's no evidence of any crime. Who would believe you, a discredited radical who feeds on the carcass of society. Who would believe Rachel, a wife besotted with her husband and jealous of her sister's happiness. Both of you trying to protect your Jacobin actor friend."

Guy was silenced. They knew, but how could they hope to prove anything against the heir of Arundel. Then Margaret Hever appeared at Rachel's side. "Father would believe *me*." There was no sign of reproach in her face, only shock and a great sadness.

Justin gave a start of surprise at the sight of his sister, but his voice showed nothing but mild amusement. "Would he, little Meg? You who've been making sheep's eyes at Rachel's brother?"

Margaret gasped but held her ground.

"It will be awkward for you, Meg, if this taradiddle gets around. Have you thought of that?"

"I don't care," Margaret said with unaccustomed fervor. "I heard you, Justin. You think Father won't believe me, but he won't dare not believe me either. He won't want you

374

around. He won't be able to bear the sight of you."

A look of uncertainty passed across Justin's face. Then, quick as a cat and with a cat's silence, he was at the table and the dagger had disappeared. Guy's eyes had been on Margaret, and he cursed himself for his inattention.

"Justin?" Her face drained of color, Christine walked slowly into the light and approached her betrothed. "It's true, isn't it? You killed Edmund."

"Of course it's not true." Justin reached for her hand but she drew away. "It's a vicious lie, concocted by your brother-in-law to save Brandon Ford. He hates me, you know. He hates me because I have you, because you're going to be my wife."

The blood flooded into Christine's face. She gave a bitter laugh. "Your wife? Do you think I would ever be your wife? You're a monster."

Justin grasped her arm and drew her to him so she was forced to look up into his face. "Am I? What's changed, Christine? Was I a monster when you agreed to let me make you the future Duchess of Arundel? Was I a monster when you took me to your bed?"

Christine made a frantic effort and broke away. "You've changed, Justin."

"No." He came toward her.

"Don't touch me. Don't ever touch me again. I can't bear it."

She turned toward Guy, but Justin caught her wrist and swung her back to him. "Nothing was wrong between us till Guy's return. You ache for him still, don't you? You want him because you can't have him, and you can't bear not having what you want. You believe his flimsy fabrications because you want an excuse to turn from me. He's wrong, Christine. *You're* wrong, and I won't let you profit from your folly. We'll wed tonight. I've had a special license for weeks. Anyone can marry us. And then it's the Continent for us, my sweet, till this idiocy your would-be paramour has raised drifts into the obscurity it deserves."

"Justin, stop!" Margaret's voice was sharp with fear. Her

375

brother was distracted and in that instant Christine wrenched free and backed toward the wings. Guy placed himself between Justin and the women.

"Burley!" Rachel called. "Burley, stop him!"

Guy did not dare take his eyes off Justin's face. Burley was here. Rachel had come prepared. She'd learned something, she'd guessed at Justin's guilt, and she'd brought Burley to witness his unmasking. Guy heard the measured steps and knew Burley had come out of the gloomy recesses of the wings.

"James Burley, Bow Street runner." Justin's voice was filled with contempt. "Do you have a warrant for my arrest?"

"No, my lord, not at the moment. But we'd like to ask you to step along for questioning."

"I have another engagement this evening."

"Ah. Well, I know where to find you, Lord Deaconfield."

Guy turned round with fury. "He'll be out of the country by morning."

"I understand, Mr. Melchett. But it's a question of proof, isn't it?"

"You're a sensible man, Burley," Justin said. "Now listen, all of you. I'm leaving with Christine. I want no trouble and I want no interference."

"No!" Christine's face was white. "Leave if you must, but not with me. I never want to be in the same room with you again. I despise you, Justin Hever."

The look of fury returned to Justin's face. He moved quickly, put his arm around Margaret as though in a brotherly embrace, and swung her round in front of him, clasping her with his left arm. His right arm went behind his back and emerged with the dagger which he held to his sister's neck.

Guy made a move toward him, then checked himself. This was no longer talk about what might or might not have happened two years ago. This was happening, unbelievably, now, and a false step could put Margaret Hever's life in danger. Guy met Rachel's eyes and saw her fear.

"You'll do as I say, Christine," Justin said. "Walk to the table. Pick up the candle and walk to the stage door. When we're in my carriage, Margaret goes free." He looked round at the others. "No heroics, now. I don't want to injure my helpless little sister, but my life is at stake as well."

Christine looked at Margaret's terrified face, then walked slowly to the table and picked up the candle.

Guy glanced at Burley, who shook his head. No heroics. But Justin must not be allowed to take Christine.

Justin and the two women went a few steps into the darkness that led to the passage to the stage door. The candle flame sent tall wavering shadows, hobgoblins of their real selves, onto the high wall. Then the light went out. Guy heard a curse and a scream and the sound of running. Christine, bless her impetuous self, must have thrown down the candle. They were her footsteps, running through the theater. Darkness would pose no obstacle. She knew the Tavistock like the house in which she was born.

Margaret's voice came out of the darkness. "He's gone!"

Guy grabbed one of the lamps and ran forward. Burley took the other lamp and followed him, Rachel close behind. They found Margaret half lying on the floor where she had fallen or been pushed, dazed but apparently unharmed. Rachel dropped down and put her arms around the girl. "Where's Justin?" she whispered. "Outside?"

Margaret shook her head. "That way, I think." She pointed toward the front of the theater. "It's Christine he wants."

They could hear it now, heavy footsteps in the passage behind the lower boxes. There was no trace of the lighter sound of Christine's running. She was being cautious or had gone to earth.

Burley said, "I'll see to the carriage," then vanished quickly into the passage leading to the stage door.

"Stay together," Guy whispered to the women.

"He has the dagger," Rachel said.

Guy smiled and touched her face. "I know. I'll be careful." Justin had no light. He would make lumbering progress. But Guy's light would give him away and make him an easy target. Better do without. He could go blindfold through the theater and never miss his step. Guy put the lamp on the floor by the women, slipped off his shoes, and moved swiftly in the direction of the footsteps.

They had stopped now. Justin must be waiting for Christine to give her presence away. Guy waited, too, panic rising in his throat. He forced it down. An endless moment later he heard a faint scuffling from above, then the sound of someone lurching and stumbling to the stairs leading to the upper boxes. It was black there. Justin wouldn't be able to see Christine, not before Guy found him. Guy moved quietly to the stairs.

And then he heard the other sounds. Justin had reached the second tier and was flinging open the doors of the boxes, letting the faint glow from the footlights shine through into the corridor. Guy saw him emerge two boxes from the end. Justin opened the next door, but there was no telltale gleam of light. All at once Guy understood. It was the box fitted up for the royals, two of them thrown together, the furthest just above the stage, the near one covering both stage and pit. The curtains must be drawn, thick velvet that would let no light through.

There was a clatter from the nearest door. Justin must have stumbled on the benches inside. He emerged shaking his head and looked back down the corridor. Guy pulled back into the cover of a doorway, then looked out cautiously to see Justin fumbling with the far door. He must not realize the two boxes were one. The faint gleam of metal told him the dagger was still in Justin's hand. If Christine had taken refuge there—

Guy moved swiftly and entered the nearer door. He stayed completely still, keeping his breathing shallow, listening for the telltale sound that would tell him if Christine was near. Justin was standing by the door farther down the box. Guy could hear his breathing, harsh and ragged with the violence of his effort.

Guy waited, his senses heightened, hearing nothing but

Justin's breathing and his own. Then he caught a faint familiar scent. Justin must have caught it, too, for he shouted, "Christine!" and stumbled forward. Guy heard the crash of a bench, followed by a curse. He felt rather than saw Justin lunge toward the curtains and rip them open, right and left, letting in the light from the house. It had been so dark that the effect was one of intense illumination, though Justin and the benches and royal chairs were drained of color in this dismal twilight.

There was no sign of Christine. Had he imagined her? Or was she hiding in the folds of the curtains at one side or another? Justin grasped the curtain on the left and swung it aside. "Christine, I know you're here. You're coming with me." There was something chilling about the assurance in his voice. Even now Justin did not doubt he could order the world as he pleased.

If Christine were in the box, she was hidden in the curtain pulled to the right-hand wall. Guy stepped forward, keeping himself between Justin and the end of the box. "It's not Christine. It's Guy."

Justin swung round, his face contorted with rage. "You hound from hell, you've interfered once too often!" He raised his arm and lunged at Guy, the blade of the dagger a thin streak of silver light falling quickly in an arc ending in Guy's heart.

Guy was ready. He lifted a chair—the Regent had sat there earlier that night—raised it to the height of his head, and held it to receive Justin's blow. He could hear the dagger tearing the rich fabric of its cover and losing itself in the stuffing beneath.

The impact took both men down. The chair fell against one of the benches. Guy reached for it, his fingers splaying out over the seat, searching for the dagger. He found it, pulled it out, and sent it clattering into the pit below. At this moment he couldn't trust himself not to kill.

"Enough, Justin." Guy pulled himself to his feet. He'd wrenched his ankle in the fall, and the pain shot through his leg as he tried to stand. "It's over. Don't you understand? It's over."

"So it is. Christine and I are leaving."

Guy heard a movement in the curtain behind him. "Let her go. Then I'll meet you, hand to hand."

"Sporting of you, but I don't have the time." Justin launched himself at Guy. Expecting it, Guy did not take the full force of the blow, but it was a moment before he regained his balance. In that moment Christine emerged from the curtain behind him. Justin saw her and turned from Guy.

"Chrissie, run!" Guy called, moving to place himself between her and Justin. "Find Burley."

She didn't leave. She pushed Guy aside and walked toward Justin. There was pity in her eyes, and wonder and disgust. "You heard Guy," she said. "It's over. Go where you must, but leave me alone."

"Go without you?" There was a trace of the familiar mockery in Justin's voice. "No, Christine. We're going to the Continent." He reached out to seize her.

Guy moved forward, but Christine was before him. Her face filled with fury and revulsion, she pushed Justin away with a force Guy had not known she possessed. "Never. Never, never, never." Justin fell back against the railing at the front of the box and balanced there a moment, a look of disbelief on his face. Then in a long, slow movement he fell backwards over the railing and disappeared from view.

There was an instant of absolute silence, followed by a muffled sound that echoed round the theater like the crack of a gun. Guy heard a scream from the stage. He supposed it was Margaret, but he could not take his eyes from Christine. She stood very still, swaying slightly, then lurched to the railing and leaned over. Guy caught her and turned her into his arms. "It's all right, Chrissie, it's all right. It's over. You can go home."

Chapter Twenty-three

When Justin fell, Rachel and Margaret ran to the edge of the stage. He lay sprawled on the floor of the pit, just beyond the screen that hid the orchestra. Rachel would have gone down to him, for the pit was in near darkness and it was impossible to tell whether he lived or not. But as she strained her eyes to see, Burley burst through the pit door beneath the boxes, carrying a lamp that made it all too clear. Justin lay in a contorted position, arms and legs akimbo, his head twisted at an improbable angle. The fall must have broken his neck.

Burley got down on his knees and brought the lamp close to Justin's face, then placed his ear against Justin's chest. He looked up and shook his head. Rachel became aware of Margaret standing stiffly at her side and then became aware of the smell of burning fabric. Margaret had got too close to a footlight. Rachel pulled the girl away and beat at her smouldering skirt. This small misadventure broke through Margaret's rigidity, and she began to tremble. The trembling grew worse and soon shook her entire body. Rachel drew the girl into her arms and held her close in the same protective gesture Guy had used with Christine. "It's all right," she said, echoing his words. "It's all right, Meg, it's over."

They met a few minutes later on the stage, Burley, Guy and Christine, Rachel and Margaret. Margaret was composed now, but Christine, helpless and disoriented, clung to Guy. "I've sent your coachman to Bow Street," Burley said.

"And I've sent Deaconfield's coachman to fetch the duke." He looked at Christine as though judging whether she was fit to talk. "I think I'd better know what happened."

"I followed Deaconfield to the boxes above," Guy said quickly. "He was flinging open doors, searching for Lady Christine. He found her in the royal box, but not at once. I distracted him, and we had a brief skirmish. I took the dagger from him and flung it away. You'll find it somewhere in the pit." Guy paused, then went on deliberately. "Lady Christine appeared and he went for her. I moved to cut him off. He stumbled and fell back against the railing, then lost his balance and went over."

"I pushed him," Christine said in a light, toneless voice. "I pushed him away and he disappeared."

Burley appeared not to hear her. "An accident," he said. "A tragic accident. Mr. Melchett was protecting Lady Christine from attack, and Lord Deaconfield lost his balance and fell to his death. Is that what you saw, Lady Margaret? Lady Rachel?"

"That's what I saw," Margaret said firmly. "It was very dark, but I could see that much. Justin was distraught. He had confessed to killing Edmund and he was trying to kill Mr. Melchett. His mind was obviously unbalanced." Margaret raised her chin. "That's what I will tell my parents, Mr. Burley. They need to know how Edmund died so they can put his death behind them." For the first time a note of uncertainty crept into her voice. "Perhaps it will not be necessary to make all of this public?"

Burley's eyes held admiration and compassion. "It is not up to me, Lady Margaret," he said. "Your father has pushed this inquiry, but we have kept it very quiet. If he is satisfied, I see no reason why it should not be closed." He looked round at the others. Rachel nodded assent as did Guy. Christine's head was buried against Guy's shoulder. She did not seem to hear.

"Well, then," Burley went on. "I must wait here, but the women should go home. Can you handle the ribbons, Mr.

Melchett? Good. I'll send Collins on when he returns. And I'll see that Mr. Ford is released tonight."

Guy retrieved his coat and shoes and moved toward the stage door with Christine. Rachel looked back at the pit. Was that all then? The end of a life. The end of their troubles. Or would there be new ones, for none of them would be unchanged by this night. It was Margaret who turned her to the door. "It's all right," she said. She was outwardly calm, but Rachel judged her too stunned by the events of the past half-hour to be fully aware of her reaction to Justin's confession and death.

Rachel remembered little of the journey to Parminter House. She held Christine, unresisting, in her arm. Across from her Margaret sat erect, her eyes focused on some place only she could see. None of them spoke.

As Guy turned the carriage into the brilliantly lit forecourt, Rachel came back with a jolt to the reality she had left behind—when? an hour ago? two? It seemed an eternity. Guy brought the carriage to a halt, and Thomas hastened down the steps to hand the women out. If he was surprised that Rachel's husband was on the box, he gave no sign of it.

They mounted the steps to the great double doors and found the hall still bright with candlelight. Magnus appeared at the head of the stairs, Arlette close behind him. Rachel felt a wave of gratitude for her brother's sanity. "Have they all gone?" she asked when they met in the middle of the staircase.

"Not quite. The Fords are here, and Reilly." Magnus glanced at Margaret's white face.

"Justin is dead," Rachel told him.

Arlette gasped. "Good God," Magnus whispered. He looked at Christine, then turned his eyes to Margaret. "I'm so very sorry," he said, offering her his arm.

Christine moaned and turned to Guy. "My poor Christine," Arlette said, moving forward and putting an arm around her daughter. "Come, I will put you to bed." Gently, but with unmistakable authority, she detached Christine from Rachel's husband and led her up the stairs.

Rachel felt curiously detached during the scene that followed. Magnus told her that her absence had been remarked by the royal party when they were ready to leave, but Arlette had managed to convey the impression that she herself was their hostess, leaving the entourage fully satisfied that protocol had been observed. The Fords were full of questions, but hesitant to ask them. No one commented on Margaret's damaged skirt nor Guy's disheveled appearance. Rachel told them that Justin had died in an accident at the theater and that Brandon was to be released as soon as possible. She did not explain the connection between these events. She would tell them later, when Brandon had been released. He should hear the story, too. For Dorinda's sake, Rachel added that the investigation into Edmund Hever's death was closed.

The Fords and Patrick, subdued by the story of the tragedy but relieved by the news of Brandon's release, took their leave. Rachel saw them to the door of the blue saloon where they had been waiting for her return, then turned to the others. Guy was speaking quietly to Magnus, telling him what had happened in the theater. Margaret looked at Rachel. "I want to know." She was standing absolutely still in the middle of the room as though movement would shatter her fragile self-command. Magnus urged her to a chair but she shook her head. "I don't understand what happened," she went on. "I have to know. I have to know it all. You mustn't keep anything back."

It was no time for sympathy. Rachel walked briskly across the room and led Margaret to a small settee near the fireplace. The ice blue satin of the settee was cold to the eye and touch, but a fire had been lit. Margaret would need its warmth. She looked chilled to her very soul.

Rachel sat down by the girl. She would have put an arm around her or at least taken her hand, but she sensed that Margaret needed space with which to armor herself against the coming revelations. Watching her with obvious concern, Magnus took a chair across from the settee and waited for the others to speak.

"How did you know?" Guy asked Rachel. He was standing by the fireplace, and the light from the candles on the mantel deepened the hollows in his eyes and cheeks. He looked exhausted and feverish, and he could scarcely contain his impatience.

"I didn't know," Rachel said. "I only guessed. There was no reason to suspect Justin. Edmund's death would have brought him a small inheritance, but it seemed too paltry a gain for something as consequential as murder. But tonight Margaret told me something that made me think Justin could have had real cause to do away with Edmund."

Margaret turned a startled face to Rachel. "*I* told you?"

"Not directly." Rachel turned to the others. "Margaret's father has been pressing her to accept Lord Winchester's suit."

Magnus frowned, then looked at Margaret in inquiry. Margaret kept her eyes on her lap.

"Which is probably what led her Cousin Elizabeth to bring the matter up," Rachel went on. "Marriage, I mean. From what Margaret told me, Elizabeth Hever was not happy in her marriage to the late duke. She told Margaret to be careful in her choice of husband. Men, she said, can do things that bring unspeakable harm to their wives and children. She was very bitter about it."

Margaret looked up. "Cousin Henry was known to have a fearful temper. In the last years of his life it grew much worse."

"Yes, that's what you told me," Rachel said. "I remembered my conversation with the dowager duchess at our dinner party for Arlette. Her younger daughter had come down with a rash and she was relieved that it was nothing but chickenpox." Rachel smiled. "I own I would not have been relieved by such a diagnosis. And then I remembered what you told me, Meg, about those last months when the duke suffered from migraines and had to walk with a cane."

"He didn't like to use the cane in public," Margaret said. "He didn't want people to know he had gout."

"That's understandable. But I don't think it was gout."

Guy turned startled eyes on Rachel. "The French pox."

As she realized what Guy had said, Margaret blushed. Then she drew a breath and sat up a little straighter on the settee. "Cousin Henry died of an accident while cleaning his gun. At least we thought it was an accident. But if he knew how ill he was and how much worse it was going to be . . ." She could not complete the thought.

"It's possible," Rachel said, "though of course we'll never know. This is where it becomes pure conjecture, though it accounts for the duchess's anxiety about her children's health and her own. It accounts for the duke's symptoms as well, the sudden rages, the difficulty in walking, the headaches. If he knew that his brain was affected—"

"Poor devil," Magnus said.

They were silent for a while. Then Margaret said, "You think Justin knew?"

"That his father would soon become the Duke of Arundel? I suspect he did," Rachel said. "The fourth duke might have lived for years, but Justin must have guessed he was not a man to surrender easily to madness."

"I see." Margaret had not quite taken it in.

"Why should Justin know?" Guy asked.

Rachel glanced at Margaret, then turned to Guy. "I assume the duchess told him. Margaret told me they had been lovers."

"She would have been obliged to tell him if she thought she might be infected herself," Margaret said. "I expect she wouldn't have—I mean, there wouldn't be any more children. Cousin Henry would never have a son. So Justin would know—" Margaret covered her face with her hands and began to cry quietly but with great wrenching sobs that shook her slender frame. Rachel gathered her into her arms.

386

Guy finished her thought. "So he would know that Edmund would soon be heir to a dukedom. It was bad enough that Justin had to spend his life rescuing Edmund from his own folly. To learn that Edmund's reward would be one of the oldest titles in England . . . It must have been a great temptation, Lady Margaret, greater because it could bring Justin Christine as well."

"Christine has escaped in more ways than one." Magnus was on his feet, pacing restlessly about the room. "She could have lived with the same uncertainty that now plagues the dowager duchess."

"Oh, don't, don't!" Margaret broke free of Rachel's embrace and stood up, swaying slightly on her feet. "I'm sorry," she said, putting her hands to her temples. "I don't mean to make a scene, but it's all so horrible, so sordid."

Magnus was immediately at Margaret's side. "Forgive me, I'm a clumsy fool. Please believe me when I say that all men are not like your brother and your cousin."

Margaret looked up at him, her face now free of emotion. She looked at once fragile and strong. Rachel had never admired her so much. "I would appreciate the use of a carriage, Lord Parminter. My family will need me at home."

Rachel watched as Magnus escorted Margaret from the room. "I'm sorry she had to hear it," she said to Guy, "but there was no way to keep it from her." She was quiet for a moment, thinking of what Justin had done to his brother, then with sudden horror remembered where it had been done and why. "Guy," she said, her voice shaking, "Justin knew that Cadogan planned to set the explosion. He knew about the meeting as well. How could he do it? Had he no feelings? No sense of honor?"

Guy shrugged. "He was the most arrogant man I've ever known. Arrogance doesn't need to justify itself."

Tears welled in Rachel's eyes. "Oh, Guy." She wanted to run to him for comfort, but she did not trust herself.

"Justin got Charles the living in Suffolk," Guy said in a

detached voice. "I was surprised, for they'd never been particular friends."

Rachel caught her breath. "You don't think Charles knew Justin was in the theater that night?"

"No, but I think Justin knew Edmund was meeting Charles there. Justin would think it prudent to have a hold over him in case he'd seen something he shouldn't."

Before Rachel could respond, the door opened and she turned to see Arlette, her eyes filled with concern. "Christine is asleep," Arlette said, coming toward them. "I gave her something and she should be safe till morning. She has had a great shock and is not responsible for what she says." She turned to Rachel. "I think you have had a shock, too." She put her arms about her eldest daughter in an embrace that was incongruous but curiously comforting. Rachel stayed there a moment, then pulled away, feeling awkward in her mother's arms. How strange. Her mother had hurt her cruelly, but tonight she had been kind. Confused, she murmured good night and fled the room.

Guy watched her leave, longing to follow her, but fearing he would be turned away.

"Go after her, Guy," Arlette said. "She needs you."

Guy shook his head. Needed him? No. He had nothing to give his wife, not even the words to tell her how he felt. Nor did he have the courage to face her rejection. "She needs to be alone," he said.

Arlette gave an expressive shrug. "My poor Guy. You are a fool. You will be doomed by your folly."

" 'Tis not my first," he said with a rueful smile. "And I fear 'twill not be my last."

Arlette rounded on him with sudden fury. "Ah, I have no patience with you. You mock, you are clever, you hide your feelings with words. Forget words, Guy. Act. Rachel is the woman for you."

"I know she is," Guy said, suddenly sober. "But I'm not the man for her."

"You are wrong. You are stupid and you are wrong. I

388

have seen you together. I know. Ah, Guy, do not let Christine come between you. It may be your only chance."

Guy hesitated, wanting and fearing to believe her. Who was Arlette to see into Rachel's heart? And yet, at this moment, her eyes seemed to hold all the wisdom of the world. He seized her hand and brought it to his lips. "I think you are a good woman."

A faint blush tinged Arlette's face. "Pah! I am not good at all. But I have lived many years, and I have not repeated my mistakes. Go. Go, *mon ami.*"

Guy left the room and quickly climbed the steps to the second floor. He paused at the door to Rachel's bedchamber, then entered his own and crossed to the door that connected it to hers. He wanted this assumption of intimacy. There was so much at stake. There was too much bitterness between them, too much hurt.

Guy knocked softly, then knocked again. After a moment Rachel opened the door a fraction, looked into his face, then opened it wide enough for him to enter. She had removed Magnus's pearls and the combs that bound her hair. She had also removed the gauze tunic. She stood before him in the red satin underdress, her hair tumbling over her shoulders. Guy looked at her with wonder in his eyes. She was the most beautiful woman he had ever seen.

Rachel stood very still and returned his gaze. Guy's cravat was askew, his coat hung badly, and his hair fell in disordered locks over his forehead. He seemed at once purposeful and uncertain. The sight of him made her heart turn over. Because she feared what he might say, she hastened to break the silence between them. "I'm sorry: I was wrong. Badly wrong. I swore Justin was innocent, and he was not. I swore Christine would never leave him, but she did. She wanted to come back to you, and I—Oh, Guy, I want you to be free. Tell me what I must do to make you so. I would give anything to undo what I have done."

It took a moment for Guy to realize what she was offering, to understand how badly she had construed the scene in the Tavistock. If he had been frantic to protect Christine, if he had held her in his arms when it was over, that was only the residue of the past. Rachel. He wondered how long he had loved her. He knew every contour of her face as he knew his own. He was bound to her by more than friendship and affection and familiarity. Hers was the face he would rather see before him than all the faces in the world.

Rachel, my muse, my fire. He moved toward her, seeking some echo of his own feelings. Her eyes were wide and deep. He could step into their darkness and lose himself forever. "Rachel," he said. Her name was an invocation. "You must do nothing. I would not loose the ties that bind us. Not for the world. Unless," he added, fearing he might have misunderstood her words. "Unless *you* want to be free."

"I've loved you for years," Rachel whispered. "I'll never be free." She was suspended in time and space. The room had dropped away and there was nothing to cling to but Guy and the faint thread of what he claimed was between them. Faint but strong, oh, so strong. If she could trust it, it would support her all her life. "Why?" she asked, not yet willing to believe the promise in his words. "Why me?"

"Because your eyes hold my soul," he said, the words coming unbidden to his lips, "and your mouth gives me breath, and on your sweet breast I shall know eternity."

Her eyes widened in surprise and wonder. It was true then. She felt a great welling of joy. Her body trembled and she was unable to speak.

Guy could not bear the silence growing between them. "My love," he whispered, "give me a sign."

And Rachel, beautiful, wondrous Rachel, walked straight into his arms.

Epilogue

"What a glorious place," Rachel said, looking out over the smooth slate blue expanse of water.

Fiona laughed. "There's something wonderfully liberating about life in the country, even on as grand a scale as this."

They were walking along the bank of the natural lake which stood on the grounds of Sundon, the country estate which had been the symbol of the Melchett family's greatness for four generations. The August sun was warm, but there had been showers the previous night, and the air was filled with the scent of damp earth and rain-drenched grass. A water bird called overhead, then circled back over the lake. Shouts and laughter and sounds of splashing came from the small strip of beach which Robert Melchett had added when his children were young. Rachel and Fiona's children were making use of it today.

Fiona stopped and lifted her face to the sun. Like Rachel she had removed her bonnet and her hair was beginning to escape its pins. "To own the truth, I'm quite beginning to like it here." She laughed again. "There, I've finally admitted it. And I don't feel the least bit guilty."

Rachel smiled and turned to look across the lawn at the house which ran the entire length of the lake. The sandstone was warm and golden in the sunlight as in the painting which hung in her room at Parminter House. With its pilasters and cupolas and glittering central dome, the house should have seemed impossibly overdone, but it had a kind of majestic beauty. "It's wonderfully theatrical," Rachel said. "That skyline would make a superlative backdrop."

Fiona lifted her skirt to avoid a bramble bush. "I have no intention of giving it up, but I'm going to do something with the income. It's not just Sundon, there's the house in Cornwall and the Irish estates and the money in the funds. I've worked for my living too long to simply sit back and live on the income now."

A gardener's boy was pushing a wheelbarrow across the lawn at the end of the lake. "Good morning, Tim," Fiona called. The boy stopped and tipped his hat, obviously pleased at having his name remembered. This was only Fiona's second visit to Sundon, but she was unquestionably mistress here, just as Rachel was at the Tavistock. Whatever Fiona's feelings about her inheritance, she was no longer afraid of it.

With one accord the two women turned and began walking back toward the children. Rachel swung her bonnet, which she was carrying by its ribbons. She felt carefree and very young. "Magnus settled some money on me when Guy and I were married," she said. "The principal is tied up for my children but I can draw upon the interest. I haven't wanted to—some silly scruples about taking my brother's charity, I suppose."

"It's hardly charity," Fiona said. "Magnus is trying to live up to his responsibilities as head of the family. The least you can do is allow him to play the role."

Rachel laughed. "Three months ago I never thought I'd say this, but there are times when I miss Parminter House. I'm glad to be back in Ormond Street, but I don't see why our life shouldn't be a little more comfortable than it used to be."

They could now see the narrow strip of beach where Gideon and thirteen-year-old Peter Carne were helping Jessica and Beth build a sandcastle. Guy had waded into the water to retrieve Teddy's sailboat which had become tangled up in

392

some reeds. Teddy was watching anxiously from the shore, but Alec glanced back toward the house and gave a sudden shout. "Uncle Magnus!"

Rachel turned and saw her brother striding across the lawn in their direction. He was expected at Sundon today, but they had not looked for him till evening. "The footman told me you were by the lake," he said when Rachel and Fiona met him. "I said I'd announce myself."

Magnus kissed Fiona on the cheek, then hugged Rachel and held her at arm's length for a moment. He was grinning, a self-conscious grin that made him look, improbably, like a sheepish little boy. "You can congratulate me, sister."

Rachel had not seen Magnus since she and Guy left London a fortnight ago. She had known the journey to Sundon would take Magnus past the Arundels' house in Hertfordshire, but she had not dared ask if he meant to stop there. "I'm so happy," she said. "For Margaret as well as you."

Fiona added her congratulations to Rachel's, but there was little time to say more, for the children, wet and sandy and enthusiastic, fell upon them with cries of greeting. The Carnes held back, but Alec and Jessica, who had learned during their sojourn in Parminter House not to hold Magnus in awe, were eager to share news of the day's excitement.

"We're building a castle," Jessica said proudly, "with battlements and a tower—"

"—and then Teddy's boat got away, but Daddy got it back for us so it's all right," Alec explained, sounding far more like a boy of eight than he usually did.

"Uncle Magnus has some news," Rachel said when she could make herself heard.

"You're going to have a new aunt," Magnus explained. "Lady Margaret. Do you remember her?"

"I do," said Jessica. "She was at the wedding. She's nice."

"Congratulations, sir." Peter was old enough to know what these occasions required.

"Congratulations," Alec echoed.

By this time Gideon and Guy had followed the children across the lawn. "My dear fellow, that's splendid news," Gideon said warmly.

Guy grinned. "All things considered, Lady Margaret isn't getting a bad bargain. Congratulations."

The pleasantries continued a while longer until the children began to grow restless. Beth tugged at Gideon's hand. "Castle," she whispered in a small voice.

"Right," Gideon said. "Tell you what, let's go and finish it and then the others can come and have a look."

Jessica had no fault to find with this plan, and Teddy and Alec were eager to try the boat again. Gideon and the children returned to the beach while the others moved toward a stand of chestnut trees on the edge of the lake. "When is the wedding to be?" Fiona asked, sinking down on one of the metal benches which stood beneath the trees.

"Late September. Meg doesn't feel she can leave her family before then." Magnus looked at Guy and hesitated for a moment. "I'd like you to stand up with me if you've no objection."

Guy regarded Magnus in surprise. Then he smiled. "That's one role I've never played. I'd be honored."

Rachel sat beside Fiona and leaned back contentedly against the sun-warmed metal. She had never thought to see her husband and brother on such friendly terms.

"What did the duke say?" Guy asked quietly.

Magnus's face turned serious. "Very little. He's a changed man since he heard about Justin. All his bluster is gone."

They were all silent for a moment. Rachel had told Fiona the story behind Edmund's murder, though Conant and Sidmouth had kept it from becoming common knowledge. As far as the world was concerned, Justin had died in a tragic accident as had Edmund.

Guy perched on the arm of the bench and drew Rachel

against him. He was barefoot and in his shirtsleeves, his trousers rolled up to the knee and dripping water. He looked thoroughly disreputable and impossibly attractive. Secure in his arms, Rachel turned to her brother. "Did you see Christine before you left?"

Magnus nodded. "I drove down to Richmond the day before yesterday."

A week after Justin's death, Arlette had taken Christine to the Parminters' Thames-side villa. However much she had neglected her children in the past, Rachel acknowledged that in this Arlette had done a great service, not only for Christine but for Rachel and Magnus as well. "Christine was in much better spirits than the last time I saw her," Magnus continued. "Philip Weston has visited her several times, and the Fords drove down last weekend. And," Magnus added, a smile playing about his lips, "Bertram Hever called on her twice when he was in London seeing to some business for his father. I'd say there's a chance Christine may be the Duchess of Arundel yet."

Rachel stared at her brother. "I knew Bertram admired her, but . . ." The thought of yet a third Hever brother courting Christine seemed wholly absurd.

Guy began to laugh. "It must be something in the Hever blood. From what I've seen of him, Bertram is by far the best of the lot."

"He's certainly risen to the occasion since Justin's death," Magnus agreed.

Rachel shook her head. " 'If this were played upon a stage now, I could condemn it as an improbable fiction.' "

"*As You Like It*," said Guy.

"*Twelfth Night*," Rachel retorted. "You're slipping."

Magnus turned to Fiona. "I'm sorry, we've spoken of nothing but ourselves. You're looking very well." He hesitated, uncharacteristically awkward.

Fiona laughed. Her simple cambric gown did not conceal the fact that she was in her fifth month of pregnancy. "Men never know how to address a woman who's increasing. I'm feeling very well. Gideon worries more than I do. It's a common failing of husbands, as I'm sure both of you will learn." She looked from Guy to Magnus with a mischievous smile. Then she turned serious. "There's something you should know, all of you. With the baby coming I've had to do a lot of thinking about the future. There are Gideon's children to provide for as well, and I hope we'll have more than one of our own. I've decided to break the entail on Sundon and Parminter House and the other properties."

Fiona regarded her three cousins, her chin slightly raised, as if to indicate she was aware of the audacity of what she had just said. Rachel smiled. "Lady Parminter may never forgive you, but I can't think of a more sensible way to settle things."

"Nor can I." Guy grinned. "I'm all for the redistribution of wealth."

"And the entail has already caused problems enough," Magnus added. "What does Carne say?"

"Oh, he agrees with Guy," Fiona said. "It's far too much of an inheritance for any one person. And it can't be good for siblings to have things divided so unequally. Sundon will go to the one who most appreciates it, boy or girl." She turned to look through the trees at the house itself and the others followed the direction of her gaze.

Sundon looked solid and serene, unruffled by the changes of the past year. Rachel found it difficult to believe that it was only a year since Magnus had summoned her to his lodgings and made the astonishing announcement that he was going to become Marquis of Parminter. Magnus and Fiona had both changed a great deal since they had learned of their legacy. Rachel turned from the house and rested her head on Guy's shoulder. One didn't have to come into a title or inherit a fortune to change. She had changed as well. As had Guy. All four of them had had to confront the past, to accept it for what it was, to look ahead to the future. Rachel reached for Guy's hand and felt his arm tighten reassuringly around her.

"Mama!" A lusty cry from Jessica broke the stillness. "The castle's finished."

Laughing, the four adults got to their feet and started down the slope to the water.

Historical Note

The Tavistock Theater did not exist, nor did the Olympique. Neither did the Levellers who met at the Angel, but the seventeenth century group from which they took their name was a real one. There were many radical groups in nineteenth century London, though most did not include so many well-born young men. The Home Office is known to have made use of agents provocateurs.

The visit of the Emperor of Russia, the King of Prussia, and their entourage was a major event in June 1814. The incident of their attendance at the Tavistock Theater and the appearance of the Princess Caroline did take place on June 11, though it occurred at a performance of the opera *Aristodemo* at the King's Theatre in the Haymarket.

The Emperor's cousin, the Princess Sofia, is a fictional character, as is William Mountjoy.